I0712366

BURN WITH ME

D. L. DARBY

Copyright © 2023 by D.L. Darby

Identifiers: Print - 979-8-9869973-6-0

All rights reserved.

No part of this book may be reproduced in any form or by any electronic or mechanical means, including information storage and retrieval systems, without written permission from the author, except for the use of brief quotations in a book review.

This is a work of fiction. Names, places, and events are either products of the author's imagination or used fictitiously. Any resemblance to persons living or dead, organizations, or events is purely coincidence.

Edited by Virginia Carey

Cover created by Aster with Asteriellydesigns

 Formatted with Vellum

Content Warning

This book contains the following:

- SA of a minor by a minor
- Emotional abuse
- Attempted SA
- CNC
- Edging
- Assault
- Gun violence
- Death from cancer (off-page)
- Homicide

If you have any questions, please feel free to reach out.

Please read responsibly.

Help is Available

If you or anyone you know is in trouble and suffering from
abuse, the National Domestic Violence Hotline is open 24/7
800-799-7233
https://www.thehotline.org/

For the readers who dream about being railed by a man in a mask.

Playlist

"comatose" – søde ven

"stranger" – Tove Lo

"So It Goes..." – Taylor Swift

"In Good Trouble" – India Arie

"Here Right Now" – Lindsey Ray

"Lipstick" – Charlie Puth

"Wildfire" – Demi Lovato

"Still Love You" – Sofia Carson

"Love Like Ours" – Aron Wright

"We Go Down Together" – Dove Cameron, Khalid

"THE DEATH OF PEACE OF MIND" – Bad Omens

Have you ever had a desire so dark you wouldn't dare speak it out loud? You've buried it so deep in the depths of your soul, but it's always there.

Wanting.

Waiting for the moment you set it free.

Our Temptangels will awaken your deepest hunger.

Here, you can feast until you're satiated.

Here, you can be whoever you want and do whatever you wish—with consent, of course.

Whether a woman or a man, or both if you prefer, your pleasure is their delight. Take a mask, pick your angel, and let your dreams take flight.

Welcome to Désirer

From the moment we met, your passion consumed me. A slow lick of blue flame set aglow the recesses of my dark mind. Setting my skin ablaze. Twining around my limbs to leave scorch marks on my soul. And when that scalding blue met the innocent glimmer in my chest, it sparked until we were bathed in an incandescent heat that burned down the world around us. My light. My love. My searing blue flame. My heart will forever beat for yours. And all I ask in return is that yours continues to burn only ever for mine.

D.L. DARBY

Prologue

GINNY

Age 10

I've always hated my appearance.

Deep copper hair. Sky blue eyes. Ivory skin with a distinct dusting of freckles across my nose and cheeks. People have always looked.

No one has ever made me feel the way Christopher Calloway is making me feel right now.

Like I'm dog poo on the bottom of his shoe that he just stepped on when he came inside his house and found his parents with the social worker and me. As if it was *my* fault his parents signed up to be foster parents. *My* fault my mother died last night after losing her battle with cancer, and now I need to be placed somewhere.

The rage on his face is poorly concealed, but his parents and Mrs. Trech aren't paying attention to him. His eyes flit up to his mother as he pushes off the wall before making his way over to me. Gripping my backpack tightly, I try to make myself smaller as he comes closer until he's towering over me. He glances back at his parents once more before looking me over with his lip curled in distaste.

"I don't want you here," he says between clenched teeth, voice low so his parents won't hear him.

Shrugging slightly, I peek up at him and respond, "I don't want to be here."

Letting out a soft snort, he reaches out and grabs a lock of my hair, tugging it hard enough to make me wince. "Don't fuck with me."

His words are lost on me. From what I've gathered in the short amount of time I've been in the Calloway's home, I've learned that Mr. Calloway is a very successful surgeon, and Mrs. Calloway stays at home. Christopher is four years older than I am and is their pride and joy. But Mrs. Calloway has always wanted a daughter, and I suspect Christopher isn't too happy about having to share his parents' attention.

"If you try anything, I'll make your life a living hell," Christopher sneers quietly, just before his parents and Mrs. Trech appear behind him.

"Christopher, are you welcoming Guinevere to our home? We're so sorry to hear about your mother, dear. Come, I'll show you to your new room." Mrs. Calloway holds her hand out for me to take as her son beams up at her like he's the poster boy for the welcoming committee.

Fighting the urge to roll my eyes, I don't take the offered hand but take a step closer to her to show her I'm ready to go.

I can feel Christopher's eyes burning a hole into my back as I walk away.

Age 12

There are shadows outside my bedroom door.

Ones I've come to expect at least once a week.

They belong to Christopher and will remain there for a few minutes before he pushes the door open softly, so it doesn't creak and alert his parents.

My chest tightens as I pull the blankets beneath my chin and turn toward the wall, pretending to be asleep.

Just like I always do when he comes in late at night.

There's a scratch in the pink wallpaper. I stare at it, letting my mind wander to anywhere other than here, as I hear the soft sounds of his footsteps while he crosses the room.

"Ginny? You awake?" His voice is soft and quiet. Sometimes, I think he knows I am, but it's easier for us both to pretend I'm not.

My mind roams to other places. Happier places. Places where my imaginary friend shows up and distracts me from Christopher's shallow breaths and the wet sound of skin on skin as he touches himself.

Christopher's view of me went from angry and annoyed, to angry and obsessed in the first year I lived with the Calloways. He was always picking on me, pinching my skin, or tugging my hair. And I dare not say anything because, as far as foster homes went, I had won the golden ticket. What was dealing with a bit of bullying?

But then, as we got older, his friends started to notice me. They'd make comments about my appearance, like boys their age do, and all of a sudden, Christopher's attention turned from bullying to possessive.

A few months ago, he started coming to my room, asking if I was awake. I've always pretended to be asleep, and sometimes I wonder what he would do if I met him with a wide-eyed stare and said, "Yes, I'm awake. Why are you in my bedroom?"

So, I started to make up places in my mind. And since I didn't really have any friends, I made up one of those, too. My imaginary friend is a boy because I think it's easier to cope that way. He's taller than me, with golden brown eyes, milk chocolate hair, and an English accent.

When he visits me, I can imagine I'm somewhere far away. In another part of the world where what's happening to me can't happen there.

Sometimes, we'll play on a playground or run through the sand on a beach. Once, we went on an Arctic expedition and played with some penguins. But for all the months I've been imagining him, I've never given him a name. And he's never offered me one.

He's just…my stranger.

Age 14

"God, your sister is fucking hot, dude," Richard Barnes says as he openly stares at me from where he and Chris are throwing a football back and forth in the pool.

It's the end of summer, and the sun is scorching. Mr. and Mrs. Calloway are hosting a pool party barbeque, so I'm in a bathing suit, reading a book in a chair as I dry off from a swim.

"She's not my fucking sister. Don't call her that," Chris snaps back at him before turning his dark eyes to my figure.

I'm wearing sunglasses, so they can't tell that I'm watching them. But somehow, I think Chris knows anyway.

"If you don't think of her as a sister, then why'd you tell the whole football team that if anyone goes near her next year, you'll kill them? Screams big bro energy to me, dude."

Hearing what Richard says doesn't surprise me in the slightest. It isn't because he thinks of me as a little sister. It's because he thinks of me as *his*.

Every night, his shadow shows up at my door, and I curl in on myself, wondering if it will be the night he finally takes what he thinks belongs to him. He's about to head off to New York for his first year of college in a few days, and he's warned off every boy in school from ever pursuing me romantically.

Everyone thinks he's just being a protective big brother.

But big brothers aren't supposed to put their hands on you.

They aren't supposed to sneak into your room and peel off your blanket. Touch you over your clothes while they touch themselves. I stopped pretending to be asleep a long time ago once he told me he knew I was awake.

All I do is stare at a spot on the ceiling and imagine that it's my stranger touching me instead. Because no matter how unwelcome Chris' touch is, my body reacts to it, so he thinks I like it. It's confusing for us both, I guess. He's started to say dirty things while he touches me. Things that make my body feel tingly all over. I don't like it. But it makes my body feel good.

I'm ashamed of it.

It's disgusting, and wrong, and I *hate* him for it.

But his parents treat me like I'm their own even though they won't adopt me because Chris asked them not to.

Because in his fucked up brain, he thinks if they do, it will solidify that what he's doing is wrong. That as long as we don't share a last name, it validates his actions.

Chris sends me a look that tells me to expect his presence tonight. "None of those fuckwads even know what to do with their dicks. The last thing my parents need is a teenage pregnancy scandal. They don't need to take care of another stray."

His words send ire through my veins. I clench my teeth and flip a page to make it look like I'm not paying attention.

Tonight, this *stray* is going to bite back.

I'm sitting on my bed when Chris walks in around midnight. My bedside lamp is on, casting a glow over the room as I read, and I look up to see him freeze for a moment before silently shutting the door behind him.

"What are you doing?" he asks.

"What are *you* doing?" I challenge, turning my attention back to my book.

Powerful would be the way to describe how I feel right now, but when I glance at him, that feeling turns to lead in my stomach. His lips turn up in a grin as he runs a hand through his dark hair and continues to walk closer to my bed.

Swallowing, I place my bookmark in the book and set it on my nightstand before swinging my legs over the side of the bed and fixing him with a mean glare. "Go away, Chris."

Faster than I can blink, he knocks me back, covering my mouth with one hand while the other holds my wrists. He's straddling my waist, and as I start to struggle, I can feel that it's making him hard.

"Do you think just because I'm leaving for school, that means you're going to be rid of me, Ginny?" He leans down so that his lips rest against my ear. "Maybe I should give you something to think about until I come back at winter break."

His hips press into mine, and tears prick my eyes as he starts to rub against me. Shouting against his hand, I begin to thrash my body against his, trying to throw him off me, but he's much stronger than I am. Chris laughs as his hips keep rolling against me, his penis rubbing between my legs and causing a sensation that I fight against with every fiber of my being.

"Just fucking lay there and take it, Gin. Too bad you're not old enough for me to fuck yet. Or I'd ruin your hairy snatch before I leave," he grunts into my ear.

He's careful not to go too fast so the bed doesn't squeak. And his hand is pressed so hard over my mouth and nose that I struggle to breathe. His other hand grips my wrists so tightly that I'm sure there will be bruises I'll have to hide.

Shutting my eyes tightly, I imagine a different body above me. A different boy whose name I don't know and whose face is always blurry in my mind. A gentler touch–more experienced. The pressure between my legs grows, and with each passing second, the line blurs between what I know shouldn't feel good and what does.

Maybe this will be the last straw, and I'll finally tell Chris' parents what he's been doing to me for the last two and a half years.

Chris buries his face in my hair and grunts as his hips start to slow. The ache between my legs dies as he pushes up off of me and looks down at my face. For a split second, he looks alarmed. Tears are streaming down my cheeks, and the straps to my night camisole have slipped down my shaking shoulders. My pajama pants have a wet spot on them that matches the one on his gray sweats, and I almost open my mouth to scream.

But I don't.

Because soon he'll be gone, and I'll be free.

Age 17

For the first time since I stepped foot into the Calloway home, I'm witnessing Chris try desperately not to cry.

Tears line his eyes as he grips my jaw roughly, though not hard enough to leave bruises. His other hand wraps around my neck, forehead pressed hard against mine, pushing me into the wall as I claw at his hands.

"You fucking *bitch*. You stupid fucking bitch. How could you do this to me?!"

His breath reeks of alcohol. It's winter break of my senior year, and Chris' parents are out of town because his dad has a conference to attend in Boston. I didn't think Chris would come back this year because he hasn't spent much time at home since he left for college.

Ever since that night in my room three years ago, he hasn't touched me or touched himself in front of me. Part of me has always wondered what made him stop, but I never wanted to dwell on it. The fact that he stopped was all that mattered.

Imagine my surprise when he walked in the door five minutes ago. Drunk and very much *not* supposed to be here.

He'd distanced himself from us–typical college boy behavior, according to his mother. Whatever the reason, I was glad for it. It took some time, but I started to come out of my shell with him gone.

I have friends now. Kids at school have stopped thinking of me as his weird little foster sister. The boys have started to pay attention to me.

And suddenly, it hits me why Chris is so angry.

"It was supposed to be *mine*, Guinevere. *MINE!* And you went and gave it away like a dumb fucking whore!"

"Stop it! You're hurting me! Let go of me, Chris!" My voice is shrill as my nails scratch at his flesh. But it doesn't even phase him.

"How'd you let him do it, huh? Did you let him fuck you in the back seat of his truck? Or did he bring you to his house when his parents weren't home and take his time with you in his bed?"

His grip tightens, and I whimper in pain, digging my nails into his hands. The air in my throat is cut off, blood rushing to my head as I struggle to breathe.

"Did you let him fuck you in the ass like a dirty little slut? Was it worth it? Did he make it good for you?" He slurs his words as he nuzzles my neck before speaking against my cheek. "Because you'll never know what it's like to be fucked again. Do you hear me? I am going to make sure no one ever so much as *thinks* they can fuck you. And if you think I'm going to touch your filthy, tainted cunt now, you're wrong. So tell me, was it worth it?"

Pushing off me, he drops his hands away from my body, and I crumple to the ground, gasping for air. One hand braces my weight on the floor as the other reaches up to gingerly touch my neck. My eyes raise, and I watch him from beneath my lashes as he paces the length of my bedroom, gripping his hair tightly.

"FUUUUUCK!" he shouts, causing me to jump.

Seconds later, his fingers tangle in my hair, yanking my head back as he shouts in my face, "Did you think I wouldn't find out?!"

Find out that I gave my virginity to Timmy Rhodes. A sweet boy who doesn't have a lot of friends and who I don't find attractive. A boy who stumbled his way through the act and didn't mind that my eyes were closed the whole time as I imagined that it was *my stranger* I was giving my innocence away to.

So that Chris couldn't steal the only shred of it I had left.

"Let go of me!" My watery screams match his as I wonder how I let it get this far. There's something sick and twisted in his mind, and any other foster home would have been better than letting this depraved man in front of me think he *owns* me.

His tears dry up as he locks down at me, and his lips twist in a grin. "You know, I probably would have lost interest once I fucked you."

His hands pull my hair harder, contorting my neck at an uncomfortable angle. "Now? Now, I'm going to make your life a living hell, just like I promised I would when you walked into this house seven years ago. You're a sickness, Ginny. A sickness that only *I* can cure. But now? Now, I'm going to enjoy watching you rot."

A cry escapes my lips as he tosses me away from him like a rag doll. A toy he's done playing with. All I can think of as I watch him walk out of my room and slam the door is how I can't wait to graduate and get as far away from him as I fucking can.

Age 18

"A full ride?" My mouth drops in awe as Mr. and Mrs. Calloway beam at me from across the kitchen table.

"Of course, dear girl. And with Christopher starting med school, he'll barely be home. It only makes sense that you two live together. No rent. We'll still send a check every month to help out with utilities and groceries. You won't have to worry about a thing," Christine says with her full lips parted in a smile, her chestnut hair perfectly coiffed.

Panic grips me at the thought of living with Chris full-time with no one else around. Briefly, I wonder what would happen if I open my mouth and tell the Calloways what their son has been doing to me all these years. But the thought of breaking Christine and Calvin's hearts is too much. Their son is *everything* to them. He's the perfect all-American football star I've never seen be aggressive toward anyone other than me. He's always worn his mask well and fooled anyone he's ever wanted.

Except me.

And if there is one thing I've learned from him that I'm thankful for, it's how to fool people into thinking you're something you're not.

So, I'll put on a show for the Calloways, and I'll make all three of them think I'm going along with their little plan. Part of me feels terrible for using their money, but I'll get a good education. I'll keep myself busy so I don't even have to be home with Chris. Then, once I've graduated, I'll get as far away as possible.

My eyes glitter, and my lips turn up in the best genuine smile I can feign. "That's so generous of you guys. Thank you so much. I promise I won't let you down."

Jackson

"**S**uck *harder*."

Fuck. What does a guy have to do to get a woman in this city to suck his cock like she's a fucking Hoover vacuum?

The woman on her knees, I don't even remember her name, looks up at me with annoyance painted on her overly dressed up face. It makes me smirk as I slap her cheek lightly. "What's wrong, sweetheart? Thought you were gonna get fucked slow and sweet and that I'd let you stay the night?"

She pulls back off my cock and wipes at her mouth roughly as she gets to her feet. "You're a fucking asshole."

"Not news. And *you* signed an NDA, so if a word of this gets out, I'll make sure you're doing this as a job for the rest of your life. And you *won't* be getting paid." My phone vibrates on the coffee table in front of me, and I tuck myself back into my slacks before leaning forward to grab it.

The woman makes a high-pitched huffing noise as she gathers her stuff and makes her way across the hardwood floor of my living room. "It isn't news that you're an arrogant playboy, but I didn't think you were the type to leave a woman unsatisfied."

She's baiting me, and I'm not stupid enough to open my

mouth and bite the hook she's dangling like she's trying to catch a big, fat, billion-dollar fish. Ignoring her, I open my phone and groan when I see it's a text from my uncle.

There's a *ding* that signals the elevator has taken the desperate female out of my penthouse, and I glance behind me to make sure she's actually gone before letting my head fall back on the couch. Part of me feels slightly bad about how I treated her. But every woman I've brought home lately is the fucking same. They pretend like they know what they're doing and then try to act demure, as if somehow going slow and acting shy is going to do the trick for me.

Slow and shy has never been my thing. I don't want an inexperienced virgin, or a woman pretending to be one. I want a woman to ride my dick like she's trying to split herself in half with it. Hard, raw, and primal is what gets me going. Graze my cock with your teeth. Tell me to fuck you harder. My idea of a good time is breaking a fucking bed frame.

And sure, there have been plenty of women who have left me satisfied sexually, but they don't keep my interest beyond that. They think that alone earns them a right to be on my arm. A right to the title of *girlfriend*, eventually leading to *fiancée*, then *wife*.

Men in my position shouldn't have wives. Or girlfriends, for that matter. It always ends messy. So why even bother? Love doesn't exist for men like me—men of power with billions at their fingertips and the world at their feet. We're greedy bastards, and one woman will never be enough.

If that were really true, you wouldn't feel the way you do, you lonely prick.

Regardless, this life has grown dull. I'm bored with the same routine over and over. No one ever says *no*. No one ever *challenges* me.

My phone buzzes again.

Checking my watch, I realize that if I'm gonna be early, I need to leave now. I don't even know what this stupid meeting my uncle wants me at is about. Or why it has to be at some restaurant he partially owns instead of at the office where they usually are.

"Fucking stupid. Like I don't have better things to do on a Friday night." Standing, I pull my shirt over my head and head upstairs to my bedroom. The intense floral perfume of the woman is clinging to my skin, and I need to wash it away if I plan on bringing someone else home tonight.

The word Decadence beams down at me in neon cursive as Robert pulls my black town car up to the curb. I've never been here, or even heard my uncle talk about it, but as soon as I step through the doors, I can see why he insisted on meeting here.

It's dimly lit, but I've always thought that makes a woman more attractive. And attractive is definitely the word I'd use to describe the waitresses.

"How can I help you today?" A pretty brunette beams up at me from the hostess stand—a blush already staining her full cheeks as she does her best to maintain eye contact.

"That depends. What time do you get off work, gorgeous?" The way her whole face flushes, I'll bet she just creamed herself.

Before she can answer, a stunning dark-haired woman wearing a cream-colored pantsuit appears behind her with an unapproving glare like an overprotective mother. "That won't be necessary, Jackson. Your uncle is in the back. You can follow me."

"And you are?"

"My name is Carmela." Her tone makes me think she doesn't like me, and I wonder what she has to do with the meeting and how she knows anything about me to begin with.

Carmela saunters through the tables, pausing to say hello to a few patrons, while I check out the waitresses and try to decide which one I'll let finish the job the no-name woman from earlier walked out on.

As far as restaurants go, this is a nice one. Exposed brick, distressed wood, bronze furnishings–for the area, it's not exactly upscale, but it's better than Serafina's. A flash of rust catches my eye, and I turn my gaze.

It's been a long time since a woman took my breath away. But this one, there's something about this one that's special. Dark copper hair that curls down below her breasts, bright blue eyes that are piercing–even in the dim lighting. Full, bubble-gum pink lips.

She throws her head back and laughs at something a customer says before nodding and moving away from the table she's at. Distantly, I hear my name behind me, but I've already turned and started walking toward the ginger goddess.

If I have to guess, I'd say she's about five-six. Her back is to me as she types something into the computer system, but she doesn't startle when I give her my smoothest, "Hi, there."

Looking over her shoulder, she doesn't appear phased at all as she gives me a once-over and turns back around. "Can I help you with something?"

Her tone is ice cold, and my eyebrows knit together in disbelief. Women don't ever respond to me like this. Affronted, I scoff, "What's your name?"

Sighing, she spins around and locks eyes with me like I'm a rodent she just caught sneaking into the kitchen. "Scarlett. And you are?"

Scarlett. Appropriate.

Now that I'm closer, I can see she has freckles over her

cheeks and nose. They make her seem endearing. Innocent. The one thing that I *don't* want in a woman.

But her fiery attitude tells me that even if she's innocent, she's got some bite to her.

Sticking my hand out for her to shake, I flash my best *fuck me* smile and respond, "Jackson Tailor."

Her contemptuous look drops, lips opening in surprise, as her eyes widen a fraction. A rosy hue breaks out on the apples of her cheeks, and she's about to say something when I hear my uncle speak behind me.

"Jackson, leave Ginny alone and let her do her job."

My eyebrow raises as I smirk at her before mouthing *'Ginny.'* She glares at me before her eyes snap to my uncle as he walks up and places himself between us.

"Shit, I'm sorry. I'm still getting used to the name tag thing," he tells her quietly.

The way her eyes soften and warm when she looks at him doesn't sit right with me. She's gotta be in her mid-twenties, at least. My uncle may be a good-looking man for his age, but he's *ancient* compared to her.

"It's okay, Mr. Tailor. Don't worry about it. Can I get you anything?" Her tone is hopeful and doting, and it makes my stomach roil.

"Are you trying to get one up on Aunt Sadie? Fooling around with a younger woman because she went and married her little boyfriend already?" It's a low blow, but I'm irrationally angry that the old man obviously got to the little gingersnap before I could.

Only a year has passed since he signed the divorce papers my aunt gave him. He had the perfect woman. If there is such a thing, my Aunt Sadie is it. And instead of treasuring her like a dragon with its gold, he fucked around on her publicly and drove her into the arms of a man that's twenty years younger than her.

"That's enough, Jackson," he warns.

Ginny's face is crimson as she furiously shakes her head. "It isn't like that!"

Uncle Scott jerks his chin in the direction behind me and says, "Let's go."

Pushing around me, he heads to the other side of the restaurant, where there's a long hall, but I don't follow him. Instead, I step closer to Ginny, lowering my head and asking, "What's it like, then? Because that look you were giving him was definitely a little too eager, if you ask me."

"You're disgusting. He's my boss, and older than my father. Not my style," she grits out as she glares up at me. She's gripping the pen she's holding so tightly that it might snap at any moment.

"What *is* your style? I'd love to find out." Taking another step toward her, I smirk as she takes one back, yet the fight never leaves her narrowed eyes.

"Not *you*. That's for damn sure." She straightens her spine, attempting to make herself look taller.

"I'm a man of many talents, *Scarlett*. Why don't you give me a chance to show you?" Reaching out for a lock of her hair, my hand freezes mid-air when she flinches. It's minimal, as if she catches herself and steels her body against it, but her breathing has picked up, and her eyes are wide as she looks at me. Hardened, as if she's bracing herself for impact.

Who hurt you, my fiery little ember?

Dropping my hand, I step back and stick my hands in my pockets. "Okay, I'm sorry. I'm not usually this much of a dick. You caught me on a bad night. Why don't you join me for a drink when you're off work? I'll make it up to you."

She searches my face silently for any sign of insincerity before her posture relaxes, and she lets out a long breath. Shaking her head, she reaches up and tucks her hair behind one ear. "I don't think so. I have to get back to work." Then she turns and walks into the open-concept kitchen.

Watching until she disappears, I slowly turn and follow my uncle to where he's impatiently waiting outside a bronze-finished door. When I reach him, I extend my hand. "I'm sorry, that was uncalled for."

He smacks it away, then lightly hits me upside the head. "You're damn right it was. And you embarrassed the poor girl. You better apologize."

"I did! And I asked if she wants to get a drink after work so I can apologize again."

"With *words*, you jackass! Not with your dick!"

Well, he's got me there.

Ginny

"**S**mug, cocky bastard!" The cooks in the kitchen give me weird looks as I pass by them and head to the walk-in fridge in the back.

I've heard about Jackson Tailor, both from his uncle and from the women I work with. From everything people say about him, he's an arrogant asshole who thinks too highly of himself and too little of the fairer sex.

He certainly lives up to his reputation.

Milk chocolate hair and hazelnut irises flash behind my lids as I close my eyes and lean against the wall in the cooler. It was only a matter of time before I met him, but the way his uncle talked about him left me hoping for...I don't know, more *depth.*

"My nephew is gonna be around a lot more here soon. Jackson's a good kid. He's just lost right now. He's got a chip on his shoulder waiting for someone to fill it up with gold and make him whole again. It's gonna take a special person to make him want to change his ways."

Not that I want to change the ways of a billionaire playboy, but if he's going to be around more, I certainly don't need another perverted man in my personal space thinking

I'm a plaything he can throw in a toy box and pull out whenever he feels like it.

I already have to deal with that at home.

Home.

It's been six years since I moved to New York—six years since I decided to take the Calloway's offer of a full ride to NYU.

Six years since I moved in with Chris.

At first, it was a nightmare. He'd been angry all the time, like he didn't know whether he wanted to strangle me or fuck me. We were both busy with school and really hadn't seen each other all that often, but on nights he was home, he'd go into my room and do the same things he did to me as a kid.

And it hasn't stopped.

Chris never does more than touch me. He made it very clear that he'll never fuck me and that he will never allow another man to put his hands on me. Touching me is only for his pleasure, and as soon as he comes, he leaves my room as if he'd just popped in to say goodnight.

Most nights, I close my eyes and imagine it's *my stranger*, just like when I was a kid, as I finish the job he started. Some nights, the ones I'm ashamed of the most, I beg him to let me come–because he never, *ever* lets me come. I have not one ounce of attraction or love for Chris, but it's like my body is a Rubik's Cube that no one else can figure out except him.

The tight grip of fingers on my skin, the way he handles my body roughly and then stops abruptly—denying me any sort of completion or satisfaction—that part I don't like.

He's stayed true to his word all these years and never fucked me, at least not in the literal sense. His fingers have been in me more times than I can count, and I'm mortified that I continue to let it happen.

My degree has taught me that I have developed a very particular taste in reaction to the trauma Chris has inflicted on me. A taste you don't just go around trusting any regular man with. And I have *tried* to date other men, keeping it from Chris, of course. But as soon as they touch me, there's no spark. No ignition of the flame that lights up my body when it's being slapped or pinched or bitten, so I make an excuse to leave.

Some days I wonder if I've developed some sort of fucked up Stockholm syndrome.

Now, the deeper into medical school he gets, the less I see him around the SoHo apartment his parents bought for him. He's in his second year of residency, and I've graduated with my sociology major.

Chris thinks I have a job as a counselor at a clinic uptown, not far from Decadence. He doesn't know I work at the restaurant–or my *other* job that I start tonight.

This is as close to freedom as I can get right now. Though not for any reason other than my own damn self. When I tried to leave years ago, after barely living in New York for a few months, my feet wouldn't move.

Door open, bags packed and waiting to be rolled down the hall to the elevator, I froze. Aside from the shit with Chris, my life was comfortable, and though I knew what he was doing to me was wrong, I realized I was afraid to be on my own.

Here I am, six years later, and the only thing I can bring myself to do is lie to him about where I work.

Which is why tonight, I'll be starting at the club that Carmela and Mr. Tailor own.

A sex-positive club where people can explore all of their dreams and desires.

It's high-end, invite-only, and extremely exclusive. The people who work there get to call all the shots, so I figure it's a way for me to take back my power. Or try to find it, anyway.

If Chris ever finds out, he'll probably lock me up.

Or kill me.

Jackson

"A sex-positive club? What the fuck is that?" No wonder my uncle didn't want this meeting at the office. When the fuck did he invest in a sex club?

And why the fuck wasn't I invited before?

"Désirer is about people being able to explore who they really are inside. Safely and without judgment. The masks are required to protect the identity of the people who work there and the patrons," Carmela answers, still annoyed at me for "*harassing*" Ginny.

"Why French?"

"Because English is ugly," she snaps back.

"So let me get this straight, Uncle Scott. You've been attending a sex club for over a year now, and you haven't thought to invite me *once*?" Sitting back in my chair, I kick my ankle up on my knee and fold my hands over my stomach.

He's standing on the opposite side of Carmela's office, hands in his pockets as he gazes out a window that overlooks a small courtyard. It's getting dark, and there are lights strung up in the trees that give off an orange glow, illuminating his face. "It's business, Jackson. Not pleasure. I want you to learn the ropes so that when the time comes, you can take over my share of it."

Carmela rolls her eyes and sighs dramatically as I get to my feet to pour myself a glass of scotch from the minibar in the corner of the room. "You act like you're dying, old man," she grumbles.

"I just want you to start learning the way we run things. Is that gonna be a problem, Jackson? Do you think you can act like an adult for once and just do as I ask?" He turns from the window and fixes me with a hard stare.

Shaking my head, I shrug and wave him off. "Keep calling me a child, and I'll keep acting like one."

"You *both* sound like children right now. Jackson, this is serious. This is *my* club, and it has run smoothly thus far. Can I trust you to treat this as a *job* and not a playground? Because if you can't behave yourself, I don't want you there." Her arms are crossed, and there's a stern look on her face.

Briefly, I imagine what she'd look like in leather with a whip.

As if she can read my thoughts, her eyes narrow, and she shakes her head. "Scott, I don't like this."

"Relax. What time should I be there? And where is it?" Like, I'm going to pass up an opportunity to go to a sex club. I'll bet there are tons of women there who like it rough.

Maybe being around a large group of people who like the same things is just what I need.

"I'll pick you up at midnight. You'll be blindfolded until we get there, and you won't complain or say a word about it. If anyone asks who your sponsor is, you'll tell them the owner. Don't tell anyone your name. And, Jackson, the girls are *off-limits*," my uncle demands.

Oh, come on!

"The blindfold is a bit much, don't you think?"

My uncle lets out a sharp laugh but doesn't respond as he

guides me into a building. Or what I assume is a building. As soon as I got in the car, he put the blindfold on and instructed me not to remove it until he said so.

There's a shuffling of feet and a few murmurs, before I hear the unmistakable sound of a door opening. As I step over the threshold, I'm hit with the sweet scent of cigars and roses, so thick that I'm sure it will stick to my suit once I leave.

We take a few more steps, and I hear the door close behind us, before my uncle pulls the blindfold off, and my sight is returned. It takes a moment for my eyes to adjust to the dim lighting, but once they do, I see we're standing in the middle of a long hallway.

Floors made of deep mahogany wood gleam under our feet as we make our way down the quiet hall. The walls are dark, perhaps black or navy, with a cream damask pattern that seems to shine like gold the longer I look at it. My eyes flit up to the ceiling, where there are crystal chandeliers that look like petals suspended in the air, spaced out enough to ensure that the lighting stays low.

My uncle reaches out and pulls me back into the middle of the hall, saving me from walking right into a small table against the wall. There are dozens of them spaced between shiny black doors, housing large vases filled with white roses.

"What's with all the roses?" My attention turns from the decor to him. There's a distant hum of voices and music coming from ahead, where the hall ends at another door.

"There's a different color rose for each wing, as well as different Angels. It'll take you time to figure it all out. I'm taking you to the Grand Room now–it's where everyone congregates before the activities begin."

"Angels?"

As we reach the end of the hall, he turns to me and holds out a plain black mask that I didn't notice he was holding before. Motioning to it, he puts one over his head, concealing the top half of his face. "Yes, Angels. There are three tiers of them–gold, black, and platinum. *Gold Angels* are for this wing, the Confessional wing. They talk and put on a show if they want to. But there's no touching allowed. *Black Angels* work in the Dreamers wing–you can touch them, but you can't fuck them. *Platinum Angels* are in the Desires wing. Anything goes in that wing as long as all parties consent.

"Masks have to be worn at all times. We have a variety to choose from for the clients, and if you want to bring your own, you can. But for tonight, this should be fine."

Reaching up to secure the mask around my face, I mull over the information he gave me with a smirk. "I still can't believe you've kept this from me for so long. You don't know me very well if you think I'm not gonna have fun in this place."

"Carmela is right, Jackson. This isn't a playground!" he snaps back. "These aren't the type of men who want their dirty laundry getting out, and these aren't the type of women you fuck and kick out of your penthouse. Everyone respects everyone here. Mick and I don't even know who half the people here are. Carmela is the only one who knows the identities of everyone. It's best kept that way. The last thing I need is for you to go sticking your cock in places it shouldn't be."

"Why bring me then?" I try to keep the annoyance out of my voice, but fail miserably. "Why is it so important to you that I get brought into this as a partner? I'd rather have a good time."

"And I'd rather you grow the fuck up already!" His voice echoes in the empty hall, and I grit my teeth to stop myself from replying.

All I am is a fuck up in his eyes. Even if he has faith in me, the disappointment always shows more. It's why the board of our company wants me out. Because they can see that not even he thinks I can do my job correctly.

The thing is, I'm damn good at my job. The company makes more money because of me. *I'm* the one who makes the deals, buys the companies, and breaks them down to sell them off. *I* make the merger deals. Tailor Industries is a multi-billion dollar conglomerate. And it's *me* who has my hands in every part of it.

My extra-curricular activities have no bearing on how well I close a deal. For years, they've continued to treat me like a child, and just like I told my uncle earlier, keep treating me like one, and I'll keep acting like one.

If they would just leave me be, then maybe I wouldn't go out of my way to prove them right. You'd think I'd want to prove them wrong, but I don't. I'm a Tailor, and Tailor men don't beg for approval.

My silence must placate him because, without another word, he reaches out and opens the door. Suddenly, the hall fills with soft instrumental jazz and chattering voices. Following him, I abruptly stop just inside the door to take in my new surroundings.

The Grand Room is brighter, though just barely–the larger-than-life chandelier in the center of the room and a giant circular bar directly underneath it are the only things giving off light. There are various sectionals, sofas, and loveseats scattered throughout the large space, all crushed velvet the color of cinnamon.

But that isn't what catches my immediate attention.

Women–and men–are walking through the crowd, wearing nothing but lingerie…and *wings*.

Shimmering gold, shiny black, and silvery platinum feather wings.

This must be what my uncle meant when he said *Angels*.

"Quite a sight, isn't it?" he asks lowly.

There are a lot of questions I want to ask, but I settle for, "Why are the wings so big? Doesn't that defeat the purpose of getting close to the clients?"

He chuckles and claps me on the back. "This is why I want you on board, Jackson. I pull you into a room full of half-naked women, and the first thing you ask is a question driven by a client's experience that may have them deciding not to return."

Glancing at him out of the corner of my eye, I shrug, not caring about anything he just said and only wondering why they'd make it harder to touch the Angels.

"The wings stand out a foot on each side, purposefully making it harder to reach out and grab. If a client gets handsy, they get removed immediately. Remember what I said about consent? The Angels have full control here. If they want to be touched, they'll invite you to a room. If you ask for them and they decline, you leave it at that. Not that *you'll* be sampling the fare."

Fuck if I won't be.

There are enough leggy blondes and brunettes to keep me busy for days. Even though everyone is wearing masks, I don't miss the way eyes light up, or darken, as we walk further into the room. We go straight to the bar, and he orders two Macallan neats as I turn around and continue my perusal.

"There are more clients than I thought there would be." Taking the glass he offers me, I take a sip of the smokey, sweet amber liquid and appreciate the path of fire it burns down my throat.

"There's a show tonight. There are viewing windows in the Desires wing. Occupants can open the curtains if they'd like so that people can watch. But, once a month, there's an actual show. Think of it as one big orgy that clients can walk around and join if they want to."

"I'm assuming you guys screen for STIs?" Looking over, I'm a little surprised to see that he's facing the bar, hunched over his drink, instead of appreciating the view of scantily clad women.

"Everyone gets tested weekly, Angels and clients. And there is no barebacking it here. Everyone has to use a condom. That's a hard rule."

Well, at least that's a rule I can get behind. It's too easy for people to lie about having a sexually transmitted disease. And women, in my experience, *will* lie to get what they want. When you're rich, everyone wants a piece of the pie. Doesn't matter how they get it.

A flash of russet catches my eye, causing my head to snap in its direction so quickly that I hear my neck crack. My eyes bounce around, seeking the color out, but just as quickly as it appears, it's swallowed by the crowd.

The majority of the group is moving toward the back of the room, so I assume the show is about to start. Still searching for the redhead, I notice that there are now three men stationed outside each of the doors that lead away from the main space. Two are dressed in all black–standard security guards, I'm guessing–while a third is in a tuxedo holding a clipboard.

My uncle must notice my curiosity because he tells me, "Each wing gets security and a booker. If a client sees a woman or man they like, they ask the booker to secure them for the evening. When it's time to go into the rooms, security goes with the Angel, so if they don't wish to entertain the client, they simply leave without causing a scene."

Taking another sip of my drink, my brows furrow as I look back at him. "That seems highly complicated. Why not let the clients and Angels work that out themselves first?"

He smiles, more to himself than at me. "Another great observation."

Raising his glass to his lips, he's about to take a drink before a series of coughs erupts from his throat. Turning my attention back to the crowd, I glance back at him a few times while he struggles to get his breathing under control.

In the back of the room, the door is propped open, and only a quarter of the clients and Angels remain. Immediately, my eyes catch on a mane of glossy red hair. Pushing off the bar, I try not to catch my uncle's attention as I focus mine on the woman standing across the room.

She's dressed in black thigh-high stockings with garters

that disappear beneath the black lace skirt attached to her satin corset. Delicate champagne-colored wings grace her back while her long sex-kitten waves settle down the middle of them.

Her hair is longer, but her height is the same, as is the creamy complexion of her skin. Silently, I urge her to turn around so that I can see her face. Even masked, I could tell if it was the woman from earlier.

Ginny.

"Jackson, why don't you go enjoy the show? There's something I need to take care of. I'll find you when it's over." My uncle's voice is gritty, and he's wiping at his mouth with a napkin when I turn and look at him.

"Thought you didn't want me to treat this place like my playground?" My attention snaps back to the redhead just in time to see her turn her head and laugh at something another Angel wearing black wings says.

It is her.

"I didn't say join the show. I said enjoy it. Just...*behave*, for once." He walks off without another word, and as soon as he disappears behind a door, I head over to the booker standing outside the wing we came in through.

"Good evening, sir. How can I help you tonight?" The booker is probably in his seventies, and his eyes look wary as if he realizes he's never seen me here before.

"I'd like to book the redhead over there for the evening," I say with a slight English accent. Voice acting is one of my many talents.

"Ah, yes. Miss Scarlett is free tonight. May I see your card, please?" he asks smugly, as if he already knows I'm not going to know what he's talking about.

If I hadn't been sure it was Ginny before, I certainly was now that he just used the name she gave me at Decadence. "It's my first time. My sponsor is the owner."

That wipes the smirk right off his face. "Very well, sir."

He writes something on his clipboard before nodding to

each security guard. One heads off toward Ginny, while the other opens the door and motions for me to follow him.

When the door closes behind me, he angles his body so that his back isn't to me as we walk. "Rules are simple. No going beyond the curtain. You can ask her to do things, but if she refuses, don't push it. You can touch yourself, but only if she gives you permission. If at any time you make her uncomfortable, she can leave, and you will wait to be escorted back to the Grand Room. Understand?"

"Seems simple enough—don't be a dick. Got it." Reaching up, I loosen the tie around my collar. If I can ask her to put on a show, might as well get comfortable watching it.

The security guard lets out a chuckle and nods his head as we stop in front of a door. "That's right. Don't be a dick."

He opens the door and steps aside for me to enter. "Go to the far side through the curtain and get settled. It'll be me bringing her back, so don't get any funny ideas about ambushing her and leaving the curtain open. Curtain stays closed until she wants to open it."

Once I'm in the room and the door closes, I look around while removing my jacket. The flooring is the same as the hall, and the walls are the same dark color without the gold pattern. There are matching black, crushed velvet, clamshell loveseats on opposite sides of the room, with a black lace curtain that cuts the space in half. In here, there are no chandeliers. Instead, there are fluted, frosted glass wall sconces that give off light at both ends.

Pulling the curtain closed behind me, I toss my jacket on the loveseat in the back of the room. My tie quickly joins it before I unbutton my cuffs and roll the sleeves of my white dress shirt as I sit. The mask on my face is itchy, but I don't entertain thoughts of breaking the rules and removing it.

Wouldn't want my uncle to find out I didn't listen on more than one account.

A few more minutes pass, and I take the time to settle back on the couch, kicking a foot over one knee and spreading my arm out along the back of the loveseat, the other hand resting in my lap. When the door opens after a few more minutes, the security guard peeks his head in to make sure I followed his directions before moving aside for Ginny.

Her eyes seem to glow from behind her intricate mask as she peers at me for only a moment through the curtain. She turns and gives a slight nod to the guard. Her movements are unsure, as if this is her first time doing this.

But perhaps that's just a persona.

Once the door closes again, she takes a deep breath before turning to face me.

Smirking, I settle into *my* persona. Enjoying the way her eyes widen as I greet her.

"Hello, Little Ember."

Ginny

I've been preparing for tonight for over a year. My best friend, Valentina, has worked here for a few years now, and she's the one who suggested I try it. She doesn't know about everything with Chris, but she knows enough to know I'm trying to take back my life.

Carmela and Mr. Tailor offered me the job the first night I auditioned, but it's taken an entire year to work up the courage to actually do it. That's the nice thing about this job, though; it's entirely at *my* pace.

Since there's a show tonight, I thought it was the perfect night to start. Get a feel for how things work. Watch the other girls during the show to see what they do and how they act. Then, when the time comes to get to work, I won't feel like a fish out of water.

But the bookings aren't supposed to happen until after the show.

So, when security approaches me and says I've been booked already, the anticipation hits me like a bullet train. The guard makes it clear that I can say no if I want to wait, but I hear myself say it's okay, and before I know it, I'm being ushered through the Confessional wing door.

Electric shocks run from my chest to my stomach as security brings me to my room–the sound of my heels on the floor echoing in the empty hall. As I got ready in the changing suite earlier, one of the girls told me I'd go fast tonight because of my hair, because I look exotic in a sea of brunettes and blondes. I just wasn't expecting it to be *this* fast.

The guard opens the door and steps aside to let me in. Barely giving the man on the couch a glance, I nod to the guard, signaling it's okay for him to leave.

When I turn around again, my breath catches in my throat.

Even though a curtain separates us, it's sheer enough that I can see him clearly. This man looks exactly like the imaginary friend I dreamed up when I was a child.

It's him—my stranger.

A plain black mask is covering the upper half of his face. He's freshly shaven, chocolate hair neatly swept out of his face, but not gelled back. Golden brown eyes stare at me from behind the mask as his lips tilt up at one corner.

"Hello, Little Ember."

His words send a shiver down my spine. My eyes widen at the nickname and his slight English accent, just like the man I've dreamed of all my life.

I've never considered myself a very sexual person. I've never had the chance to really explore that side of myself. However, there is something utterly gratifying and thigh-clenching about the way he's looking at me.

"Good evening, sir." Slowly, I make my way to the curtain, deliberately swinging my hips the way I was trained to. He smirks and leans forward to rest his elbows on his knees as he watches the show I'm putting on.

It's liberating.

My hands raise, running over my thighs as I slowly lift my skirt to give him a peek at what's underneath–a simple lace thong–before continuing their journey up my body. "What brings you here tonight? Do you have something you want to talk about? Something you wish to confess?"

His eyes follow my hands, Adam's apple bobbing as he

swallows. "I just wanted to admire the beautiful view for the evening. Tell me, Little Ember, is there something *you* wish to confess?"

His question takes me aback. Carmela, and most of the girls who work in the Confessional wing, told me that the men here either like to talk like it's a therapy session or they like to confess their dirty secrets while watching the Angels touch themselves.

"It's my first night," I hear myself say. Why I think he needs to know that, I don't know. My cheeks burn as embarrassment floods my veins, and I drop my hands back to my sides.

Suddenly, I'm self-conscious. It must show on my face because the man leans back on the couch and motions to the matching one on my side. "There's nothing to be nervous about. Why don't you take a seat?"

Grateful that he seems not to be a jerk, I settle on the edge of my loveseat. It vaguely reminds me of the night I auditioned to be a Confessional Angel. Mr. Tailor had been the one on the other side of the curtain that night, though the curtain had been pulled back, and he'd told me to put a robe on immediately.

He hadn't been interested in what my body looked like. Instead, he was more interested in having someone to talk to. He'd made me feel comfortable, and we've had standing weekly "appointments" ever since.

This man, though...this man clearly enjoys the view of my body. Slowly, I arch my back and straighten my shoulders to draw his eyes to my chest. Crossing my ankles, I plaster a smile on as I ask again, "So, what brings you here tonight?"

"You," he states simply. He's still smiling, and where a few minutes ago it was charming, it's now starting to become unnerving. It's making me feel like a rabbit being hunted by a fox.

"Me? If this is my first night, then how could it possibly be me you came here for?" My tone is playful. More curious than nervous now.

"Have you ever done something but you don't know why you're doing it? Then, all of a sudden, something happens, and it all falls into place. Everything starts to make sense, and you know, at that moment, you were always meant to be doing it?"

My throat is dry, and I have to force myself to swallow. Nodding slightly, I whisper, "Yes."

"I was invited here tonight. It's also *my* first time. And I had no idea why the fuck I needed to be here...until I saw you. From the moment I laid eyes on you, I knew you were a firestorm waiting to happen. And I desperately wish to be burned by you, Little Ember."

His words *do* create a storm within me. But I can't let every man who books me make me swoon with pretty prose. Shaking my head, I stand and take a step toward the curtain. "This isn't the wing for that, Mr...what can I call you?"

He stands and takes a step toward me as well. I can see well enough through the lace to decipher he's tall, and his body is toned without being overly muscular. He puts his hands in his pockets like he's going to stroll forward casually, but doesn't take another step. "You can call me whatever you'd like. And I'm well aware that this isn't the wing for such carnal desires. I'm happy to just talk to you...for now."

"And exactly what type of carnal desires are you into?" My hands lift to my body again, sliding up my chest and into my hair.

One of his hands slides from his pocket to the front of his pants like he's going to touch himself before it stills, as if he remembers he's not allowed without my express permission.

"Go ahead if you want," I tell him softly. Eager to see what's under his dark slacks.

Too eager.

As if all my self-control has stolen my golden wings and flown away.

Instead of touching himself, though, he only adjusts his cock through his pants before taking a step back. "My tastes are very…particular."

I'm hungry for more, desperate to know what is so particular about them. Part of the allure of this job was potentially finding someone who could give me what I crave. Or at least what I *think* I crave.

As soon as I open my mouth to ask him to explain further, he asks, "Why are you here?"

"Here, with you?"

"Here, in general. Why are you working here? What is the appeal?" He turns his back to me and grabs his jacket, reaching into the pocket of it for something.

My body freezes, and my nerves alight with panic for a moment. None of the members are supposed to bring anything in. Phones and other things are supposed to be checked at the door when they enter. My stranger must have bypassed all that, though, because a phone appears, and he checks the screen before shoving it back into the jacket.

Annoyance courses through my veins. At him for asking me a question and then promptly ignoring me, and then at the fact that he managed to sneak a phone past security. We're supposed to be safe. It could have been a gun, a knife, or any other weapon.

"Clearly, you have more important things to worry about, so why don't I excuse you?"

Turning, I head for the door but halt when he bites out, "Stop."

"Turn around and look at me," he commands. His tone is sharp and smooth. A few seconds pass while I decide if I want to do as he says, but eventually, I acquiesce.

"Good girl." His words send a fire straight between my legs, and if my body could turn to liquid and spill into his side of the room–it would. A flush ignites my face, creeping lower down my neck as I bite the inside of my lower lip–mindful of the merlot-colored lipstick I'm wearing.

His lips tilt up in a smirk before he asks, "You like to be praised, don't you?"

Opening my mouth to reply, I close it again, realizing I don't really know.

The way my body lights up at his words, the way I'm eager to hear him tell me how good I am again, I must.

Maybe I'm not ready for this job. I feel woefully underprepared for how badly I want to pull the curtain to the side and pounce on this man.

"I...I don't know." Another truth I'm not sure why I willingly give him. Perhaps it's because he's like my stranger come to life, and I feel a connection to him even though he's *not*.

My corset feels too tight, and I bite the inside of my cheek to keep the tears that are threatening to make an appearance at bay. All I wanted was to feel powerful. Like I was in control of my body.

Now I just feel stupid.

He tilts his head to the side as if he's mulling that information around in his head. "I'll ask again, then. Why are you working here?"

Closing my eyes, I inhale, letting the air fill my lungs as I ground myself and try desperately not to fall apart. I'm gonna get fired before the night is over.

He's patient while I pull myself together and think about what I could possibly say. Standing there with his hands in his pockets, his eyes are like molten gold against the inky darkness of his mask.

Taking my time to get it all out, I decide to just be honest. "I don't have much experience with this sort of thing. I wanted a way to feel in control. And to...to find someone who could...teach me...things."

It might be a trick of the light, but I swear a shudder goes through his body. The muscles of his arms flex–a clear giveaway that he's clenching his fists in his pockets. "Are you a virgin?"

Shaking my head slightly, I clasp my hands together behind my back. The masks keep our identities hidden, so might as well just go all in with the truth-telling tonight. "No. But I might as well be."

He lets out a noise that's somewhere between a hoarse cry and a laugh. "Oh, you're just a rare gem, aren't you?" One of his hands lifts to run through his hair. "Tell me, what must I do to ensure only *I* can book you?"

My lower belly tightens, and there's a flutter in my stomach like a hamster just got on its wheel and started running furiously. "I'm not sure that's a thing you can do," I say breathlessly.

The room shifts, as if the air itself is coiling around us, tightening with tension. "I assure you, it will be before the night is through. That is…if you want it to be."

"Yes." My reply is immediate. It's bad enough that I lost my composure the moment he started talking, but I can't imagine doing this with another man.

It's irrational to think of him as my imaginary childhood friend, but he feels so familiar–the coincidence is too extreme–and I want more time with him.

"Then I'll make it happen. For now, I think it's time for you to clock out for the night." He turns to grab his jacket and then watches me expectantly.

"When will I see you again?" I'm anxious, like a puppy whose owner is about to leave it alone for the first time.

A genuine smile takes up his whole face, and I long to see what's underneath the mask. He motions to the door behind me. "Good night, Little Ember."

Hesitantly, I step back, still facing him, and reply, "Good night, My Stranger."

His head cocks to the side. "My stranger? Interesting choice of name."

My lips tilt up at the corner as I continue backing up to the door. "Maybe I'll tell you about it one day."

The guard is standing right outside when I step out, and

he ushers me down the hall before I can even catch my breath. But there's a permanent smile on my face as I immediately make my way back to the changing suite.

I have no idea if it's even possible for one client to book an Angel all to themselves, but I really hope that whoever he is, he's able to.

Jackson

"Where did you disappear off to last night?" my uncle asks as he breezes into my penthouse unannounced.

I'm still sitting at my breakfast bar enjoying my coffee, for Christ's sake. "Got bored, came home. Why are you here so early? Shouldn't you have jetted off somewhere for the weekend with a girl from the club?"

Snorting, he helps himself to my fridge, pulling out a container of sliced strawberries that Claudia had prepared for me a few days ago. Since Aunt Sadie moved to Jacksonville permanently, their housekeeper has been staying busy by coming to my place to cook and clean. She reminds me of my grandma, in a way, and I can honestly say that she's the only woman, besides my aunt, who doesn't grate on my nerves after an hour.

"I made a list of things that need improving at the club. How Carmela has kept that place running for so long without anyone causing major issues is beyond me." The dregs of my coffee are bitter as I finish my cup and move to rinse it out in the sink. Before I left Désirer last night, I had a long conversation with the booker. It took some convincing—and a wad of hundreds—to ensure that Ginny wasn't to be booked by anyone other than me.

Whoever the old man was in charge of that wing, he hadn't been so easily bribed. But, in the end, took the money, making it clear he wanted my ID number the next time he saw me, which would be no problem since the man in charge of issuing the cards *had* been easily bribed. Two shiny, black metal cards were now tucked away in my wallet. One with the slightest scratch on the stem of the feather on the front, so I knew which one to use for my alter ego and which to use when I was with my uncle.

The greasy ID man looked like a kid who hadn't seen the sun in months. Like he lives in the underground room that was set up for him to prepare the cards. There'd been a bed, a kitchenette, and a bathroom, along with multiple machines to make the exclusive cards. I'm not sure where they're getting the people who work for them, or who is in charge of vetting them, but if I'm going to have any hand in the club from this point forward, some things are going to change—just as soon as they've all served my purpose.

"Morroni's men took care of everything. There was never any word of disturbances because they got cleaned up quickly and quietly. Since Mick kicked Morroni out last year, things have been tense. Half his men are still there because Carmela needs the security, and because Morroni thinks Mick is gonna cave and ask him to come back. Either way, it's been a power struggle."

Vinny Morroni. Head of one of the families that run the Mafia and not someone to mess with. Why on Earth had my uncle gotten involved with him?

After he pours himself a cup of coffee, he unlatches the lid to the strawberries and starts to eat straight out of the container. It reminds me of when I was younger, when he used to drop by my grandmother's house unannounced on a Saturday or Sunday afternoon. She'd always have fresh fruit

ready for him to pick at while he and I caught up with whatever was happening at boarding school.

Back when he was still head over heels in love with my
aunt and they made me believe in happily ever afters.

"What are your plans for today?" he asks as he checks the
vintage Rolex on his wrist.

Should I tell him I planned on going into Decadence to see
if Ginny is working? After last night, I can't get the little spit-
fire out of my head. Seeing her at Désirer without her
knowing it's me will be fun. And I plan on using everything I
learn at the club outside of it to get her into bed.

It's been a long time since a woman has made me work for
it, and I have a feeling she's gonna work me like a sheep dog.

"I'm meeting up with Tripp to go over some acquisitions."
The lie rolls off my tongue easily, and there's only a slight
twinge of guilt for not telling him the truth.

As if he can sniff out the lie on my scent, he narrows his
eyes and holds my stare for a moment before I finally shake
my head and raise my brows. "What?"

"It's Saturday. You expect me to believe you're working?"
He looks at me like he can see right through my facade as
easily as looking through a clean glass window.

Pushing off the counter where I'm leaning, I don't meet
his eyes as I head for my bedroom. "Work hard so you can
play harder, Uncle. Isn't that what you always taught me?"

And I intend to play hard today. *Very* hard.

Decadence is busy with the Saturday morning brunch rush.
Which is exactly what I was hoping for, so it's less likely for
Carmela to see me and rat me out to my uncle.

The hostess this morning is another pretty brunette who
flashes me a smile as fake as her veneers. "How many today, sir?"

My eyes bounce around the room–looking for Ginny while trying to avoid Carmela. "Is Scarlett in today?"

Her smile falters for half a second, eyes guarded as she sizes me up. "Who's asking?"

Annoyed by how long this transaction is taking, I hone in on her hard chestnut eyes as a group of people step into the space behind me—a cold gust of the New York spring air accompanying them. "Jackson Tailor."

Recognition blooms across her face and the corner of her plump bottom lip disappears behind her teeth. Normally, I would think that was a genuine reaction to my name, but the sly smile she's now wearing tells me that isn't it. "Ginny works at the clinic on Saturdays. Chillard Women's Center on Lexington and 63rd, close to Equinox."

Warily, I eye the name tag the woman is wearing. It says *Bianca*, but I have a feeling that isn't her real name, just like Ginny's says Scarlett. It was too easy, the way she gave up where Ginny is, to a man she doesn't know, which makes me wonder if the reason is because Ginny told her about our little encounter yesterday.

"Do you always give out the locations of women who work here, and their real names, *Bianca*?" Another cool blast of air causes the tiny hairs on the back of my neck to stand on end as I fight the shiver that wants to roll through me.

There's nothing I hate more than the cold.

It reminds me of the mornings at boarding school when I would get bullied by the older boys who weren't scared of my last name and unending wealth. I'd been tied to the flag-pole in nothing but my underwear more than once before I finally hit puberty and began to fight back.

Bianca drops her voice to a whisper so the customers around us don't hear. They're getting restless at being ignored and I can hear a male behind me muttering something under his breath about me *flirting with the hostess*. "She told me all about your little run-in yesterday, *Mr.* Tailor. So I already know you know her real name. As for telling you *where* she's at? Well, let's just say that I have a feeling she can use some friendly banter today. Just don't piss her off too badly."

Reaching into my suit jacket, I pull my wallet out and discreetly hand her a crisp, fresh hundred straight from my safe at home. "Thanks for the information."

Her eyes light up as she plucks it out of my grasp and tucks it away down the front of her button-up blouse and into the top of her bra. "Anytime, bossman."

Chillard is a beige brick, three-level walk-up that looks like it's seen better days. As soon as I walk in, a cheerful sandy blonde-haired woman in a neon pink and blue windbreaker greets me with a Southern accent as thick as her waistband. "Why, hello there, handsome. What can I do for you today?"

She's sitting behind a glass window and beyond her I can see a few other women mingling and working away on computers. "I'm looking for Ginny."

Instantly, her bright gaze darkens as she peers at me over the top of her horn-rimmed glasses. It feels like I'm about to be scolded and an uneasiness settles between my shoulders as I tense for her to tell me I've already been put on a no visitation list. "Ginny's in with a client right now, young man."

"Does she have a break?" I don't know why I'm bothering. All I have to do is go to the club tonight and I'm sure she'll be there. But she doesn't know *that* man is me, and I want to obtain her as a client of the club *and* as myself.

The lady looks at me skeptically before she checks something on her computer. "It looks like she has something coming up at eleven. It's not a break, but you look like you could use some couch time."

Grinning, I let out a small laugh, earning a scowl in return as she scolds, "*Therapy*, son."

That wipes the grin right off my face. "Sure. I'll take her eleven," I respond with a roll of my eyes.

"Well, go on and take a seat on the couch. What's your name? I'll put you in the computer."

Briefly, I wonder if I should just leave. The last thing I need is it getting out that I was at the Women's Center for a therapy session. It's clear that this lady doesn't know who I am just by my face, but my name might jog some recognition.

"Simon." The name is out of my mouth before my brain can catch up—the name of my late father.

"Last name?" she prompts.

But I've already turned away to go sit on the worn blue corduroy sofa, and she doesn't press the issue. Taking a seat, I scrub my hand over my face and back through my hair. Inexperienced women are not my thing. Slow, virginal, unsure of what they want or like.

My nightmare.

However, when Ginny admitted last night that she was working at the club because she wanted to find someone to teach her—it suddenly became my wildest fantasy.

She'd said she was nearly virginal, and where I'd typically run because virgins end up thinking you're going to get married and that they're in love with you, I found myself enraptured.

Ginny is a gold mine that has yet to be explored—all her treasures, mine for the taking.

For the first time in my adult life, it appeals to me. It hit me with a raw, primal hunger—the *need* to be the one who teaches her what makes her feel good, and shows her how to take and give pleasure. That fiery temper of hers is just waiting to be unleashed.

"Good night, My Stranger." She'd said. She'd been eager for more and desperate not to leave.

My stranger.

Well, me as the *stranger* will teach her things, while me as *Jackson* will reap the benefits.

44

"What are *you* doing here?" Her tempestuous tone cuts through my thoughts like lightning.

Lifting my eyes to hers, I stand and offer my best charming smile, ignoring the irritated glare the lady at the front is sending me through the glass. "I'm your eleven o'clock."

Her hair is piled on top of her head, and she's wearing a simple forest green turtleneck and a pair of jeans that do nothing for her figure. Baggy with frayed bottoms that hover above a pair of tan suede ankle boots. She shakes her head furiously. "I don't think so."

"Afraid so." Making a show of checking my watch, I walk toward her, relishing the way her eyes widen and her throat constricts as she swallows. "Now, why don't you show me to your office so we don't cut into my hour?"

Ginny's cornflower blues dart to the glass where the lady at the front all but has her face pressed up against the surface as she watches our exchange. "How did you find out I worked here?"

"A little birdie at the hostess stand at Decadence sang your location oh so sweetly," I whisper.

Her eyebrows relax as she rolls her eyes and turns to open the door to the rest of the office, muttering about someone named Lenni. "Whatever, let's go. You know this is a waste of resources. This is a *women's* center."

"Ah, but I love women. So I think this is just the place for me, Litt—" I cut myself off abruptly as I almost call her little ember. Playing the two roles is going to be more challenging than I thought.

She pays no attention to it, though, and mumbles, "Gross."

We make our way past free standing cubicles, earning curious looks from more than a few of the men and women who are working. It should make me uneasy, the thought of this getting to the gossip rags before I've even stepped foot outside again, but I'm paying more attention to the way

Ginny swings her hips as she walks in front of me. My cock stirs behind my slacks and I'm glad I'm wearing a long peacoat to hide that fact.

Following her down a hall to the left, I nearly run into her when she stops outside an open door and turns to motion me inside. "This is us."

"You sound *so* happy to see me. Tell me, do you treat all your patients like this?" Once inside, I sit on the small gray couch that's tucked against the wall, catty-corner from a plain black desk. There's no photos on the wall, no plants on the small windowsill that overlooks the sidewalk below. No character or charm. Nothing that makes it feel like it's *her* office.

"I'm *not* happy to see you, Jackson. Why are you here?" she asks in a clearly pissed off tone.

Today, she asks the question with ire, instead of the curiosity she had last night. Such opposites, Scarlett and Ginny.

One, a pile of dying embers just waiting to be stoked to a full flame. The other, an explosive inferno I want to unleash in the confines of my bedroom.

"I'm here to apologize again for yesterday. I know I came off as quite a dick. So, I'd like to ask for forgiveness again, and see if you'll let me take you out as a way to make it up to you."

She crosses the room, leaving the door open, to take a seat at her desk. "I know all about you, Jackson Tailor. And I am not interested in whatever it is you think you want to offer me for the night."

Shifting back to rest against the plush cushion, I fold my hands together behind my head and nod to her. "And what exactly have you heard, Ginny?"

I'm very aware of the way her eyes dart down my body quickly, as if she thinks if she's fast enough, I won't catch her checking me out. She blows a breath out, disturbing the pieces of hair that have fallen out of her bun and frame her face. "Look, it's no secret that you like women. And if that's working out for you, then great, but I'm not into it. I'm not dazzled by your charm or your good looks or your money. There is literally nothing about you that appeals to me."

Ouch.

"And that is, in fact, most likely the only reason you are even here, isn't it? Because I won't say yes, and you aren't used to that. You're just like your uncle in that aspect—you hate the word *no.*"

The last part is said quietly, as if more to herself than it was meant for me, but it catches my attention, nonetheless. Leaning forward again, I ask, "What is the deal with you and my uncle? Thought you said you haven't slept with him?"

Her creamy skin turns pink as her eyes grow wide. "I haven't!"

"I call bullshit."

Goading her is causing her to get all flustered, and it's making me imagine what she'll look like between my sheets with that same look on her face. Setting my elbows on my knees, I try to discreetly bite my knuckle in order to have something else to focus on, because all my cock wants to do right now is stand at attention.

"You know you're doing an awful job of convincing me that I would want anything to do with you. I think it's time for you to leave. You came, you asked, I declined. I'm not a plaything that you can use and throw away when you're done, Jackson." She launches herself out of the chair she's sitting in and strides across the room, catching me by surprise when she reaches out to grab my arm.

She's not strong enough to pull me up, but I oblige her by standing. However, I underestimate how close she is, and when I stand, my erection brushes against her thigh. Ginny sucks in air as her eyes drop to the bulge in my pants. She's still holding onto my arm, and I don't miss the way her fingers flex and her nails dig into my arm marginally. My head dips, breath skating over her cheek as she continues to stare.

"I never called you a plaything, Ginny. As for throwing you away when we're done. Something tells me that would be quite *hard* to do." My voice is deeper, huskier, and my fingers itch to reach out and grab ahold of the back of her neck and sit her up on her desk so that I can fuck her into next week.

Her eyes meet mine, chest rising and falling with her quickened breathing, cheeks reddening with either embarrassment or excitement. Something tells me it's now the latter.

Long, dark lashes flutter against her cheek as my hand lifts slowly, not wanting to see her flinch like she did last time. Just as my fingers are about to curl around a lock of her hair, the sound of glass shattering resonates from somewhere out in the space where all the cubicles are.

Ginny lurches back, the red flush on her cheeks spreading down her face and disappearing beneath the material of the turtleneck. Pushing her fallen strands back, she stammers, "I'm not…I won't be…a notch in your long…carved up bedpost. So, put that thing away and please leave."

She gives me her back and makes no move to turn around as she sets a hand on her hip while the other clutches her neck. Turning my back to the door, I quickly adjust myself before pulling my peacoat tighter around my body and exiting without another word.

As I walk back out to the front, I mentally make a note of all her little tells. The way she sucked in a breath when she felt my length against her leg, the way her eyes widened when she saw it straining against my pants, desperate to be inside her. She's wound tighter than the lid on a pickle jar.

Time for her *stranger* to give her some sweet, sweet release.

Ginny

"I can't believe you told him where I work!"

The rest of the day went by agonizingly slow after Jackson left my office. As soon as I closed the door behind him, I wanted to rush to the bathroom, shove my fingers beneath my panties, and get myself off to the thought of his impressive length.

No wonder he's so cocky.

"He's way hotter in person, Gin. I couldn't help myself. Figured you could use something to get you riled up for tonight. I totally get not wanting to be a notch in his belt, but damn. How could you *not* want him to roll you around in his sheets?" my best friend, Lenni, says through the phone.

Taking a pause from folding my laundry, I reach up to rub my eyes as I think about last night. I'd asked when I would see the stranger again and he'd just told me *goodnight*. "Yeah, he's hot, but he's a complete fuckboy. I'm not interested in that. As for my stranger, he may not even be there tonight. And he may not have gotten them to book me exclusively with him."

The faint click of a lock and the door opening makes me freeze, my heart pounding in my chest so hard it's almost painful.

"Gin?" I hear Chris call out.

"I have to go, I'll see you later," I whisper to Lenni before cutting the call. She's used to it. She thinks I just have an overly protective big brother who acts more like dad.

I've never felt comfortable admitting the truth to her.

The smell of Chinese takeout filters from down the hall as I head toward the kitchen. "Smells good. You're home early."

Chris is unloading the cartons from a bag, not bothering to look up as I enter the room. "Grabbed Mazu on the way home. It was a slow night, so I asked if I could take off early. I got those sesame noodles you like, and the lemon chicken."

He doesn't sound mad, he actually sounds tired, and it doesn't surprise me that they let him come home early. He's been working overtime, getting in as many hours as he can before he leaves with Doctors Without Borders in a few weeks.

Still though, I hadn't expected him home. And I wasn't about to miss my shift at Désirer.

"Sorry, it's bingo night with Michelle." Bracing myself for his attitude, I quickly grab the sesame noodles and a pair of chopsticks and turn back toward my room.

"It's no big, I'm beat. Gonna head to bed after I eat and shower," he replies, causing me to pause in shock.

No argument? No million questions about where it's at and who else will be there? He *must* be tired. He *always* questions me when I say I'm going out.

Michelle is the woman who works the front desk at my clinic. The *same* clinic Chris thinks I work at full time. She covers for me, no questions asked, when he comes around looking for me. Always telling him I'm with a client and he can leave a message. She's never asked why I lie to him, but has always told me she gets a bad vibe from him.

Sometimes we actually do go play bingo.

Turning back around, I watch as Chris empties his lo mein into a large bowl and attacks it with fervor. "I'll probably be late, so don't wait up."

He doesn't so much as blink as he slurps his noodles loudly while nodding.

Okay, then.

The next thirty minutes are spent going over my clinic notes for the day while I eat my dinner and try to stop thinking back to Jackson in my office. *Why* are the most frustratingly annoying asshats complete and utter babes?

Jackson Tailor can have any girl he wants—I don't know why I've caught his eye.

Yes, I do. It's because I keep saying *no.*

And I will continue to say no to him. Until he gets the picture and understands that in no way, shape, or form, is he going to ever hear the word *yes* come out of my mouth.

"Yes!"

The word is sharp and instant, and the acoustics in the small room make it sound as though I've shouted it.

My stranger *was* able to book me exclusively.

So, here we are again. The only thing separating us is the material of our masks and the curtain that divides the room. To my dismay, however, he's shown up tonight in a full face mask. It's pure black, and shines with intricate detailing. The nose and lips are formed but solid, his eyes the only part of his face I can see.

He's asked again if this is what I want and chuckles lowly at the reply I've given.

"Well then, Little Ember. How to proceed? What is it that you wish to learn?" His accent is thicker tonight, but I imagine that happens when you're away from your home for long periods of time. Sometimes your cadence wanes and other times it grows stronger.

Leaning back in his seat, he crosses an ankle over his knee and spreads his arms wide on the back of the loveseat. Like before, his suit jacket is discarded and his white-collared shirt is unbuttoned and loose at the top, with the sleeves rolled halfway up his toned forearms.

It feels hot in the room tonight. And I wish I hadn't taken Lenni's advice with the heavy clip-in extensions that are curled around my face. At least I'd picked more breathable clothing—a simple black silk slip trimmed in lace. I'd been bold and decided not to wear anything underneath.

Before I can answer, he asks me another question. "How many partners have you had?"

My mind soars back to that night. Fifteen seconds, almost as many awkward thrusts, and an apologetic, *"I'm sorry. We can do it again in a little while so you can get off too?"*

Ducking my head in embarrassment, I mumble, "Only one. When I was seventeen."

"And how old are you now?"

"Twenty-four." The words are barely audible as I make my admission.

Seven years. It's been seven years since I lost my virginity.

"Fuck, I'll bet your cunt is so fucking tight." His crass words send a flood of warmth between my legs. He reaches for the glass tumbler on the table beside him and takes a sip of amber liquid. "Do you ever touch yourself?"

My whole body feels like it's on fire. I'm stretched out on the loveseat on my side of the room; legs pressed together to keep the liquid heat between my thighs–afraid it might pool out and make a mess on the crushed velvet.

"Sometimes." My answer is meek. The truth, screaming to be let out. For me to tell someone, *anyone,* the hell Chris puts me through from time to time. But that isn't what this man is here for. He's here for a sexual conquest and a depraved unleashing of his innermost desires.

At least, that's what Carmela always says.

"Little Ember, if you're going to learn what you like, you have to stop being so embarrassed. Now, tell me, what do you think about when you touch yourself?"

You. Even when I didn't know it was you.

"Someone I don't know watching me. Sometimes I imagine them standing over me. Close, but never touching me." My voice grows stronger as I speak. The way he's responding makes me feel good, knowing that he's imagining me touching the most intimate parts of myself.

He adjusts his legs so that they are spread wide. He's hard and if this is going where I think it's going—where I'm *hoping* it's going—then I wonder if he'll oblige me and show me what's under those pants. His knee starts to bounce as he brings a hand to his mouth, biting the knuckle. "So you like to be watched, do you?"

Nodding, I suddenly feel daring, and stand to remove the wings strapped to my back. He watches as I slowly peel the straps down and discard them on the floor before stepping toward the curtain. "Do you want to watch me do it?"

He lets loose a long breath. "Fuck, yes."

When I make it to the curtain, I pull it aside slowly, before moving back step by step, doing my best to appear sexy, until my calves hit the edge of the seat. As I start to lower myself, his words send me to my feet again.

"Come here."

Instantly my chest is filled with a rush of adrenaline. It's one thing to be on my side of the room and do this, do what I was trained for, but to do it so close to him?

Can I do this?

Hesitating, I anxiously finger the hem of my slip. He shifts and motions for me to sit by his side. "I won't bite, I promise. At least not tonight."

His words make it easy to imagine a smirk on his lips as he says them, and it makes me relax a little, moving to sit next to him. The seats are wide and deep, giving us enough room to face each other.

Now that we're closer, I can smell him. Fresh laundry, and a spicy undercurrent of citrus. It drifts across the space between us and coils around my senses, causing my nipples to harden and more arousal to pool between my thighs.

"Lay back," he commands.

I'm hesitant, only because I don't know how that is going to work without us touching each other. As if he's reading my thoughts, he instructs, "Lay your head on the pillow. Keep your legs bent. Let's see if that cunt is as pretty as you are."

A flame licks up my core as I do what he says, the velvet caressing my skin as I keep my legs pressed together. He shifts to kneel, getting close without touching me, just like I said I like to imagine.

"Now. Drop your knees to the side. And let me see how wet this is making you."

Oh, fuck.

Doing as he says, he echoes my silent sentiments. "Oh, fuck. Look how glorious you are."

Watching from between my spread legs, a fresh wave of arousal unfurls and his eyes seem to glow as he inspects me. Silently, I'm cursing the mask that hides his whole face. Because I desperately want to see his facial expression.

"Now, Little Ember. Touch yourself."

Jackson

It amazes me how Ginny is so dead set against letting me take her out, but here—as Scarlett—she's so eager to spread her legs for a stranger.

Not just any stranger, though. *Me.*

If I ever decide to reveal this secret, *our* secret, to her, it's very likely she'll try to kill me.

Although, she might as well be trying right now.

Pussy is pussy. Yeah, there's all different sizes and colors. Some are tighter than others, and some I wouldn't touch with a ten-foot pole. But I've never had a virginal, or nearly virginal, one before. Not even when I was a virgin myself. It's never interested me.

I've seen too many of my colleagues get wrapped up in the appeal of a fresh, never been touched before woman. And after, they have to deal with the clingy, when are we getting married, I'll file a sexual harassment suit if you don't give me what I want, attitudes.

No fucking thank you.

But Ginny's pussy?

As far as they go—and I've seen a lot—is what I consider perfect.

Small and pink, the clit enlarged and peeking up from

under the hood. Wet. So *very* wet, shining with her arousal, and she hasn't even touched herself yet.

Her cheeks are flushed and she starts to squirm the longer my eyes are glued to her cunt. "I told you to stop being embarrassed. Show me what you like. I wish to see what makes you feel good."

Slowly, her hand drifts down her body, nails lightly scraping her skin, leaving goosebumps in their wake. Even though her voice is soft, her tone bites as she says, "It's not like I can just turn off the embarrassment. This is extremely vulnerable."

There's that fiery attitude.

A smirk plays across my lips even though she can't see it. "It's just us, Little Ember. There's no one else here to see this spectacular sight. If I had it my way, no one else would get to see this again. This view would be *mine* for the rest of eternity."

Women love to hear this shit in the moment. Waxing poetic about all the ways you want to keep them and make them yours forever. You don't have to mean it, most of them just want to hear it in the bedroom.

Ginny is no different.

A little moan escapes her lips as they part, her teeth biting into the bottom one. Her fingers find her clit and circle slowly, before she dips a middle finger down between her lips and smears her arousal around that little bud.

My cock is painfully hard, but I refrain from touching myself because she hasn't given me permission. Usually, I wouldn't listen to the rules, but there's something about this entire situation that is really doing it for me and I don't want to fuck it up.

When she lifts her finger, a trail of wetness extends and the sight of it makes my mouth water. What I wouldn't give at this moment to delve between her legs and lap it up with my tongue. "You *do* like being watched. Does it make you feel like a dirty girl? All I want to do right now is slam my cock into you and fill you with cum. Does that make you feel powerful?"

"Yes," she moans as her hips lift against her fingers. Continuing to circle them, her other hand drifts to her breast and I blow out a breath as she pinches her nipple through the lace trim of her slip. "Do you want to touch yourself?"

Her middle finger slides down and my teeth find my bottom lip as it disappears into her slick entrance while her thumb continues to rub at her swollen clit. "As badly as I do, I won't. Tonight is about bringing one of *your* fantasies to life."

"What if my fantasy is to do this while I get to watch you do the same?" Her head tilts to the side as she continues to play with herself, growing more comfortable with every passing second.

"If I take my cock out right now, there won't be any watching. I'll break all the damn rules and there will be sucking, fucking, and coming inside that sweet cunt. But there sure as fuck won't be any watching."

She throws her head back with another moan as she pushes a second finger inside, stretching that tight passage around her petite digits. "I like it when you talk like that."

"I'll bet you do, you dirty little slut." The second the words leave my mouth, she stills. It's like all the air has been sucked out of the room, the moment frozen in time.

"I don't like that." Her tone is hard as the hand that was playing with her breast pushes up into her hair.

"Okay," I say softly. "I'm sorry. Dirty girl is alright, though?"

I've *never* apologized once in the bedroom. I've never had to. Hell, I don't apologize in general, and actually mean it.

But I find myself wanting to fix the moment I've ruined with a simple phrase.

She doesn't respond. Her eyes are closed tightly and wherever she's taken herself in her mind—she's no longer here. The hand between her legs falls away to her side and she wipes it on her slip.

"Scarlett–" Pushing up off my knees, I get off the couch and take a step closer to her.

"No, no, it's okay. I'm sorry. That's what this is, right? Finding out what I like and don't like?" When she removes her hand from her hair, I can see that her eyes are glassy.

My erection diminishes. Feelings and emotions don't belong in the bedroom. But here? This situation makes me realize that if our arrangement continues, there's a possibility of this happening a lot.

The sudden need to gather her in my arms is overwhelming.

It's a foreign feeling, the sharp sting in my chest as her tears start to fall. She sits up, pulling her knees to her chest as she wraps her arms around them and lays her cheek against their smooth surface. "I'm so sorry."

"You have nothing to apologize for," I tell her, though anger is coursing through my veins. Not because I'm upset that the moment is ruined. But because *someone* is the cause of this reaction she's having. Phrases like that don't make you cry unless they've been directed at you in a negative way.

Abruptly, she bolts from the couch as if it's burned her. "I completely understand if you don't want to see me exclusively anymore. There are lots of other women here who can give you what you want."

As she makes her way across the room for the door, it makes my heart skip a beat and a panicked feeling bursts in my chest. If she makes it out that door, it may very well be the last time I see her. Her embarrassment is getting the better of her and she has the power to make sure we don't see each other again.

"I don't want other women." My words make her stop— back to me, hand on the door. "I'm sorry for whatever happened to you for that phrase to have such an impact. If you want to talk about it, you can. That's why this is called the *Confessional* wing, isn't it?"

Turning, she lifts a hand to grab her elbow as she looks

down at the ground sullenly. "Why would you pay so much money for *this*?"

"It isn't about the money," I say while walking toward her slowly. Strangely enough, it isn't a lie. If this were any other time, if she was any other woman, it would be, and I *would* move on to another Angel. But watching her flinch yesterday, and seeing her come apart today, it's quickly becoming something I've never dealt with before. Something I've never *felt* before.

Protectiveness.

"You said you wanted a way to feel in control. This is the safest way for that to happen. And you're safe here with me, Little Ember. No one can hurt you in here. No one *will* hurt you in here. In this room, I've got you," I tell her quietly, stopping a mere hair's breadth away, our hands nearly touching.

"And what about out there?" she asks, just as quietly. Her big blue gaze pierces mine, hopeful, begging to be saved.

"Out there?" Inwardly, I curse myself because though it was my plan all along, its connotation has changed now. "Out there, maybe it's time to find someone with enough power to protect you from whatever it is you're scared of."

Oh, yeah. I'm going to hell.

Ginny

My stranger's words echo in my mind for the rest of the night and into Sunday.

Part of me was disappointed to hear him tell me to find someone else. It was silly, and I felt stupid for forming such an attachment to him in only two days. But I'd been hoping his answer would be more along the lines of *let's remove our masks and just be together in the real world.*

So. Fucking. Dumb.

It's not like me to be this delusional.

"Ginny, dear. Is everything alright? You've barely touched your breakfast," Christine's voice interrupts my self-loathing thoughts.

Chris' parents flew up for a few days to be here for some charity event Tisch is throwing on Wednesday. Even though Calvin hates the city and Christine would rather be in the warmer weather back home in Beverly Woods, North Carolina. But Tisch is treating Chris well, and Calvin thinks that throwing them a sizable donation will convince them to continue to do so.

Looking down at my plate, the Brioche French toast I ordered is indeed getting soggy beneath the berry sauce it comes with. We're at Little Owl in Greenwich Village–Christine's favorite place to eat brunch when they come to the city.

"I guess I'm not very hungry," I tell her with a fake smile and shrug my shoulders.

"Gotta make sure you fit into your dress for Wednesday night, eh, Gin?" Chris elbows me in the ribs, and I roll my eyes while scooting my chair closer to Christine.

"Oh! That makes sense, honey. It is a lovely dress. A little risqué for a hospital event if you ask me, but you do look lovely in it," she says as she picks at her asparagus salad.

The chatter from the restaurant swallows my unladylike snort as I reach for my mimosa. "Chris is the one who wants me to wear that one. Take it up with him. I'm happy to wear something different."

Chris stops cutting into his steak as Calvin and Christine share an uncomfortable look discreetly—well, not *so* discreetly—but only I see it. Chris is looking at me like I'm the most annoying thing ever to grace his life while I smile sweetly in return.

"Ginny," he stresses. "I've already told you that I want to make a good impression on the bigwigs of the board."

"And you think parading me around in a skin-tight gown is gonna do that?" I fire back.

"Oh, come on. We all know those men will be drooling all over you. That'll be enough to keep me in their good graces just to get a glimpse of you at every event they throw. You know how men like that are." He waves his knife around as he mansplains his reasoning, before plucking a bite of steak off his fork with a ridiculous grin.

Calvin lets out a long sigh and shakes his head, but remains quiet. The uncomfortable silence descends over the table, just like it always does when Chris makes comments like this. Neither Calvin nor Christine, will ever speak out against their son.

It's only gotten worse as we've grown older.

"Thanks, Chris. I love being reduced to your arm candy

even though I'm your *sister*." I'm playing with fire. His parents will only be here until Thursday. And lately, he's left me alone. But the look in his eyes right now says that once they leave, I'll more than likely be getting a visit in my room.

"You're *not* my sister," he spits venomously.

"Now, now. Let's talk about something else, shall we? Ginny, how is the clinic? Are they treating you well?" Christine intercepts.

My eyes find hers as I sit back in my chair, crossing my arm under the one holding my glass. "Yeah, things are good there. I feel like I'm really making a difference."

"That's great to hear, honey! How are you feeling about Chris leaving soon? Will you be okay on your own? I'm going to be so worried about you in that apartment by yourself." She pushes her half-eaten salad away and drains her white wine before laying a hand on my arm. "I worry about you here alone."

"I'll be fine." My eyes meet Chris' over the table. "In fact, I'm looking *forward* to having my own place for a while."

Christine *insists* we see the Moulin Rouge! Broadway show. *Just us girls.*

While the show is fantastic, and honestly sort of relatable at times, my mind keeps drifting back to Désirer and wondering if *he's* there, wondering where I am.

After the show, I suggest we walk for a little bit before catching a cab back to the apartment. "I just need some air," I tell her.

"Are you sure you're feeling okay? You've been *off* all day, Ginny. You know you can tell me if something is bothering you," Christine coos. She's paying more attention to the knock-off purse vendors than she is to me, watching them with thinly veiled disgust as she scrunches her nose.

"Yeah, I'm feeling fine. You know how Chris is. Sometimes it's just nice to get a little space." We pass by Baked by Melissa and I pull her into the mini cupcake and macaron shop for a treat.

"I need to be able to fit into my dress, too, Gin." She pats the nonexistent bump of her stomach and looks around as though the other people in the shop are judging her just for walking in the place.

Ignoring her, I tell the girl behind the counter, "We'll take two sugar cookie macarons and two snickerdoodle ones, please."

Christine lets me pay and we step out of the way, waiting for another girl to hand us our confections. "You're thin as a rail. Two tiny macarons aren't gonna kill you."

"Oh, all right, I suppose," she giggles. It makes me sad, because I know Calvin has never made her feel like she isn't thin enough.

No, those comments have always come directly from Chris.

"Don't want to get fat, Mom. Dad will leave you for someone younger."

"Mom, have you put on weight? Maybe you should start up Pilates again."

Where he gets his view on women from, I have no idea. But it certainly *isn't* Calvin.

We walk a few more blocks as we enjoy our dessert. The evening spring air bites at our cheeks, turning them a bright shade of rose as we make small talk about the newest gossip back in Beverly Woods and the things going on at the clinic— at least the things I can talk about.

"Well, I'm glad you're happy. Any thoughts on moving into your own place?" The question is leading, and honestly, it takes me by surprise. Ever since I was eighteen they've been pushing for me to keep living with Chris so that I don't have to pay rent.

At my confused look, she lets out a little laugh. "Darling, I *know* how difficult Christopher can be. And I know it isn't exactly fair that we bought him a place and not you one."

"It's fine–" I try to tell her, but she keeps going as though I haven't said anything.

"I just don't want you thinking that we love you any less than Christopher. What with school and rent being paid for, I assume you've built up quite the savings. If you wanted to use some of it for a down payment on something, I'm sure it can be arranged for whatever you want to spend to be matched." She doesn't look at me as she suggests it, but her offer nearly knocks me off my feet.

The Calloways have money, but they aren't wealthy wealthy. They already have what I consider to be a mansion in Beverly Woods, one of those timeshare things with the Hilton Grand Vacations Club, and a condo in Coronado. Not to mention the three-bedroom apartment Chris and I live in.

"That's *really* generous of you, Christine," I finally manage to say.

She shrugs as though it's not, stepping to the edge of the sidewalk to hail a cab. "My little girl isn't so little anymore. I know earlier it seemed like I didn't want you to be on your own but it's time you had your own space. In a *secured* building. And don't think we aren't making Chris take over the payments for his apartment once he's secured his place at Tisch."

Giving me a wink, she opens the door of the cab that's stopped for us and gets in, sliding over as she gives the driver the address to the apartment.

For the first time since I've become a part of the Calloway's family, I actually *feel* like family.

Jackson

It's been four days since I've seen her.

She hadn't shown up at Désirer Sunday night, which was just as well because my uncle needed me to be there for a meeting with Carmela and Mick, and I hadn't had time to slip away for as long as I would have liked, anyway.

Monday and Tuesday, work kicked my ass. Both nights, I fell asleep on my couch and didn't wake up until well after two in the morning. There hadn't even been time in my day to go down to Decadence to see if she was working there.

I consider sending my secretary, Stacey, to the clinic Wednesday afternoon, but in all honesty, I need her with me at the office. Besides, I have no idea what I would even send her for. To see if Ginny is working? Then what?

I'm at that stage before you turn into a full-on stalker.

Fixated. Zeroed in on. *Obsessed.*

It crosses my mind as I stare out the glass floor-to-ceiling window of my office that it's been nearly a week since my cock has seen any action. Ginny has given me blue balls more times than any woman has been allowed to repeatedly grace my bed.

And I can't fucking get *enough.*

"Do you need me to go pick up a suit for tonight?" Stacey's honey-laced tone cuts through my thoughts.

Swiveling around in my chair, I pin her with a confused look. "What's tonight?"

Her brows raise and her expression reads '*are you kidding me*' as she sighs. "Scott asked you to take his place at the Tisch Hospital event tonight. Remember?"

No, I don't fucking remember.

"I have things to do tonight. Can't I just send a check and put the company name on it?" Grabbing a pen off my desk, I start to open the drawers to try to find a checkbook.

"Jackson, I don't know what's been going on with you this week, but get it together. The board is already after Scott to put a leash on you and now you're distracted. Frankly, it's not a good look. What's going on with you?" She perches at the edge of my desk, concern written over her pretty features.

There was a time when I begged her to get into bed with me. She turned me down flat before revealing she preferred the company of other women. When I told her I was perfectly okay with watching, she threatened to quit.

She's the best secretary I've ever had, and I used to wonder if it's because we've never slept together, but the longer we work together, the more apparent that becomes.

Over the years, she's become more like an honorary big sister. One who I pay an astronomical amount for, on top of all the lavish vacations she squeezes out of me.

At five-foot-ten, Stacey is a knockout. Remnants of last year's Mediterranean glow still clings to her skin. Long blonde hair and Caribbean blue eyes. Big full lips that I once imagined wrapped around my dick but ended up scolding me more often than not for my *bad behavior* with women.

"Be my date?" Ignoring her question, I shoot her the best puppy dog eyes I can muster.

The sun is starting to set over the New York skyline, casting the room in an orange glow, making Stacey's eyes sparkle as she replies, "I figured that was gonna happen. Already let Kaia know I'd be going out tonight."

"Tell your wife I owe you both a weekend at the spa."

Stacey often accompanies me to these events. She looks good in photos and keeps the gossip down, even though it still isn't enough to please the board. It's actually how she met her now wife, who is a senior software engineer for Google. Kaia understands the demands of Stacey's job and beyond giving me crap every now and then for taking up most of her wife's time, she enjoys the perks I give them.

"You owe us *two*," she says, getting off the desk to leave. "Pick me up at seven?"

Checking the time on my computer, I realize it's already nearly five. "What time is the event?"

"Eight."

"Where's it at?"

"The Lighthouse. I figure it'll take nearly an hour to get there with traffic."

"Yeah, okay. Go ahead and head home to get ready." Closing out of my files on the computer, I check to make sure everything is set for tomorrow before standing to grab my jacket and briefcase.

"Already planned on it." She waves a hand as she retreats, disappearing out the door and down the hall.

Smartass.

By the time the event is over, there will still be plenty of time to go to Désirer. If Ginny isn't there tonight, I'm gonna hunt her down and make her wish she'd shown up at the club on Sunday.

When we arrive, Chelsea Piers is lit up, basking in the afterglow of the sunset as dusk settles over the city. There's a small crowd lingering outside. Ordinary people with everyday humdrum lives, hoping to get a glimpse of someone famous. As far as events go, there's likely to be no one here that would garner that type of attention unless the crowd is the billionaire buddies groupie type.

Instructing my driver to be back by ten, I offer my arm to Stacey as we walk in, smiling for the paparazzi as we enter. The DJ plays some type of house music as we pass the elegantly decorated tables and the dance floor, heading straight to the bar because I'm gonna need a drink to get through the night. "Why couldn't my uncle make it again?"

"I don't know, he just said he needed you to show up on his behalf," she answers before ordering a glass of champagne and a Macallan neat for me.

Her hair is pulled up in a simple chignon, and she's dazzling in a soft raspberry-colored calf-length sheath dress that ties around her neck in a large bow. As a punishment, she made me match my tie to her dress. If I wasn't confident I could pull off *any* color, I'd be pissed.

As it is, the only thing I'm upset about is the amount of time I need to spend *here* when I could be searching for Ginny at Decadence.

I'm like a fucking drug addict who needs his fix.

After twenty minutes of handshaking and giving bullshit excuses for why my uncle can't make it, Stacey excuses herself to the bathroom to freshen up. Turning away from the men we were talking to, I pull my phone out and send a text to my uncle.

You owe me.

Staring at my phone while I wait for his reply, I accidentally bump into someone as I move toward the terrace. Spinning around to apologize, my eyes widen, and the words die on my tongue when I see *who* I've bumped into.

Ginny stands there, mere feet away, looking absolutely breathtaking in a champagne satin gown. She seems equally shocked to see me as we continue to stare at each other as though both of us have forgotten how to speak. Her hair is pulled up in a mass of elegant curls, showing off her bare shoulder in the one-shoulder dress. There's a mile-high slit up the right side of it, showcasing the creamy ivory skin of her thigh and a cutout on her waist.

It's a lot of skin to show for an event like this, and though I can appreciate the gown, it seems very *not* Ginny.

That thought makes my blood heat as I imagine who could have picked it out for her. Does she have a boyfriend? A gay best friend? A fucking fiancé that she forgot to mention?

Taking a step toward her, I open my mouth to ask when her eyes flit over my shoulder, growing wide, and she shakes her head quickly in a sharp manner.

"Ginny, there you are," a masculine voice says behind me.

Turning my head, I catch the profile of a man with raven hair and equally dark eyes. He wraps an arm around her waist as he settles into her side, and my eyes immediately find where his fingers curl around the naked expanse of her skin.

"Who do we have here?" he asks in a clipped tone, fingers tightening as he looks at me like a fly he found in his drink.

Ginny looks terrified—like a mouse who's been cornered by a cat. And I'll bet whoever the man is, he doesn't know we're acquainted.

Extending my hand, I act as though we *don't* know each other. "Jackson Tailor. I was just about to apologize to your girlfriend here for bumping into her."

My voice is tight, relaying my irritation to her. His expression turns to surprise as he unwinds his arm from her to shake my hand. "Mr. Tailor, thank you so much for being here tonight. I'm Chris Calloway, this is Guinevere, my–"

"Sister!" Ginny interrupts him, taking the chance to move a step away and closer to me. "I'm his sister, *not* his girlfriend. It's nice to meet you, Mr. Tailor," she says politely as she extends her hand.

He's her *brother*?

It takes great effort on my part not to curl my lip in distaste at the way he was touching her. Brothers do *not* touch their sisters like that.

Chris looks at her with annoyance clearly written over his face, jerking his head as he looks back at me with a firm, fake smile. Taking her hand, I bend to kiss the back of it, relishing the way her cheeks light up. "Lovely to meet you, Guinevere? Was it?"

Ginny raises an eyebrow in amusement. Her soft pink lips turn up in a playful smirk. "You can call me Ginny."

Chris' eyes bounce back and forth between us before he motions to my nearly empty glass. He steps forward to hand her his, making it very apparent that he doesn't like our exchange. "Yeah, Gin. Why don't you go fetch us some drinks? Jackson, what are you drinking? Whiskey? Bourbon?"

Her playful face falls into one of displeasure even though she takes the glass and looks at me, patiently waiting for me to give her my drink order as the din of the room fills the space between us.

"Scotch," I finally tell her.

I'm not discreet about the way my eyes travel down her body as she turns and walks away, revealing her back to be mostly bare, save for the few straps that attach the shoulder to the other side of her lower back.

It's like I'm breathing in fresh air for the first time in days. The tension that's been settled in my muscles since Saturday night, easing with her presence.

Chris steps in the way of my view of her. "She's not *really* my sister. We aren't related. My parents took her in from foster care when we were younger. But they never adopted her."

The tone of his voice is possessive. Low, and hard to hear over the noise in the room. Meant to be a warning. He draws himself up—still falling a few inches shorter than my six-two

—and takes a step closer to me. If he's trying to be intimidating, he's failing miserably.

Leaning into me, he gives me a quick wag of his brows as he says, "We live together. If you catch my drift."

Holding his gaze, it takes everything in me not to hit him square in his smug-looking face. Briefly, I wonder if he's the one Ginny lost her virginity to. But that only makes me want to hit him even more.

"Everything alright here, gentlemen?" Stacey's dulcet voice drifts between us.

Chris steps back, his eyes snapping to her in surprise, quickly morphing into appreciation as he unabashedly rakes his gaze down her body. She allows me to wrap my arm loosely around her waist as she waits for an introduction.

Ginny emerges from the crowd at that moment, faltering when she sees me standing there with my arm around another woman. Making a huffing sound of disbelief, she shakes her head slightly and presses my drink into my chest. "Here ya go. Great meeting you."

Her eyes are heavy with disappointment, and for a moment, something akin to betrayal. Chris watches it unfold with amusement dancing over his features, while Stacey shifts slightly away from me as if to tell Ginny with our body language that we aren't together.

However, Ginny waits for no introduction as she turns and flees without another word. Chris loudly sucks air through his teeth, producing a clicking noise as he shakes his head. "Sorry about her. Bit of a troublemaker. She's got a few problems up here," he says, tapping his temple. "Anyway, it was nice to meet you. Always a pleasure meeting the financial donors."

Is this guy for real?

He takes a few steps back, running his eyes over Stacey's body once more, before turning and disappearing into the crowd.

"What was *that* all about?" Stacey asks, stepping away

from my body as she visibly shivers. "That guy gave me a serious *ick.*"

"Yeah," I agree, before tossing back my drink in one gulp. "Same here."

Half an hour later, I'm growing tired of the charade.

Ginny's actively avoiding me, running off whenever I get close enough to talk to her—throwing me shady glances across the room and staring at Stacey for long periods of time like she's plotting ways to stick gum in her hair.

I'd be annoyed with how juvenile she's acting if it weren't for the fact that it was making me want to drag her into the bathroom and fuck the attitude out of her.

She's acting jealous. Like one of the women I've fucked who acts shocked and hurt when I show up somewhere with another female on my arm.

Her behavior should be enough to wipe my hands clean.

Only, it's not.

It's making me want to *play.* I can feel Ginny's eyes burning a hole in my back from across the room.

As a man who is all but begging for a donation excuses himself to get another drink, my hand wraps around Stacey, and I lower my lips to her neck as if I'm going to kiss it. She startles and starts to pull away, but I tighten my grip and don't let her go. "Jackson, what the fuck are you doing?" she grits out between clenched teeth. A nearby couple turns and gives us a disapproving glance as the man ushers his wife away.

"Getting what I want." Discreetly, I look behind us under the guise of scanning the room, and just as I thought, Ginny is staring with a scowl on her pretty face.

Pretending not to notice, my hand drifts lower on Stacey's waist.

"Move that hand any lower and I'm going to cut it off, Jackson. Who's the poor girl this time? The redhead from earlier?" she croons sweetly through a fake smile. "You know, I expect a bigger bonus at Christmas for this shit."

Turning my attention to her, I move my mouth to her ear, making it look intimate while I whisper, "You can have as big of a bonus as you want. This one is different, Stacey."

She turns her head into mine, helping me to complete the scene, her blue eyes aglow with mock adoration as our gazes lock, and she asks, "Then *why* are you playing your normal bullshit games with her?"

Deep down, I know she's right. Dropping my arm, I take a step back and clear my throat. My head swings in Ginny's direction, but she's no longer there.

Stacey grabs two glasses of champagne from a passing tray and holds them out to me. "She went out on the terrace."

Giving her a thankful look, I step forward and take them, kissing her cheek lightly before stepping away.

It doesn't take me long to find Ginny. Her red hair summons me, like a beacon against the night sky. Making sure her *brother* isn't in the general vicinity, I sidle up against her as she leans against the rail and watches the water below. "Ginny." Her name is my only greeting as I hand her one of the glasses.

"He's going to make my life hell if you pay too much attention to me," she says forlornly, catching me by surprise at the ease with which she says it.

"Yeah, your brother is a creep. Does he always handle you that way?" Turning to the side, my elbow finds the rail as I search her profile for any sign that tells me he's the reason she broke down the other night.

"Like he owns me? Yeah," she scoffs.

Staring at her as she does her best to not look at me, I reach back over and pluck the untouched champagne from her hand, handing both our glasses to a passing woman who looks at me incredulously, but takes them, and continues walking away.

"Well then, let's fix that." Holding my hand out to her, she finally looks at it before lifting her gaze to mine.

"What are you doing, Jackson? What do you think you can *fix*?" she argues. The lights from the skyline and the pier light up the water, reflecting in her eyes as she stares up at me—the same look from Saturday night shining in their depths. Only now, there's a hardness to it. She wants to be saved. Scarlett isn't too proud to admit it.

Ginny is.

Stepping into her, I shift to shield her body from the majority of the room behind us, letting my hand drop to her waist where her brother gripped her earlier. She sucks in a breath as I gently stroke my thumb up and down her skin there, her hands moving to circle my forearms.

"I think that the only way I can erase his touch from your body is to take you out on the dance floor and spin you around for a few songs. *That* way, he can't make a scene. And later, if he does, you can tell him you secured a million-dollar donation with just a few dances."

Shock dances across her face for a moment before her demeanor relaxes at my words, body growing slack beneath my touch. "Why are you being nice to me?"

My brow furrows and I pull her into me, turning to go back inside. "I've never been mean to you, Ginny."

We catch a few pairs of curious eyes as we pass through the crowd. There haven't been a lot of couples dancing tonight, but the DJ switches the house music to smooth jazz as soon as our feet hit the floor. Looking over, I see Stacey standing at his podium, and she raises a glass to me nonchalantly before striking a conversation with a random woman.

Ginny sees the exchange and sniffs as I pull her into my arms and start swaying us to the rhythm of the alto saxophone drifting over the room. "Fuckboy," she mutters under her breath.

My, my, green is a lovely color on her.

Gently I pinch the skin of her waist, earning me a startled yelp, her eyes growing wide with an anger so tangible I swear there's red in the depths of her blue orbs. "What the hell, Jackson?"

"She's my secretary. And she's married...to a *woman*," I tell her pointedly.

The shock on her face wears off quickly. "Whatever, I don't care."

Pulling her flush against my body, I dip my head so that my lips hover closer to hers. "Your body language says otherwise. In fact, your body is telling me that you want me just as badly as I want you. So why don't you cut the bullshit and stop lying to yourself."

The crowd parts at the edge of the dance floor as I look away from the incredulous look she gives me. Her brother is standing with an older couple and two other men, his back to us. The woman, who bears a striking resemblance to him, keeps glancing over at us worriedly, and every time Chris moves as if he's about to turn around, she finds a way to keep his back to us.

"Go out with me." My eyes cut back to Ginny, a plan forming in my head that will make me seem like a bastard, but that's nothing new. She already thinks the worst of me.

Rolling her eyes, she turns her head away and says, "No." Her eyes catch on her brother, uncertainty bleeding into them as she watches to make sure he doesn't see us.

"Something tells me your brother doesn't know you work at Decadence." *Or at Désirer.* "Go out with me, or I'll march over there right now, and tell him that we do, in fact, know each other. And I'll allude that we know each other *quite* well."

Spinning her away from me, I check to see that his attention is still occupied before pulling her back and holding her tightly to my chest. "You wouldn't dare," she whispers angrily, clutching my shirt in her hands to stop me from spinning her again.

Lowering my mouth to her ear, I whisper, "Try me."

Heat radiates from her body, searing my skin as the tension crackles between us like static electricity. Our dance has become a game, both our eyes continuously darting over to her brother, neither of us wanting to admit defeat.

Letting go of her, I shrug with a smirk. "Your choice."

I've only taken a few steps when I hear her let loose a conquered sigh. "Fine!" she snaps at my back.

Such sweet victory.

Turning back to her, I flash her my charming smile. "You'll go out with me?"

She smirks, her eyes lighting up as she saunters toward me. My smile falls, uncertain of why exactly she's looking at me like *I'm* prey that *she's* hunting.

Scratch that. She's looking at me as if she's already caught me.

"On one condition," she counters.

"What's that?" I ask skeptically. My eyes roam over her shoulder to see that we've finally caught Chris' attention. He's watching us curiously while the woman, who I assume is his mother, speaks to him.

"Thirty days," Ginny says, drawing my attention back to her.

"Thirty days?" I parrot back.

Smirking triumphantly, she balls her fists on her hips and gives me a sharp nod. "I'll go out with you. After you've gone thirty days without being with another woman. No dates, no touching, and *no* sex."

Ginny

J ackson just stares at me as though I've spontaneously grown a second head.

Gotcha, fucker.

There's no way he'll agree to my terms.

"Is that all?" he finally drawls, chuckling as though I've said something incredibly funny.

Crossing my arms, I shake my head as my brows scrunch together. "Oh, don't act like it's going to be a piece of cake. You're *you*." I'm highly aware of the fact that I don't actually know Jackson at all. All I know is what I've heard and what I've seen firsthand.

In my office at the clinic and tonight on the terrace, he's shown glimpses of someone I didn't think he could be. Gentle. Kind.

But in all actuality, I feel as though I've just stepped into a giant flaming pile of dog shit.

"And you don't know *me* at all." His eyes dart over my shoulder, and he reaches into his suit jacket, pulling out a checkbook. Suddenly, I feel a heavy presence at my back, and I don't have to turn or look over my shoulder to know it's Chris.

"What is going on over here?" he sings as though he's caught me doing something bad.

"Ginny here just secured you a million dollars," Jackson says as he fills in the check before ripping it out and handing it to me.

Hesitating, I eventually take the offered piece of paper and stare down at it. He's written *thirty-day deposit* in the memo. My eyes snap to his with a pointed look, and he just smiles at me in return.

"Sh…I'm sorry, she what?" Chris stammers.

Jackson's comment has drawn the attention of the people around us, some of them clapping at his generosity. Throwing me a wink, he tucks his checkbook back into his jacket. "See ya around, Red."

"What was that all about?" Chris' voice startles me, causing me to jump and spin around to see him at the entrance of my bedroom.

"What do you mean?" I know exactly what he means, but pretending as though I have no clue what he's talking about is the way I need to play the game tonight.

Jackson's words from earlier have been playing on repeat since he waltzed out of the event with his secretary.

"The only way I can erase his touch from your body."

I don't even like the man, but he saw something in thirty seconds that most people have chosen to ignore for the better part of my life.

And he came to my rescue.

"Maybe it's time to find someone with enough power to protect you from whatever it is you're scared of."

My stranger's words have also been on replay.

The idea of someone needing to protect me from Chris is

one that leaves a bad taste in my mouth. I'm a strong, independent woman.

Only…I'm not.

My life is riddled with excuses and lies. Hiding from
Chris, hiding from the world by working at Désirer.

Hiding from myself.

There are days when I wish I could just admit *who* I've
become as a person. I'm no longer the scared little girl
watching her mother dwindle away to nothing. No longer the
child whose innocence was stolen by a boy with so many
issues, you never knew which one you were going to get.

I'm a young adult who has had a lot of her world handed
to her on a silver platter. Who is afraid to leave the comfort of
her home because the thought of being alone is *terrifying* but
also *exhilarating*.

It's like the pain and the turmoil fuel me.

I'm a fucking mess.

Jackson Tailor is the last person I want caught in my
tangled web. One day as a fly trapped in my silky spun lies
and he'd want to tell me how fucked up I am and how I
deserve everything Chris gives me.

I'm not the type of girl you just fuck and leave. I'm the
type that will drag you down and fuck your life up.

Chris crosses the room and wraps his fist around my hair,
pushing me into my closet. His face mere inches from mine,
spittle hitting my cheeks while he clenches his teeth and asks,
"Did you promise to fuck him? Guys like that don't just give
up that kind of money for a fucking dance."

"*You* wanted to parade me around tonight like a show
dog. Don't get upset when males come around and treat me
like a bitch in heat. Your boss was highly impressed that you
brought that kind of money in tonight. What the *fuck* are you
so upset about?"

My voice is low—his parents are just down the hall in
their room—but the rage is apparent. Reaching up, I grasp his

fist, which is more tangled in my curls than squeezing to hurt me. "Get out of my room."

"What did thirty-day deposit mean, Ginny?" He lets go of me, retreating to the other side of my closet. It's a walk-in, but it's still small, leaving less than a foot between us.

"I have no idea. The guy is a douchebag." The pins holding my hair up hurt now that they're all askew, so I start pulling them out one by one, massaging my scalp as I go.

My comment seems to appease him. But before he can say another word Christine appears in the doorway. "What's going on in here?"

She looks between us with apprehension written on her face. Making me wonder why, all of a sudden, she seems to have had a change of heart where her son is concerned.

"Nothing, Mother. Was just saying thank you to Ginny for whatever it was she did to get Jackson's money." His tone is still accusing, and I silently curse Jackson for the attention he bestowed upon me tonight.

"Oh, I read up about that man. Seems like he has a new girl on his arm every day. He's probably already forgotten about your sister. No offense, Ginny," Christine says as she walks further into my closet to help me remove the pins.

Her words don't offend me. It's clear they are spoken in an attempt to get her son to not waste any more time thinking about it, and it works.

"She's *not* my sister."

"She is in mine and your father's eyes." She shoots him a look I can't see, but whatever is on her face makes Chris roll his eyes and straighten up to leave.

"Goodnight," he mutters as he walks out.

Neither of us says anything as we continue pulling pins out of my hair. Once we're done, she gently urges me to turn so that she can unlock the straps of my dress. My hands catch the front so it doesn't fall off and pool to the floor.

"Thank you," I say without turning around.

She pats my back gently. "You're welcome, dear."

"I heard you had quite the night on Wednesday."

My fork pauses midway to my mouth, a drop of vinaigrette falling back onto my plate as my eyes meet Scott's across the table. Our regular Friday morning appointment was moved to the afternoon due to him flying in from California. Since I had a shift at Decadence after I worked at the clinic this morning, I suggested we have lunch together.

It wasn't completely out of the ordinary to see Scott dining at Decadence. It was just usually with Carmela and sometimes Senator Mick Charles while they went over business.

Taking the bite of my salad, around a mouthful of arugula, I tell him, "Your nephew is quite the handful."

Scott laughs and flips another piece of paper in the packet he's initialing through. "Well, if anyone can put him in his place besides Stacey, I imagine you'd be perfect for the job."

He looks tired. His skin has an unhealthy pallor, and there are dark circles around his eyes. "You look like you haven't slept in a while."

"Don't you worry about me, Ginny."

I'm silent for a few more bites. He hasn't touched his sandwich. He's barely looked up from his paperwork since he sat down.

"You need to eat something." Sliding his plate a little closer to him, I keep nudging it until the au jus threatens to spill over the little dish and onto his work.

Finally, he puts his pen down and pushes the packet away. Picking up his French dip, he takes a small bite before putting it back on the plate. He barely chews, looking like he'd rather not be eating, and it takes him a few tries to swallow.

"Have you talked to Sadie?" Setting my fork down, I push my plate back. Suddenly, I'm not that hungry anymore.

He tenses, right hand straying to where his wedding ring

still sits on that third finger on his left. "No. And I don't intend to. It doesn't make any sense to tell her now."

"She'd want to know. She'll be furious when she finds out." His ex-wife, Sadie Tailor-Michaelson, is a former model who lives in Jacksonville, Florida. They got divorced on their twentieth wedding anniversary last year because Scott had an infidelity streak a million miles long.

But the straw that broke the camel's back was the secret he's been keeping from everyone. She mistook it for another time he cheated on her—which was easy to do when he'd been photographed around town with multiple women—when in all actuality, if she knew the truth, she'd probably beat herself up over leaving him.

Which is exactly why Scott doesn't want to tell her. Or Jackson.

When he doesn't respond, seemingly lost in his thoughts, I change the subject. "So, did Jackson tell you about Wednesday?"

That snaps him out of it. A smirk crosses his face, reminding me too much of his nephew, as he grabs his papers again. "No, Stacey did. It seems like you've made quite the impression on him."

"Please, we both know if I actually said yes to him, he'd dump me the second he got his happy ending." Rolling my eyes, I pick my fork up again and stab at a strawberry. "What does his mother think about how much of a manwhore he is?"

Scott tenses, his pen stilling over the paper. "Jackson's mother isn't in the picture. She walked out right after he was born. His father—my brother—shot himself when he was a teen. He grew up watching my father and me, and how we conducted ourselves. And he idolizes his aunt. So when we got divorced, you could say that put the final nail in the coffin."

He sets his pen back down and looks me right in the eyes. "Jackson is the way he is because of me. I won't apologize for it because he's a damn good businessman, and I'm proud of him. He's a hard worker, but as far as his personal life goes? His whole life has been handed to him—women included. But the women are all after one thing—the money and the name. I'll tell you right now, Ginny. It's a lonely life. And I know for a fact that he's not happy with it. He's a good man. He just hasn't found something worth dropping his defenses for."

Well, *fuck.*

I really thought he was just an asshole.

But to have your mother walk out on you and then your dad kill himself? Most people would feel abandoned. Usually, people like that grow up with attachment issues—problems with intimacy. A lot of people put up a shield to protect themselves from the pain and hurt of those hardships.

Jackson Tailor doesn't just have a shield around him. He's got a whole goddamned fortress of coping mechanisms.

"Speak of the devil, and he shall appear," Scott mutters under his breath.

My eyes widen, head whipping around sharply to see Jackson walking through the restaurant, heading straight for our table. His hands are in his pockets as he strolls through the room, catching the attention of every woman here in his charcoal gray suit and deep bronze tie. The color of which brings out the golden amber in his eyes, and I hate that I notice that.

Turning back around, I gather my dish and start to scoot out of the booth when Jackson sits down and swings an arm around my shoulders.

"Well, look who it is. My favorite warden," he says with a grin.

Swiveling my head slowly in his direction, I narrow my eyes at him. "Go. Away."

"Now, now. That's no way to talk to your prisoner, is it?" he asks cheekily, grabbing my shoulder and squeezing me into him before letting me go.

"What are you going on about?" Scott asks, gathering the papers and settling them into his briefcase.

"You haven't heard? Ginny here put me on a leash," Jackson replies, unwinding his arm from my shoulder to reach across the table for a fry off his uncle's plate.

"I didn't put you on a leash. You put yourself on a leash. Now, let me out." He doesn't budge as I push against him.

"Apparently, Stacey didn't tell me everything?" Scott's comment is leading, waiting for one of us to explain what's going on. He has an amused look on his face as his eyes dart back and forth between me and Jackson.

"He keeps asking me out, and I keep telling him *no*. However, I told him that if he can go thirty days without dating another woman or having sex, I'll go out on *one* date with him."

"The number of dates was never determined," Jackson cuts in.

"Oh, yes, it was!"

"Kids! Jesus, you already sound like an old married couple. I have to get to a meeting. Play nice," Scott scolds before getting out of the booth, throwing a fifty-dollar bill on the table, even though my work meal is free, and he owns the restaurant.

"Jackson, good luck." He looks at me and winks. "Ginny, *well done*." Grabbing his briefcase, he ignores my silent pleas for him to stay and walks away from the table as Jackson grins at me.

"Hi, Red. Miss me?" He grabs another fry from Scott's abandoned plate before pulling the whole thing over.

"*Why* are you here? And scoot! Over!" Pushing him harder, he finally slides over an inch.

"You told me I couldn't date anyone else for a month," he says, as if that simple explanation clarifies why he's here in the middle of the day during my shift.

"No, I said you couldn't date any *women*. There's a difference."

"Well, the way I see it, if I can't spend the next month with any other women, that just means I'll be spending it with you." He shoots me another close-lipped grin around a bite of French dip.

"Ginny, your break is over. You need to get back to work. Hi, Jackson," Jacqueline, my shift manager, interrupts us.

Jackson turns to look at her, not bothering to give her a once-over or flash his pearly white teeth, sending a surge of smug satisfaction through me.

"Yeah, I know," I tell her. "I'm clocking back in now."

"Are you free tonight?" she asks him, ignoring me. "I know this great party where I'm sure we can have some fun." Her valley-girl tone grates on my nerves. Jackson's, too, if the look he gives her is anything to go by.

"Sorry, sweetheart." He stands and reaches out to chuck her under the chin softly.

His eyes slide to mine as though he *knows* the gesture will piss me off. A sharp thorn pricks my chest, spreading green poison throughout my veins. Clenching my teeth, I follow him out of the booth.

"I'm on a thirty-day cleanse," he says.

Jacqueline looks between me and Jackson, obvious confusion in her eyes as she asks, "What does that mean?"

Holding my gaze, his answer is like an antidote I didn't know I wanted. "It means I'm taken."

$$\mathcal{Jackson}$$

When Ginny steps into our room at Désirer, I nearly choke.

She's wearing thigh-high stockings, the tops trimmed in lace, with a nearly see-through thong. Her top is lace, as well, a halter style that cuts off just below her breasts. It barely conceals her rosy pink nipples, and I'm instantly hard.

The curtain is pulled back. It was like that when I arrived and was told she's asked for it to stay that way for the remainder of our time together. As soon as the door shuts behind her, she grins as her eyes immediately settle between my legs.

"That's exactly the reaction I was hoping for," she says, reaching for a drink. A bottle of champagne has been set up on her side, glass already half-full of pink fizzy bubbles.

"You walked through the Grand Room like that?" Jealousy courses through me at the thought of anyone seeing her nearly naked.

She shakes her head as she takes a sip. "I came straight from the changing room. My robe is on the doorknob outside. They're specially made to let the wings slip through the sides."

Her answer pleases me. But I'm not, and have never been, a jealous man. The feeling is unpleasant and unwelcome.

There's something about her tonight that seems different. It's only been a handful of hours since I've seen her. But to her, we haven't seen each other since Saturday—almost a week.

She seems…more sure of herself tonight: less Scarlett and more *Ginny*.

"You didn't come Sunday. It's been almost a week." Steeling my tone, I try not to sound pathetic as I take a seat on my couch, absentmindedly running my hand over the velvet arm.

"Did you miss me?" She doesn't take a seat on her side, but instead, comes to sit next to me.

Close.

So close that it would take barely a movement to reach out and pull her into my lap.

"I was worried after…last time," I tell her honestly. "I was beginning to think you'd decided you no longer wished to see me."

"Of course I want to see you!" she exclaims, sitting up straighter. "Real life just got busy…that's all."

"Anything you want to talk about?" Goading her, I wonder if she'll talk about the bet we made—the bet she and *Jackson* made.

She looks down at her glass, a little smile pulling at her lips. "No. I'd rather do *other* things."

"Not tonight, Little Ember. Tonight, I want to talk." Grabbing my drink from the side table, I shift and lean against the arm of the couch, pulling further away so that I can look at her straight on. "What happened last week?"

Instantly, her cheeks turn pink as she picks at the top of her stocking. "What do you mean?"

"Well, for starters, I'd love to know what happened to you to make you have such a response."

Her eyebrows knit together as she looks over at me. "It's in my past. What makes you think I want to relive that?"

The question goes unanswered. My fingers itch to reach for her but grip the back of the couch instead. "Scarlett, did someone hurt you when you were younger?"

Made up images of a younger Ginny and Chris flash through my mind as I wait for her to answer. The way he acted at the charity event has had me wondering, again, if it's *him* she lost her virginity to. He seems like the insensitive sort to call her names.

She's gone still. So still, I don't even see her chest rise and fall with her breath. "Why would you ask that? What makes you think someone hurt me?" she eventually asks.

Blowing out a breath behind the mask, I sit up straight. "Your answer is telling enough."

She shifts, uncomfortable with the direction the conversation is going.

But I *have* to know.

"Who did you lose your virginity to?"

Her head snaps up, annoyance gracing her features as she turns to look at me. "That is really personal. Our identities are supposed to be anonymous, you know. Why would I give up information like that?"

That fiery temper is simmering just beneath her surface, a flame shooting up every now and then before it dies back to an ember. If I'm not careful, she may just get up and leave.

"My apologies. I presumed it would be best to know about your past if I'm going to attempt to teach you how to take hold of your future."

My words are precisely what she needs to hear and she melts back against the couch with a remorseful look. "You're right. I'm sorry."

Silence stretches between us while I wait for her to speak next. When she does, her tone is soft and barely audible. "It wasn't anyone special. Just a boy I went to school with. He was sweet, and that was what I needed."

Tears line her eyes and I inwardly sigh. I've made her cry again. "So, I assume it wasn't this boy who called you by that name?"

Her legs curl underneath her, and she picks her glass up again, shaking her head. Her toes skim the fabric of my pants, the black material of her stockings sheer enough that I can see her pink-painted nails.

"Who was it? Someone you lived with?" It's risky to ask, but I can't leave this room tonight without knowing.

Lifting her glass to her lips, she nods before taking a sip.

"Did they do more than just call you names? Did they ever physically hurt you?" I press. My upper body creeps forward, leaning toward her while I wait for her answer.

She's doing her best to keep the tears at bay. But at the last question, they escape as she sighs a shuddered breath. "I don't want to talk about it anymore."

My jaw clenches, hands balling into fists at her silent admission. The need to leave the club immediately and find her bastard of a foster brother grows within my chest, but then she looks at me and all I want to do is hold her.

That fucking bastard.

"You know, I really wish that I could comfort you right now. With something other than words." What I mean is that I want to gather her in my arms, but she huffs a laugh and wipes delicately beneath the mask at her eyes, careful not to pull it off or smear her makeup.

"Yeah, all these beautiful outfits keep going to waste. I feel like all I've done is cry in this room with you." She lets out a small laugh.

"Trust me. It's no waste. I'm thoroughly enjoying the view, even if you are crying. And I mean that genuinely. But... perhaps there is something that can be done about our little dilemma?"

Her eyes find mine, questioning silently. My gaze slowly travels from hers to the golden wings she wears, then back to her face. Realization dawns when she looks over her shoulder at them.

"We could upgrade to the Dreamers wing?"

Touching. No sex. But I can touch her.

My cock stirs just thinking about it. "*That*, my Little Ember, is an excellent idea. If you're up for it?"

"Yes." Her reply is breathy. *Needy.* Her nipples pucker beneath the fabric of her top, and all I can think about is that tomorrow night, I can reach out and touch them if I want to.

"Well then, consider it done." Standing, I drink what's left of my scotch before adjusting myself with my back turned toward her. When I spin to face her, she's gotten up as well and is standing so close that I almost take a step back.

Almost.

"I'll see you tomorrow then?" she asks, eyes wide and hopeful.

"Yes." My hand itches to reach out and touch her. "Yes, you most certainly will."

Ginny

"Why am I just hearing about this *now*?" Lenni asks as we fill saltshakers at an open table in the back of Decadence.

My best friend fills in once in a while when Carmela needs her, but her primary job is Désirer. She's one of the best Angels they have, switching between the three tiers depending on her mood.

And excelling at every one of them.

Lenni is their most sought-after Angel. She's five-eight, has long chestnut hair, and ochre eyes. Her skin is in a perpetual state of looking as though she spent the day at the beach, and her way with men makes me wish I had her confidence.

"It isn't true. We *aren't* dating," I tell her as I grab another half-empty saltshaker.

"But are you fucking? If you're not, when is *that* gonna happen? And believe me, Gin, it *needs* to happen. It's been too long, babe. You need some dick. Who better to give it to you than Jackson Tailor?" Lenni flips her long hair over her shoulder and scowls at one of the other women as she passes by and gives me a dirty look.

"Valentina!" Using her full name in hopes of conveying

my exasperation, I quickly look around to make sure no one heard her.

It's bad enough all our co-workers are being catty after Jacqueline went and told everyone that Jackson basically alluded that we're dating.

"Since when are you so enamored with the rich and famously dickheaded?"

"Oh, please. He's gorgeous. If he wasn't so *enamored* with you, I'd climb him like a tree and swing from the branches." She screws a cap back on her last shaker before pushing everything away from her and folding her arms on the table. "Is he really so bad, Gin?"

My thoughts stray to Wednesday night.

No. No, he's not.

"I don't want to be someone's one-night stand." I shrug as I finish my last shaker. "I don't know, I feel like I deserve *more* than that."

My eyes dart to my friend, who bristles at my comment and says dryly, "Well, gee, thanks."

Rolling my eyes, I sit, reaching across the table and container of salt to grab her arms. "You know that isn't what I mean, Lenni. There's nothing wrong with having one-and-done meet-ups. It just isn't what *I* want."

She places a hand over mine and gives me a warm smile. "I know. And you do deserve more than that. It's just...it's *Jackson Tailor*."

Laughing, I open my mouth to respond when her eyes grow wide as she looks over my shoulder. "Ginny!"

But her warning is too late as something ice cold hits my back. It pours over my shoulders like a waterfall, dripping down my back as it ruins my white button-up, and the scent of coffee fills the air.

"Oops," a snotty voice says behind me.

Slowly, I turn to see Rebecca, another co-worker who drools over Jackson regularly, glaring down at me. Her pouty, cherry-red lips turned down in a scowl.

"You fucking bitch!" Lenni cries out as she jumps up to grab a bunch of napkins from a nearby table. Quickly, she unrolls the silverware and hands them over one by one to help soak up the mess.

Rebecca cackles, and some of the other women across the room join in, watching as Lenni and I attempt to dry me off.

"Ladies! What is going on here?" Carmella's sharp tone cuts through the empty restaurant.

Everyone goes silent as she looks from Lenni and me to Rebecca, then to the other women. "Ginny, why don't you take the rest of the day off? Go home and clean yourself up. Rebecca, you're fired."

Lenni starts to laugh as Rebecca stammers, "B-but, Carmela! It was an *accident*! I swear!"

Our boss doesn't spare her a second glance as she turns to head back to her office. Rebecca's eyes find mine again as she spits out, "You're going to regret this! Jackson doesn't care about you! You aren't anything special! He'll grow tired of you, eventually. A man like that can't be pleased by only one woman."

Huffing, she turns and storms out. The other females all glare at me as they loudly whisper to each other while I continue wiping myself off.

"My place is closer. You can shower there before you go home if you want," Lenni offers.

Nodding my head, I tell her, "Yeah, that would be great. Thank you. Do you mind if I borrow some clothes, too?"

"Of course not. Mi casa es su casa," she says. "You know the code."

As I leave, I'm grateful I have such a wonderful friend who lives nearby. It would take forever to go back to my apartment and shower, and then there's the possibility of running into Chris before I left again.

Because home is not where I'll be spending the afternoon.

Jackson Tailor is about to get a piece of my mind.

After showering at Lenni's, I quickly dry my hair and throw it into a messy bun on top of my head before changing into a pair of light-wash skinny jeans and a dusty blue oversized knit sweater that keeps falling off my shoulder. I don't care about looking good. I'll just be going to Jackson's home to yell at him.

Finding the address on Google is easy, but I figure it will be harder to actually get *in* the building—let alone up to the penthouse.

Turns out I'm wrong.

As I get out of my cab, staring up at the gigantic building with mirrored windows as I walk to the door, there's an older woman with a bunch of grocery bags in her arms who gets there at the same time as me. The doorman, who is shutting the door of a black town car, rushes over to open it for her, but I beat him to it.

"Thank you, young lady. Who might you be here to see?" he asks.

"Yes, thank you," the lady echoes him.

At the same time, I reply, "Jackson Tailor."

They share a look, and my eyes bounce back and forth between them as they share a smile.

"Well, Miss Claudia here can you take you on up," he says, ushering me in behind the woman named Claudia as he waits for the elevator doors to open. The lobby of the building looks more expensive than the mini-mansion I grew up in. The black and gold floors shine as though they've just been waxed. There are geometric sculptures throughout the floor plan, matching the gold design of the flooring. A desk made of cream and tawny marbling is home to a concierge, the light from the giant dripping light fixture casting a warm glow over the space.

Once the elevator arrives, the doorman reaches in and

swipes his card, hitting the button with PH etched into it. "Have a nice day, ladies."

As the doors shut, Claudia looks at me, and I reach out, gesturing for her to hand me a few bags. "Here, let me help you."

"Does Mr. Jackson know you are coming to see him?" she asks as she hands two over. Her accent reminds me of Dorota from *Gossip Girl*.

"No. It's a surprise," I say sheepishly as I examine the boxed-in area that's taking me to the devil's lair. Even it's opulent, and now I feel like I should have put more effort into my appearance.

Claudia looks at me as another soft ding signals that we're passing another floor. She openly gives me a once-over before smiling and saying, "Mr. Jackson will be pleasantly surprised, I'm sure."

I think it's a compliment.

When we arrive at the top, I'm not prepared for what I walk into.

Claudia moves with purpose into the large open space while I follow slowly and take everything in. When I thought about Jackson's home, I assumed it would be all broody and masculine. Grey marble and deep-toned walls. Low lights and dark floors.

But that isn't what I step into at all.

The walls are a light gray, host to a few obscure paintings that are by artists whose work I don't recognize. Floor-to-ceiling windows let in the sunlight, shining on the simple glass coffee table and large dark gray sectional in the living room. The hardwood is a light walnut, warm beneath my bare feet since I slipped my ballet flats off once I stepped inside.

With all the sunlight streaming in, the lights are off, but the fixtures are recessed and spread throughout the large area. There's a staircase off to the right of the living room that leads upstairs, with the kitchen—where Claudia went—nestled beneath it. That area *is* dark. The charcoal cabinets and island match the stairs, and all the appliances are a black stainless steel.

Above the island are silver glass pendant lights that hang from the ceiling. It's the only extravagant lighting fixture in the whole place.

I don't know why I expected chandeliers shaped like boobs.

"Mr. Jackson will be in his game room. But I doubt he will hear us go in. Follow me," Claudia says, leaving the bags on the kitchen counter.

She leads me down a hall and opens the second door on the right, the noise hitting us like a bullet train as he yells at something. When I step in, I notice it's like a large theater. With a flatscreen that takes up nearly the whole wall, a black couch that sits four cushions wide and two deep, and a minibar in the corner, complete with an impressive array of liquor.

Jackson is playing some sort of game, yelling at someone through his headset, and looking the most comfortable I've ever seen him in gray sweatpants and a plain white shirt.

"Coming up on our flank. Watch our flank! Tripp, what the fuck are you doing?!" His hand flies out toward the screen as if whoever is on the other end of his headset can see him.

Claudia grabs the remote from the minibar counter and points it at the TV. Suddenly the giant flat screen goes dark, and Jackson yells out, "What the fuck?!"

"Hold on, the TV went black." Pulling his headset down around his neck, he starts to look for the remote.

Claudia clears her throat, causing him to spin around and see us standing behind the couch. Standing quickly, something that looks like horror flashes across his face, and I reach up to stifle my laughter behind my hand.

He looks embarrassed, cheeks growing bright red as his eyes bounce back and forth between me and Claudia—at a loss for words.

"Nerd." It escapes my mouth through a fresh fit of giggles.

"What are you doing here?" he asks, throwing his controller and headset down on the couch. I can barely make out someone on the other end yelling at him, but he ignores it and continues to stare at me.

For a moment, I forget why I decided to come here as I take him in. His casual shirt is stretched over his muscles, his hair mussed up instead of perfectly styled. I've caught him off guard, and as much as I don't want to admit it, off guard looks good on him.

Then I remember *why* I came.

"You're a jerk!" My voice is loud and shrill, making Claudia jump.

"I'll just be going back to the kitchen now," she says, scurrying out the door and closing it behind her.

"Why am I a jerk?" Jackson asks, still staring at me as if he doesn't quite believe I'm standing in his home.

"Because you told Jacqueline you were taken and made it seem like it was by me! Now the girls at work won't stop being catty bitches, and they are saying and doing ridiculous things. One of them tried drowning me with her coffee!" Swinging my arms out, I point to my hair. "Do you know how many times I had to wash my hair to get it all out?!"

Jackson blinks, then erupts into laughter. It catches me by surprise never having heard him let out a genuine laugh before. When he sobers up, he looks at me and shakes his head before collapsing back onto the couch.

"You know, you're the only woman alive who would get mad at me for saying I was taken by you," he says to the blank screen in front of him.

Marching around to stand in front of him, one hand finds my hip as I point at him with the other. "Jackson, this isn't funny!"

"Sure it is. Tell the girls to get a life. Better yet, I'll tell Carmela to fire them all." He rubs his face before swinging an arm above his head to rest on the back of the couch. He's half lying down, one leg propped up with a clear outline of his penis against his sweats.

My eyes dart back to his face, but I know he caught me looking by the look he's giving me. "Carmela *did* fire the one who dumped coffee on me. All it's gonna do is make my job harder."

"You're making something else hard right now, Red." He grins at me and wiggles his eyebrows.

I will myself not to look back at his dick. "I can't stand you."

Claudia reappears with a tray filled with bowls of cut fruit, yogurt, and granola. None of us say anything as she rounds the couch and sets the tray on the cushion at Jackson's stretched-out feet.

As she leaves, he singsongs, "Thank you, Claudia."

She's muttering something about Scott and Sadie before the door closes and cuts off her voice. Jackson pushes off the back of the couch and leans forward, grabbing an empty bowl. "Hungry?"

My mouth waters, and my stomach clenches. I haven't eaten since last night before the club. But do I want to stay here and share a meal with him?

Sighing, I plop down onto a cushion and grab the other empty bowl, silently thanking Claudia for assuming I was staying.

"This doesn't mean I like you," I grumble as I put together my parfait, layering up yogurt, granola, and strawberries in the bowl before scooting back so that I can stretch out next to him.

Well, nearly next to him. I *do* make sure there's a respectable distance between us.

"So, tell me, Red. Is it really so bad being attached to me?" Jackson asks. He's lying on his side, the bowl in front of him filled with more fruit than anything else.

It occurs to me how bizarre this is. Me in his house, eating a meal together while he's in lounge clothes. Surely, this can't be something he does often with women because this is *normal* behavior, and his reputation wouldn't be what it is if he acted normal.

"Well, now that I know you play video games in sweatpants on Saturday mornings, I'm beginning to think the masses have it all wrong. You're just a nerd who can't get a woman to stick around once you bust out the Xbox controller, aren't you?"

Grinning over at him, I laugh at the look he's giving me, like the bite of melon he just took is sour. "Listen here. You came to *my* house, unannounced, on a weekend. Just to yell at me because some of the girls at work are *picking* on you? What are you really doing here?"

Well, when he puts it that way…

"I think you just wanted an excuse to see me again. Tell me, Red, will *you* be able to handle thirty days around me with no sex?" He's observing me with a predatory gleam in his eyes.

A warm shock zips down my spine and settles between my legs. My teeth find my lower lip, and his eyes track the movement. I don't have to look down to know what's going on in his pants. He's not ashamed of it as he openly stares, waiting for me to answer him.

"I-I think I'll get by just fine," I finally manage, clearing my throat and breaking eye contact to stare at what's left of my food. "Besides, the deal was that *you* had to go without. Not me."

My lips tilt up as I look at him from beneath my lashes. Sitting up, he sets his bowl on the tray at the end of the couch, edging closer when he settles back down. The movement makes me painfully aware of his erection, which looks like it's attempting to escape his pants.

I'm thankful—and also not—for the material of the jeans I chose to wear. Thankful that they are thick enough to keep the arousal that's seeping from between my legs from soaking through. And not, because as I shift to ease the feeling, the rough material rubs against my clit, and a noise escapes my mouth that I can't describe.

A gasp. A moan. Whatever it's called, it causes Jackson's eyes to darken.

It isn't going to be easy, denying him. I have eyes—I know he's the most gorgeous man I've ever seen. I want to believe our banter and chemistry is ours alone, but it's probably not. This is all a game to him.

And I hate playing games.

I always lose.

"Let me fill you in on a little secret, Ginny. If *I* have to go without for an entire month. *So. Do. You.* If gossip is already spreading that I'm off the market, I'll be damned if the object of my desires is seen around town with another man. Can't have people thinking I'm leaving you unsatisfied." Somehow, he's managed to get even closer without me realizing it.

"When did this become 'let's let the world think we're dating'? That wasn't the deal." My instincts are telling me to back up, but I'm frozen as I look down at him. He's still on his side, but holy hell…when did he get so close?

Jackson hasn't even touched me, and yet my body is strung tighter than a violin string about to snap. This is…*bad.* We aren't even a week into this deal. Why does my body want me to fail? I can't give in to him.

"Don't you want that? Or would you rather they think you're running around on me? The woman who finally got Jackson Tailor to stop his roguish ways steps out on him with another man? I can see the headlines now. Maybe I can spin the narrative and make it seem like you broke my heart. I'm sure that will get me plenty of pus-"

"Oh! You think you're so smooth, don't you?" I cry out, my tone laced with disgust as I make a face like now I've eaten something sour. His words are like a bucket of ice water hasn't just been thrown on my head, but like I've been fully submerged in a frozen pool.

He laughs. "We can go to my bedroom right now so I can show you just how smooth my mouth can be."

"Ugh, you're so *gross*! *Why* are you so gross?!" The moment has definitely been broken. Which, honestly, is probably better anyway. All the pent-up sexual frustration he's causing me can be fuel for the club tonight.

"I haven't heard any complaints before." He shrugs and moves to his back, wearing a smug smile as he laces his hands behind his head on the plush pillow back.

"I'm sure they say things behind your back." Picking up my bowl, I lean over to place it on the tray and start to get off the couch.

"Yeah, while they're down on their knees suc–"

"Stop!" Changing direction, I lunge at him without a second thought. My hands shoot out to cover his mouth, and I laugh at his surprised expression. "I seriously do *not* get the appeal."

Caught up in the moment, we're both frozen for a beat before he reaches up and grabs my wrists, hauling me up his body and into his lap. Jackson unabashedly lifts his hips, pressing his hard length into me before his leg finds its way between mine.

The air catches in my throat as he places my wrists on the pillow behind him, stretching my body out over his. My nipples harden painfully as that feeling between my legs shoots straight to my clit. Our lips are mere inches apart. The surprise melts from my face as he moves his leg, rubbing against me. My body arches into his with its own volition, and suddenly, I couldn't care less about what a player he is.

If Jackson tries to fuck me right now, I like to think I'll say no. But with every passing second, it looks more like I'll be putty in his very experienced hands.

"Your body seems to get it," he whispers as his hands let go of my wrists to trail lightly down my arms.

His scent engulfs my senses—sharp spices, sandalwood, and a warm, musky vanilla that wraps around my body and settles into my skin. I'm breathless, eyes fluttering closed as his hands move further south to my butt. Gripping it in his hands, he draws me down onto him as his hips shift upward. The way he presses against me, the way his warm breath caresses my face. The way I feel as though I could come just by him doing that again.

It's too much.

It's too much to feel for *him*.

All of it overwhelms me, and I sit up abruptly. "Yeah, well, my body is a traitor."

His hands fall away, a reproachful sigh escaping his lips as I scramble to remove myself from his body and the couch. Flying through his home, part of me feels relief that he lets me go without any attempt at getting me to stay.

As the elevator closes behind me, I can't help but recognize that part of me is also feeling the sting of disappointment.

There are more women being led to rooms in the Dreamers wing than I've ever seen in the Confessional one.

Vibrant, deep pink roses fill the vases in this hall. Their fragrance thick and sweet, but not cloying.

My regular security guard walks in front of me, taking me to my new room, and I appreciate that we are assigned personal guards, instead of the guards only being assigned to the wings. For some reason, it makes me feel safer—even though I know I have nothing to fear from my stranger.

I'm wearing another slip tonight. Emerald green satin with black see-through lace throughout the top. Instead of going commando, I put on a flimsy thong—though I might as well be wearing nothing.

Memories from the first time I touched myself in front of him surfaced while I was picking out my outfit. If something like that were to happen again, it's easier to cover myself with a slip than an intricate set of lingerie.

My nerves feel frayed, each ending lit up and sending electric pulses through my body.

Hyperaware that I'm seconds away from touching him.

Still overstimulated from my afternoon at Jackson's.

The anticipation has been building all day, even though Jackson's words haunt me. *"If I have to go without for an entire month. So. Do. You."*

There's no part of me that feels guilty for this, though.

As the guard opens the door to let me in, I hold my breath and step over the threshold, letting it out as he shuts it quietly behind me. My stranger is standing on the other side of the room, hands in the pockets of his black dress pants.

There's a large circular bed between us, draped in black silk with multiple pillows. Polished black tables line the walls, nothing on their surfaces, but I know the drawers hold an array of toys and instruments used for creating pleasure.

Or pain.

The thrill of it all sends goosebumps down my arms and legs. Walking further into the room, my stranger's eyes roam my body, his throat bobbing as he swallows. Finally, he removes his hands from his pockets and begins to walk around the bed.

"I've been thinking about this all day," he murmurs.

"So have I."

He stalks toward me like a big cat on the prowl. Sleek, graceful.

Ready to pounce.

"Get on the bed," he quietly commands, his accent nearly causing me to melt into a puddle on the floor.

"What? No small talk tonight?" Shooting him a smile, my hands nervously play with my hem as my feet stay planted to the floor.

"Get. On. The. Bed, Little Ember. *Now.*"

He's nearly to me, only mere inches between us. His size

dwarfs my petite frame, and I have to crane my neck back to look up at him. Our eyes hold each other for only a moment, before I go to the edge of the bed and begin to climb on.

"Slowly. Crawl to the middle."

He wants me to *crawl?*

I'm torn between being turned on and wanting to turn around and ask why he wants me to do something so degrading. But as I start to do what he asks, I hear him blow out a breath behind me and realize he has a perfect view of my bare ass and nearly naked pussy.

It's not degrading. It's fucking sexy.

"Does crawling make you wet?" His voice is low, the timbre sending shivers along my spine.

Nodding, I stop on all fours when I reach the middle of the bed. "Now what would you like me to do?"

"Arch your back, ass in the air. Grab a pillow for your head." The edge of the bed dips, and I glance behind me to see that he's sat down, eyes zeroed in where I'm exposed.

Slowly, I reach for a pillow and lay my head on it. The air on my naked skin feels thick and charged with energy. The scrap of fabric I put on for underwear is already soaked.

When he finally touches me, there's an actual shock, and I jump in surprise as he chuckles. His fingers skim the sides of my thighs, up and up, until they hook the band of the thong and pull it down slowly.

"Fuck, you're so beautiful. I could stare at this cunt all day." His words make me squirm, so keenly aware that he's closely inspecting every inch of the most intimate part of my body.

"Touch me. *Please,*" I beg him. I'm not ashamed of how needy I sound. How desperate I am.

"No, Little Ember. Touch yourself, and let me watch you make yourself feel good."

Turning my head, I see that he's kneeling on his knees behind me. My fingers snake down the front of my body between my legs to gather my arousal and smear it across my clit. "It would feel even better if you did it."

Suddenly, my fingers still as I feel him moving off the bed. Turning to look again, I'm startled when he grabs my shoulders and directs me to sit up. "Come here."

My back is still to him, and he grabs me around my waist and pulls me into him further until my back rests against his thighs. His cock pokes between my shoulder blades, and I press against it lightly while rubbing my thighs together.

"Spread your legs and touch yourself," he commands.

Before my hand can find my skin again, his is lying on top of mine. He directs my fingers to circle and presses down on my clit as my head falls back against his stomach.

Moaning, my hips chase our fingers as he slides them down and through my center. "Push two inside."

Between the wings and all the extra hair I pinned in, my back starts to grow slick with sweat as I do what he says. His fingers pump against my skin, pushing mine deeper as I continue to press back against his erection. My other hand reaches up to grab his forearm, my nails digging into his skin through his shirt.

The sound of us fucking myself with my fingers reverberates throughout the small room. His other hand finds my chin and tips my head back. "I want to see your face when you come."

"I want to see *your* face. Why did you cover the entire thing?" It's an odd moment to ask, but I really want to know.

He answers by maneuvering a third finger at my entrance. "Another."

It's slightly difficult to fit another finger. I have to shift my hips, and the heel of his hand presses down into the top of mine, causing our hands to move against my clit roughly.

"Spread your legs wider. I want to see everything." He sounds hoarse, like he's struggling not to come himself.

I'm still rubbing my back against him, his hand collars

around my neck just below my chin, forcing me to look up at him. "Don't you want to touch me yourself?"

He grunts and tears his eyes away from my pussy to look at my face. "I want you to come for me."

My eyes flutter closed as his hand strokes my jaw. "Come for me, Scarlett."

Our fingers move faster, the sloppy wet sound pairing with our harsh breathing. It's like an ocean wave unfurls in my body, rushing south and breaking at the surface between my thighs. Letting out a quiet, raspy cry, I push back into him as he releases my throat.

His hand still rests on mine as I sag against him, my entire body growing slack with my release. Gently, he helps me so that I'm lying fully on the bed instead of back on his thighs.

"You did well for your first lesson," he whispers close to my ear.

Shifting my head, I notice he's moved to his knees beside the bed. He begins to stroke my hair, pulling the sweaty locks off my forehead as I ask, "And what lesson was that?"

His voice proposes there's a grin on his face as he answers, "You like being told what to do."

Jackson

Tuesday morning finds me turned around, staring out the window of my office instead of finalizing a merger contract like I should be doing.

I'm perplexed.

Any other woman I would have flipped them around and pounded it out until I got my release, too. But aside from not being in the right wing of the club for that, I was content with helping Ginny find hers.

Not that I didn't leave that fucking room with blue balls. At this point, I'm surprised I didn't come in my pants from the way she was rubbing against me. Nearly two weeks without sticking my cock in a tight, warm pussy, and all of a sudden, I'm back to my juvenile days of nearly nutting whenever a pretty woman looks at me.

But not just any woman. *No*, my cock is apparently now only partial to *her*.

Ginny. Scarlett. Red. Little Ember.

Nearly a virgin. Inexperienced. Unwilling to let *me* have her. But oh so very willing to let *him* teach her.

Never in my life have I wanted someone like Ginny. Now, she seems to be *all* that I want.

That will change once you fuck her.

Will it, though?

A knock on the door cuts through my inner musings, and I spin to see my best friend, Tripp, enter my office, thumbing through a stack of papers without looking at me. "Have you finished that merger contract yet?"

My eyes flicker to my computer screen where the contract sits, only three-quarters of the way complete. "Not yet. I'll get it done by the end of the day."

"Jackson, you're killing me. This was supposed to be sent over first thing Monday morning." He collapses into a chair on the other side of my desk and rubs at his face. It looks like he hasn't shaved in a week, and his brown, curly hair is in need of a cut.

"When are you gonna get over Emily and get your shit together?" I ask.

His eyes snap to mine, serious, no sign of the happy-go-lucky guy he used to be before his fiancée left him because of his *'weird fetishes.'* Making a mental note to ask my uncle if I can extend an invitation to Tripp for the club, I shoot him a smile and shrug.

"I'm sorry, man. But you look like shit. It's been four months. Tell me you're getting laid, at least."

"Yes, Jackson. I'm getting laid. Which is more than I can say for you, apparently. Since when do you *date*? She doesn't even look like your type," Tripp says as he scrolls through his phone before tossing it on my desk.

A photo of me and Ginny dancing at the Tisch event stares back at me from the screen. I clench my jaw in annoyance at his blatant disrespect regarding Ginny's appearance. "Pussy is my type."

"That's not true. We both know you're picky as shit. But in all the years I've known you, I don't think I've seen you fuck a redhead. You always like to go for the pretty brunettes or the leggy blondes, like Stacey."

"Like Stacey, what?" The woman herself interrupts as she breezes into my office without so much as a knock. "Daniel's firm just called. They said they haven't received the counteroffer for WhirlTech?"

"Oooooh, sounds like this one has you whipped. Fucking up at work? *Not* fucking any women? Tell me you're at least getting it from her?" Tripp prods.

The sound of Stacey berating him for his choice of words becomes background noise as the image of Ginny laid out on the bed Saturday night while I pumped her fingers into her crashes to the forefront of my mind.

Her little whispered moans, the way she felt beneath my hands. The way she looked up at me as she came.

"Jackson?" Stacey snaps her fingers, jerking me from the memory.

They both stare at me like they asked a question, and I haven't answered it yet. Looking at Tripp, I tell him, "I'm getting enough."

"Huh? Getting enough what?" he asks as I push my chair back and stand.

"I'm going out. I might be back later. If I'm not, I'll finish the contracts at home," I inform Stacey, grabbing my jacket.

"No. No, you need to finish them *now*, Jackson," Tripp says as though he's my boss and not the other way around.

At the same time, Stacey chimes in, "What about the counteroffer?"

Heading for the door, I lift a hand, addressing them both. "I'll take care of it. Don't worry."

"What are *you* doing here?" Ginny frowns at me from her desk at the women's center, though her tone lacks its usual bite.

"Was in the neighborhood and decided to stop in and see if you wanted to join me for lunch."

Lie.

Her hair is down and curled around her face today. Barely a stitch of makeup. Like a sunset, she's naturally beautiful. Stunning without even trying.

It makes me wonder why I always go after women who are so heavily put together.

What the fuck is wrong with me?

Is this what happens when women tell you no? Would I be so obsessed if I hadn't seen her bare pussy up close and personal?

"No thanks." She stands and crosses the room to where her long camel-colored peacoat and bag are hanging on the coatrack.

Her dark jeans cling to her legs, while a simple black turtleneck hugs her like a second skin. At the sound of her clearing her throat, I tear my eyes away from my perusal of her to see her inspecting me in the same manner.

"I'm actually leaving for the day. Looking at apartments here in a little bit," she explains as she shrugs on her coat.

That catches my attention. "Ready to move out of *brother dearest's*?"

"He told you we live together?" Her face falls as she asks.

Amongst other things.

"Where are you looking?" Ignoring her question, I pull out my phone and text Stacey, letting her know I won't be returning to the office.

Her quick reply is a facepalm emoji.

"I have a bunch of studios lined up in Murray Hill today. It's slim pickings out there for a girl on my budget."

Murray Hill is an acceptable neighborhood. Crime is low. It's reasonably close to the restaurant, Chillard, and Désirer. "Who's your realtor?"

"I don't have one." She looks sheepish as she says it. "I was just going to go attend the open houses."

Moving out of the doorway so she can pass, I relish the way her face lights up with the smile she throws over her shoulder at me. "Wanna come?"

Following her, I open my mouth to reply, but she cuts me off without looking back, "Don't be gross, Jackson. You're lucky I'm feeling nice today."

I'll bet you are after you got off Saturday night.

"And what, pray tell, has you in such a good mood, Red?" We exit the building—after I throw Michelle at the front a wave as she watches us leave through disapproving eyes—walking down the steps side by side.

Looking over, I see that Ginny's cheeks have turned pink, and her lips are pulled up at the corner. "Nothing in particular. Just having a good day, I guess."

"I sure hope another man isn't the reason for those pink cheeks." Holding the door to my car open for her, when she goes to slide in, I step in her way and whisper, "Otherwise, I may just have to bend you over my knee and give you a pink ass to match."

Instead of her usual disgusted sneer, she smirks and leans into me. "Keep dreaming about my ass, Jackson. 'Cause you're never gonna touch it."

She gets into the car, giving my driver, Robert, an address as I shut the door behind me. As soon as we're on our way, I lean over and whisper back, "Have you already forgotten, Red? I got a handful of it Saturday morning."

"No." My answer is firm as I turn and walk out of the studio, grabbing Ginny's arm as we retreat from the monstrosity she was about to make me walk through.

"Jackson!" she whines. "That's the second one you haven't even let me *look* at!"

Looking down at my phone as it goes off, I see that Stacey has emailed me a list of *suitable* apartments in the area. "Let's go. There's one on fifty-fourth I *will* be okay with looking at."

During the drive, she pouts with her arms crossed as she

stares out the window. "Ginny, those places were dumps. The lock on the door was broken at the first one, for Christ's sake."

I have a feeling the reason she's looking at places like that is because it's all she can afford. Making a mental note to find out just how much she makes at Désirer, I hand her my phone with the new list Stacey sent over.

"Here. Browse those and see if you want to look at any of them."

The fact that I just handed her my phone isn't lost on either of us. She stares at me wide-eyed before she starts clicking through the links. "Jackson, I can't afford these."

"We can negotiate the price." *And if that doesn't work, I'll buy the damn building.*

"I don't really have time to do all that. Chris is leaving for Doctors Without Borders in a week and a half. He's gonna be gone for a few months, but I wanted to have everything ready to move out while he's gone."

Watching her while she scrolls through listings, something feral curls in my chest, listening to her talk about her foster brother.

"Ginny…are you in trouble? Does your brother—does he, uh, hurt you?" It's an uncomfortable question, and I struggle to ask it without sounding pissed off.

I don't imagine she'll tell me the truth, especially if she won't tell *the stranger*. But her body language tells me enough, just like it did at the club.

Still, I want to hear the words come from her lips.

"Why would you ask me that?" Her voice is soft, with no sign of defense or outrage.

Leaning closer to her, I angle my body so that I can look at her profile. She's still absentmindedly scrolling through listings, not pausing to look at any of them. "At the charity event last week, he alluded to the fact that you two are together. Your rush to leave while he's gone kind of makes me think you're trying to escape him."

"We've arrived, Mr. Tailor," Robert announces.

Ginny bolts from the car, my phone still in her hand. Climbing over the seat, I get out and watch her as she looks up at the building in front of us. "Ginny…"

"I'm fine. Come on."

Following her into the five-story walk-up, I keep quiet. She takes her time, looking around the studio with mild interest before shrugging her shoulders. "It's nicer than the others."

"It has a Murphy bed." *And it's 300 square feet of cold floors with a bathroom that looks like it belongs in a prison.*

"It was on your list," she argues back, her temper returning to its normal temperature where I'm concerned.

Yeah, she's got me there. I don't know what Stacey was thinking when she added this to the list I asked her to drop everything and make.

Sighing, Ginny motions to the door. "Tomorrow is another day."

"Why don't you let me hire a realtor?" I ask as we exit the building and get back in the car.

She ignores the question but says, "I'm hungry. Are you hungry? Can we stop somewhere real quick?"

The fact that she still wants to spend time with me isn't time I want to waste, so I motion to Robert and tell her, "Of course. Where do you wanna go?"

"Bryant Park, please." She settles into her seat and takes my phone out of her pocket right as it dings. Her eyes scan the screen quickly before she hands it to me with a smile. "It's for you."

"Gee. You think?" I say dryly as I read the message.

STACEY

You really like her, don't you?

We spend the rest of the ride in silence. She gazes out the window while I try to work on my phone to draft up a counteroffer for a company Tripp and I want to acquire.

When we get to Bryant Park, I tell Robert to go park on a side street nearby. As he drives off, my eyes stray to the skyline across the park, and I get an idea.

"Ooh, I love these things," Ginny gushes as she walks toward the Wafels & Dinges hut. "Wanna split one?"

"Sure." I'm not really thinking about food or the fact that she offered to share a meal with me. My eyes are glued to my phone, where I'm furiously typing out separate messages to my aunt and uncle.

Uncle Scott responds right away.

> It's not even a question, of course, I'm okay with it. Your aunt may be harder to convince.

My phone dings again, proving my uncle wrong as I read my aunt's surprising response.

> We have no plans to come up there anytime soon. If we do, I have no problem getting a hotel. Proud of you. Xoxo

Relief rushes through me as I look up to see Ginny approaching with a paper tray filled with whipped cream. Her eyes are lit up, and she's the happiest I've seen her all afternoon. "You're hungry and wanted whipped cream? Is there a waffle under there?"

She laughs, scoops some of the sugary fluff onto her finger, and sticks it in her mouth. "Mmmm, it's so good. There's strawberries under there somewhere, too."

Watching as she attempts to pick the waffle up from underneath so she can take a bite, I try to stifle my laughter when she pulls back with a dollop of cream on her nose. Reaching out, I swipe it off before sticking it in my mouth, loving the way the action makes her cheeks flush again.

Cocking my head to the side, I turn to start walking across the park. "Come on, I wanna show you something."

"Do you want a bite?" She holds the tray up to me as we make our way through the throng of people.

Looking down, I see she's scraped off some of the cream to expose the strawberries and waffle underneath. She's got the waffle pinched at the edge, holding it slightly up for me to take hold of. Instead, I stop walking. Without breaking eye contact with her, I lean down and take a bite, wrapping my lips around her fingers.

She swallows hard as I withdraw, reaching up to wipe the cream from my lips. Slowly, she brings her fingers to her mouth and sucks them clean.

"You're aware that was just touching my mouth?" The air is cool, but the space between us is heated, charged with an electric energy I can't see but can certainly feel.

"I know." Her words make my dick jump as her eyes fall back to the tray. "So, what did you want to show me?"

Remembering my plan, I will away my erection and reach for her hand, which she lets me take. "It's this way."

Kids are screaming as parents watch them skate in the rink. The different smells of the food stands mingle together to make one giant delicious aroma. Shoppers make their way through the walkways, bags smacking into other patrons as they admire the wares. Ginny lets me pull her through it all as she finishes the waffle, feeding me a few more bites while we exchange heated glances.

When we reach our destination, she stares up at the large building. "The Bryant? Jackson, why are we here?"

She hasn't let go of my hand, and I continue holding it as the doorman opens the door for us. We pass by the concierge, who just nods in greeting. It's not the first time I've been to my aunt and uncle's apartment, having stayed here quite a bit after boarding school when I was first settling into the city and the business.

"Jackson!" Ginny whispers as we enter the elevator.

Once the doors shut, she tugs at the sleeve of my jacket. "What are we doing here? I swear to god if you think I'm going to sleep with you–"

"Good lord, Red. Give me more credit than that. Bringing you to an apartment and expecting you to take your clothes off? I have more class than that."

Her reflection in the doors gives me a pointed look, causing me to shrug. "But I mean, if you want to–"

"Jackson!" she shouts, hitting me playfully in the chest as I smirk down at her.

We get off on the twenty-fifth floor, and I take her to apartment B. Fishing the key from my wallet, I step aside as soon as the door opens, letting her walk in first. "It belongs to my aunt and uncle, but neither uses it. I just okayed it with them. If you want it…it's yours. For as long as you need."

I don't know why the thought didn't cross my mind earlier when we were looking at old, worn-down buildings and places where she wouldn't even have space for her belongings.

"Jackson, this is…wow. This is beautiful." She lets out a long breath as she admires the place.

"It's a two bed, two bath. Floors are heated. You get views of Bryant Park and the Empire State Building. Lots of storage and natural light."

Setting the key on the Calacatta marble countertop, I stick my hands in my pockets and follow her through the apartment, watching her face light up as she checks out every room.

"Jackson, this is too much. I can't afford to live here," she says eventually, wrapping her arms around her middle as she ends her viewing at one of the windows that overlooks the park.

"No one's asking you to pay, Ginny. You need a place. They have one. My uncle loves you. He said yes quicker than I could blink." My eyes look out at the skyline as the sun begins to set.

"You know, I used to live here. Back when I first moved to the city and started working with him. This place has killer views. I used to love watching the sunset. My aunt and I would sit on the balcony and discuss life and the future. Though it turned out vastly different than what either of us imagined back then."

Ginny leans against the terrazzo wall and looks up at me. "What happened between them? Your aunt and uncle? He seems to still love her a lot. Why couldn't they make it work?"

"Honestly? Because Scott is stupid. They *were* happy. He worshipped her, and she adored him. But it wasn't enough. He went and fucked it all up because men like us are never *truly* happy. Always thinking we need *more*." I don't look at her as I say it, afraid of what I'll see in her eyes if I do.

"As much as I hate to ruin what I'm sure is supposed to be a *deep* moment, you're not exactly making me want to go on that date with you when you say things like *that*," she deadpans.

Grinning, I remind her, "*Dates*. Plural."

"That is still a hard no for me." She pushes off the wall, swiping the key from the counter as she heads toward the door.

"Is it, though, Red?" I call after her.

After all, if today is anything to consider, we've already gone on one.

Ginny

The unmistakable sound of furniture being pushed across a hard floor fills the hall as I make my way to my new room in the Dreamers wing. Either someone is moving something, or the people occupying the room are getting very, *very* rough with each other.

My guard lets out a small laugh as we approach the door, the noise growing with each step, and I realize the sound is coming from within *my* room. "Should we tell him that he can ask to have the room rearranged?" he asks.

Opening the door, he turns his back so I can disrobe, the squeaking stopping the moment my eyes meet my stranger from across the room. We watch each other silently as I peel my robe off, placing it in my guard's waiting hand before stepping into the room while he shuts the door behind me.

"You look breathtaking," my stranger says, eyeing tonight's outfit with approval.

"You look like you've been busy," I remark.

The bed that once sat in the middle of the room has been pushed to one side, and a small loveseat I didn't notice last time is now at the head of it.

"I wanted us to enjoy a more comfortable position tonight." His words send heat blazing south as my bottom lip disappears behind my teeth. He's wearing his usual white button-up tucked into dark dress pants tonight.

He sure seems to like staying fully clothed for as many clothes as I try *not* to wear.

"Come here," he commands.

His order sends a sensual chill through me and makes my nipples harden beneath the see-through material of my gown. It's all I'm wearing tonight. Floor-length, navy mesh with slits on both sides and simple straps to hold it up. I left the hair extensions in my area in the changing room, not wanting to deal with the extra heat they cause.

Tonight, I plan on getting hot enough.

His eyes are trained on me as I slowly walk through the room, my heels echoing loudly against the floor. When I reach him, I fist my hands in his shirt, glaring at it as though it offends me.

"Why do you always wear so much clothing?" My fingers slowly reach up to undo the top button, but his hands catch mine before I can finish the task.

"You're awfully bold tonight." His full-face mask skims my hair affectionately as he lowers his head. Stepping into me, his hands cradle mine between us as he walks me backward to the bed.

"I've had a good week."

It's true. My afternoon with Jackson on Tuesday left me feeling lighter than I've felt in years, and I've seen him twice more this week. Once, on Wednesday, when he attended a meeting at Decadence with Scott and Carmela before insisting he drive me to Lenni's after my shift. And again earlier today, when we went back to The Bryant to give the building my information—he'd even bought me another waffle at the park afterward.

Not to mention that when I had his phone on Tuesday, I added my number to it—which he uses often now—even before I saw Stacey's message.

While my Friday and Saturday nights belong to my

stranger, my weekdays are beginning to be possessed by Jackson.

As hard as I try to fight the flips my insides do whenever he shows up at Decadence or Chillard unannounced, my chest and stomach have become home to a whole damn gymnastics team where he's concerned.

Lowering me to the bed, my stranger lets out what sounds like a chuckle as he asks, "Tell me about your week, then."

He lets go of my hands and moves to the couch, sitting down and spreading his legs wide as he motions for me to sit between them. My lips pull up in a sly grin as I get on all fours and crawl to him slowly, appreciating the low, gravelly laugh he gives me in return.

Once I reach him, he gently slides the straps of my wings down and discards them on the floor before positioning me so that my back is to his chest. His arms wrap around me after he pushes my hair off one shoulder. "Tell me, Little Ember. What has put that glowing smile on your beautiful face?"

Without hesitation, I tell him, "Not *what*. *Who*. I did what you suggested—found someone out there to help me. I got a new apartment. Moving in will take a little bit, but it's a huge relief."

"I'm glad to see you so happy. It's a nice change from seeing tears fall from your eyes." He attempts to nuzzle my neck, but the mask makes it awkward. It's cold against my skin, causing me to shiver against him.

"You aren't upset?" My fingers lift to trail down his arms, tracing random patterns over his shirt.

"Not at all. I cannot do for you out there what I can do for you in here."

"Could you remove your mask? Not fully, but maybe change back to the one you wore the first night?" Looking over my shoulder, it's not lost on me the way he looks away quickly, as if afraid of me looking into his eyes when we're this close.

Shaking his head, he pulls me back to lie against him. But

as soon as I do, I jolt up again, jumping from the bed and racing over to the door. "I have an idea!"

Quickly, I pull it open, startling my guard. "Everything okay, Miss Scarlett?"

"Yeah, I just need the sash to my robe. Would you mind?"

Chuckling, he retrieves what I need. As he hands it over, he whispers, "That's what the drawers are for."

My cheeks flush as I realize I just ran across the room in a see-through gown when I could have easily grabbed a blindfold from one of the tables. "Thanks."

Closing the door, I shyly turn around and hold up the sash. "You can blindfold me?"

Walking back to him, I sit at the edge of the bed, where it meets the couch. "If you blindfold me, you can remove your mask. That's what you're worried about, isn't it? Me seeing too much of your face."

"Precisely, though I can't say I hate your idea. Turn around." Taking the sash from me, he scoots closer so that he can tie it around my eyes.

"Lift your mask for a moment so that I can secure this."

"It seems silly to keep the mask on if I'm going to be blindfolded. It covers just as much as my mask." My heart starts to race. The idea of us both removing our masks—even if we still won't be able to see each other's faces—has me feeling giddy, like Christmas morning when I couldn't wait to see what Santa put under the tree.

"If that's what you wish, remove your mask."

I all but tear it from my face, barely a second passing before he places the sash over my eyes and secures it tightly around my head. "Is that okay?" he murmurs.

Nodding, I whisper, "Yes."

He takes my mask from my hand, and then I hear the slight clink of his against the table. When his warm lips touch my bare shoulder, it makes me jump. Now that my sight is gone, all my other senses are heightened.

"What is it that you wish to learn tonight?" he asks against my skin as his lips skate across my shoulder blades.

"I don't want to offend you…" I tell him, my voice trailing off, because there's one thing that I really *do* want to learn, and I'm hoping he'll be the one to teach me.

How to be sexually confident.

There's another gentle caress of his lips on the nape of my neck. "Why do you think I would be offended?"

My nipples pebble as my back arches, head rolling to the side as he finally nuzzles my neck like he tried to earlier. "I don't want you to think I'm asking for *him*."

His lips freeze against my skin, breath warm as it blows out on my back. "And what is it that you're asking?"

"I want to know…how to be confident with my body. How to…not seem so…*virginal*."

Laughter sounds against my shoulder as his hands slide under the straps that hold my gown up. "Oh, Little Ember. *Nothing* about you in this outfit says virginal. But this is what we'll do. Tonight, you're going to tell me *exactly* what you want. I want to hear you use your words, every single dirty thing that pops into this exquisite head of yours."

He slowly starts to lower the straps, as if to give me time to refuse. But I don't want to. My pussy clenches as the night-gown reaches my nipples, catching on them before he pulls it down the rest of the way, letting it pool at my waist. I can feel him as he bends over me, warm breath hitting my collarbone, thumbs coming up to flick my nipples.

"Can you do that for me?" he whispers against my ear before lowering his mouth to my neck as he palms my breasts.

Throwing my head back on his shoulder, I suck in air and arch my back, pressing my chest further into his hands as my clit starts to pulse. "Yes. I want to feel your hands on me. Everywhere. *Please*."

The bed shifts, and then he pulls me to stand, letting the nightgown drop to the floor. Naked and unafraid, I reach for him, sliding my hands up his chest as his find my waist before moving back to cup my ass.

It reminds me of when Jackson grabbed me last weekend, and the thought of him, while my stranger touches me, sets the fire inside my body ablaze.

He turns us, getting back on the bed and guiding me by my hips to sit down and scoot back against him like we were earlier. His hands move over my thighs, gripping the insides before spreading my legs wide.

"You're not talking," he whispers against my neck.

I can feel from how his fingers run up my skin that I'm so wet. I've already made a mess between my legs. "I told you to touch me."

"I am touching you. Be more specific."

My pussy clenches, more wetness dripping from it as his fingers ghost over where I want to feel them. "Right there! Please! I want your fingers inside me."

Blowing out a breath against my neck, his forehead drops against my back for a second before he pulls me back further. I assume it's so he can watch over my shoulder. Two of his fingers swipe up my center as one of my hands reaches back to twist in his hair, the other twisting in the sheets. "*Yes*, just like that. Only a little higher."

"How high, Little Ember?" he asks, moving his fingers against my flesh to my belly button, trailing my arousal along my skin. "This high?"

Shaking my head, I squirm against him. "Lower."

He dips his fingers through me again before they travel further down between my cheeks. "Here?"

"I want your fingers inside me, but also, I want them on my clit." I cry out. I'm torn between humiliation and such need that I feel like every dirty word I know is about to explode from my mouth.

There's a sharp nip to my earlobe before he says, "Good girl."

The praise causes me to whimper as he pushes two fingers

inside me, slowly, as his thumb begins to circle my clit. His other hand reaches around to palm my breast, letting the weight of it sit in his hand as he rolls my nipple between his thumb and forefinger.

My hips rock against his hand as his fingers move inside me, his thumb swirling around my needy bundle of nerves. An errant thought crosses my mind that his fingers are much more experienced than Chris', which jolts me out of the moment.

As if he senses the change in my demeanor, he slows his fingers and asks, "Are you okay?"

When I don't answer, he grabs my chin and turns my head toward him. "Get out of your head, love. Wherever you've gone, come back to me."

He starts to move his fingers again, and slowly, like pouring white paint on a dark canvas, the present bleeds back into my mind, pushing back my dark past. "Tell me what you're feeling right now."

"It feels good, but I want *more.*" The need to feel something rougher, more intense, overwhelms me.

"Can you take a third?" he asks as he teases another finger where the other two are already knuckle deep. His hips are rocking against my butt, erection pressed into my back.

It makes me feel powerful.

Sexy.

Using my hands, I lift myself to sit back on his lap, directly on top of his dick. The movement earns me a groan as I start to grind on him wantonly, spreading my legs even wider.

"Yes, give me another. I want to feel full."

"Fuck, love. That mouth of yours just needed to be unleashed, didn't it?"

A cry leaves my throat as he enters a third finger, stretching my walls and making me feel impossibly full. I'm riding his fingers now, my hips jerking over his cock. "I want to make you come."

"Keep riding me like that, and you'll get your wish," he groans against my shoulder. His teeth gently scrape against my skin, as if he's holding himself back from sinking them into my flesh.

My hands lift to tangle in my hair, pulling it up to bare my naked back to him. Letting go of all abandon, I let whatever comes to mind fly out of my mouth as I fuck his fingers and ride his cock through his pants. "I want you to make me come, then I want you to get undressed and fuck me."

He grips the skin of my hip and says, "No, Little Ember."

Thinking it's just another way to get me to talk, I ask, "No? No, as in, not now? Or no, as in, never?"

My hips jerk as my breasts bounce in the air. The hand that isn't fucking me wraps around my shoulder, pulling me down into him with every thrust of his cock into my backside. I feel in control. It's like he's caught up in how *I'm* making *him* feel, and he's getting pleasure *from* me instead of only giving it *to* me.

"No, as in, not tonight. I want to savor this moment. There will be time for other things."

I can feel my orgasm beginning to crest, but I still need just a little more to push me over the edge. My hand snakes down to where his thumb is pressing against my clit, and I begin to rub my fingers over his digit, using him to fuck myself harder.

"Fuck!" he shouts, hips shuddering against me as he comes.

The fact that *I* did that to him, before he could get me off, allows me to let go. Crying out, I come as his fingers sink into me as deep as they'll go, and I press his thumb against my clit as hard as I can.

My hips slow, eventually coming to a stop with his fingers still buried inside me. Sinking back against his chest, I let out a little giggle at his harsh breathing against the crook of my neck. "I made you come."

"Proud of that, are you?" He sets his chin on my shoulder and slowly pulls his fingers out.

"I am." Even though I can't see, I spin around to straddle his lap and lean down to lay my head on his chest.

His arms wrap around me as he lays back against the pillows on the couch, legs stretched out as he holds me to him. Our hearts beat erratically, thumping against our chests like drums, trying to create their own music together.

"You know…I've never been able to get off with someone other than myself," I mumble against his shirt.

His fingers start to draw lazy patterns on my skin. "I'm honored you agreed to let me help."

Something seizes behind my ribs as Jackson flashes through my mind unwittingly. "Are you okay with me seeing someone out there? Do…do you have someone you go home to?"

His answer is immediate. "There's no one I go home to, Little Ember. But if someone out there catches your fancy, he's a lucky man to have your attention. I'm not the jealous sort. In here, you're *mine*."

I wonder at his words, my head warring with my chest over how I feel. If I'm his in here, I'm beginning to wonder if out there…I'm Jackson's.

The building that houses Tailor Industries is a giant, futuristic architecture with mirrored windows and darkly painted steel beams.

Still riding Cloud Nine from my weekend at the club, and from the fact that Chris is leaving in three days, I spontaneously decide to stop by Jackson's work to surprise him. But from the look the woman at the front desk is giving me, it's going to be harder to see him than I thought.

"I'm sorry, who are you?" she asks in a snobby tone. Her unimpressed eyes take in my outfit before she clicks something on her computer. I'm wearing a cream knit dress with tan suede boots that reach my thighs. The late-spring air is starting to turn—not quite warm enough to put away my heavier clothes in favor of lighter ones, but enough that wearing dresses is no longer uncomfortable.

"Ginny. He isn't expecting me, but-"

"Jackson doesn't take unsolicited visitors, and he's in the middle of a very important meeting," she interrupts me as though she's on a first-name basis with him.

And who knows, maybe she is.

Jealousy flits through my chest as I try to smile nicely and calm my temper as I read her name plate. "Nikki, is it? If you just call up there, I'm sure–"

"It's a no from me. Sorry. You'll have to wait until he's off work when the rest of the other kitty cats come sniffing around," she drones on as if bored by my mere presence.

The fact that she put me in the same category with all the other women vying for Jackson's attention pisses me off. Seconds away from saying some not-so-nice words, I pull my phone out and type out a message to him instead.

> Parole officer here for random check-in. Your guard dog won't let me up.

Not even ten seconds go by before Nikki's desk phone rings. She barely gets her greeting out before abruptly halting as her eyes whip to me. "Absolutely, of course, sir. I'm sorry, I didn't know."

Hanging up the phone, she looks at me with a mix of annoyance and surprise. "Top floor, on your right."

Giving her a smile so saccharine it could cause cavities, I say, "Nikki, it's been *such* a pleasure. I'll be sure to put in a good word."

During the elevator ride to the top floor, there's time to reflect on where my sudden attitude came from. I've never been this way with men before—especially not men who are known for sleeping with half of New York. Not only has Jackson gotten under my skin, but it's becoming easier to think of him as *mine*.

Only, he isn't.

Once the thirty days are up, when he gets what he wants…

I'm not sure I want to go down that thought road right now.

Jackson is waiting for me as soon as the elevator doors open, his greeting sending a possessive thrill through me. "Aww, honey. You brought me lunch?"

"Only if you agree to walk it off with me in the park after," I say, holding up a bag with paninis from Zaid Gourmet.

There are people at desks who watch us curiously as we interact, as if this isn't normal for Jackson to be out amongst them. Some look at each other with grins, and some raise their phones to snap photos.

Where I once would be terrified of Chris finding out from a random gossip column about me and the billionaire spending time together, now I'm beginning to feel like there's no problem of mine Jackson can't handle.

He puts his hand on his chest as if he's surprised. "I'm sorry, Red. Did you just ask me on a date?"

Pushing my way past him with a roll of my eyes, even though I have no idea where I'm going, I tell him, "Yeah, yeah, yeah. Thought you were in a *big important meeting*?"

"I was." His tone is deadly serious.

Spinning around again to face him, my lips stretch into a grin, but his expression makes me stop as I realize he's not kidding. "Shit. I'm sorry, I didn't mean to interrupt."

He prowls toward me as though I'm the only one in the room as he reaches out to cup my cheek. The first time he ever tried to touch me, I flinched. Now, his touch is welcome and has me thinking dirty, dirty thoughts of all the things we can do in his office.

His thumb caresses my cheekbone as he reaches for the food bag with the other hand. "You never have to apologize for stopping in for a little *afternoon delight.*"

Laughing at his joke, I relish the genuine smile he shines down on me as his hand drops away from my face to grab mine. "That's a dessert, right? I *love* dessert."

As he pulls me through the maze of desks and down a hall, he replies huskily, "Yeah, sure, Red. It's a dessert. One I'll eat right on my desk if you let me."

A lady scrutinizing a file looks up sharply at his words as we pass. We try to muffle our laughter as we look at each other, almost running straight into his secretary because we're paying more attention to one another than where we're walking. She's standing in the middle of the hall as if she saw us coming and wanted to stop us.

"Jackson, you realize that you just walked out of the meeting that could make or break this deal with WhirlTech, don't you?" she chastises.

Stacey makes me feel extremely inadequate. She's tall, beautiful, and can command the attention of any man in any room with a simple look. If Jackson hadn't told me she was married, I don't think I'd be able to handle how close their relationship is.

"Sorry, it's my fault. I didn't know he was really in a meeting. I thought the girl downstairs was just being difficult," I tell her while guiltily looking down at the carpet.

"No, *you* don't apologize for anything. *He* should have sent me out for you while he finished up in there. Hi, by the way. I'm Stacey. We haven't been properly introduced." She holds her hand out under my line of vision. My eyes lift to her hand before moving to her face to see her smiling warmly at me.

Reaching out, I shake her hand and return her smile. "Ginny."

Her eyes find Jackson's again. "I get it. I do. But can we please just get through this deal first?"

The way she speaks to him sounds more like a work partner than a secretary. It kinda makes me wonder if most big businessmen's secretaries are the ones pulling the strings all the time.

"Probably not the best time to tell you I'm leaving for the day after we eat lunch—but that's what I'm doing," Jackson tells her.

He steps around her, pulling me along with him. Disappointment crosses her features as she blows out a breath and hangs her head back. Digging my feet into the carpet, I pull him back. "Why don't you go finish your meeting? I'll just wait in your office for you."

Jackson looks annoyed as Stacey turns around and nods, walking past us as she says, "I think that's a great idea. I'll show her where it is. Follow me, Ginny."

"Go do your job. Such a slacker." Making a tsking noise with my tongue, I take the food from his hand and start walking backward in the direction Stacey went.

His jaw clenches, but he's smirking at me as he watches me with heated eyes. A perfectly chiseled god in a four-figure suit. "You're asking for it, Red."

Waving my fingers at him, I turn around to follow Stacey.

Soon, I feel like I'll be begging.

Central Park is bathed in vibrant green hues as spring gives way to early summer. Lilacs are starting to bloom, gracing our path with their sweet fragrance. The leaves on the trees are young and thin enough that the sunlight filters through them, shining down on us as we make our way through Sheep Meadow, heading in the direction of the skating rink.

"I feel bad the meeting didn't end well. I shouldn't have

just shown up like that. I'm sorry," I apologize for the umpteenth time.

Jackson laughs as he swings his arm around my shoulders casually. Without hesitation, I lean into his side, relishing the comfortable nature of the gesture. "Ginny, stop apologizing. It's not that big a deal. We have them backed into a corner anyway. If they say no to us, their company is gonna fold. I'm not worried about it."

We pass an elderly couple who look at us with big smiles as they take in the scenery. It causes a thought to flutter through my mind, resulting in a giggle escaping my throat.

"What's so funny?" he asks, voice lowering for only me to hear.

"I just realized this is probably as close to a normal date as we've ever had. And by we, I mean separately," I tell him.

"What do you mean?" he asks.

"Well, *you* don't date. So, I'm guessing you've never gone on a walk in the park with a woman who wasn't Stacey or your aunt. And *I've* never gone on a walking date with a man. It's always dinner—where they feed you sexual innuendos all night, a movie—where they try to grope you, or a party— where they try to get you drunk and then fumble around your body and pretend to know what they're doing."

Jackson pulls me to a stop. His arm falls from around my shoulders as his hands find my waist beneath my open peacoat. "Have a lot of guys pretended to know what they're doing when it comes to your body, Ginny?"

A shiver runs through me, and it's not because of the breeze. Just the way he says the words, low and husky, and his eyes darken, even though the sun highlights every streak of caramel and green in his irises. Nonchalantly, I cross a booted foot over the other to discreetly clench my thighs together.

"Not really. I'm particular about who I spend my time with. Which is more than I can say for *you*."

Letting out a laugh because it's meant to be a joke, I'm not prepared for the way he lets go of me and steps back. His hands burrow into his pockets as he continues walking, leaving me behind to hurry after him.

"Aww, Jackson, you're not upset, are you?" A bark sounds up ahead, followed by more that join in and draw my attention toward Wollman Rink.

"Is that an adoption fair?! I *love* animals! Come on!" Looping my arm through his without waiting for an answer, I pull him toward the rink.

Pet adoption fairs pop up every now and then, and I've always loved coming to pet the animals. We never had a cat or dog growing up. Not even so much as a fish. I used to wonder why, but the older I got, the more I thought it was because Collin and Christine feared that Chris would harm them.

If only they would have been as considerate toward me.

"I don't want to go see animals in cages. How depressing," Jackson says, but he continues to let me pull him along.

From one of my sessions with Scott, I happen to know Jackson loves cats. Scott's mother had no less than four at a time, so Jackson grew up with them. Scott also mentioned that regarding charities, Jackson threw a lot of money at animal shelters and programs around the city.

"They're so cute, though! I like to pet them through the bars. Let them know they're loved and will be okay." We make it to the entrance, and I instantly drag him over to a litter of puppies in an open-wire kennel area.

People are perusing cage to cage as kids run around screaming at their parents about which animal they want to take home. Jackson hangs back as I pet the puppies, checking his phone while looking like he'd rather be elsewhere.

Squishing a pug puppy against my cheek, I ask him, "Isn't this the most adorable face you've ever seen?"

He regards me for a moment before taking a step forward to say, "As a matter of fact, it is. The puppy isn't so bad either."

"Oh, so smooth," I tell him playfully before setting the pug back down.

Jackson's eyes stray down the walkway to where the cats are stacked in kennels four high. "A cat makes for a much better pet than a dog."

Grabbing his hand, I pull him down to where there are multiple litters of kittens and adult cats. Some are rubbing their furry faces against the bars, and some look scared, which breaks my heart. A glance at Jackson's face tells me it's making him uncomfortable.

"You should get one. Caring for something other than yourself might do you some good." Reaching up, I stroke the cheek of a beautiful, long-haired tabby.

Jackson answers with a laugh. "I don't have time for a cat. They're needy. I work too much."

"Cats aren't needy. They are perfectly independent," I argue.

"See, people *think* that, but it's not true. Some are, sure. But cats are actually very loving creatures. Many would rather be with their owner than by themselves." He moves down the cages until one catches his attention.

Walking away from the tabby, though it shatters my heart to leave him, I join Jackson to see what he's looking at. "Maybe having something at home to depend on you would be a good thing. You're obviously not the settling down kind of man, but a cat might keep you a little more grounded."

"You really don't think highly of me, do you?" He doesn't look at me as he asks. He's staring into one of the cages where an old, rough-looking cat with patchy cream fur is hunched over with its nose in the back corner.

Nudging his arm with my shoulder, I smile up at him. "Come on, you're telling me you're gonna pass on having pussy at your house all the time?"

That gets him to crack a smile. He shakes his head and raises his hand to the bars, clicking his tongue at the cat. In the softest voice I've ever heard from him, he coos, "Hey, little guy. You look like you've seen better days."

The cat's ears swivel around, but other than that, he doesn't pay Jackson any attention.

"That one doesn't really like people much. Can't blame him, though. Owners dumped him on the street and left him out in the cold." A lady holding a clipboard appears on the other side of Jackson, wearing a red shirt with the adoption clinic logo on it.

"If you guys are looking for a friend for your little one, that one isn't the guy you want," she continues.

Jackson looks at her sharply, and I assume it's because she alluded to us having a kid, but instead, he surprises me. "His owners *dumped* him on the street?"

The look in his eyes is telling. If he wants to, he'll find out exactly where this cat came from and make its previous owner's life a living hell. Something feels warm in my chest as I watch the way he looks at the cat. More upset about the creature's circumstances than the lady's assumption of us being together.

"How tragically sad. Babe, I think little Jackson Jr. would very much appreciate a friend. He's been so lonely lately," I lilt, brushing the hair off his forehead. It's soft and thick, and I imagine what it would be like to grasp it and pull while he's on his knees in front of me.

His gaze whips to mine, clearly not amused. Continuing to grin up at him, I push his hair back again and pout. "Think of how happy you'll make him, honey."

Clearing her throat, the lady tells us, "I'll give you two a moment."

"No need," Jackson snaps without breaking eye contact with me. "We'll take him."

"Oh! Excellent! I'll just need you to fill out this paperwork then, and then you're free to go." She fumbles with a paper packet on the clipboard before handing it to us. Jackson takes it and tucks it under his arm as she moves away to help a family.

As soon as she's gone, Jackson grabs my waist and turns me so my back is against the cages. I'm instantly wet between my thighs as he steps into me, leaning down to whisper, "When we get home, you are in so much trouble, *honey*."

Two hours later, I haul four large bags into Jackson's penthouse while he brings in the other two and the largest cat tree I've ever seen.

After filling out the paperwork, he called Robert to pick up the cat—whose name ended up being Mr. Piddlesworth— to bring it back to his house while Jackson and I went shopping for it.

Having never owned an animal before, I didn't realize there was so much that we would need to get. Though, I have a feeling Jackson went just a tad overboard.

Setting the bags down in the kitchen, I notice Mr. Piddlesworth has already made himself at home on a deep windowsill in the living room. "Aww, I think he likes it here."

"Considering most cats would be hiding right now, I'd say you're right." Jackson sets down his bags and the tree before taking a few steps toward the cat Instantly, Mr. Piddlesworth tenses as though he'll bolt if Jackson moves any closer.

Seeing this, he puts up his hands and turns around. "You do you, little guy. You'll come to me when you're ready."

"Pawtherhood looks good on you," I joke, unloading the food to put it in an airtight container. It's black with little white paw prints *'to match the kitchen decor.'*

Turning to find a good place for it, I let out a startled squeak when Jackson grabs me around the waist, picking me up as though I weigh nothing and sitting me on the kitchen counter. "So you think Jackson Jr. is lonely, hmm? I can tell you right now that you're not wrong about that, *honey*."

My knees part as he jerks me to the edge of the counter, stepping between my legs to prove that *Jackson Jr.* really is looking for some attention. He takes the food container out of my hands and pushes it away from us as he leans into me. I have to grab his shoulders to stop myself from falling back.

"It's been nearly three weeks since he's had any attention." His nose nuzzles mine as one hand pulls my leg around his waist and the other braces on my lower back.

"Oh no, whatever will you do?" My body feels like it's been lit with a cool blue flame—nipples hardening as my pussy involuntarily clenches. There's a weight in my lower throat, like my heart has climbed into it, and I feel every rapid beat in my esophagus.

I *want* him.

I want him so badly that I don't mind as his erection presses into my center. My dress rides up as he pulls me closer, nearly off the edge as my other leg wraps around his waist. Our breathing quickens as his forehead rests on mine, his hand sliding up my leg and around the inside of my thigh.

His lips are almost on mine as his fingers skate beneath my dress and ever so lightly over my core. "Tell me you want this," he says quietly.

Leaning my head back, I gently press my mouth to his as my hands wrap into his hair. When our lips part, we look at each other as everything melts away, and suddenly, he's all I can see.

In a burst, our mouths collide. I'm pulling him closer as his hands grip my ass and drag me onto his body. Fingers dig into scalp and skin, as lips part and tongues tangle. I've never felt so alive kissing before.

Jackson kisses me as though he's trying to devour every part of my soul. Deeply. With purpose.

My legs squeeze his waist, trying to create the friction I desperately need between my thighs. He walks us to the living room, lips never parting, and turns to sit on the couch with me straddling his lap.

Once he's sat, his hands leave my thighs—one traveling up to fist in my hair while the other journeys between my legs to rub at my clit, with more intention than before.

My hips roll into his fingers, searching for more, as I pull my lips from his and move to kiss a trail down his neck. Firmly, but with care, he pulls me back by my hair to look me in the eyes. The little bit of pain that shoots from my scalp down my spine causes me to grow even more wet, and with the way his fingers are moving against me, there is no way he hasn't noticed.

"You didn't answer me. Before this goes any further, you have to tell me you want this," he tells me.

There's something in his voice, a frantic need that matches my own want. My hips chase his fingers as he pulls them away from my underwear, a whimper escaping my lips.

"Let me be very clear, Ginny. All you have to do is give me the green light, and I will take you upstairs and fuck you the way no man before me ever has, and no man after me ever will."

It's meant to be so promising—a turn-on.

No man after me ever will.

As much as I want him, his words convey that this is still just a game to him—something to win.

Something to walk away from *once* he's won.

Fury flashes through me, but I'm beginning to learn how to play this game by his rules.

A smirk lifts the corner of my lips, and suddenly, he doesn't look so sure that he's about to have me. Lifting onto my knees, I let go of him, pulling my dress down and backing off him.

"I think I'm good." Swiping my thumb across my lower lip, I walk around the couch, ignoring his incredulous stare.

"You think you're good? What does *that* mean?" he calls after me.

Turning, I can see that he's standing, his erection pointed straight at me. Giving him a shrug, I grab my purse from the counter and start toward the elevator. "Have a good night, *cats*anova."

"Ginny! Wait! *Where* are you going?"

Throwing him a wink, the elevator doors shut on the image of him staring across the room at me as though I've lost my damn mind.

To me, though, it feels like I've just won my first game.

Eat your heart out, Jackson Tailor.

Jackson

Big blue eyes glazed over with lust.

Her nails scrape against my scalp as her tongue tangles with mine.

The weight of her on top of me as her hips chase my fingers.

My fingers, drenched, even through her underwear.

"That creepy guy from the Tisch event is here to see you. Christopher Calloway? Should I let him up?" Stacey's voice interrupts my daydreams of the other day, drifting through the open door from her desk just outside my office.

What the fuck is that asshole doing here?

My fingers still over the keys of my MacBook. I'm right in the middle of working on *another* counteroffer because Whirl-Tech is playing hardball dirtier than I thought them capable— though I can hardly make sense of the last few sentences because my Little Ember took over my thoughts.

There's no way I should stop what I'm doing to entertain him.

But he's leaving tomorrow for the Doctors Without Borders program, and I have a feeling there's a significant reason he's here to see *me*.

Probably the same reason my aunt texted me earlier with a message that read:

A photo taken of me and Ginny at the adoption fair had gone to print the next day, capturing the moment when she was holding the puppy up to her face as I watched with what appeared to be fucking stars in my eyes. The headline read, *'Take two Tailor: Jackson Tailor has been seen around town numerous times with a mysterious redhead. The playboy billionaire has never been photographed with a woman more than once.'*

The psycho probably wants to have *the big brother talk* before he takes off for a few months. Although, I'm sure his intentions are anything but brotherly.

"Sure. Send him in," I call out to Stacey.

Finishing up the clause I'm working on—no, you *can't* have casual Fridays—I don't even look up from my screen as she escorts him into my office before closing the door behind her as she leaves. "What can I do for you, Mr. Calloway?"

The fucking weirdo is silent for so long that I finally tear my eyes away from my screen to find his dark beady eyes glued to me—a snarky grin on his ugly face.

"Did you just come here to waste my valuable time?" I ask, eyes returning to my computer.

"With all due respect, Mr. Tailor, I think you know why I'm here."

Sighing, I make sure my progress saves before I shut my laptop. "No, I really don't. Care to enlighten me?"

"You were photographed with Ginny in the park a few days ago. Ring a bell?" His eyes grow wide as his brows rise. He's the picture-perfect image of a looney toon, and something unfurls within my chest at the reminder that Ginny had to grow up with him.

"I wasn't aware it was a crime to talk to your sister." Folding my hands in my lap, I lean back in my chair.

Relaxed. Unbothered.

Annoyed.

140

"She's *not* my sister!" he all but shouts while taking two quick steps toward my desk.

It doesn't phase me, and I give him a bored, unamused expression. "Is there a point to this?"

"I want you to stay away from her. She's not right in the head, and you're going to confuse her. See, she belongs to me, and I happen to be leaving for a while for work. So I wanted to make it clear that she's off-limits."

Fuck this guy. She *belongs* to him? She's not fucking property. But if she's going to belong to any man, it's going to be *me*. Not some fucked in the head asshole with some serious boundary issues.

If she'd let me, I'd move her out of their apartment tonight. How the fuck does she handle being around him?

As it is, I respect her decision to do things her way.

Which is why I continue letting her walk away when I really want to rip the clothes from her body and chain her to my fucking bed.

"I wasn't aware they let medical students participate in the MSF." Completely ignoring his warning, I fix him with a cold gaze. "Seems like a pretty big opportunity for someone like you."

He makes a face and shrugs as if it's no big deal. "I'm a talented surgeon. They made an exception. It'll look good on my resume moving forward with my career."

"You know what won't look good on your resume? Threatening a Tailor when my uncle is a top donor for the hospital—not to mention my *generous* contribution."

The smug smile drops from his face, and his lips curl into a sneer. "I'm not threatening you."

It occurs to me that this little interaction could very well convince him to stay, no matter how good of an opportunity it is with the medical program. And that is something that just will not do. I want this fucker as far away from Ginny as possible.

So, I decide to deal with him in the only way he apparently knows how. The only way disgusting men like him understand.

"Regardless of what you or the tabloids think, I'm drowning in pussy. I have no interest in chasing after your sister. Simple women like her can't hold my interest, and I'm not into redheads."

"She's *not* my sister!"

"Either way. We ran into each other in the park, and she helped me get a good photo to make it look like I cared about the animals. Gotta keep up the charitable image, after all. And you gotta admit she takes a pretty picture." Shrugging, I open my laptop and pull the counteroffer back up. "You have nothing to worry about from me. Good luck on your trip, Mr. Calloway."

You vile prick.

Chris seems placated by my answer. Smoothing out the jacket of his navy checkered suit, he gives his head a sharp nod. "Thank you, Mr. Tailor. For telling me *exactly* what I needed to hear."

After I finish the counteroffer, the rest of the afternoon is spent catching up on emails and skimming contract negotiations—though my thoughts continue to stray to the other night on my couch. After I reread the same paragraph for the fifth time, I will my erection away before heading out of my office.

Stacey isn't at her desk, so I don't have to deal with her disapproving regard and questions about where I'm going at three in the afternoon.

"Where are you going?"

Spoke too soon.

Turning, I see her holding a stack of files and tapping her foot as though she already knows where I'm headed.

Busted.

"What? I got all my work done," I tell her as though she's *my* boss and not the other way around.

"What are you doing with that poor girl, Jackson? Because if you're serious, then I will get behind it, but if you're just waiting to wear her down and then drop her–"

"It's not like that!" Cutting her off, my voice is sharp and final.

Stacey's eyes widen a fraction before she shakes her head. "Okay then. I hope you know what you're doing."

As the elevator doors open, I watch her for a moment—mumbling to herself as she walks away—before stepping through them.

No, I have absolutely no idea what I'm doing.

Michelle stares at me like I'm a fly she just found in her cup of coffee. The lime green neon jumpsuit she wears is a glaring monstrosity, and I have to wonder if she genuinely likes wearing the clothes she does. "Ginny sure is popular today. She's down in the big room with the families. I'm guessing you're here to *help out*?"

My eyebrow raises, and I'm about to ask what she's going on about when I hear, "Jackson? What are you doing here?"

Turning, I see my uncle coming through the door that leads to the rest of the building. "I could ask you the same thing?"

It hasn't escaped my attention that something is going on between my uncle and Ginny. At first, I thought that it might be sexual. There was even a point where I wondered if something had happened at the club between them. Then he mentioned forgetting about the names the first day I met her, so he knows she works at Désirer.

But the more time I spend with her, I no longer think

that's the case. However, it's starting to unnerve me that they act as if they're in on a secret that only they know about.

"Dropped by to make a donation. Ginny organized the whole thing, but the resources are limited, so I thought I'd help out a little." He buttons up his black peacoat and wraps a dark gray scarf around his neck, even though the temperature outside is nearing sixty-five.

At my confused look, he points behind him. "The little carnival for the kids they set up downstairs? She's been working on it for weeks."

"Funny, she never mentioned it." Looking back at Michelle, I see she's watching our interaction through the glass window, a giant Starbucks Frappuccino in hand, as though we're a live version of a trashy reality TV show.

"Ah, well. What *are* you doing here?" My uncle makes his way to the entrance while waiting for me to reply.

"Just wanted to see Ginny." It's not a lie. But it's not *me* either. The honesty has him drawing his eyebrows together as he looks at me with consideration.

"Be careful, Jackson," he finally says. "It's a dangerous thing…love. It will turn you into something you don't recognize faster than it takes you to realize you're even in it. As much as I'd hate to see Ginny get hurt, I don't wanna see you suffer because you ran headfirst into something you don't understand. If that's where it's headed, take it slow."

"You married Aunt Sadie after four months."

"And look how that turned out. If I could go back and do it over again, I would. I'd still marry her. But I'd do it properly, after a respectable amount of time dating. Give her a chance to know the *real* me, instead of the front I put on trying to impress her."

A sudden series of coughs racks his body, and he pulls a handkerchief out of his pocket to cough into it. When he's done, he continues, "Maybe if we'd spent a little more time getting to know each other, I wouldn't have taken her for granted. I would have realized she deserved better than me and wouldn't have put her through the hell that I did."

His admission jars me. It's the first time I've heard him speak of my aunt this way. I know he misses her, and I know he still loves her, but I didn't know he actually regrets the way he treated her.

"She's happy now. That's all that matters. All I'm saying is, if you think Ginny is a woman worth getting serious with —and make no mistake, I'm very fond of her and believe she would make you a better man—then take things slow. Navigate it together. You both deserve that."

A loud slurping sound has us both turning our heads to look at Michelle, who is watching us with wide eyes as she sucks the rest of her slushed coffee through the straw. "Don't mind me," she says.

My uncle and I let out a simultaneous chuckle. Nodding my head toward the interior of the building, I tell him, "Your words are noted. Thanks for the advice, old man."

"No problem. Oh, I was gonna text you later, but since you're here, I need you to go with me to California this weekend for the Schlemming merger."

Going to California means no time with Ginny at Désirer. But it isn't like I can tell *him* that. He'd be suspicious if I made a big deal about it.

Fuck.

"Yeah, okay," I sullenly agree.

He gives me a nod before turning to leave. "Thank you."

"Uh-huh." *God fucking dammit.*

Michelle makes no protests as I walk through the door to the back like I own the place. I have no idea where I'm headed, but there are balloons with signs that guide me, and after a few turns down random halls, the smell of cotton candy and hot dogs assails my senses. Descending the wide set steps into the basement-turned-gym of sorts, Ginny's shock of red hair stands out in the crowd, drawing my eyes to her immediately.

Her hair is pulled half-up out of her face, and her left cheek is adorned with a giant glittery butterfly. She's got a toddler on her hip, and her lips are pulled up in a smile that brightens the room as she attempts to hold the little girl's attention while someone paints the kid's cheek.

Something in my chest warms—at the same time, my hands grow clammy.

Being a father was never something I wanted to experience. It isn't that I don't like kids. I just don't want to raise them. I didn't grow up in the traditional sense—I'm not really sure what a father is.

But watching Ginny as she interacts with another group of small children who rush up to show her the prizes they've won from the games…

It paints a picture in my mind.

Broad strokes with bold colors.

A canvas filled with reds and oranges. Yellows and blues. Tiny footprints and even smaller hands. Lazy Sunday mornings wrapped in silk sheets until a toddler interrupts and demands pancakes while we all watch cartoons.

The mangy cat I've quickly become attached to curled up on Ginny's round, swollen belly.

Cornflower blues drift across the room as if in slow motion, and our gazes lock. Smiling at me, she signals for me to come to her.

Like a dog, I willingly obey.

"Hi! What are you doing here?" she asks brightly, reaching out to hug me.

Wrapping my arms around her, I lean down and kiss her unpainted cheek softly. "Finished work early and thought I'd come to see if you wanted to join me for dinner later."

Ginny laughs as she pulls me away from the face-painting station. "After the last time we saw each other, I didn't think you'd be that eager to see me again."

"Are you kidding? You left me with a raging hard-on in

the middle of my living room. I nearly chased after you and demanded you finish what you started." My fingers stroke her side through her thin black shirt. She's wearing tight black pants that look as though they've been painted on her body and knee-high black boots with heels that bring her eyes level with my mouth.

"*I* started?! *You're* the one who grabbed me and put me on the counter!" She looks around as she whisper-yells at me, a playful smile gracing her lips.

"And it was *you* who kissed *me* first." I pull her closer, bending my neck in hopes she'll let me kiss those luscious pink lips of hers.

Shrugging, she places a hand on my chest to stop me. "Can't argue with that, I guess. Not here, Jackson. This is my job."

"If I recall, you showed up at my job and promised me some afternoon delight just the other day." My fingers continue to stroke her side as I brush my thumb across her cheek with the other hand.

A rosy hue graces her entire face as her lips part slightly, eyes drifting to my mouth. Just when I think she's about to let me kiss her, something runs straight into me and wraps its tiny arms around my legs. Shocked, I look down to see a little boy staring up at me. He unwinds his arms and holds them out, silently asking to be picked up.

My first thought should be to look around for his mother or father. Instead, I find myself letting go of Ginny to lift him. "Well, who do we have here?"

Setting him on my hip, I look back at Ginny to see her trying to hold back a laugh. "This is Geoffrey. He doesn't speak much," she informs me.

"Ah, a man of few words. Some of the most powerful men I've ever met are that way, too," I speak to the boy, who continues to stare at me.

His hands pat my cheeks as he opens his mouth to make a

clucking noise with his tongue. My eyes find Ginny's as he continues. She's watching the interaction with something I can't quite interpret in her eyes. Geoffrey pulls on my cheeks, strong for such a little guy, and I bend my head in compliance as he rests his forehead on mine, his big brown orbs staring into my soul.

"Oh my gosh, I'm so sorry! Geoffrey, you can't just run away like that!" a female voice breaks the spell.

Suddenly, he's being pulled out of my arms, and I find myself agitated. "He's no trouble, ma'am."

"He loves Ginny. I've never seen him take to a stranger before, though. You must have some sort of kid superpower," the lady jokes before throwing a smile at Ginny and walking away without another word.

As I watch them go, Geoffrey observing me over his mother's shoulder, Ginny steps into me and palms my cheek, guiding my gaze down to her. "That was extremely hot," she says before pressing up on her tiptoes to lay a gentle kiss against my lips.

"Oh, do dad bods get you going, Red? Or is it the image of me with a kid?" I whisper into her ear as I scan the crowd of kids and parents. It seems as though the event is far from over, but I wonder if I can get away with whisking Ginny off to her office for a little action.

As if she knows exactly where my thoughts are heading, she smirks up at me. "Maybe if you're good, I'll go home with you."

"Can I chain you up so you can't leave again?"

I'm expecting a hard no. What I get is a coy little smirk and a shrug of her shoulder. "Sounds like it could be fun."

"*Fuck*, you're going to kill me."

Spiders' nests. Being stuck outside in a winter storm. The market crashing.

Thinking of anything that will chase away the erection that is straining against my pants, I hold her to me so that her body shields it from everyone else in the room. The last thing

I need is a headline saying something about getting hard at a children's event.

Ginny just giggles.

Hours later, we're sitting across from each other at one of the long tables set up for people to sit and eat at. Most of the families have gone home with their sleepy children, arms loaded with bags full of stuffed animal prizes and candy.

"So you thought of this whole thing on your own? What made you do that?" I'm ready to leave with her, but she wants to stay until everything is cleaned up. If I hadn't forced her to sit for a moment, she'd still be running around like we've done for the past few hours.

From operating games to helping pass out prizes, even going as far as to cut a kid's food up for him, I've been Ginny's obedient sidekick for the better part of the afternoon.

I've enjoyed her bossing me around—more than I thought I ever would enjoy taking orders from a woman. It gives me an idea for our weekend ahead at the club, but then I remember my uncle said he needs me in California this weekend.

"I don't know, really. It just kinda came to me. A lot of these families are low-income and could never afford to bring their kids to the fair. As far back as I can remember, my mom took me every year until she died."

Her eyes turn glossy as she goes somewhere in her mind, playing memories of happier times. There's a small part of me that's jealous. She at least had time with her mother.

But her mother didn't choose to leave her.

"I'm sorry for your loss," I murmur, reaching across the table to grab her hand.

"Sorry to interrupt—we just wanted to say thank you again for today, Ginny. It was really wonderful." Geoffrey's mother appears behind her. She's holding the little boy, who is holding an overflowing tray of nacho chips and cheese. There are two more kids behind her, shyly peeking from behind her legs.

"Of course! I'm so glad you guys had fun!" Ginny gushes, the sad moment forgotten.

Geoffrey's mom reaches out a hand toward me. "Thank you again, as well. For being kind to him when he grabbed you earlier."

"It was no problem at all, really." I extend a hand to shake hers, and as I do, Geoffrey tosses the nacho tray in the air to reach for me.

Chips and cheese go flying, landing directly on top of Ginny's head.

She flinches, then lets loose a long breath, trying not to react poorly.

No one says a word. All of us are stunned as the little boy continues to squirm in his mother's arms as he tries to get to me.

"Oh, my god. I'm so sorry." His mother finally jolts out of her stupor.

Shrugging, Ginny slowly reaches up to wipe a gob of cheese from her forehead before it drips into her lap. Her hair is covered in the yellow sticky substance, but instead of being upset, she smiles. "It's not a big deal. That's what they make showers for."

As the family scurries away, the mom's cheeks flaming, Ginny rests her chin in her hand and smirks at me. "Your place is closer than mine. Care if I clean up?"

My answering grin is positively feline. "Depends. Do I get to help?"

The space between us is charged with energy. A palpable electric current that wires us together as we keep sneaking glances at one another across the back seat of my car.

The elevator ride up to my penthouse is stuffy, and my skin prickles with awareness.

We want each other—even if she is covered in nacho cheese.

But neither of us wants to make the first move.

"You can use the bathroom in my bedroom," I tell her as I motion up the stairs. "Towels are in the cabinet. I'll lay out a clean shirt for you."

The thought of her in my clothing has my cock straining against my suit pants. Her demure smile as she slowly ascends the steps, drives my need ahead at full force.

She doesn't invite me to join her, so I wait until I hear the water running before heading upstairs to pull out a white dress shirt for her.

I could have picked a plain shirt. However, her wearing nothing but one of my button-ups will fuel a fantasy that I can put in my spank bank for when I'm alone in my bed.

I've gotten well-acquainted with my hand over these last three weeks.

While she's cleaning up, I go back downstairs and put together a charcuterie board. Ginny didn't eat the entire time I was at the clinic, and I have a feeling she probably didn't eat much before I arrived, either.

Once the fruit, meats, and cheeses are arranged haphazardly on the tray—because I don't give a shit what it looks like, just that she eats—I head back up to my bedroom.

The water is off, and I can hear soft humming coming from the bathroom. There's steam pouring through the cracked door, and I shamelessly take a peek from across the room. Creamy skin wrapped in a towel—wet red strands flowing over her shoulders—a blue glass bottle in her delicate fingers.

Wait.

Shit.

That's the cologne I use for the club, so she doesn't recognize my regular scent.

"Everything alright in there?" I call out.

She jumps, startled, and quickly places the bottle back in the medicine cabinet, where it is hidden behind a mirror. Which means she was snooping.

"Yeah," she replies. Pulling the door open, she freezes and looks down at herself, realizing she's only wearing a towel.

A jingling sound tears my eyes from her body to see my cat—I've renamed him P-Kitty—as he whacks one of his toys aggressively underneath the long dresser against the wall.

He flops on his side, batting at it, but it's too far for him to reach. Getting down on my knees, I hear her trying to stifle a giggle as I retrieve the toy and toss it down the stairs, watching as he goes bounding after it.

Without moving from the floor, I look at her over my shoulder. "What's so funny, Red?"

She shakes her head, smiling as she plays with the hem of her towel. "Just admiring the view."

Heat blazes in her eyes, igniting a spark low in my spine. Turning on my knees, I'm aware I may look funny as I walk slowly on them to her, but she doesn't laugh, watching me intensely. "Do you like looking down at me?"

When I reach her, I lift my hands to her waist and guide her to sit on the edge of my bed. The towel is short and rides up as I pull her knees apart so that I can kneel between them. "Do you wanna find out just how good the view can be? With you up there and me down here?"

Ginny swallows thickly, brazenly standing again to unwrap the towel from her body. I can only stare as her naked skin is exposed, my Adam's apple bobbing hard as she bares herself to me. My eyes travel down between the valley of her breasts, over the flesh of her stomach, and finally settle on her naked pussy that's almost at my eye level.

She's like a monarch butterfly in a chrysalis—just as it's

become transparent and you can see the colorful wings showing through. Gone is the caterpillar. Something even more beautiful in its place.

Her confidence.

"Fuck, you are beautiful," I murmur as my hands find her hips again. My eyes never leave her swollen center as I push her back to the bed. She widens her legs, causing a low moan to escape my throat as she leans back on her elbows and offers herself to me.

Her cheeks are like glowing cherries as I lick my lips. "I'll bet you taste just as good as you look."

"Why don't you have a taste and find out?" She's channeling Scarlett with every passing second. My instruction at the club is paying off.

"Don't be afraid to ask for what you want."

"Men appreciate confidence "

"Fuuuuuck," I moan, wasting no time to lift her legs over my shoulders. Leaning down, I swipe my tongue up her drenched slit, flicking her clit when I get to the top. Her hips lift to meet my face, wanting more, as her head presses back into the bed, and a gasp is wrenched from her chest.

"Fucking divine," I whisper against her.

Ginny's hands rake through my hair as my mouth encloses around her. Long, languid strokes as my tongue caresses her core, dipping the tip into her before moving back to flick against her clit. My fingers press into her inner thighs as I pull her wider, moaning against her slick center.

"Jackson," she whimpers, rotating between pulling me closer and pushing me away. But with every push, I fight against her and attack her lower body with more fervor. Her breathy moans grow with every stroke of my tongue as I eat her out with an unbridled passion.

Licking and sucking, grazing my teeth so gently that she cries out for more. "Harder," she begs.

"Fuck, Ginny, you're gonna make me come in my fucking pants if you keep talking like that." My cock is rock solid, weeping to be close to her. Ready to sink into her warm depths.

She looks down between her legs, gripping my hair roughly as she pushes my face back toward her pussy. Grinning against her, I attack her clit again, sucking harder, as she asked. Her feet press against my back, and I'm not even concerned about breathing as she holds me to her with impressive strength—her body beginning to shake with her impending orgasm.

"Jackson, I'm gonna come!" she whispers to my ceiling.

I've never been more turned on by a woman than I am right now. My mouth closes around her as I moan loudly, sending vibrations ricocheting through her center. Her limbs seize up, and her hands tighten painfully in my hair as her mouth opens in a silent scream while she climaxes. I watch her with raw want as her hips ride my face through it, and I gladly continue to work my mouth against her until it becomes too much, and she gently pushes me away.

Chuckling, I begin to climb up her body, mouth and chin glistening with her cum. Chest heaving for air, her foot darts out to catch my shoulder, and she pushes me back, sitting up as she does.

"What are you doing? I'm not done with you yet," I tell her, reaching to remove her foot.

Quickly, she stands, knocking me back to sit on my feet. Staring up at her with frenzied lust, I watch as she smirks, reaching for the clothes I laid out for her on the corner of my bed. "You look good on your knees, Jackson," she says breathlessly. "You should get on them more often."

My mouth drops open in surprise as she slips back into the bathroom, changing into her pants and my shirt before she walks back out, passing me without another word but throwing me a wink as she exits my bedroom.

"What the fuck just happened?" I ask myself out loud. Bewildered that she just fucked my face and left me, yet again, with another raging erection.

Speechless, I remain glued to my spot instead of chasing after her.

"Have a good night!" she yells from downstairs just before the elevator lets off a ding, signaling she's leaving.

I don't know whether to be pissed or proud.

Ginny

A ll I wanted to do last night after Jackson gave me the best orgasm of my life was crawl to the head of his bed, wrap myself in his silk sheets, and take a nap.

But the look on his face was oh-so worth leaving and going home instead.

Strangely, I'd been excited to tell my stranger about it—about how I took control and asked for what I wanted. Okay, well, I didn't necessarily ask, but I kinda did.

However, when I got to Désirer last night, I was told that he had to cancel our entire weekend—no note from him, no message. Just the booker telling me I was free to do as I wished.

I didn't like the way he said it—as though my stranger said it was okay to entertain someone else for the weekend. I didn't *want* anyone else. Really, I just wanted to talk to *him*. To confide in my teacher that our lessons are paying off.

When disappointment coursed through my veins, it was because I had no one to talk to about it. Not because I looked forward to another lesson, which I stowed away in my mind because it seemed important, but because I wanted to talk to him more than be touched by him.

Jackson's hands are the ones I want touching me—his

hands, his lips, and other parts of him that I yearn to discover. Where Jackson is concerned, I feel like I'm scaling a rock wall with no proper equipment to catch me when I fall.

And I *will* fall.

No matter how much I fantasize about a future with him, I know there is none.

But even though I know that, my mind has once again set me up for heartbreak. A heartbreak that I'm running toward at full speed.

Trailing a hand down the crisp white shirt Jackson let me borrow—the one I'm currently wearing with a pair of thigh-high wool socks as I lounge in my bed—a small smile pulls at my lips as I reminisce about yesterday.

That is, until I hear footsteps down the hall. Then my lips drop as I stare at my open door in horror.

Chris was supposed to have left early this morning. I thought that he just hadn't said goodbye and was glad for it. But his smarmy face appears before he pushes the door wider so that he can step into my bedroom.

"You didn't think I'd leave without saying goodbye, did you?" His eyes scan my shirt, and where I expect fury to burn through them, I find...pity?

He sighs. "Oh, Guinevere. You really are so delusional, aren't you?"

His hands are in the pockets of his navy dress pants, but he pulls one out to reveal his phone. Holding it in the air, he gives it a shake before pulling the other hand from his pocket to press the screen.

Suddenly, Jackson's voice fills my bedroom.

"I'm drowning in pussy. I have no interest in chasing after your sister. Simple women like her can't hold my interest, and I'm not into redheads."

Something tight grips my chest. My throat seizes, and I have to work very hard to ensure that my face does not fall in front of Chris. Swallowing the rock that's lodged in my throat, I shrug. "Is that supposed to mean something to me?"

"Don't pretend like his good looks and playboy charm haven't swept you away. I just wanted to remind you that you're *nothing* to him. Men like him don't fall for women like *you*. However, sick as you are, you are everything to *me*. You. Belong. To. *Me*. So don't go getting yourself into trouble while I'm gone. I have eyes on you, Gin."

Walking further into my room, he stalks slowly around the bed and sits on the edge near me. Reaching out, he gently pushes some of the hair that's escaped from the bun piled on top of my head out of my face, fingers ghosting my cheek down to my chin, where he grabs me roughly.

Jerking me toward him, he smashes his lips to mine. His other hand winds into the loose bun, threading his fingers through the strands and squeezing tightly, causing tears to spring to my eyes.

I don't struggle.

I don't kiss him back.

Not until his fingers ease and he's about to pull away. Only then do I part my lips slightly and suck his lower lip into my mouth, nibbling gently—just like he likes it.

There's no pleasure in it. I do it so he doesn't leave me crumpled in pain like he usually does when I resist.

His grip turns gentle, caressing my skin and massaging my scalp to soothe the sting. Even though tears fall from my eyes, I give him a small smile when he pulls back.

Resting his forehead on mine, he looks into my eyes and says earnestly, "If you're a good girl while I'm gone, when I return, I just might have to fuck you finally. I'm tired of punishing you, Ginny. I want to start a life with you. That means giving each other everything—body, soul, and mind. Your mind is already beautifully broken. And I've tasted and touched most of your body. But our souls have yet to fuse together. I think it's time we consummate this relationship and call it what it really is."

Bile rises in my throat, but I force it down as I continue to smile at him, tears still streaming down my face. There's no need to reply. He's not looking for a response. He pulls back and lays a gentle kiss on my forehead.

"I'll only be gone for a few months. Until then." He lays another chaste kiss on my lips and gets up from the bed, not bothering to look back as he walks out of my room, down the hall, and out the front door.

Releasing a shuddered breath, I let out a sob and stumble out of bed to run to my bathroom, throwing up the contents of my stomach until there's nothing left.

Vigorously, I brush my teeth before stripping down to get into the shower. As I scrub his touch from my skin, I recall Jackson's words.

When did Chris even talk to him? Jackson never mentioned seeing him. Did his words have any truth to them? It certainly seems like something he'd say—but that was before. It seems like something he'd say *before*.

Not now.

Right?

Six days.

It's been six days since I heard from Jackson.

Sure, leaving him on his knees wasn't exactly nice of me, but he's the type of guy who thrives on a challenge. Who likes a chase.

So why isn't he chasing me?

I'm torn between breaking down and sending him a text or simply trying to ignore it and hold out for one more day when I can see my stranger at the club.

I'm feeling needy and very alone right now, having not seen either of them in days—my stranger in almost two weeks.

I'd assumed Jackson would come calling at the clinic or the restaurant. But after a well-placed, discreet question to

Carmela, I found out that Jackson hasn't even been at Decadence when I'm not there.

He's MIA.

And I'm over it.

Where are you?

Gripping my phone tightly, I stare at the screen, awaiting a response. It's a Thursday afternoon. He should be at work, but getting past Nikki probably won't be as easy since Jackson isn't responding to me.

Hours pass. I'm ashamed to admit that I spend more time watching my phone and shooting off more unanswered texts than I do listening to my clients.

Jackson, answer me.

Why haven't I seen or heard from you in six days?

I'm acting fucking crazy. Certifiably loony. Like one of those girls I swore I'd never be. One of those girls I always pitied because I never thought men were worth getting this upset over.

Is it because I didn't let you fuck me? Is that it? Tired of the "playing hard to get" routine?

Finally…. I send the nail in the proverbial coffin.

Did you really mean what you said to Chris?

All of them go unanswered.

As the day winds down, entering into late afternoon, I tell Michelle I'm not feeling well and head out. It's a gloomy day, the clouds heavy with promises of rain. The air is cool as it kisses my skin. I forgot a jacket today, and even though my top is long-sleeved and my boots are thigh-high, my skirt is short, and none of the layers do anything to keep out the chill. Burrowing into the blanket scarf I *did* remember, I hurry down the streets toward Jackson's office.

Nikki be damned.

Try me today, bitch.

By the time I make it there, I'm cold and angry, and it must be apparent because Nikki doesn't even so much as say one snide word. She barely glances at me as I storm past her desk to the elevators. While I wait, I think I hear her on the phone with someone, warning them I'm on my way up, but it only fuels my anger as I assume it's Jackson she's talking to.

But it's Stacey who greets me when the elevator doors open at the top floor.

"Where is he?" I grit out.

"He's not here. He called out today," she says simply, eyes appraising me with worry.

My body deflates. It was pointless to come here. If he called in, he has his phone. Which means he's blatantly ignoring me. Which means he's probably over my shit.

"Figures. God, I'm so stupid," I mutter while shaking my head and turning to leave.

"Why are you stupid, Ginny?" Stacey asks softly.

Spinning back around, I throw a hand up and narrow my eyes at her. "Don't pretend like you don't know, Stacey. I haven't heard from him in days. He hasn't answered his phone at all, yet he called in? He's probably at home with some leggy blonde between his legs, doing what he does best —being a fuckboy."

A grin spreads on Stacey's face, making me even angrier. Even though Jackson's secretary has been nothing but kind to me, she's still under his employment, and I'm sure my little outburst will make its way to him.

"I don't have fucking time for this." I'm about to leave again when her hand on my arm stops me.

"Jackson hasn't been with anyone since he met you,

Ginny. I can promise you that." She shrugs. "He doesn't so much as touch a woman until she signs an NDA. And I'm the one that drafts them up for him."

He sure as hell has touched me, and I didn't sign shit.

Scoffing, I look at her incredulously. "Do you honestly expect me to believe that? That he isn't the type to just pick up a random girl in a bar and fuck her wherever he can? Don't treat me like I'm stupid."

The pretty blonde looks momentarily insulted before taking her hand off my arm. "Believe what you want. Jackson is careful about who he *fucks*. Yes, he sleeps with women often, but he's not the type to just pick a woman out and fuck her in a random public place."

"Why are you defending him?!" My voice borders on hysterical, drawing attention from the rest of the floor.

"Because as much of a man-whore as he is, you don't know him. And I'm a little offended that you think *I* would lie to you. I've known Jackson for a long time, and I'm telling you, you're the only woman he's been spending time with," she explains soothingly.

Searching her eyes for any hint of deceit, I relax a little as I realize she has no reason to lie to me. She must be telling the truth.

"Well, then, *where* the hell is he?"

Stacey looks at me solemnly. "It's the anniversary of his father's death. He and Scott normally spend the day visiting Simon's grave before drowning their sorrows in a bottle of bourbon. He's most likely at Scott's. Or with Tripp."

Shame and guilt sweep through my body.

I'm an awful person. Here I am, acting like a jealous girlfriend when I have absolutely no right to be behaving this way, and he's spending the day in pain.

Stacey watches as I flounder for something to say. In the end, I choose to stay silent because there's nothing that I *can* say. Her features turn to something that resembles skepticism.

"You know, Ginny, he likes you. I'm not sure if he's even

aware of it yet. But I've watched him do more for you these past few weeks than I've ever seen him do for anyone. So, maybe it's time you decide *what* exactly it is you want from him."

"What is that supposed to mean?" Suddenly, the urge to defend myself from whatever she's alluding to is strong.

Straightening up, she looks me dead in the eye. "It means that if this is just a game to you, to be able to say you brought Jackson Tailor to his knees before you leave him, I'm telling you to walk away now. As much as I have seen Jackson use women and never give them a second glance, I have never seen him look at one the way he looks at you. I'm beginning to think you have the ability to hurt him. And I refuse to let that happen."

I'm torn between flattery and anger. The fact that she thinks Jackson could feel anything for me is absurd. It's not who he is. And he's torn apart plenty of hearts, yet she's going to get mad if he gets his broken?

But the fact that she thinks I even have the power to do it. That I would even *want* to. That was never my intention when I made the thirty-day deal with him. I never expected him to go through with it—I didn't think he *could*.

It never crossed my mind that he would *actually* want to give up his playboy ways for a month. And never in my wildest dreams did I think *I* would mean anything to him other than a difficult conquest.

While I war with myself in my head, she smirks and half turns to leave. "I'll send you Scott's address."

The words leave my mouth before I can stop them. "I know where he lives."

She gives me a funny look before shrugging and heading back to her desk.

I'd never been to Scott's penthouse, but after his ex-wife came to the restaurant last year, I'd gone down the rabbit hole of their lives on Google. It's surprising how easy it is to find rich people's addresses.

As I leave the building, Stacey's words replay in my mind.

To be able to say you brought Jackson Tailor to his knees before you leave him.

She's delusional if she thinks I would do something like that.

I've had Jackson on his knees. If he wants to stay, I'll let him stay there forever.

I arrive at Jackson's with the intention of waiting for him to get home.

P-Kitty greets me as soon as the doors ping open, just like a dog greets its owner. He's sitting pretty and patiently waiting for head scratches, stretching his neck as if to show me the collar Jackson was finally able to put on him. It looks like a bow tie and is lined, *'so it doesn't rub against his skin and cause more hair loss.'*

"Hi there, pretty kitty. You got yourself a good daddy, don't you?" Picking him up after I set my bag on the counter and remove my boots, I snuggle my face against his patchy fur and sigh.

As I walk further into the penthouse, the dim sound of voices drifts down the hall, coming from the game room. Curious, I set the cat down and watch as he pads to the room, pushing his way through the crack in the door.

"Jackson?" I call out, but there's no answer.

Pushing the door wide when I reach it, I'm surprised to find a movie playing on the giant screen on the wall—a rom-com featuring the actors that play Fat Amy and Bumper from *Pitch Perfect.*

Stepping into the room quietly, I whisper, "Jackson?"

Peeking over the back of the couch, I find him curled up on his side, face toward the back cushion as he dozes. He's dressed in a pair of black sweats and a plain white shirt, smelling of smokey scotch and something that is utterly *him*.

That musky scent a man has that only belongs to him—not the gross body odor kind, but the kind that makes your toes curl and your lower body tighten with want. I reach over the cushion to brush the hair out of his eyes, mine straying to where his phone is lying further down the couch as it lights up.

P-Kitty jumps up on the couch, immediately going to curl against Jackson's neck, setting his head in the space between his chin and shoulder. Comforting the best way he knows how.

Jackson's phone lights up again, so I round the couch to see who it is. There's a missed call from Scott and two from Tripp. A text from Stacey asking how he's doing, and one from someone named Viki that says 'thinking of you today' with a crying face and a heart.

Who the fuck is this?

Beneath all of those are my crazy messages, and if there were a way to unlock his phone and delete them, I would. While at it, I'd delete hers too.

Okay, Gin. Now you're really starting to go crazy.

Jackson shifts, his hand reaching up to scratch the cat on the head as he carefully turns so as not to scare him. His eyes find mine as he pulls the cat into his chest and curls his other arm under his head. "What a nice surprise to wake up to. Am I dreaming? Or did I die? Because I'm pretty sure I went to bed alone, and here my angel is to save me."

He's slurring his words, obviously still drunk. Eyes heavy and half-lidded as he reaches out for me. "C'mere, angel."

Shaking my head, I sit at the far end of the couch and tuck my leg underneath me. "How are you?"

His hand drops, startling the cat, who jumps up and dashes off. "No! P-Kitty, come back! I'm sorry I didn't mean to scare you, buddy." His eyes sway to me with a scowl. "You're no angel. I forgot you have horns, not a halo."

I can't help the giggle that erupts from my throat. "Oh? I'm the devil now, am I?"

"You're a fucking little dream minx is what you are. Are you here to suck my dick? Because *real* Ginny would *never*." He rolls to his back and drapes his arm dramatically over his eyes.

"All I think about day and night is real Ginny taking my cock between those sweet, sweet lips of hers. But noooooo, she's a taker. Not a giver. And you know what, little dream minx?" He peeks at me from beneath his arm, words running together as his pitch switches from high to low.

"What's that?" I bite back a laugh as I ask. There's a slight ache between my thighs at his words, but the fact that he's drunk acts as a dam, holding the pleasure back.

"I'm okay with it." He shrugs, flopping his arm out to his side with a big sigh. "I've never been a giver. Always a taker. Now she's serving me my own shit on a platter, and I can't get enough."

"Do you plan on telling real Ginny this?" Playing with the frayed end of the scarf that's still wrapped around my neck, I smile to myself at his candor. Turns out Jackson is a funny drunk—a far cry from the serious, calculated man he's used to showing everyone else.

I wonder how many people have seen this side of him?

He giggles. *Giggles.* "Noooo."

"Why not?" I press, curious to hear his answer.

Jackknifing to a sitting position, he doesn't reply, climbing off the couch with all the grace of a toddler and swaying on his feet when he stands. Jumping to help him so he doesn't fall over, I lead him from the room and further down the hall, where there's a bathroom. There's no way in hell I'll be able to get him up the stairs, and I'm hoping a lukewarm shower and some coffee will sober him up.

"You smell nice, dream minx." He takes a whiff of my hair.

"Thank you." Because what else am I supposed to say?

It crosses my mind that in order for him to shower, I'm going to have to undress him. While I feel that he wouldn't mind in the least bit once he's no longer drunk, part of me doesn't feel right about doing so without his non-intoxicated consent.

That part of me wins out as I turn us and head back out to the living room, helping him to sit before moving to the kitchen to try and find things to make coffee. The sun is setting, casting a tangerine glow over the room. It's kind of magical, and I make a mental note to enjoy it with him another time.

After the coffee starts, I locate a medicine cabinet—luckily in the kitchen—and bring him a large glass of water and some ibuprofen. "Here. Take these and try to drink this whole glass, okay?"

Jackson does as he's told before his head lolls back against the cushion. "I'm tired."

"I'll bet you are. As soon as we get some coffee in you, you can go back to sleep." Who knows how long he's been drinking. I almost think to call Scott and ask if he was with Jackson at all today, but just like Jackson lost a father, Scott lost a brother. So, instead, I decide I'll message him later to ask how he's holding up.

"If you put coffee in me, does that mean I get to put me in you?" He smiles lazily at the ceiling, chuckling as I let out a very unladylike snort.

Once the coffee is brewed, and he's forced down a strong plain cup—fun fact: Jackson takes his coffee so sweet it might as well be liquid sugar—we end up back in the game room. He climbs back to the spot I found him in, patting the space in front of him and grinning up at me like he's on Cloud Nine.

"Watch a movie with me, dream minx."

No part of me wants to leave. And it takes no further convincing for me to unwind my scarf and toss it on a random cushion as I climb on and settle back into his chest.

The movie playing earlier is still on, with the beautiful Priyanka Chopra taking up the screen.

Jackson wraps an arm around my waist, pulling me back into him further so our bodies are flush. With as much as he obviously drank, I'm surprised to feel his erection pressing against my butt. Instinct makes me wanna push back against him, like I did with my stranger at the club. But again, he's drunk, so it's not appropriate.

Besides, his breathing evens out within a few minutes, the soft puffs of his breath against my hair lulling me to sleep as well.

When I wake, it's to Jackson's palm, warm against my skin, as his fingers draw lazy patterns against my bare thigh. Sometime during our nap, I must have rotated around. My arms are now wrapped around his waist, and our legs are entangled while I use his arm as a pillow.

"Hi there, Red." His voice is even. Sober.

Letting out a soft hum, I start to move away, but his hand grips my leg tighter. My hands find his chiseled chest as I lean back and look up at him. How he removed his shirt without waking me, I don't know.

"What time is it?" I ask.

Something vibrates, and my eyes stray to his phone on the back of the couch as he answers me. "Almost nine."

"Shit, we slept for three hours? Well, *you*, I understand. How are you feeling?" I slide a hand up to stroke his cheek but almost pull away as he chuckles.

"I'm fine. Woke up twenty minutes ago. Checked my phone while you were still sleeping. *Someone* went a bit overboard with the texts." He raises an eyebrow as a smirk pulls at his lips.

Hitting his chest playfully, I'm not even embarrassed

anymore as amusement drips from his gaze. "You ignored me for *days*. What did you expect?"

"You left me on the floor after coming on my tongue," he says huskily, his voice still laced with sleep.

Now I'm embarrassed. However, I also feel emboldened.

My teeth find my lower lip as I trail a finger down his stomach before I say, "Do you wanna have your turn now?"

He snatches my hand up so quickly it startles me. "Not tonight. Tonight, I just want to lie here with you, if that's okay."

Jackson's expression is serious. There's a heat between us, but instead of smoldering, it's tempered. Controlled.

Comfortable.

It's surprising. Almost unbelievable that he's turning down a blow job. Though, I can't help but feel a little relieved because I've never had a cock in my mouth and wouldn't know the first thing to do with it.

Adding that to my mental list of things to ask my stranger for, I wind my arms around his neck and pull myself up his body to lay a gentle kiss against his coffee-flavored lips. "Of course, that's okay. Whatever you need, Jackson. I'm here."

"Are you hungry? We could order takeout?" He shifts to get up, pulling me with him off the couch.

"Sure, that sounds great." Clearly, he isn't ready to talk about his father, and I don't want to push him.

"Menus are in the drawer next to the fridge if you want to find a place. I'll run upstairs and grab you some clothes that are more comfortable."

Laughing, I follow him out of the room and toward the kitchen. "Dear god, please don't run anywhere. I'm not equipped to lift you if you fall."

Settling on Thai, we place an order, and I change into a pair of his boxers and an Oxford University shirt.

"Why Oxford?" I ask as I walk back down the stairs.

He tenses for a moment before shrugging. "All the Tailor

men go to Oxford then finish at Harvard. I did it because it was expected of me."

Thinking about my stranger, I try to hold back a smile, but Jackson sees and gives me a funny look. "What?"

"Nothing," I answer, hopping onto a stool and propping my chin on my fist. "I just totally have a thing for English accents."

"Sorry, Red. I couldn't do an accent to save my life," he says before quickly changing the subject. "How was your time at NYU?"

We spent the rest of the time waiting for our food, talking about my days at NYU and how I always knew I wanted to go into my line of work because I've always wanted to help others.

I just don't tell him why.

Once we're finished eating, we clean up and go back to the game room to pick another movie. At this point, it goes unspoken that I'm going to stay the night. It doesn't go unnoticed how easy the night has been, but something still holds me back from completely opening up to him.

Later, when he's spooning me as I'm spooning P-Kitty, I summon the courage to ask, "Who is Viki?"

"Someone from my past. No one I want to have a future with," he answers immediately.

He kisses my neck softly, and I close my eyes, just relishing the closeness that we're sharing. How normal it all feels. Him, me, and the cat. I want this all the time, but when I try to open my mouth to tell him, the words don't come out.

It's frightening, the idea of being so honest and the possibility of him shooting me down. His words and actions tell me that maybe he wants it, too. But he's still *him*.

And I'm not sure he's capable. Or even wants to be.

As I drift off to sleep again, he nuzzles my neck and whispers in my ear, "I said what I did to your brother to ensure he left. I didn't mean a word of it. I promise."

"Shh," I tell him softly, though a smile now graces my lips. "Go to sleep, little dream minx."

"Teach me how to give a blow job."

Amber liquid spews from my stranger's lips, dripping from the inside of his mask as he coughs and beats his chest to clear his airway. "Come again?"

Tucking my legs underneath me, I sit up on my knees, eagerly looking at him. "I've never done it before. I don't want to be bad at it."

After I woke up this morning, wrapped in Jackson's arms, I tried once again to initiate oral sex. Again, he turned me down. Kissing my forehead, he told me I could shower in his bathroom while he used the one in the hall.

Jackson—the man who makes sexual innuendos every chance he can.

The man who oozes sex and can probably make a woman come just by looking at them.

Has now turned me down *twice*.

It left me wondering if he could tell I'd never done it before. Fearing that the reason he keeps saying no, is that he doesn't want an inexperienced woman testing out her lack of skills on his prized joystick.

We'd showered separately. Then, he dropped me off at my apartment before going to work. His eyes were glued to his phone the entire ride, making me feel like the night before had been a dream.

He was affectionate but not overly so. Attentive, but not suggestive.

Very unlike himself.

"I don't think you could be bad at it if you tried, Little Ember." My stranger laughs. His crisp accent is throaty from the coughing but doesn't hide the amusement dripping from his cadence.

"But I need to learn how to do it," I pout, squeezing my arms together to push my boobs higher.

I discarded my wings as soon as I stepped foot in our room. My outfit tonight consists of a tight black leather bodice with an attached lace bra and skirt. Black bows sit on the garter straps attached to thigh-high stockings. It's more cute, instead of sexy—at least I think so.

So, I try to look more appealing as I beg my stranger to let me suck his cock while he instructs me on how he likes it.

It isn't lost on me how off it is that I'm asking another man to teach me something to please Jackson. But it's been four weeks now, and besides the one time he came while I rode him reverse cowgirl through his pants, all the pleasure has been mine.

Jackson said I'm a taker. I want to give as good as I get.

"Then ask your boyfriend." He holds his tumbler up to his temple as though trying to soothe a headache.

"He's not my boyfriend." The words are out of my mouth before I can stop them.

He's *not*. We haven't discussed being exclusive, though I believed Stacey when she told me he hasn't been with anyone else. Still, that doesn't make him *mine*.

My stranger sighs and presses his glass harder into his skin. His body seems tense yet tired. Depleted of energy and clearly not in the mood for any type of lesson tonight.

"Where were you last weekend?" I ask, changing the subject.

"I had business to attend to out of town."

"Did you mean what you had the booker tell me?" Suddenly, I'm self-conscious and want to cover myself with my robe, even though he's seen me more naked than I am now. Wrapping my arms around my middle, I lean my weight back until I'm off my knees and settled against my side of the loveseat.

"What do you mean?" He sounds tired, too. Tone dancing on the edge of annoyance.

My voice is small when I answer. "You told the booker to tell me I was free to do as I wished."

"You are free to do as you wish."

"I thought we were exclusive." My voice is flat, and I tear my eyes away from his overly large mask to stare at my stocking-clad feet.

"And if you wish otherwise, I will acquiesce to any request you make of me. You've come a long way this past month, Little Ember. It's been a pleasure watching you come into your own...but I've always known I'd have to let you go one day."

"You keep saying you'll give me whatever I want, yet you keep turning me down." Why are both of my men being so stubborn?

My men.

Yes, I think of both of them as belonging to me.

And neither wants to fulfill my wishes.

"Men like him don't fall for women like you." Chris' words echo so loudly in my mind that I can almost swear they bounce off the walls of the room.

Maybe I'm just not good enough. Maybe both my stranger and Jackson have grown to see me for what I really am. What Chris has always called me.

Rot.

A disease.

"I think we're having an off night. I'm not feeling well, if I'm being honest. I think it best to call it a night," he says quietly.

Before he can say anything else, I'm off the loveseat and through the door, grabbing my robe and wrapping it around my body as I storm down the hall, not bothering to wait for my guard. Tears flow freely down my cheeks, and when I get back to the changing room, black mascara smears the delicate skin under my eyes.

A pretty woman with green eyes and dark hair pauses in my mirror. "Are you okay? Do you want me to grab someone for you?"

Shaking my head, I wipe the tears from my face and begin to undo the garter straps. "I'm fine. Thank you, though."

"No problem. This line of work isn't easy. Just know you always have a choice to stop whenever you want to," she informs me kindly before walking away, her gold wings glittering as she leaves.

Staring at my reflection, I remind myself that she's right. It's all *my* choice. In here with my stranger, and out there with Jackson.

As freeing and comforting as that is supposed to be, though, they both continue to take the choice from me by telling me no. And the events from the entire last week have all but bled the confidence from my soul.

Leaving me feeling like I'm back at square one.

Jackson

"**M**y god, woman. How much clothing do you own?"

We're on our fifth trip down to the moving truck I hired to bring Ginny's things to her new apartment. All the boxes were from her closet, and I thought *I* had a lot of clothing. I'd have to build an entirely new closet if she lived with me.

I don't hate the idea of that—her moving in. We haven't even slept together yet, but after waking up with her on Friday morning, it made me feel...*scared*. It was so domestic, and I've never been the domestic type.

It honestly sort of spooks me how many times this week I've thought of a future with her. At this point, I've filled an entire album of portraits I've drawn in my mind of how a life together could be. Thinking of how much I wanted it to be like that every morning, I shut down, trying to process every-thing while I got ready for work with her just a few steps away.

But I fear my aloofness yesterday morning may be a problem *now*.

Ginny's been relatively quiet all morning as we moved her things from the SoHo apartment to The Bryant.

She's past pouting and is full-on acting like a puppy who got kicked. Stepping out of every embrace I try to give her and turning away from every kiss I attempt.

So between turning her down Thursday night, my actions Friday, and then with what happened at the club last night, I'm sure she's feeling unwanted.

There are reasons I turned her down Thursday night as myself and Friday night as her stranger. Thursday, I'd been caught up in my own shit and afraid that if we went there, I'd hurt her. I wasn't in the right frame of mind to do anything other than hold her to my body and breathe in her lemon sugar scent.

Yesterday, my head was pounding, and I couldn't call into work a second day in a row. Even if I was the boss. The migraine lasted all day and well into the night. At the club, Ginny's eagerness to please me grated on my frayed nerves for the mere fact that she was asking to suck another man's cock. Even if it was to learn for *my* pleasure.

It's quickly becoming more complicated to keep that line between the club and reality crystal clear. According to Ginny, I said some interesting things to her when she found me drunk out of my mind. It's a goddamned miracle I didn't say anything about Désirer.

I want to tell her the truth, but I'm not ready to lose her.

If there were any possibility in my mind that she would forgive me for tricking her, I'd consider coming clean. However, I still think she's too fragile to handle the truth.

Before, when this all started, it was thrilling. *Exciting.*

Now, it makes me sick.

Yet I continue.

Because I fear that if I were to walk away as her stranger, she'd break. And she doesn't trust *me* enough to pick up the pieces.

"Should we take a break and go grab a waffle?" I suggest as she all but tosses a box labeled *clothes* on the floor. She doesn't answer, and I try not to wince as the box hits the real oak floors with a resounding thud.

Grabbing her by the wrist as she storms past me, I ask gently. "Ginny, what is going on with you today?"

She yanks her hand out of my grasp, but I catch her around the waist, walking her backward until her back hits the wall. "Hey. I thought you'd be happy to move in here, but all morning you've been acting as if you don't have a choice. Would you rather not stay here?"

"Doesn't matter, does it? Anytime anyone says I have a choice, I never really do," she bites out quietly, refusing to look up at me.

It's clear she's upset that I keep turning her down on her offer for oral sex. The urge to push her to her knees and force her pretty mouth to take my cock is so strong I have to take a moment to steel myself before I speak. "Tell me what's bothering you."

Glaring up at me, she sneers, "You know what's bothering me, Jackson. If I were any other girl, you'd have let me do it, so what's the problem? Don't think I'm good enough?"

"If you were any other girl, I wouldn't have laid you out on my bed and eaten your pussy like it was my last goddamned meal, Ginny. Besides, is that what you want? To be like *every other girl*?" I bite back.

Her cheeks glow at my statement, and some of the fight drains from her eyes.

"If that's what you want, *actually* want, I'll take you to the bedroom right now and fuck you till you can't stand. But I'd rather wait, because in less than a week, the thirty days will be up. I'll have passed your little ultimatum, and you can sleep better at night knowing that I worked my ass off to earn my place by your side in that bed."

"And then what, Jackson? Once I let you fuck me, you walk? Go back to your old ways of bedding a new girl every night?" she spits angrily.

She's being a fucking brat, and it's pissing me off.

Grabbing her chin, I force her to look up at me while my other hand digs into her hip. "Is that why you're begging to get on your knees, Ginny? Because you think I'm going to walk away? You don't have to prove anything to me. When will you realize I'm here because I want to be? I get that I have a reputation, but you'll have to get over it if we're going to be a thing."

"A thing?" The corner of her lips pulls up even though the anger is still evident on her features.

"Isn't that what you want? Exclusivity?"

Something I've never offered another woman. Something I wouldn't even offer the only *serious* girlfriend I've ever had.

Something I'm willing to offer to Ginny because she deserves it.

My thumb moves from her chin to her lips, stroking them softly before I lean down to kiss her gently. When I pull back, tears are lining her eyes. Frowning, I ask, "What is it?"

Her hands reach up to fist my shirt as the tears fall down her cheeks. She hangs her head as she speaks, not able to look me in the eyes when she says, "I don't think you're capable of being exclusive, Jackson. It just isn't who you are."

Ouch.

Well deserved. But it stings nonetheless.

Yes, I know I haven't been the picture-perfect image of a man who can be trusted with a woman's heart. But I've been *trying* to be better for *her*. They say people don't change that quickly, but I have. So why can't she see that?

Letting her go, I step back. Her hands grip my shirt tighter, and I lift mine to remove them. "Robert will help you with the rest of your stuff. Feel free to use his services for the rest of the day."

Sticking my hands in the pockets of my dark gray sports jacket, I turn to leave. Ginny darts in front of me, silent tears still falling as her eyes grow wide. Placing her hands on my chest again to stop me, she cries. "Jackson, wait, I'm sorry—"

"It's fine," I interrupt her, reaching up to rub the two-day-old scruff on my cheeks. "You don't have anything to apologize about, Red."

She shouldn't feel the need to apologize for feeling the way she does. If the roles were reversed, I'm not sure I'd trust me either.

We stand there, her searching my eyes for something I'm not sure exists yet, while I search hers for any trace of trust. All I find, however, is a powder blue wall a mile high. And right now, I don't feel like trying to break it down.

Stepping back, her hands fall away as I head toward the door.

"Jackson!" she cries out behind me. But I don't stop.

Just because she feels that way doesn't mean it doesn't hurt to hear. Never in my lifetime did I think I'd find a woman worth changing for. It's new territory for me, and apparently, I suck at it. It will take time, but I just have to continue proving to her that she's more than just a fling.

As much as her confidence is growing, I have a feeling that the past week has knocked her progress backward. And if I'm going to take her to my bed next week and make her mine in every sense of the word, she needs to be prepared for it.

Which means her stranger is going to have to put in some work tonight.

Arriving at Désirer early, I speak with the booker and arrange for a package to be delivered to Ginny in her changing room. A forest green lace teddy from La Perla with an underwire to push her tits up to her ears and no crotch for easy access.

I've seen her completely naked, but there's something about watching her while she's still clothed that does it for me. A good lingerie set can make all the difference if you're into that sort of thing.

Tonight, I am.

After wrestling an all-expenses-paid trip to Florence for her and Kaia out of me, Stacey spent the afternoon discreetly retrieving the items I asked for, which not only included the lingerie, but also the array of toys I've laid out on one of the tables.

Sex toys aren't something I'm familiar with. I've never used them—never needed them. I've always thought that if I can't get a woman off with my cock, then there's something wrong with me. A woman shouldn't need anything other than a man's experience, and if she *needs* a toy, then she needs a better-trained man.

Sex is something I'm good at, not something I need help with.

Fucking Ginny isn't something I'm able to do as her stranger, though. I plan on having her become thoroughly acquainted with my cock, and can't risk her recognizing it. Not all cocks are created equal, and mine is as superior as my pedigree.

And I do plan on fucking her when our thirty days are up. But if she hasn't had sex since she was seventeen, I'm going to have to prep her. So, tonight she'll get fucked by me—it will just be with one of these damn toys.

But I digress.

Stacey did not disappoint in her selection. There are at least three realistic-looking penises, curved, and oval-shaped toys—some with tongue-looking things on one side. And penis-shaped dildos with "rabbit ears" to stimulate the clit as well as internally.

Ginny gets to pick her poison tonight. At least what we'll start off with.

I'm well aware that the club provides toys in the rooms, but I'm not leaving my health in the hands of whoever is in charge of cleaning them. I really should ask Carmela what the protocol is for that.

The sound of the door opening pulls my attention. Ginny

steps through, wearing her gift but not her wings, and even through the mask, I can tell she looks guarded.

"Good evening, Little Ember. I see you got my gift."

"I did, thank you. It's beautiful. What are those?" she asks curiously as I step aside to let her view the other presents.

"I think it's time we see just how much your pretty cunt can take, don't you?" My arms settle on either side of her as I grip the table, caging her in. She doesn't seem to notice, instead reaching out to inspect her toys.

"You got all this for me?" she whispers.

"For *us*, yes." I long to sink my teeth into the flesh of her neck. But since the large mask I wear is in the way, I reach for her hips instead, digging my fingers into the lace that covers her skin. "Which one would you like to start with?"

Sliding my hand up her side, I glide it back down over the curve of her ass and continue moving until my middle finger is sliding through the opening in the lingerie to tease her entrance.

A gasp flies from her mouth, her head falling back on my shoulder while I continue to slide my finger along her already slick lips, moving higher toward that tight bundle of nerves with every pass. Her hands fly out to brace on the edge of the table as she lets out a long moan.

"More," she whispers just as the tip of my finger teases her clit.

"Choose a toy," I respond before pulling away entirely and going to stand at the edge of the bed.

It doesn't take her long to choose one of the "Rabbits" and crawl on the bed with it in hand. "Are you going to watch me?"

Chuckling, I hold a hand out for her to give the toy to me. "No, you're going to watch *me*."

Her confusion shifts to clarity as a shiver of excitement rolls through her body, making her look as happy as a kid on Christmas morning. "What do you want me to do?"

"Lie back and spread your legs," I command.

Ginny does as she's told. Grabbing a pillow to prop under her head, she lies back and unabashedly spreads her legs, revealing her glistening pussy. Instantly, my cock is hard, and I readjust myself before crawling on the bed between her legs.

There's no need for lubricant, so I swipe my fingers up her center, relishing the way her back arches off the bed as I spread her arousal over the head of the toy before turning it on. The little ears start to shake, the purple silicone lighting up from within as the head starts turning in circles.

Her eyes widen as she watches it. Her knees begin to close, so I quickly settle between them so they can't. Gripping the edges of the pillow under her head, her big blue orbs glow with unrestrained lust.

"I'm going to go slow, so just relax," I instruct.

She draws her bottom lip between her teeth as she watches me lower the head to her pussy, rubbing it up and down between her lips before pushing in slightly. Sucking a breath in, her back arches off the bed, her legs squeezing my sides as she tries to draw them together.

"Relax, Little Ember," I repeat.

I reach up to rub her clit slowly and begin to stroke her insides with the dildo. My eyes bounce back and forth between watching the toy enter her slowly, little by little, and her face as she twists her head to bite her knuckles.

She's fucking glorious.

"How does it feel?"

"So good," she moans. "So fucking good. Don't stop."

Once her walls are stretched around the toy—which is much smaller than my cock—I angle it so that the ears of the Rabbit can flick against her clit.

"Oh my god! Fuck!" She squirms, hips thrusting off the bed.

"Can you take more?" My voice is hoarse, my accent slipping, but she doesn't seem to notice. Too lost in her euphoric haze to hear.

"More? How much more can there possibly be?" she cries out.

Oh, baby. You have no idea.

"Tell me if it's too much." I click the button that causes the part inside her to move more quickly and withdraw the toy slightly, pulling the ears away from her.

"No, bring it back," she whines. Her eyes are screwed tight as she writhes on the bed, angling her body in different positions to try to get the stimulation back.

"Patience," I chuckle as I slowly push it back into her. I'm watching for any sign of blood, any sign that tells me it's hurting her, but all I get is resistance as her tight walls try to accommodate the size of the toy.

Edging has always been something I enjoyed. It prolongs the pleasure, making the orgasm more intense when you finally reach it.

Every time Ginny looks as though she's about to come, I slowly pull the toy back. Her frustrated cries spur me on as I drive her toward a pleasure that will leave her boneless. "Please let me come!" she begs.

Reaching up, I pinch her nipple before slapping her breast. "You'll come when I say you can."

I keep alternating the toy between speeds, sometimes turning the clit stimulator off entirely. Her brows pull together as her lips turn down in a frown. "No, I don't like that."

"Trust me, you'll love it." I pull the toy out completely and slap her clit lightly. If I had her in my bed, I'd devour her in between sessions with the Rabbit before making her taste herself on my tongue as I drove it back into her.

Her hips lift to meet every thrust of the toy as she grips my forearms, attempting to keep me from pulling it back. "I don't like it. I want to come!"

"Not yet."

"Stop!" she shouts so sharply it startles me. Getting off the bed, I remove the Rabbit and step back, turning it off as she scrambles across the bed.

When she looks over at me, tears shine in her eyes, causing my chest to tighten. "Why are you about to cry again, Scarlett? I feel like I'm always making you cry."

"I know. I'm sorry-" she sniffs.

"Don't apologize. I'm not angry. I'm concerned."

"It isn't you…it's *him*." Her tears start to fall as a sob escapes her throat.

Him? Surely she doesn't mean *me*?

"Him who, Scarlett?" I toss the toy on the loveseat behind me and move around the bed to go to her.

Pulling her knees up and wrapping her arms around her legs, she buries her face against them. "My foster brother," she sobs, "he did this when we were kids—touched me and never let me finish."

The hair on the back of my neck stands up as all the sound is sucked from the room. She's sobbing, but I can't hear it— only the rush of my blood as it comes to a raging boil throughout my veins. Expelling air through my nose, I start to count slowly, until the sounds of her cries creep along the edge of my hearing.

That fucking bastard. I'm going to kill him.

"You must think I'm disgusting," she says through her tears.

Rushing toward her, I scoop her into my arms and sit her on my lap as I sit on the loveseat. She buries her face in my neck as I stroke her hair. "I could never think you were disgusting. *He's* the disgusting one."

We sit there for so long that I lose track of time while I come up with all the ways I can kill Chris. Ginny's sobs eventually subside as I continue to stroke her hair and her back, attempting to soothe her with words of comfort.

"May I ask when it started?" I ask when she's finally calm.

It takes her a long time to answer. "When I was twelve— he was sixteen. It's why…it's why I call you my stranger. I used to imagine it was someone else, someone that looked like *you*. My stranger even sounded like you. I used to imagine visiting him so I could be far away from home. It was a way to deal with what was happening."

Removing my hands from her body, I flex my fingers to relax my muscles so I don't hurt her. Struggling to stay in character and not give away that I know her brother, my voice is deep—accent thick—as I ask, "Are you still in touch with this man? Your foster brother?"

"I've lived with him all my life."

I knew he was cuckoo, but I never would have guessed it was *this* bad. I replay every interaction I've had with her. "He's the one who hurt you. He's the one you're afraid of."

She was just a kid.

It feels like there's a hammer in my chest as I tighten my arms around her. The signs were there—I should have known. The second he said they were together at the Tisch event, I should have forced her to leave with me and kept her far away from him.

"I'm safe now. It just brought up bad memories. That's all." She tries to play it off. The hammer bangs against my heart, cracking the steel around it.

She says she's safe, but it has to be because he's gone *now*.

With how he acts, there's no way it isn't still happening. But I can't press her for those details, because they aren't things her stranger would know.

"God, I really suck at this, don't I?" She lets out a harsh laugh against my chest before pushing off me to wipe at her eyes.

"You went through something terribly traumatic. It's okay not to like something sexually because it's triggering." I let her go, even though I want to keep her close to me.

"I shouldn't have admitted all that. I'm sorry." Ginny gets up to rush across the room, putting distance between us.

"Please stop apologiz–"

"I'll see you next week, that is, if you still want," she cuts me off, hand on the door, ready to leave.

She's not looking at me, so I simply say, "Yes. Of course."

Then she's gone.

Running my hands through my hair, I remove my mask and fling it to the other end of the loveseat. My foot starts to tap as my forefinger and thumb stroke my chin, contemplating whether I should arrange for something to happen to Chris while he's gone, or draw it out when he gets back.

Tap. Tap. Tap.

How can I treat her the same now? She's so fragile. And I tear women apart.

Tap, tap, tap. Tap, tap, tap.

No. It doesn't matter. I won't hurt *her*. I've been helping her in here. She's taking control of herself when he's had control for so long. Gripping my hair, I lean forward to rest my elbows on my knees.

The thought of his hands on her, the thought of him *fucking* her.

Tap, tap, tap, tap, tap, tap....

When my foot starts to bounce uncontrollably, I shoot up to grip the edge of the loveseat, adrenaline pumping through my veins as I flip it angrily. My mask and the pillows go flying as it crashes into the wall. Then, moving to the table where everything is still laid out, I swipe everything from it before throwing it across the room.

The resulting crash as the wood splinters is joined by my outraged cry. "FUCK!"

Ginny

"Miss Scarlett, is everything okay?" my guard asks as I race from the room, forgetting my robe in my hurry to get as far away from my stranger as possible.

I *know* it wasn't Chris touching me. I tried so hard to keep my eyes open and focused on my stranger. But *anyone* could be behind that mask.

Jackson even appeared when I closed my eyes and tried to focus on anything other than the feeling of coming so close to release and having it taken away. And it was enjoyable for a little while…until it wasn't.

It was too much like all those nights with Chris.

Thankfully, the Grand Room is nearly empty as I rush through it and into the changing suite. Sympathetic looks are cast my way as I tear the mask from my face, but I ignore them. Locking myself in one of the bathrooms, I sink to the floor and pull my knees up to my chest, resting my forehead against them, sobbing as quietly as I can.

I begged my stranger to let me come, but he wouldn't— just like Chris.

My stranger isn't a bad person, but in that room—on that bed—there was no difference between them.

Then, to admit *why* I was having a meltdown? The words had flown from my lips because I'm so tired of holding it back, of not being strong enough to admit I've been letting it happen for years.

Letting it happen.

I'm an adult, and I *let* Chris do this to me. Let him turn me into a shaking leaf when I could be a great tree that shelters others from storms created by men like him.

Lying down, the tile of the floor is cool against my cheek. There are whispers from some of the women just outside the door, and I hear one of them tell another to get Lenni.

She may be my best friend, but she's not who I want right now.

Sitting up, I wipe the tears from my face and unlock the door. No one asks me what's wrong, but I can feel the curious stares. Getting dressed quickly, I grab my bag and rush out, having one of the bouncers at the employee entrance hail me a cab.

As soon as I'm on my way home, I pull out my phone and send a message to Jackson, even though it's just past midnight.

> I don't want to be alone tonight. First night in a new place and all…

It isn't until I'm walking into The Bryant that he answers me.

> Be there soon.

Warmth floods my chest knowing that regardless of how we left things this afternoon, he's still dropping whatever he's doing to come to my side.

Part of me wonders what it is he *was* doing, though. Why is he up this late?

All my clothes are still in boxes, so I don't bother changing out of my leggings and oversized NYU sweatshirt while I brush my teeth and wash my face. When there's a knock at my door, I race from my bedroom to answer it.

Jackson is there, wearing dark gray joggers and a plain black shirt, with his hair ruffled as though he crawled out of bed to come. We're both silent, just staring at each other for a few seconds before tears line my eyes, and I launch myself into his arms.

"I'm sorry," I cry.

"Me too." He doesn't ask me what's wrong as I grip his shirt like I did earlier when I didn't want him to leave, soaking it through with my tears. He bends and scoops me into his arms, kicking the door shut before bringing me to the bedroom and laying me down on the Egyptian cotton sheets.

As soon as he gets in the bed with me, I wrap my hands in his hair and attack his lips, needing to feel something other than the misery that's taken up the last two hours of my night.

Jackson molds his mouth to mine, slowly caressing my tongue with his as we lay on our sides, his body cradling mine—protecting me like a sanctuary I've gone to for refuge.

When we pull back for air, it's *then* that he asks, "Is everything okay?"

"No," I answer immediately. "I'm a mess. I'm confused and unsure of absolutely everything in my life right now. It's like I'm the only one on a train and can see that the tracks have been removed up ahead, but there's no way to stop. And a voice keeps telling me to jump, but I'm scared. I'm fucking terrified even though the voice is saying it's okay. That everything will be fine if I just jump. But I *can't*."

A fresh batch of tears fall, and I wipe them away angrily, frustrated that I've been crying so much today. Jackson pulls me to him, and rolls onto his back so that I'm lying on top of him. "You can, Red. You can jump when you're *ready*. I'll be right there to catch you when you do, I promise."

Hugging him like a koala, I bury my face in his neck. His

spicy sandalwood scent smells different, a sharp freshness buried underneath where there's normally sweet vanilla. It makes the space between my legs clench as I nuzzle further into him, inhaling deeply.

My legs squeeze around his waist as I press my center directly over his growing length, eliciting a groan from his lips. "What are you doing, Red?"

Dragging my lips over his skin, I kiss my way up his chest. "Just give me this, Jackson. I *need* this tonight."

His hands cup my ass as I roll my hips. "Ginny…."

My lips find his, and I kiss him passionately as I continue rocking into him through our clothes—working into a frenzy so that, hopefully, he gets lost in the pleasure before he can turn me down.

He breaks our kiss and grins up at me. "What are we in high school?"

Jerking my hips, I relish the way his eyes glaze over as his mouth falls open. "You seem to like it just fine. It's called compromise, Jackson. Since we have four more days till the month is up."

A tingling sensation starts to bloom in my spine as he thrusts upward. The ridge of his head pressing against my clit, and even though it's through our clothes, I swear it feels just as good.

"Three," he rasps. He's helping me ride him, fingers clenched into the sides of my upper thighs. "It's technically Sunday morning. So, there's three days left. And we can spend every one of them compromising if you want."

Leaning deeper over him, I get the friction I need and feel my orgasm drawing closer. "Jackson, I'm gonna come."

"Let go, baby. *Jump*. I got you," he whispers into my hair as I bury my face against his neck once more, crying out as my release tears through me.

A tidal wave of emotion crashes against my skin, and Jackson holds me through it, letting out a quiet, "Fuck," as he comes, too.

Breathing heavily, neither of us makes a move to get up. He smooths my hair away from my face and kisses the top of my head as I lay my cheek on his chest. "Do you want me to stay?"

Nodding, I squeeze my arms around him tighter. "Yes, please."

No other words are spoken. Nothing else needs to be said. We fall asleep to the sound of each other's breathing, and I feel safe.

I feel *safe*.

"I didn't know you could cook. I assumed Claudia did all that for you." Picking up a wrapped wheel of Spanish Manchego, I wince at the price and gingerly put it back, giving it a few pats on the top.

Good for you, cheese, knowing your worth.

Jackson laughs as he places a block of parmesan in our cart—the last of the ingredients we need for dinner. "I watched my grandma cook when I was home from boarding school. I picked up on a *few* things."

"Well, I'm excited. Who doesn't love pasta? And to have Jackson Tailor cooking me dinner, excuse me while I swoon." Laughing, I place the back of my hand against my forehead and pretend to fall over into the cart.

"I can't tell if you're making fun of me or being serious, but I *did* offer to take you out for dinner. You're the one who said you wanted to stay in but were sick of takeout." He picks up a jar of spicy fig jam while he waits for me to right myself, then starts to push the cart toward the checkout.

"Jackson!" Both our heads turn in the direction of a rich, sultry feminine voice.

Instantly, my hackles rise as a leggy blonde weaves her way through the stands until she reaches us and throws her arms around his neck. He looks taken aback, and his eyes dart to mine as he half-returns her hug awkwardly.

The blood in my veins heats, and it's not from pleasure.

"How are you?! It's been so long. I just moved back. We simply must do dinner," she gushes as she lets go of him and steps back.

Not nearly enough.

There's an edge to her voice, an accent of some sort. Russian maybe. Her perfectly curled hair bounces around her shoulders as her sparkly, ice-blue eyes stare up at him adoringly. She completely ignores me, but Jackson takes a step back so that he's closer to my side. Only then do her eyes focus on me, sharp as an icicle.

"Viktoriya," Jackson greets as though he'd rather be talking to anyone but her.

Her icy blues bounce between us as her smile goes from saccharine to sour. "Who do we have here? Training a new housekeeper?"

"Excuse me?" My words sound incredulous as they leave my lips, but before I can say anything else, Jackson cuts in.

"No, this is Ginny. She's my…friend."

There's a sharp sensation that zips through my chest. It hurts, and it takes everything in me not to turn my eyes to his. He could have made it clear I wasn't a staff member in training, and he could have said friend without the pause. He could have said girlfriend, but then again, how can I expect that?

"Oh. Oh, I see. Well then, I'll let you get back to it." Viktoriya's smile is triumphant as she goes back to ignoring me, reaching out to lay a hand on Jackson's arm. "You have my number, darling. Call me so we can set something up for dinner. Will I be seeing you at the Kennedy's party?"

"Yeah, I'll be there." Is all he says, neither agreeing nor disagreeing to the dinner she keeps trying to push.

"Well, hopefully, I'll see you before then," she lilts suggestively. Her eyes drift to mine once more before adding, "If not, I'll see you there."

She turns and leaves, without so much as a *goodbye* or a *nice to meet you*, hips swaying in jeans that look painted on her modelesque figure, while her Louboutins click loudly on the hard floor in her retreat.

Jackson expels a long breath before he begins to push the cart once more. Our earlier playfulness is forgotten as my mood turns bratty. "Who was that?"

"No one."

"Jackson, I'm serious." Folding my arms over my chest, I stop in front of the cart and stand my ground.

His eyes burn into mine. Clearly, this is a conversation he doesn't want to have, but he eventually sighs. "I'll tell you in the car on the way home."

Home.

Earlier, I would have been elated to hear him say that instead of *my place*. Right now, though, I'm irritated and can't get past what just happened.

When we get into the car, he raises the partition that separates the front of the vehicle from the back. Rubbing at his eyes, he lazily drapes his arm over the back of the seat behind me. "She's my ex-girlfriend."

Girlfriend?

"I thought you didn't date," I reply lamely. There's never been any talk of him ever having a girlfriend that I know of.

"I don't. She's the closest thing I've ever come to a real relationship." His knee starts to bounce as he loosens the tie around his neck.

"What happened?" My voice is small as I ask. His eyes dart to the side as he notices me lean away a little before he turns to look out the window.

"When I imagined a life with her, it wasn't what I wanted. I wasn't ready to settle down—this was almost ten years ago. We were too young. I was too wild, and she was desperate to get her hands on my money. It would have never worked out. So, I ended things before they got messy."

Snorting, I turn to look out my window as his gaze turns to me. "Seems like she's still desperate to get her hands on you. Take *her* to dinner tonight if you'd prefer."

Jackson shifts. When he speaks again, his voice sounds right against my ear as he whispers, "I'm right where I want to be tonight, Red."

Our noses nearly collide from how close he is when I whip my head around. I try to keep the anger out of my tone as I ask, "Why did you introduce me that way?"

His brow furrows as confusion seeps into his expression. "What other way should I introduce you, Ginny? We're friends, aren't we?"

"I think we're more than friends, Jackson. You've spent the last three nights in my bed, making me come with everything but your dick. I think that deserves a title stronger than *friend*."

Studying my face, he lifts a hand to brush an errant strand that has fallen from my messy bun out of my eyes. "You told me you didn't think I was capable of being exclusive. I thought calling you my girlfriend would be presumptuous of me."

Softening at his words—because he's right—I think about how I'm being. I'd been so intimidated by Viktoriya that I was acting threatened when it wasn't my place. Did I want him to see her for dinner? *Fuck no.* But did I have a right to ask that of him after telling him I didn't think he could be monogamous?

Also, a big fat no.

I really need to get my shit together and sort out my feelings. Today is *the* day. Today marks a month since we made the deal—well twenty-eight days anyways—close enough. Neither of us has brought it up since he picked me up at The Bryant once I'd gone home and showered after work.

I spent an abhorrent amount of time meticulously shaving

and plucking, picking out a sexy bra and underwear set, and making sure everything was perfect because, in my mind, tonight is the night we finally sleep together. But Jackson hasn't so much as made one crude comment about it since we've been together.

At my silence, something hardens in Jackson's hazelnut orbs before he pulls back. "Right."

Words fail me, and I spend the rest of the drive to his place gazing out the window while he taps away on his phone. Lead fills my stomach at the possibility of him messaging Viktoriya. Perhaps he is already setting something up for after he fucks me.

Does that change my mind?

As much as I want to say yes, the answer is undoubtedly no. I'm ready to be with him. I'm ready to feel something other than his fingers and his tongue filling me. And if it means I only get it this once, if it means he forgets about me after it's happened, I'll just have to find a way to deal with it.

Jackson is an experience I want to have, even if we part ways afterward.

Looking at him across the car, Jackson looks irritated, and my anger melts away, wanting to comfort him instead of being mad at him.

No, parting ways isn't what I want, I have to stop lying to myself. Even though I'm afraid he's going to hurt me, I *want* to be his.

"Here, try this." Jackson lifts a spoon to my lips after blowing on it to cool the homemade Alfredo down.

"Feeding me now? Is this your idea of foreplay?" I laugh.

"Try it and tell me if it's working." The smile he sends me is enough to make me melt into a puddle on the floor. All my senses are in overdrive, wondering when—*if*—he's going to make a move.

He's still in his work clothes, sans jacket, with his sleeves rolled up to his elbows. A sight I've been salivating over for the last thirty minutes while I sip white wine and watch him from where I'm perched on the counter next to the stove.

As soon as we made it into the kitchen, he'd forbidden me from even so much as lifting a finger to help. Telling me my job was just to enjoy my wine and let him do all the cooking. It seemed like as soon as he was within his own four walls—well, a figurative four, not literal because I'm not sure exactly how many walls this place has—all his tension dissolved away because he was back to acting normal.

In the last half hour, he's boiled pasta, baked garlic bread, and pan-fried chicken for the Alfredo he's now finished.

"You're going to put me in a food coma." Groaning as the delicious sauce hits my lips, I chase it with the wine while watching him turn off the burners.

Laughing, he starts to pull out the plates. "Good, we can eat in the game room and put on a movie."

Watching him for a moment, I realize I'm not exactly starving. So, I ask quietly, "You do know what today is, right, Jackson?"

He pauses in plating our food and looks over at me. "Today?"

Setting my wine down, I hold my hand out across the space between us, summoning him to me. Jackson puts the pot of sauce down, taking his time by picking up his wine glass to drink from it while watching me with heated eyes.

Finally, he walks over to me, and I waste no time grabbing his shirt to pull him closer. "Yes, today. Today marks a month. Our deal is up."

Stepping between my legs, he places his hands on either side of me on the counter and leans into me. "It's only been twenty-eight days."

"Close enough." My voice is breathless as I all but beg him to take me upstairs.

He smirks. "So it is. Where would you like to go on our first date?"

My arms encircle his neck, one of my hands twisting in his hair as I squeeze my legs around him. With a soft, throaty tone, I ask, "We've had enough first dates, don't you think?"

Tilting my head up, my lips find his as his arms wrap around me to pull me to the edge of the counter. Our kiss is like a soft current, ebbing and flowing, until he grips my hips and lifts my body against his.

"What do you want, Ginny?" He breaks our kiss to ask while just holding me against him. His chest is heaving, and there is unrestrained lust shining in his eyes.

Tightening my legs around his waist, I use the leverage to roll my hips against him. "I want to go upstairs, and I want to have sex with you." Blunt and to the point. My stranger would be proud.

"Is that what you really want?" He's asking, but his legs are already moving in the direction of the stairs.

"Mmmhmm." I nod before lowering my mouth to his again, my tongue dancing to meet his.

Jackson all but throws me on his bed once we get to this bedroom, pulling a little squeak from my mouth as I land. It's barely a moment before he's lying on top of me. "Do you know how many times I've thought about this?"

"Not nearly as many as I have." Tugging his shirt out of his pants, I run my hands beneath it, scraping my nails over his bare skin. Pushing it up, I kiss his chest as he balances his weight onto his forearms before pulling back from me.

He gets off the bed as I sit up to pull my sweater over my head and the hair tie from my bun. As my hair falls around my bare skin, he blows out a breath as he finishes unbuttoning his shirt and pulls it off. "God, you're fucking beautiful."

My cheeks warm as he reaches for the button on my jeans,

quickly ridding me of them before pulling at his buckle. Reaching out to help, I unzip his dress pants and push them down his legs, loving how he chuckles at my hurried motions.

It's the most naked we've been with each other.

As he steps out of his pants, he reaches out to cup my cheek, causing my eyes to meet his. His thumb swipes along my bottom lip slowly, eyes half-lidded as he nods for me to continue undressing him.

I'm wet and needy and just want him inside me already. There's been so much foreplay over this last month that I'm ready for him to absolutely destroy me.

His hand falls away from my face as I pull the band of his boxer briefs down, staring as my eyes lower from his to the impressive cock that is revealed as I get him completely naked. Licking my lips, I hear him suck air through his teeth sharply. "Don't do that while you're staring at my cock, Red. You're not ready to have me in your mouth yet."

Glaring up at him, I reach out quicker than he can take a step back and wrap my hand around his length. Leaning forward, I swipe my tongue along the head, where there's a drop of precum shining at the tip. It's salty, and I relish the taste as a sharp, "*Shit!*" leaves his lips.

Attempting to take him into my mouth, I hate that he's right because I don't know what I'm doing, and instead of a lesson in giving head, I really want him to fuck me. Just as his hand reaches up to fist in my hair, I pull back and move higher on my knees to kiss him again.

He consumes me. Pulling soft whimpers from my throat as he bends my head back so far it's almost uncomfortable. Suddenly, he releases me and pushes me back so that I fall against his navy silk sheets.

My wetness spreads along my inner thighs as I rub my legs together and watch him walk around the bed to pull a condom from a drawer in his nightstand. His proud length bobs as he walks back to me, looking too big for the condom as he pinches the tip and rolls it on.

My mouth fills with saliva when he crawls on the bed and pulls my legs apart. His eyes stare directly at my pussy as he pulls my underwear down my legs and flings them behind him. "Take off your bra."

I sit up and do as he says while he hooks his hands around my legs and pulls me wide to lick up my center. My body jerks at the sudden pleasurable feeling, and I fall back to the bed once my bra is somewhere on his floor, hands flying to his hair as I swallow my moans.

"Don't do that," he says between swipes of his tongue.

"Don't do what?" My voice is breathless as I look down to see him watching me.

"Don't try and be quiet. I want to hear you. I want to know how good this makes you feel." His mouth closes around me and sucks.

Tightening my fingers in his hair, I cry out, "It feels so fucking good, Jackson! Don't stop!"

As his tongue flicks against my clit, he pushes two fingers into me, working me toward an orgasm by pumping them leisurely while he devours me. "Come for me, Ginny."

My body writhes against the sheets, hips rocking against his face as I reply, "I want you inside me."

Chuckling against me, he whispers, "After you come for me. Did you think you'd only be getting off once tonight? Give me more credit than that."

Looking down at him between my legs, I stop trying to hold back my release, and it crashes through me as his fingers pick up their pace. With one final lick up my center, Jackson crawls up my body to kiss me deeply.

I taste sweet on his lips.

He swallows the sounds I make when the head of his cock nudges at my entrance, and he pushes in a little. My nails dig into his skin as the size of him stretches my walls slowly. He's being careful, eyes intensely watching for any sign of discomfort on my face.

"*Fuck*, you're so tight."

My eyes screw shut— body so tense that he pauses, giving me a moment to relax with the tip of him nestled just inside me.

He's trying to be so gentle. And I'm thankful for that because his size is so much bigger than the toys at the club, his fingers, and even the stranger's fingers when he put three of them inside me. Jackson is thick and long, and it takes a few seconds for my body to mold around him.

Lowering his mouth to my neck, he kisses my skin gently before whispering, "Relax, baby. The more you tense, the more it's going to hurt."

My eyes flutter open, and I look up at him, heat flooding my cheeks as I try to do what he says. "I'm sorry. I know you're used to women who are…more experienced."

His cock twitches inside me as he groans. "Don't you dare fucking apologize, Ginny. You're perfect just the way you are."

Lifting himself higher, he presses his hips further into me as I start to settle. "Now open up, baby. Let me in."

If I'd heard it in a movie, it would have been a cheesy line. But hearing it from Jackson's lips as he whispers it into the space between us, it's practically perfect as my body eases the further he pushes into me. He doesn't sink all the way in before moving back slowly and repeating the motion.

My eyes roll back as his hips continue to push in and out of me. But when he lowers his head, kissing over one of my nipples before sucking it into his mouth, I let out a sharp gasp and look back down to watch him. As I cradle his hips with my legs, he grabs just behind my knee to push one leg up, letting him thrust into me even further. The new angle presses at something deep inside, and a strangled cry leaves my lips as my hands grasp his shoulders.

"Are you okay?" he asks, slowing slightly.

My arousal makes it easier for him to slip in and out of me, leaving me wondering what it would feel like if he were fucking me harder, instead of so gently. "You can let go. I know you're holding back, Jackson."

Our eyes connect, and I try to convey what I want with my gaze. But his fingers flex around my knee as he lets out a sharp moan. "I'm not gonna hurt you."

His hips snap faster and continuously hit that spot deep inside, the tingling feeling in my spine spreading lower as I near another climax. My inner walls start to clench around him, and he lets out another low moan.

"Fuck, baby. You keep doing that, and I won't last at all." His head drops into the crook of my neck, and my arms move from his shoulders to wrap around his neck, cradling his head to me.

I don't know what it is I did, but I squeeze my walls again, earning a low throaty chuckle from him. The hand that's holding my knee slides down my thigh and beneath my ass to shift my lower body up slightly.

Stars explode behind my eyes as the new angle allows him to hit a spot that convinces me I've died and gone to heaven. "Jackson, I'm coming!"

The words are barely out of my mouth as another orgasm crashes into me right on top of the other, and I cling to him as he rides me through it. "That's it, baby. Squeeze my cock."

Doing as he says, we both let out a strangled, "Fuck!"

There's still a pressure deep inside me that's like an orgasm but...*more*. I can't explain it. All I know is that there is no me and Jackson. There's only *us*—no beginning and end, just an endless circle of passion and ecstasy.

Sliding a hand from behind his head to his cheek, I pull his lips to mine and kiss him deeply.

After a few more thrusts, his hips shudder against mine as he comes.

He continues to slowly rock into me, my hands tangling in his hair while our tongues dance together until he's finished.

Rolling onto his back, he pulls me into his side as we both lie there, breathing heavily. "Are you okay?" he asks again.

"Mmmhmm," I hum contentedly. It was everything I expected, yet not, at the same time.

Jackson is caring and gentle with me when he has the reputation of being anything but.

I *know* he held back for my sake.

Just when I'm about to ask him why he was so gentle, he kisses the top of my head and gets out of bed, heading into his bathroom. I assume it's to get rid of the condom and clean up, but then I hear the water running for an extended period. Too tired to move, I curl up against a pillow and watch as steam starts to roll out of the bathroom.

A few minutes later, Jackson appears again. "Come here." He motions for me to go to him, so I lazily crawl to the edge of the bed, where he scoops me into his arms.

Giggling, I wrap my arms around his neck and ask, "What are you doing?"

But as he pushes the door wider with his foot, my breath catches as I realize he's drawn me a bubble bath. Gently, he sets me into the water and kisses the top of my head again. "I'll go get your wine glass. Soak as long as you need, and come downstairs when you're ready."

I'm utterly shocked as he leaves again. Nothing about tonight went the way I thought it would—though I'm certainly not complaining. I will always count *this* as my first sexual experience.

And Jackson definitely did *not* disappoint.

But I wasn't expecting him to be gentle or soothing with me. I wasn't expecting a bubble bath and to be doted on. That *isn't* Jackson.

Then again, I built tonight up in my head. Built it on rumors and gossip and perhaps even a little of my own desires from the only sexual encounters I've ever had—which were *not* healthy ones.

P-Kitty comes into the bathroom and jumps onto the tub's

ledge, curling up in the corner as he watches me. Leaning forward, I scratch the cat on the head as I contemplate.

So, it *could be* Jackson. But the look on his face throughout it, the way his fingers flexed against my skin, itching to sink deeper into my flesh, that's Jackson *too*.

Maybe I just need a lesson from my stranger that involves how to ask for a little bit of a rougher touch because I'm craving...*more*?

And I know Jackson can give it to me—he just needs the green light.

Jackson

"Well, it happened. We had sex finally." Ginny is slumped against the far end of the loveseat, looking anything but lovestruck as she sips her champagne.

It hasn't even been two days since I've seen her, and I'm not sure how I feel about her seeing *her stranger* before *me*. Especially not with the way she's talking about our first time so cavalierly.

"It was…nice."

My drink gets caught in my throat, rerouting down the wrong pipe and causing me to spew liquid everywhere. Since I'm wearing the mask, half of it gets caught on the backside and drips down, causing me to reach beneath and wipe at my face angrily.

Nice?

"Don't laugh! It was more than nice. It was…*sweet*." She takes another sip with a nonchalant shrug.

She came in here tonight—clearly bothered—but I certainly didn't think it was going to be because I didn't fucking *satisfy* her. It would make sense why she's been distant since we had sex on Wednesday.

Ginny had seemed *thoroughly* satiated when she left my

house Thursday morning. I'd been careful not to hurt her. Even going so far as to run her a fucking bubble bath afterward so that she wouldn't be sore.

Yet, here she is. Making fun of me with another man?

"You sound as though he didn't satisfy you at all." My voice is gritty as I continue trying to clear my throat from swallowing my drink wrong.

"He did! I just…I don't know. I expected something different?" She curls her legs beneath her and then settles back against the arm of the couch. There's no sexual energy between us tonight, but if there had been, it would undoubtedly be gone now.

"What do you mean?"

She shrugs. "He gets more pussy than most men get in their lifetime. I don't know if he was just trying to be nice or what, but he was gentler than I thought he'd be. I guess I figured since he finally got me into bed, he'd pull out all the stops and try to impress me? But he was caring, and kind, and thoughtful. And while I *appreciate* it, I guess I was looking forward to being *fucked*."

I blow out a breath and hang my head over the back of his couch. "What am I going to do with you, Little Ember?"

Her words are like a slap in my face. I thought our relationship had been progressing to the point of us actually being together. But the way she's talking about me right now makes me feel like a fool.

She stretches her legs over my lap, and I pull my head up to look at her as she says, "I know, I know. *Ask for what you want.* I just didn't know how to ask *him*."

"Was there no part that was enjoyable for you?" My hands rest on her legs, thumbs stroking the dips in her inner ankles.

"It *was* enjoyable! He's like a fucking *sex god*," she mumbles.

Regardless of wanting to preen under her affectionate nickname, the fact that she seems so upset is making me feel uneasy. "So why the regretful expression? Go back and tell him what you want."

"There won't be a next time," she says sullenly.

The fuck there won't be. "And why not?"

"I'm no one special, just the girl that told him no. Now that he's had me…I'm sure he'll toss me away just like all the other women he fucks. We haven't even seen each other since that night."

She grows angrier as she speaks, and a little feeling in my chest pricks the spot where my heart lies encased in steel.

"Perhaps you should give him more credit."

We haven't seen each other because work has gone late for me the last two nights. I've done nothing to make you think I'm going to just toss you aside now that I've gotten you into bed.

She sets her glass down and slides a foot across my lap, bending her knee and letting it fall to the side to reveal the small strip of fabric that covers her pussy beneath her simple slip dress. "Perhaps *you* can just give me what I want?"

It stings—only for a second—that she was just in my bed Wednesday night, and here she is, asking for another man to give her what I didn't—what I *couldn't*. What I so desperately wanted to give her, but cared more about her fragility than unleashing my monstrous desires.

Only, she's no longer fragile.

Sure, she has her moments. But through our meetings at the club and my undivided attention outside of it, she's grown from an ember to a fiery little goddess.

And I'm a fucking arsonist—ready to set everything in our path ablaze.

But I'm also the idiot who treats her like she's glass.

The next time I see you as myself, you better be prepared to get exactly what you wish for, Ginny.

> We lost the WhirlTech deal. I expect to see you in my office ASAP. I don't give a damn that it's the weekend.

Tripp

> WhirlTech went with the other guys. You dropped the ball, dude. This was such a big fucking deal. I get you're obsessed with this new girl, but it's affecting your job, man. Thought money came before everything? Something we need to talk about?

Stacey

> Scott is...less than thrilled. He's already called me twice, and I'm not even his secretary. Good luck today. If you need anything, let me know.

Well, this Saturday already sucks, and it's barely ten in the morning.

Slumping down on the couch, I wipe the sweat of my morning workout from my face with the towel around my neck.

Losing the deal with WhirlTech is not a complication I foresaw. I thought we had them in the bag. But if they want to go with a company that offered them less money, if it means they can keep their casual Fridays, then fuck them.

Is it really that big of a deal?

Sighing, I rub at my face.

It is.

Jackson Tailor doesn't lose deals.

Scott Tailor doesn't like to lose money.

"Fuck!" Throwing my phone against the other side of the

couch, I go upstairs to take a quick shower before heading to the office.

When I arrive, my uncle is waiting for me. He's turned around in his chair, staring out the floor-to-ceiling windows as I walk in. "You wanted to see me?"

"Are you really going to act like this isn't a big deal?" he asks as he spins around and fixes me with a hard stare. He looks tired—angry—but worn down, nonetheless.

Shrugging, I continue into the room and take a seat in the chair across from him. "I'm sorry. I don't know what the appeal was with the other company. I didn't deny too many things they asked for, and we offered a hell of a lot more money than they were worth."

"You walked out in the middle of a fucking meeting with them because Ginny showed up?!" he roars back.

Opening my mouth to respond, I quickly shut it because I have nothing to say. Eventually, I nod with a sigh. "Yeah, I did that."

"What the fuck, Jackson?"

Shrugging sheepishly, I reply, "She surprised me. And I wanted to see her?"

His eye twitches as his teeth clench, causing me to swallow hard.

Any other day, any other time, I am calm, cool, and collected. But sometimes, my uncle intimidates the ever-living fuck out of me, and it humbles me real quick. This is about to become one of those times.

"When are these childish games of yours going to end?" His tone is stern, nothing I haven't heard before.

Only this time, I have a different answer.

"It's not like that with her. She's different."

"Oh, really?" he bites back. "If she's so different, tell me why you've been sneaking into the club under your *father's* name to book her?"

At my silence and look of utter shock at the revelation that he knows, he barks out a harsh laugh. "Oh, yeah. I know,

Jackson. For someone who is supposed to only be there on Sundays, I noticed you were a little too friendly with the staff. It only took a little digging and the threat of people losing their jobs to find out what you've done. Probably would have gotten away with it longer had you not destroyed a room last weekend."

I have the grace to look embarrassed. That cost me a pretty penny, but I settled up before leaving that night. I should have known word would have gotten back to him about it.

Before I can say anything, he delivers the question that makes me feel even worse. "Does she know it's you?"

"What does it matter? You have no idea–"

"DOES SHE KNOW?" He slams his hands on the top of his desk as he shouts. He hasn't raised his voice to me like this in years. With all the shit I've pulled, I haven't seen him *this* mad in a very long time.

"What does it matter to you? What is the *deal* with you two? She claims nothing has happened, but there's something *off* about the way you treat each other."

"Don't do that, Jackson. Don't deflect. Ginny is a good girl. She doesn't deserve the shit you're pulling."

"I told you things are *different* with her!"

"If they are so different, then why are you playing your bullshit games with her?"

His question makes me freeze, recalling that Stacey said that exact thing to me the night Ginny proposed our deal a month ago. An entire month and I still hadn't brought myself to tell her the truth about our time at Désirer—about me being her stranger. But there are reasons I haven't come clean about it. We've only just gotten to a place in our relationship —if you can even call it that after the way she was talking at the club last night—where she's beginning to trust me.

I'm not ready to throw that all away.

Her trust is fragile.

"I'm not playing games with her. I know it seems like it, but that isn't what's going on. You wouldn't understand."

Crossing my arms, I focus my attention out the window behind him.

"I wouldn't, huh? Well, here's something I understand, Jackson. I understand that you better tell her the truth, or *I* will. How about that? Is that something *you* understand?" He shifts his head so that he's in my line of vision.

Pushing out of my chair, I start to leave. He's not going to bully me into telling her. I'll tell her when I'm damn good and ready—when *she's* ready.

"I don't even recognize you anymore!" he yells after me.

Yeah, I don't recognize myself either, old man.

The afternoon bleeds into the evening. After leaving the office, I walked around to clear my head and ended up back at my place, not feeling any better than I had when I left earlier that afternoon.

My email has been going off all afternoon with new counteroffers drafted by companies we've nearly closed deals with. News articles highlighting our loss are being blasted all over the internet. Losing the deal with WhirlTech hit harder than I initially realized. While that particular company isn't a significant loss, the fact that we *did* lose them is causing other companies to think they can drive up their stakes, knowing we aren't going to want to lose multiple deals at once.

How the fuck did I let this happen?

Ginny's been consuming all my time and attention, that's how.

Sighing, I dial Tripp's number while pouring myself a finger of scotch, tossing it back as the phone rings.

And rings. And rings.

"Come on, Tripp. I know you're not *that* mad at me. Pick up your phone." Leaving him a voicemail, I pour myself another.

And another. And another.

Even Ginny doesn't answer when I call her instead.

"Why would she?" I ask myself out loud. "Apparently, you weren't that impressive. It's not like she's been begging for more."

Throwing back another drink, I slam the glass back down on the counter.

Why *would she throw herself at her stranger? Okay, he makes her feel comfortable, but she fucked* me.

Was I really not good enough?

Anger starts to build the more I think about it. The thought of her laughing—of mistaking me choking on my drink as *me* laughing. It makes me want to throw my fucking glass at the wall.

She's different.

Yeah, she's different, alright. She made me wait an entire month to sleep with her and then laughed about it with another man.

I'm losing deals because of her. Fucking up left and right.

Still, I'm not good enough.

It wasn't enough for her.

Why is it never enough?

And why is no one ever here for *me* when I need them?

Catching a glimpse of myself in the mirror that hangs on the wall by the entryway, I pause in my quickly spiraling soliloquy. The glass in my hand is nearly full, the liquid about to slosh over the side.

"There's nothing wrong with you," I whisper to my reflection. "You are who you are. You're Jackson *fucking* Tailor. You don't need *her*. You don't need *anyone*."

And I certainly don't need to drink away my fucking sorrows alone.

Bemelman's has been quiet all night, but it's exactly what I need.

Dinner for one.

Sober-ish.

Drinks for two?

Waiting for someone to catch my eye.

Raising my fingers to signal I want another scotch, the bartender walks to my end of the bar like he'd rather be helping anyone else.

"I think you've had enough tonight, sir."

"'Scuse me? I'm doing just fine. Now give me another."

"I don't think so." He shakes his head and sets a glass of water in front of me instead.

Dick.

"Do you know who *I* am?"

But he's halfway down the other end of the bar by the time the question passes my lips.

My phone hasn't lit up the entire time I've been here. Tripp hasn't answered me. Ginny isn't answering me.

By now, she's probably getting ready for her night with her stranger.

Well, guess what, Red? He's not coming tonight.

"Hey there," a sultry voice sounds to my left, and I turn my head, coming face to face with a giant pair of fake tits encased in bright pink glitter.

Big blonde hair, too much makeup, and a silicone rack I can stick my dick between while she sucks me off.

"Can I help you?" I drawl in a bored tone.

She'll do, I guess.

The blonde takes a seat next to me as she purrs, "I was thinking maybe *I* could help *you* tonight, Mr. Tailor. You look pretty lonely."

I am fucking lonely.

"You know this will go nowhere, right?" I motion for my check, tossing back the water as she nods while tacking a giant ass smile on her overfilled lips.

"Wouldn't dream of expecting more. Though *you* might, once I'm done with you," she coos as we stand and make our way to the exit once I've signed my tab.

Robert is waiting for me as we approach the car, unable to hide the disgust that crosses his face once he sees the woman walking in front of me. After she gets in the car, I tell him, "Don't leave. This won't take long."

"Whatever you say, sir." His tone is judgemental, but I let it slide.

The second I'm in my seat and the door closes behind me, the blonde launches into my lap and attempts to kiss me. Turning my head at the last second, I raise my hand to the top of her head, fingers twisting in her coarse, overly hair-sprayed hair, and roughly push her to her knees in front of me.

"I'm not sure what you've heard about me, but I imagine none of it's true. You won't be getting fucked tonight, sweetheart. You're here to do a job, and that's it."

Cold. Detached. Unfeeling.

Her eyes don't even flinch as she starts to giggle. "I can do that for you, Jackson. Here, though. At least enjoy the view while I do it."

I don't know if she's trying to sound like Marilyn Monroe or what, but the breathy words aren't working for her. She reaches up to undo the tie around her neck, letting the top of her dress fall down, revealing her chest.

My cock is as flaccid as a wet noodle.

Everything about this feels wrong.

Pushing through it, I close my eyes and lean my head back as she starts to unbuckle my belt.

Cornflower blues flash through my mind, and my hands seize into fists as I will the images away.

The woman lets out a whimper as my fingers tighten in her hair, but I ignore it. She's gotten my pants unbuttoned and is pulling my shirt up. Her lips meet the skin of my stomach, and it causes the contents to churn.

Pulling her back roughly, she cries out as I push her away. With her arms cradling her chest, she stares at me with a *what the fuck is your problem* look on her face.

I can only stare back as I process my thoughts.

What the fuck is right.

Big, round tits that I would have spent the night biting, sucking, and pinching until they were black and blue. A face that I would have blown my load on, watching with satisfaction as her mascara smeared when she tried to clean my cum from her lashes.

Hollow.

Meaningless.

Empty.

All I want is *red hair* and *blue eyes.*

Something pricks my chest.

It doesn't fucking matter that I lost the deal. It doesn't matter to me that I'm spending more time thinking about Ginny than I do my job. None of it fucking *matters* because the only thing that does is *her.*

Stacey once told me I'd regret my ways one day...when someone came along and turned my head for longer than a proverbial second.

That second has turned into weeks of infatuation that hasn't waned even the slightest bit. I'm obsessed with Ginny for reasons I don't fully comprehend. Yes, she's the only woman ever to tell me no. But she's also the only woman who hasn't given two fucks about my wealth and whatever status I can give her. The only one to allow me to cook her dinner instead of expecting to be taken to a fancy restaurant. The one who–*somehow*–talked me into buying a mangy cat and volunteering at the clinic, doing things for *others* instead of only myself.

She's settled herself into my life in a way no one else has even tried. Without meaning to, and without my realizing it, she's started to melt the shell around my heart. The thought of being tied to *her* isn't as terrifying as the thought of being held down by *anyone* once was.

It doesn't matter that it's fucked up my life. That was life as I knew it. This is life *now*.

She's become my captor. Bound me in chains that I willingly bear.

Because from this moment on, no other woman will hold any appeal to me. My world has become engulfed in her flames, and it is with startling clarity that I realize I will *gladly* burn for her.

The last bit of steel casing melts away with these reflections. My heart warming in my chest—beating only for *her*.

Ginny is the only thing I want. She's the only thing I *need*.

And here I was—about to fuck everything up.

Reaching across the seat, I open a side compartment and pull out a basic NDA. "Hand me your purse."

The blonde looks at me oddly while she ties her dress back around her neck. "What for?"

"Your ID. Before you get out of this car, you'll sign this NDA. I want to make sure you sign the correct name." Pulling a pen from the pocket inside my suit jacket, I reach out and grab the offensive pink sparkly bag as she holds it out.

"I won't say anything. Promise," she swears. But behind her bubblegum pink lips is a hidden smirk I've seen on far too many faces before hers. I learned early on that those faces were always masks that hid lies and deceit.

"Not gonna take that chance." I write in her name from her ID and hold the paper and pen out for her. "Sign here."

While I button my pants back up, she reluctantly does. And for being such a good sport about it, I pull a couple hundreds out of my wallet and hand them to her when I give her back her bag.

"I'm not a hooker," she pouts, but takes them anyway.

"Coulda fooled me, sweetheart. Have a nice night." Opening the door, I motion for her to get out.

Just when her bright pink heel hits the pavement, a camera flash goes off, followed by the sounds of someone running away as fast as they can.

Fuck.

My phone is out faster than I can blink to start calling in favors at every gossip column and paper that will try to buy that photo. After a few calls going to voicemail, though, I realize Stacey is the one who usually deals with all of this, and she's the one who will have the correct numbers.

Dialing her quickly, I shut the door and tell Robert to drive me home.

"Jackson? What's wrong? Is everything okay?" Her voice is sleepy, but I'm grateful she answered.

"Stacey. I fucked up. I fucked up big. Someone got a photo of me with a random woman. I don't know who it was. But I need it killed. It can't go to print."

She sighs while I hear her wife asking what's going on. "Jackson, why would you–"

"Because I was stupid, okay? Between losing the deal, Tripp not answering me, Ginny not picking up her phone, I just…I fucked up."

"Okay, okay. I'll deal with it. Go home. *Alone.* And pray that I can find out whoever it was."

"Thank you."

After we hang up, I bite my knuckles the entire drive home. P-Kitty meows at me for attention when I make it inside my penthouse, but I go straight for the full glass of scotch I left earlier, gulping it down like its water.

I don't doubt Stacey will take care of everything, but I try Ginny's cell again, half tempted to just show up at her place.

Again, she doesn't answer.

Fuck it.

Might as well just get completely shit-faced.

Alone.

Like always.

216

Ginny

The pounding in my head is persistent as it rouses me from sleep. Laying there, waiting for the pain to pierce my temples, I groan as I realize it's coming from someone pounding on the front door. *Not* my head.

Rolling over, I see it's just after eight in the morning. Reaching to tap the screen on my phone, I'm reminded that I have an old as-hell iPhone that decided to take a dip in a rain puddle yesterday afternoon, and it's currently still sitting in a container of rice on my kitchen counter.

"Ginny, open up. It's me!" Lenni yells through the door.

What the fuck is happening?

It is way too early for her to be up. She normally closes down the club and isn't home until well after four.

Scrambling out of bed when she starts shouting again, I go to answer the door before she gets me kicked out of the building. Yanking it open, I jump back as she storms in. "That fucking bastard. I'm so sorry, Gin. I came as soon as I saw the article."

Article?

Rubbing the sleep from my eyes, I yawn and ask, "What article? Lenni, what are you talking about? Do you know what time it is? It's my only day to sleep in."

And I desperately need the sleep after staying up worrying about why my stranger stood me up last night.

Turning, I head back to my bedroom and crawl into bed as she follows me, kicking off her shoes and pulling her jacket off to reveal a maroon flannel pajama pant set. "You haven't seen it? *Fuck*, Ginny. I'm sorry. Actually, no, I'm not. I'm happy that I got here before Jackson shows up and tries to bullshit his way out of it."

That gets my attention.

Things have been tense between me and Jackson since I left his place Thursday morning. I'll admit it's entirely my fault because I haven't known how to navigate our relationship from here. He's been busy at work, and I haven't wanted to bother him. I meant to message him yesterday about them losing the deal he was so sure they'd get, but then my phone went swimming, and I never got the chance.

My breathing grows shallow, and it feels like something sharp is stabbing my heart. Breath tight, I ask, "Lenni, what are you talking about?"

She types something into her phone before handing it over to me. There, brightly lit up on the screen, is a picture of a busty, leggy blonde stepping out of Jackson's car. Her lipstick is smeared. His face is frozen as he stares at the camera with his shirt pulled out of his pants.

'Can't hold Tailor down! Jackson Tailor was seen with a mysterious blonde after only a few weeks of being off-market.' The article is full of lines such as, *'Guess a leopard can't change its spots,'* and, *'Can't keep a good dog down.'*

Bile rises in my throat, and I press my hand to my mouth in an effort to keep it at bay. Tears rise and fall from the depths of my eyes, my body quaking as Lenni pulls me into her arms.

It was all a game.

A stupid game I thought I could play—but I lost.

I always do.

Everything becomes blurry as the room starts to spin.

The soothing, dulcet tones of Lenni's meant-to-be comforting words are taken over by Chris' voice, echoing in my head.

"Men like him don't fall for women like you."

"You're nothing special, Guinevere. No man will ever want you because you're a sickness. You worm your way into the hearts of men with your crimson hair and come fuck me eyes, and then you rot them from the inside out. It's what you did to me. You caused me to turn into what I am. You created the monster inside me. It's all because of you."

Wet flesh slapping on flesh. Whispered words of, *"What have you done to me?"*

Me, begging him to let me get off. *"I'll be good. I promise I'll be good."*

Someone is whimpering, rocking back and forth so hard that the bed is shaking.

"Fuck, Ginny. Calm down. Calm down, babe. Ginny, you're having a panic attack."

Something is shoved into my hands, but my fingers don't work, so it falls to the bed.

"Ginny, I need you to breathe. I need you to breathe and repeat after me. It's going to be okay."

No, it's not.

"...Ginny!"

Why *would* anyone want me?

A freak.

A monster.

I'm disgusting.

I'm disgusting.

I'm disgusting.

Jackson

BANG! BANG! BANG!

"I'm coming up the stairs, so you better be dressed!"

BANG! BANG! BANG!

"Make it stop," I mumble from beneath my pillow. My head is pounding, and whoever is in my house is making it worse.

"Jackson, I've been calling you all morning. Jesus Christ, it smells like a distillery in here. Please tell me that isn't vomit." Stacey's voice drifts through the silk-covered cushion on my head.

"Go away."

"Jackson, you have to get up. This is important."

Nothing is important today. Nothing except me sleeping off this fucking hangover.

"The photo went to print. I thought I had squashed it, but the photographer took the money, turned around, and still sold it. It ran on every major media outlet this morning."

Adrenaline rushes through my veins, causing me to sit straight up. The room spins, and there are three of Stacey as I hurl myself over the side of my bed and throw up in the trash can.

Or at least where the trash can used to be.

"Dear lord," Stacey says on a gag. "How much did you have to drink last night? You haven't thrown up in years."

"Who was the photographer? I'll make sure he never gets work in this city again." Spitting the last of the vomit from my mouth, I wipe my arm across my lips before glaring up at her.

"I think there are more important things to consider right now, Jackson. Something like this right after the WhirlTech deal…. It looks bad. Scott is pissed, again, and rightfully so, but I don't need to tell you that, do I?"

"He's always pissed at me. What the fuck do I care anymore? He's not my fucking father." Getting off the bed, I storm into the bathroom and turn on the faucet, splashing cool water on my face before grabbing my toothbrush.

"And Ginny? If she hasn't seen it yet, she will."

My eyes find my reflection in the mirror. If Ginny's seen it, I'm fucked.

I knew I should have just gone to her last night.

Anger pours through me. At myself, at my uncle, at the fucking photographer.

Glass shatters as I let out a roar while dragging my arm along the vanity, sending everything on it crashing to the ground. Dropping my elbows to the surface, I dig the heels of my palms into my eyes. Acid burns in my stomach, in my chest, and up my throat.

She's never going to forgive me.

Wire coils along my lungs, squeezing as I try to even my breathing.

This was her biggest fear when it came to me. I let her down.

"Maybe you should go to her."

Opening my eyes, I see Stacey standing in the doorway, eyeing the mess I've made. A soft meow sounds from the bedroom, pulling me out of my daze.

Motioning for her to close the door, I tell her, "Don't let him in here. I don't want him getting glass in his paws."

Doing as I ask, she pauses before she shuts it entirely. "Get cleaned up. I'll start some coffee and tell Robert to have the car ready."

I don't answer her. But when I'm showered and dressed, downstairs and ready to go, I tell her, "Stacey, I don't know why you stick around with me, but thank you."

She shrugs and sends me a sly smirk. "You definitely keep things interesting, Jackson. But seriously, how else will I continue filling the pages of my passport?"

We ride the elevator down in silence, taking the back exit of the building since the front has a few paparazzi waiting to get another photo. Before I get into my car, she touches my arm to get my attention. "Next time you're feeling that way, call. I told you I'd be there if you need anything. You're not alone, Jackson. You have friends."

Snorting, I pat the pocket of my sports jacket where my phone is. "They didn't pick up when I called."

Walking away, she calls over her shoulder, "You didn't call me."

There are also a few photographers hanging around outside The Bryant, and I wonder how they found out Ginny is living here. Giving Robert instructions to get rid of them, I make my way inside, ignoring the numerous calls of my name.

Once I step out onto her floor, I take a moment, bracing an arm against the doorframe before finally knocking.

My chest feels like Swiss cheese, punched through with holes I'm not sure how to fill. Soft footsteps sound behind the door, and I straighten up, tensing as it opens to reveal Ginny's friend instead of her.

"What are *you* doing here?" She glares at me, dressed in flannel pajamas. If looks could kill, I'd be dead.

"I take it you've seen the article?" Pushing my hands in

my pockets, I nod behind her. "None of it's true. I'd like to talk to Ginny."

"Sure as hell looked true enough," Lenni deadpans, not budging an inch.

"Ginny! I can explain!" I call out into the apartment.

Lenni rushes out the door, causing me to take a few steps back as she pulls it closed behind her. "You can't see her. You *broke* her. She's a fucking mess because of you. She doesn't want to see you."

"I think she can make that decision for herself." Standing here arguing with her mouthy friend is doing nothing but wasting time, so I push around her, ignoring the fact that she grabs my arm and tries to pull me back.

Her efforts are futile, but she continues to yell at me as I push the door open. "She doesn't want to see you! Haven't you hurt her enough? Do I need to call security, you big brute?!"

"I own the damn place–good luck." Not entirely true, but she might not know that.

"Ginny!" I call out, walking past the kitchen toward the bedroom, thinking that maybe she's just out on the balcony.

But what I see instead stops me in my tracks.

Ginny is curled into a ball in the middle of her bed, her hair splayed out with some falling over her face, half hiding it from my sight. The half that isn't hidden, though….

Her pale skin is splotchy, with red patches smeared across her face. It's evident she's been crying, but her eyes are dry. She doesn't so much as blink when I walk in. Her eyes don't shift to me. No evidence she even registers that I'm here.

She's breathing through her mouth, deep breaths that come in shattered gasps.

A piece of me dies inside, knowing I did this to her.

Kneeling next to the bed, I reach for her when Lenni's voice sounds so shrill it startles me. "Don't touch her!"

"Will you leave and give us a minute alone, *please*," I stress the last word with an emotion I'm unsure what to call. All I know is that it's foreign and unwelcome.

"No. I mean, she'll freak out if you touch her. I've just been lying here with her. She's been this way for a little over two hours now," Lenni explains.

Letting out a long breath, I settle for resting my arms on the bed as I speak to Ginny. "Hey, Red. It's me. I know I'm probably not your favorite person right now, but I need you to hear me when I tell you the article wasn't true. There's an explanation—"

"Get out." Ginny's small voice sounds cold and detached. It's a tone I recognize all too well, having used it quite a few times myself.

"Ginny, I promise—"

"Please leave."

"Just listen to me." Pushing up on my knees, I start to get on the bed, but her sharp cry stops me.

"Don't! You got what you wanted, Jackson! I'm no one special! I get it!" Her voice cracks as tears line her eyes.

"That isn't true at all!" I argue, frozen where I'm still half-kneeling at the bedside. A panicked feeling grips my lungs with cold fists, squeezing until it's hard to breathe.

She's shaking, hugging her knees tighter as she says, "Men like you don't change. You'll never change. You're *not* capable of it."

Nothing comes out of my mouth when I open it this time. She's not listening to me. Not even willing to hear me out. Though, in this state, I'm not sure she could, even if she wanted to.

All of this is causing her obvious distress, and all I want to do is take it and make sure she never feels this way again.

Making a decision not to listen to Lenni, I stand and reach across the bed for her. "Ginny, you have to listen to me."

The second my hand touches her, she jerks back and smacks it away. "GET OUT!"

I continue to try and subdue her, vaguely aware that Lenni

is back in the room and trying to pull me off the bed. "Ginny! Stop!"

"GET OUT! GET OUT! GET OUT!" Her voice is so piercing it leaves a ringing in my ears.

The sharp sound of her palm meeting my face claps through the air as my head snaps to the right.

"I hate you!" I hear Ginny cry as she pushes away from me.

Stunned, I don't move for a few moments. Then, slowly, I rotate my head back to look at her. She's glaring up at me, chest heaving, tears streaming down her face, hair matted to her flushed skin.

"I'm sorry," I whisper as I hang my head, unable to continue looking her in the eyes.

There's no getting through to her right now. And I can't stand that I'm the one who caused her to feel this way.

Feeling defeated, I turn to leave. As I pass the threshold of the bedroom, I swear I hear her whisper, "Me too."

Ginny ignores me for days.

Text after text. Call after call. Countless voicemails. Multiple bouquets of flowers—to her apartment, Chillard, and Decadence.

By the time Thursday rolls around, I'm nearly at my wit's end. Yearning to go back to her place to try convincing her that the photo wasn't what it seemed. But the look in her eyes when I left on Sunday still haunts me.

There's a nagging feeling at the back of my mind as I recall my uncle's words from Saturday. He threatened to tell her about the club if I didn't. Part of me wonders if he was being truthful, and since we're meeting for lunch, I'm going to ask him point-blank.

My knee bounces under the table as I wait for him, a glass

of Macallan in hand, even though it's the middle of the afternoon. When he finally shows, it's with a disapproving frown at my glass and a shake of his head. "I'm assuming you're not going back to the office?"

"Did you tell her?" My fingers tap against the tumbler in time with my knee. It's a warm day, and the sunlight is pouring through the glass panes, bathing me in its heat.

My uncle cocks his head to the side and asks, "Did I tell who what?"

Prick.

"Don't be an asshole right now, I've been through enough this week." Tossing what's left of my drink back, I signal for the waiter to bring me another.

"I think you're getting a healthy dose of what you deserve, Jackson. And did you really have to have that photographer fired?"

"Fuck you," I snap. "Why the fuck are you *always* on my case? You were just as bad at my age."

"Exactly! Which is why I want *you* to be better." He picks up his menu and sets it down just as quickly, ordering a simple house salad when the waiter brings my scotch.

"You should eat something. Stacey and Claudia both tell me you've been drunk for most of the week. I can smell you from here."

"Did you tell her?" I ask again.

"Why'd you do it, Jackson? The blonde? If Ginny is so different, then *why*?" He dodges my question again.

My jaw clenches, fingers tightening around the glass as I fix him with a hard glare. He glares right back, clearly not going to answer me. Finally, I tell him, "You said you didn't recognize who I was anymore."

"I didn't mean to go out and try to fuck whoever threw themselves at you first. I meant the sneaking around pretending to be someone you aren't. Fucking off at work. *Losing* deals."

"All of that is because of *her*." Leaning forward in my seat, I push my drink off to the side before I break the glass.

"No, Jackson. All of that is because of *you*. Because you don't even know what's staring you right in the face."

"And what is that?"

"You're in love with her, you idiot."

"If *this* is love, I don't want it." I've never been in love. Wouldn't know what it looked like if it slapped me in the face.

Like *she* did.

If love is going around and around, hurting each other with unspoken words and misunderstood meanings, then what is the point?

"She's hurting, Jackson. She let her guard down with you, and you hurt her. Give her some time." He falls silent as the waiter returns and sets his salad in front of him, asking if I'd decided on a meal.

Shaking my head no, I wave him off as my uncle starts talking again. "For the record, no, I haven't told her. But the longer you wait, Jackson, the worse it will be. How the hell did you even manage to get a second ID card?"

"Security in that place isn't as tight as you think it is. Trust me, I've compiled a long list of things that need to be changed." I rub my eyes, which are becoming increasingly drier with my lack of water intake this week. Setting my chin in my hand, I massage my temple with two fingers as a headache starts to form.

"How did you even know it was her?" His phone lights up from its place on the table, and I lean forward to see who it is, but it's a number I don't know.

"Easy. I'd recognize those eyes anywhere paired with her hair."

Because she calls to me like a siren to a ship at sea.

"You really do have it bad, kid. So what are you going to do about it? You can't keep something like that a secret forever. Not if you plan on trying to have a relationship with her." He's talking to me, but his attention is now focused on his phone, causing a scowl to pull at his face. "I gotta get back to the office. You need to go home, sit in the sauna, and detox while you think about how you're going to make this right."

"Yeah. Okay." Is all I say as I watch him leave.

I set my hand on the table, my fingers twitching to grab my phone and call her again. I'm like a drug addict who hasn't had his fix in days.

Tomorrow. I can wait until tomorrow. Even if it's as her stranger, I'll get to see her.

"Is there anything else I can get you, sir?" the waiter asks as he sets my bill down.

"Have you ever fallen in love?" I ask, pulling my wallet from the pocket inside my jacket.

"Love? Uh, no, sir. Can't say that I have." He looks young. Bright and wide-eyed. Probably working his way through school. I pull out a crisp hundred and lay it on the bill. It's enough to cover it and give him over a hundred percent tip.

"Good. It fucking sucks. My advice? *Don't.* That's the best tip I can give you."

Ginny

It's been almost an entire week, and still, my chest hurts as though it were only this morning.

I'm late—the only sound in the Dreamers hall is the click of my shoes on the hardwood and the soft tap of my guard's footsteps in front of me.

The last time I saw my stranger, he'd turned me down *again*. If I didn't know any better, I'd say he doesn't want me now that Jackson has had me.

But I know that's not it. He was telling me no long before I gave in to Jackson.

As it is, tonight, I'm not in the mood. Not in the right frame of mind to be sexual with him in any way. The makeup I'm wearing is waterproof because I have a feeling the moment I see him, the tears will start again.

I spend more time crying in his presence than I do anything else. I don't know why he continues to see me.

My guard holds his hand out for my robe as we get to my door, but I shake my head and wrap my arms around myself. "I'm going to keep it tonight, thank you."

He gives me a nod, not saying a word, and reaches for the door handle instead.

My stranger is already there, waiting. His full mask is ominous as he stands on the other side of the room like he's been there for a while, watching to see when I'd come through the door.

As soon as our eyes lock, mine tear up, just as I suspected they would. Wordlessly, as if he knew I'd be a mess tonight, his arms open, and I rush across the room into them.

His arms wrap around me awkwardly with the wings in the way, but I hug him tighter anyway, as I cry into his shirt. "What's wrong now, Little Ember?"

"Everything. Everything I was afraid would happen, did."

"With your boyfriend?"

My heart feels like it's getting crushed all over again as I nod my head. "I was so afraid of getting close to him, and when I finally let down my walls, he stabbed me in the back. Just like I knew he would."

The stranger's arms tighten around me just a little, and I can hear him let out a deep breath behind his mask. "At the risk of potentially giving something personal about your life away, do you want to elaborate on what exactly happened?"

Real identities are the furthest thing from my mind right now, and I go full steam ahead with my tale of what happened last weekend. As I explain, the stranger leads me to the couch and sits with me in his lap, stroking the back of my hair while he listens.

"Things were weird all week after that. We barely spoke. I thought maybe I did something...like maybe I just wasn't good at it?"

"I find that hard to believe, love."

"Then I don't know what happened. It was all so confusing. He kept acting as though we were dating, but the second we slept together, it was like he no longer cared. It was everything I was hoping wouldn't happen. When I saw that photograph of him with that woman, I had a full-blown panic attack. I...I'm not proud of this, but I *hit* him. I screamed at him like a lunatic and struck him. That isn't *me*."

"People can't help what they do when they have attacks like that. I'm sure he doesn't hold it against you." His voice is quiet. Restrained and gravelly, as though he's angry and is trying to hide it.

We're silent for a few moments before I ask, "Do you think you could just hold me tonight? Would that be okay?"

"Absolutely. We haven't been intimate since the night with the toy–"

"I know. I'm sorry, does that bother you?"

"Not at all, Little Ember. I'm here to be whatever you need me to be." He pulls me closer to his chest.

Quietly, I laugh. "That's supposed to be *my* job. I kind of suck at this. But you know what?"

"What?"

"I'm happy it was you in my room that day. You honestly have no idea how thankful I am for you." Pulling back so that I can look into his eyes, I let out a sigh when he looks away, like he always does when we're this close, and I try to peer behind his mask.

"I like to think I'd have killed any other man who tried to take you that night."

A flood of warmth rushes through my body at the possessiveness of his tone.

"You know, there's nothing wrong with you, Scarlett. It's okay for you to be upset over the circumstances—you have every right to be. But I hope you can understand *why* I won't sleep with you. It's very obvious you've fallen for this boyfriend of yours, and feelings that strong don't just go away."

Letting his words sink in. I choose not to respond, and he takes that as a green light to keep talking.

"Is there not any way he can earn your forgiveness?"

"No." My answer is instant and sharp as I pull away from him completely. His arms tighten, refusing to let me off his lap, but I turn so my back is to him, wings probably in his face.

"Maybe you should hear him out," he presses.

"Excuse me?"

"Put yourself in his shoes, Little Ember. You should hear him out and give him a chance to explain his side instead of jumping to conclusions. What if it were you that'd been photographed with another man? Would you want the opportunity to explain your side?"

"*I* don't have *his* reputation!"

"Regardless of his reputation, you fell for him anyway. Is that not deserving of a talk?"

Spinning, I glare at him before getting up from the couch and walking to the drink cart in the corner of the room. "Where were you last weekend?"

The change in subjects doesn't even phase him. "I had things I needed to attend to."

"You couldn't have given me a heads-up?" Now I'm just being bratty. Never in a million years did I think he would take Jackson's side.

I imagine he's rolling his eyes at me. He starts to chuckle and stands, crossing the space to pull me back into his arms. "You can act like that all you want, love. Your attitude doesn't phase me."

"*Nothing* seems to phase you. You paid a disgusting amount of money to book me exclusively, and all we've done is play therapist. And it's been *you* counseling *me*. That isn't normal."

"Nothing about this club *is* normal. Wouldn't you agree? If I had issues with our arrangement, I'd end it. However, I quite like our Friday and Saturday evenings."

"Yeah, when you show up."

There's a beat of silence between us before I turn and bury my face against his chest. "I'm sorry. I'm being awful tonight."

Wrapping his arms around me again, he says, "I told you it was okay. You need a punching bag? I'm happy to be that for you. But it still remains that I think you should hear him out. Promise me you'll think about it?"

He holds me for what seems like an hour, but in reality, I know it's only a handful of minutes. I've already been debating letting Jackson defend himself. In the last five days, he's had flowers delivered to almost every place I've been and has been calling non-stop. I listened to the voicemails he left as soon as they went through to my phone. They're all the same.

"I'm so sorry."

"Please forgive me."

"I promise it wasn't what it looked like. Please, just let me explain."

"I miss you."

It isn't fair. Because despite the fucking picture and all of the articles—not to mention the paparazzi hanging around outside The Bryant trying to get photos of me and comments on what happened—I still have feelings for him.

I hate that it's true, but I do.

"Yeah, okay," I finally mumble into his chest. "I'll think about it."

Sighing, I turn in bed to see the bright white numbers on my alarm clock reading three in the morning. Since I got home from the club, the stranger's words have been replaying in my mind.

My heart and head are at war—one wanting to never speak to Jackson again, the other wanting to call him and give him a chance to explain. Another fifteen minutes pass by as I stare blankly at the clock, watching as the numbers change. As it becomes three sixteen, I reach for my phone and pull up my text conversation with him.

Typing a message out quickly, my finger hovers over the send button for multiple seconds before I finally press down on my screen, telling myself that if it doesn't send on the first try—it's been giving me issues since I dropped it in the water —then I'll delete the message.

It goes through.

> Are you up?

Barely a minute passes before he responds. My heart leaps into my throat at our first communication in a week.

> For you, yes.

It's all he says. I wait for a moment, thinking he'll follow it up with something else. Maybe a *how are you?* Or *I miss you.* But nearly five minutes go by without another message.

> Can we talk?

> Do you want to come here? Should I come to The Bryant? Or do you just want to call?

Nibbling on my thumbnail, I debate what option to choose. If I go there, I can leave whenever I want, but if he comes here, it won't be that easy. This deserves more than a phone call, though.

> I can come there.

> I'll send Robert now.

> I'll take a cab.

> Okay.

It shocks me that he doesn't put up more of a fight. Then

again, why would he? I've ignored him for a week. Trying not to dwell on it, I slip out of bed and into my walk-in closet to pull on the jeans I wore earlier with a plain, long-sleeved black shirt.

The cab ride feels like it takes forever. Lights are still glowing from multiple bars and businesses that are still open. The city that never sleeps is still vibrant and bustling as the cab slowly inches me block by block toward a truth I'm not sure I'm ready to hear.

I rehearse my speech a million times in my head throughout the drive and on my way up to Jackson's penthouse. But the second the elevator doors open, my mind goes blank, and my heart drops from my throat to my stomach.

Jackson is waiting for me, dressed in a pair of gray joggers and a plain white shirt. He looks like he hasn't slept in days. The entire room smells like a bottle of expensive alcohol was dropped and left to evaporate into the air.

Our eyes connect, and I'm overwhelmed by the feeling of wanting to run into his arms and just be held by him.

Instead, I slowly step out of the elevator and slip my ballet flats off, dropping my purse next to them on the floor.

"Hi," he finally greets me when I look back at him.

Crossing my arms over my chest, I raise my brow and do my best to give him a hardened look. "Hi."

Ire melts through my veins as the corner of his lips tilt up in a smile before he squashes it down. Nothing is amusing about this situation, yet here he is, trying not to laugh at me. "You wanted to explain. So explain."

His eyebrows shoot up into his hairline. "You want to talk about this *now*? At almost four in the morning?"

"Yeah, I do. So, tell me, Jackson. Was it your plan all along?" Keeping my feet firmly planted, I glare at him in my best attempt to show him that this is not a game to me. That just because I'm here, it doesn't mean I'm going to forgive him.

I have no intention of forgiving him.

"No, Ginny. It wasn't my plan all along. It was a moment of weakness after a really shitty day. Not to mention, you barely spoke to me after we had sex, so I thought that maybe it was *you* who was done with *me*. You didn't exactly sing my praises and beg to fall back into my bed."

"Insecure much? Is that what you need, Jackson? Someone to tell you what a pro you are in bed and how good you fucked them?" Every word that leaves my mouth turns angrier and angrier. My rage bubbling beneath the surface of my skin.

"No, I don't need anyone to tell me how good I am in bed. But I didn't exactly fuck you the way I do other women. So the fact that you didn't speak to me and then ignored me all day Saturday didn't exactly feel great." He crosses his arms, mirroring my posture as he speaks to me like I'm a petulant child.

It pisses me off even more.

"My phone was sitting in a container of rice for most of the day Saturday. So sorry I wasn't at your beck and call, *sir*. Good thing you have a whole list of women who will fall at your feet and do whatever you want them to."

"It wasn't like that. I've told you that a million times, Ginny. I know it looked bad, but I swear to you that *nothing* happened. I didn't want...I couldn't do it. Trust me, I tried. I wanted to burn you from my memory. I wanted to erase the way your skin felt on mine and the way your body felt like it was made just for me. Because I thought you didn't want me, and because I thought I didn't *need* you. But the second that woman touched me, I knew it was a lie. I do *need* you."

He uncrosses his arms and walks toward me, but I veer around him and head into the living room. "Well, maybe I don't *want* you."

When I turn, he's watching me with guarded eyes. I can tell my words hurt him, and triumph floods my body because I want him to feel as hurt as I've been. "You know what I do want, though, Jackson? I want to know why you were so gentle with me."

His body relaxes, and he takes a deep breath, walking into the living room until we're nearly chest-to-chest. "Because you aren't like other women. And I didn't want to scare you away."

"What does that even mean?"

"You know what that means, Red. I was practically begging you to be mine. I would have never done that with any of those women." He reaches for my hand, but I jerk away and take a few steps back.

"Yet those are the women that you can be yourself with in bed. It was obvious that you were holding back. Even if you say it's because you wanted something serious with me, you would have had to show me that side of you. So why couldn't you? What is the appeal of those women? What do they have that *I* don't?"

I didn't even realize it until now, but *this* is exactly what I want. I want to experience sex without him holding back. Just once. Just to see what it's like. I want to know what he's keeping from me. Then my curiosity will be sated, and I can move on with my life and pretend the last month and a half never happened.

"You are *nothing* like them! And that's exactly why I want *you!* You aren't listening to me, Ginny. Nothing happened with that woman. That life isn't what I want anymore."

"But you *wanted* it to. You wanted to go back to your old ways just to prove you aren't the man you've become since we started hanging out. So show me *that* man, Jackson! Show me what I'm missing out on. Fuck me like you do all those other women!" I'm throwing my hands around like a crazy person, and I can feel the tears falling from my eyes as I yell at him.

A look I can only describe as disgust appears on his face as he shakes his head and turns away. "That isn't us, Ginny."

"There is no *us!* So show me!" My words make him freeze

before he turns back to look at me, his eyes staring intensely into mine.

"Is that what you really want?"

"Yes. I want to know what it's like to be *fucked* by Jackson Tailor," I sneer.

My chest is heaving, cheeks wet from my tears. Jackson clenches his jaw repeatedly, breathing heavily and looking like he's at war with himself.

I see the moment he makes up his mind. Something shifts in his eyes, making them appear harder—darker. His body tightens, and he draws himself up to full height.

It's like a mask slips over his entire form.

It makes my skin break out in goosebumps—the hair on the back of my neck standing on end.

The person standing in front of me is no longer Jackson.

He seems *unhuman*.

Suddenly, I'm prey about to be torn in two.

"Fine then. Upstairs. *Now*," he orders.

With a glare, I do as he says, wiping my cheeks as I ascend the staircase into his room. He's quiet as he follows me, but as soon as we enter his bedroom, it's like I'm about to have sex with a whole different man.

"Get on your knees," he commands. His voice is deeper and throatier than it just was moments ago, but it's devoid of any emotion.

Heat shoots to my center as I do what he says without hesitation. My body shivers as he walks closer, head craning back to stare up at him when he reaches me.

"Open your mouth." I think he's about to caress my cheek, but then he takes me by surprise as he clutches my jaw to squeeze my lips open.

"You look so fucking pretty on your knees, Ginny. I've thought about this moment for so long." Shifting, he pulls himself out of his joggers, his swollen head already glistening with precum.

Letting go of my face, he slides his hand through my hair,

238

twisting my strands around his fingers as he squeezes so tightly it makes me wince.

"Now suck."

The moan that leaves my mouth is silenced by him thrusting his cock between my lips. Jackson is big, and I struggle to fit even half of him in my mouth before I try to pull back.

"No, you'll take it all," he grits out, hand tightening in my hair to stop me from retreating.

He grabs the base of his shaft and forces my head onto him. My hands fly up to his thighs as my gag reflex kicks in, but it doesn't seem to bother him that there's a good chance I might throw up on his dick.

I have no clue what I'm doing, though it doesn't seem to matter.

Jackson gives me a moment to breathe before he slams further into my mouth. My tongue runs along the underside of his length, where multiple veins are popping beneath the silky skin, trying to do my best to please him like any other woman would. When he draws back, I hollow my cheeks and suck hard, licking along his slit before he pushes in again.

I'm wet between my thighs and reach down to touch myself to alleviate some of the pressure, but Jackson pulls out of my mouth quickly and slaps his cock against my cheek. "Did I say you could touch yourself?"

Too stunned to respond, I blink up at him as he rubs his head against my lips before pressing in again. He doesn't go far, barely past the head and tells me, "Suck it fucking hard."

My mouth seals over him, creating a vacuum-like effect as my tongue swirls against his slit, the tip pushing in just a little. He groans, and I like that doing as he says makes his head roll back in pleasure. He's still holding the rest of his length, so I reach up to replace his hand, catching his eyes as he looks back down at me.

Slowly, I start to pump as I move my head up and down his shaft, saliva coating him as it spills from my mouth. It's dirty and making a sloppy sucking sound, but it's honestly turning me on more, and it seems like Jackson likes it too.

"Such a dirty fucking girl, aren't you? This is what you've been begging me for. Gagging on my cock. Do you like the way it tastes?"

Nodding against him, I bob my head more enthusiastically as his other hand finds the back of my head. He pushes me down onto him, hitting the back of my throat and holding me still as I choke around him.

I can't breathe.

I don't like that I can't breathe.

Just when I desperately need air, he lets me go and steps back, his length bobbing in the space between us.

"Get up." He grabs me roughly by my arms and pulls me from the floor. He begins to unbutton my jeans while I rip my shirt over my head and unclasp my bra, stepping out of my pants and underwear as he pushes them down my body.

For a moment, I think he's going to kiss me, but then he palms both of my breasts and squeezes hard before bending to take one in his mouth.

He doesn't kiss, or lick, or even suck. He bites my nipple, and it's so painful that I cry out and try to push him back. I shove against him so hard that I fall back on the bed.

"What the fuck, Jackson?"

"This is what you wanted, isn't it? Turn around, get on all fours." He glares at me as he walks around the bed to grab a condom from his nightstand. Slowly, I turn, watching him in a stupor as he rolls the condom on.

There's no sign of the man that I've come to know. Being handled roughly is one thing, or at least I thought it was. Whatever *this* is, it feels more like a punishment when it should be *me* who is punishing *him*.

When he's behind me, I'm not prepared for the way he grabs my ass and squeezes as he pulls my cheeks apart. "Always so fucking wet for me."

There's a sharp sting between my legs as he slaps his hand against my pussy.

Then he's slamming into me with such force that I pitch forward, and my upper body falls to the bed. There isn't much time to adjust to his size, but I'm so wet that it doesn't hurt as much as it could've.

His hands anchor my hips as he thrusts into me repeatedly with such vigor that the bed shakes and groans beneath us. There's no foreplay, no gentle caresses, or paying attention to any part of my body that would make it more pleasurable for me.

Jackson sets a punishing pace. No words leave his lips. It's just him taking his pleasure. It feels okay, but not as good as the other night.

It's kind of painful.

I'm trying to enjoy it, but every time I close my eyes, I picture him with that woman from the photo, and that haze clears. Picture him doing this with more experienced women —ones who know exactly how to react to him and give him what he wants.

My body jolts as he slaps his hand against my ass before doing it again hard enough to where I know there's going to be red marks. Fisting the sheets, I suck my lower lip between my teeth and try not to cry out—a lone tear escaping my eye as I press my forehead into the bed.

Jackson slides a hand up to grab onto my shoulder, pulling my body back against him with every snap of his hips. There's a sharp sensation deep inside that blooms into a feeling I've never known before. My lower body starts to cramp, an uncomfortable flush breaking out over my face.

Shifting positions, the angle makes it almost unbearable— whatever he's hitting doesn't feel good—as he leans over me and sinks his teeth into the flesh below my shoulder blade, biting down as he rides me.

That does make me cry out. And not from satisfaction.

Our bodies slam together–the only sounds in the room are his grunts and my whimpers.

It's a far cry from the other night when he held me gently as he rocked into me, making every single moment pleasurable—making me feel special and safe and taken care of.

Now he's like an animal rutting against me—teeth digging harder into me with each thrust, to the point where I'm sure he'll break the skin. Tears line my eyes, and I let them fall, though I'm silent.

I wanted this.

I *asked* for it.

This is how Jackson fucks women.

He doesn't care about them or their pleasure. He doesn't talk to them or make sure they come. He leaves bruises and marks and makes sure they'll never forget their night with him.

I've always thought this was what I wanted—all this pain. But now that I'm truly experiencing it, I don't know what I want. I'd rather have the other night over this.

Isn't there something in between?

A small orgasm hits me unexpectedly as Jackson wraps his arm around my waist and hauls me up against his back. It feels like sticking your toe in the water to see if it's warm enough, then deciding it's not worth fully submerging your body.

He slaps my clit before his hips shudder, and he comes with nothing more than a gruff grunt against my ear. When he's finished, he lets go of me, letting me fall back to the bed as he pulls out—discarding me quickly, just like every other woman he brings into his bed.

Without a word, he walks into the bathroom. There's no sound of running water. No bubble bath to soothe my sore skin.

Wiping the tears from my eyes, I gingerly reach around to try and feel the teeth marks under my shoulder, but it's at an angle I can't reach.

Slipping off the bed, I pull my clothes back on because I'm embarrassed and ashamed, and I want to leave.

It was a mistake to come here tonight.

By the time he comes back out, he looks ashamed as he watches me get dressed. "Where are you going?" he asks softly.

"Home. Thought you didn't let women stay the night?" I'm angry. Angry that he gave me exactly what I asked for. That he got me off exactly how I always imagined I'd like it best—only I didn't.

It was too rough.

My shoulder hurts where he bit me, and the skin on my ass stings with every move I make.

"Ginny—"

"We're done, Jackson."

Walking out of his bedroom, I hurry down the stairs as he yells out behind me. "Ginny, wait! We're not fucking done!"

Looking over my shoulder, I see him stepping into his joggers before coming down the stairs after me. My heart seizes in my chest before jumping into my throat. "Yeah. We are. There's nothing left to say. I can't trust you."

And now, every time I look at you, this will be all I remember.

Everything in me just wants to turn and break down in his arms. To try to fix what we've broken. What we've ruined before it even had a chance to start.

But my head is more stubborn than my heart and tells me to keep my chin high as I grab my purse and slip into my flats.

"That's it then? You're just going to believe the tabloids and fuck everything we've been working toward?" he shouts behind me, voice desperate.

The elevator doors ping and open. Stepping into them, I turn and shrug. "You already fuck everything else, so why not this, too?"

It's probably the worst thing I've ever said to anyone.

Jackson's face hardens as if I've physically hit him again.

And as the doors start to close, I swear it looks like his eyes are glazing over with unshed tears. It's almost enough to throw my hand out and catch the door.

"Ginny, don't do thi—"

They shut, cutting him off. Interrupting his hoarse plea as he begs me not to leave.

My eyes sting, but I will myself not to cry again. I'm done crying. I'm done playing by the rules of these men who think they can just do whatever they want with no consequences.

I'm just *done*.

Jackson

y the time I make it down to street level, Ginny's gone. My chest heaves with every breath, lungs burning from the unexpected cardio of running down the fire escape stairs, attempting to intercept her before she leaves the building. But even in my best shape, there's no way I would have been able to catch up to her.

It's raining when I push the doors to my building open and run out into the street, looking both ways for any flash of red hair or a wayward cab that might be taking her away from me.

There was never another way for tonight to end except badly. I knew it from the moment she messaged me asking to talk.

Crouching down, I grip my hair between my fingers and let out a string of curses into the dusky gray sky of the early morning.

Ginny deserved better than that—even if she wanted it— she had no idea what she was asking or getting herself into.

And me?

Fuck me for getting lost in the moment. For marking her the way I did. When it was all over and done, I saw—really *saw*—what I'd done to her...what I've done to multiple women before her, and never once has it bothered me the way it did tonight.

The angry red imprints of my teeth on her skin, the broken blood vessels, and the bruises that had already started to form where I gripped her skin so tightly.

Bile rises to my throat, and I empty the contents of my stomach into the street, watching as the rain washes it away into the gutter while Ginny's words replay in my mind.

"It's over."

No. It can't be over. It's barely just begun.

As much as I don't want to be in the office today, I stay and work on all the counteroffers that are piling up thanks to our lost deal with WhirlTech. It's monotonous–the work–and I barely pay attention because my mind is still stuck on what happened with Ginny this weekend.

I hadn't expected her to message me early Saturday morning asking to talk, but it seems my words as her stranger got through to her.

But what we did wasn't talking.

What *I* did was make another huge mistake.

I should have *never* let her get in my head. All I wanted to do was give her what she wanted. Show her that side of me that everyone else sees. Show her that the side of me she gets is exclusive—only for her.

"You okay in here?" Stacey's voice cuts across my office.

Checking the clock on my laptop, I see that it's already three in the afternoon. I haven't left my office since I arrived at seven this morning.

"Yeah, I'm fine." My eyes don't stray from the screen, but she comes further into the room and sits on the other side of my desk as she types something into her phone.

"I'm worried about you," she mutters.

"Nothing to be worried about," I reply. My fingers still over the keyboard as I speak, fighting the need to dump everything that's been going on to someone who knows nothing about the club so I can get an outsider's perspective.

If I were able to tell anyone, it'd be Stacey.

"I can see that isn't true. Why don't you tell me what's going on? Is Ginny still not answering you?" Crossing her legs, she sets her phone on my desk and sits back in her chair.

"She messaged me Saturday morning. We saw each other." I save the document I'm working on and exit out of it, shutting my laptop before leaning back in my chair.

"How did that go?"

"Fucking awful. She doesn't believe me about the photo. Asked me to fuck her like every other woman because she wanted to know what the appeal of them was."

Blunt and to the point.

"Please tell me you didn't." Stacey's eyes are wide and unbelieving as she asks.

Rubbing my temple, I send her a look that answers her without words. We're quiet for a while before she finally sighs and reaches for her phone again. While she's typing, I decide to come clean about everything.

"There's more."

She finishes whatever she's doing on her phone and sets it down again. "I had a hunch. Tell me everything."

So I do. I tell her every little thing—from meeting Ginny and my uncle telling me about the club to recognizing her there and creating a fake persona to book her. I leave out the dirty details about *what* exactly we did in those rooms, but I tell her enough that she gets the picture.

"Let me get this straight. You've been spending every weekend at a sex club that Scott owns? *And* you've been pretending to be someone you aren't to gain Ginny's trust while using everything she's told you in there as a way to get her to sleep with you as *Jackson*?"

"Scott owns a sex club? Why the fuck am I just now

hearing about this?" Tripp's voice startles me. I didn't even hear him open the door. But when I look up, he's already coming across the room to sit next to Stacey.

"How long have you been standing there?" I ask him while shooting Stacey a glare. She's not startled, so I have a feeling it was him she was messaging, telling him to help her figure out what's been going on with me all week.

"Long enough to hear...pretty much the entire story. That's fucked, dude. And you know I love you like a brother, but that is some seriously messed up shit. Also, again, I ask, why am I just now hearing about this super awesome sex club?"

"It's not a sex club," I hear myself tell him. "It's a sex-positive club."

Might as well get behind the concept if I'm going to have a hand in running the damn thing one day.

"What the fuck does that even mean?" Tripp asks, mirroring my own question when I first found out about it.

"It sounds like a place where you can go and be comfortable exploring the things you like. Honestly, why does this entire thing *not* surprise me? I've worked for you for too long," Stacey answers.

"You'd actually like it," I say to Tripp.

His ex-fiancée left him months ago because he has a specific preference in the bedroom for certain things, and she made him feel ashamed of it. Désirer would be a perfect place for Tripp to get to do the things he wants to do without fear of anyone judging him or even knowing it's *him* behind the mask.

"Uh, yeah. It sounds like I would. So, buddy, tell me why you've been keeping it a secret?"

"It was on my list of things to do. I had to okay it with Scott first."

"Like he would have said no! Disappointed in you, Jackson. For not inviting me to play and for tricking your little lady. You've been talking about how she's so different, so why are you lying to her about your identity at the club?"

"Not only that, Jackson, but what were you going to do when your relationship with her progressed? You can't keep it from her forever," Stacey supplies.

"I know! Don't you think I know all of that already?" Slamming my hand on the top of the desk, I feel slightly bad when it startles her, causing her to jump in her seat.

"Falling for her was the last thing I expected when this whole thing started. I thought I could get away with never telling her."

Both of them look at me with shock written on their faces. Tripp's mouth is opening and closing like a fish out of water, and if the topic weren't serious, I'd find it comical.

"I mean, I kinda figured you'd really fallen for her, but hearing you say it out loud is weird." Stacey is the first to recover.

Tell me about it.

"Yeah, well. I'm at a loss. I don't know what to do now. We didn't see each other at the club Saturday night—she called out. Am I just supposed to wait until Friday to comfort her at Désirer? That's days away. I don't know if I can wait that long."

"Have you tried contacting her since Saturday?" Stacey asks.

"No. You don't understand. When she asked me to do… what I did, I didn't hold back. When it was over, I was afraid I really hurt her, and she made it *very* clear she didn't want anything to do with me after that. She said we were done." Dropping my head to my hands, I press the heels into my eyes to stop the foreign emotions that have been pestering me lately from surfacing.

"She's probably just hurting. Or freaked out. The first time I did…that…with Emily…" Tripp trails off as a shudder wracks his body.

I remember how much of a mess he was when she

wouldn't call him. Just as bad as I'd been all week. However, instead of drowning my sorrows with my friend, I chose to stay at my apartment alone with P-Kitty and Claudia checking on me every so often.

"Maybe you should just apologize. Simple. To the point. Tell her you respect her decision to end things and leave it at that. Put the ball in her court. She cares about you, Jackson. She may just need some time," Stacey says.

"I don't even know what to say to her."

Tripp grabs my phone off the desk and hands it to Stacey. "She just told you what to say. But here, Tace, you do it. That way, he doesn't fuck it up any more than he already has."

Stacey takes the phone with no hesitation. "I hate it when you call me that, Tripp. Here, Jackson, I'll put what I think you should say in a note, and you can choose whether or not you want to send it to her later. Deal?"

She doesn't wait for an answer as she starts to type furiously, her fuchsia nails scurrying over the screen with well-practiced agility. It takes her less than a minute before she's handing it back to me to look over.

I know you don't want to talk to me, but I wanted to tell you how truly sorry I am for what happened this weekend. I respect your decision to end things. You won't have to worry about hearing from me again.

It's simple and to the point. I don't know how I feel about it. What if Ginny never responds? If I say she doesn't have to worry about hearing from me again, I should stick to that, right?

As if Stacey reads the questions on my face, she says, "See what her reaction is on Friday at the club."

"I thought we weren't condoning him lying to her? You know how I feel about liars," Tripp asks.

Another thing his ex left him with. After telling him for weeks that there was no one else and that she just didn't love him anymore, he found out that was a lie and that Emily had, in fact, been dating someone else on the side. What made it worse was that this guy was a complete jackass. His family came from money, and he rode his father's coattails without doing any *real* work.

It had crushed Tripp.

"I'm not condoning it," she says to him before turning to look at me. "I disapprove of you lying to her. You need to end things at the club or come clean. It will be so much worse if she decides to speak to you again and later finds out you lied."

Tripp's phone goes off, and he gets up after he checks it, pointing to me before heading to the door. "I gotta get back to my floor. Keep me in the loop, got it?"

"Yeah, I need to get going, too. Let me know if you decide to send the message, okay?" Stacey says.

"Yeah, I will." Watching them leave, I stare down at my phone for what seems like hours.

Finally, I copy and paste the words into the text thread with Ginny and hit send.

Then, I prepare to have my heart broken for the first time in my life.

Ginny

A week passes without Jackson.

When I left his place Saturday morning, I had meant what I said—it was over.

But this last week has been miserable without him.

I hadn't realized just how ingrained he'd become in my everyday existence. And now, all I seem to do is wonder what he's doing with his time.

Is he back to fucking every woman that catches his eye? Is he with that bitchy blonde bombshell—Viktoriya?

Is he as unhappy as I am?

All I've done besides work at the clinic and the restaurant is mope around in my apartment. Well, it's not *my* apartment. There's something about staying at The Bryant that no longer sits well with me if Jackson and I aren't in each other's lives anymore.

Looks like apartment hunting is on the agenda for this weekend.

First, however, is tonight with my stranger. I didn't show up on Saturday, and I'm wondering how he will take my request tonight.

I want to experience something in between both of the times Jackson fucked me. Something more than the soft and sweet, but less than the harsh biting and slapping so many times it took days for his handprint to leave my skin.

The teeth marks have healed, but there's still a bruise under my shoulder that is tender and days away from returning to the pale color of my skin. It serves as a reminder of everything Jackson wants, and I hate that it also makes me think of Chris.

Carmela told me it was okay not to wear my wings tonight since they sit right against that spot, and it's nice not to have the added weight of them at my back as I walk through the Grand Room to the Desires hall.

My outfit tonight is meant to be enticing. I'm more naked than clothed—black lace outlines my bare breasts and trails down my stomach in a single strap that's attached to a small triangle that barely covers my pussy.

There are still random bruises on my skin, but the low lighting will make it hard for my stranger to see them. I have a feeling that he would have his mind made up before I even asked the question if he saw them.

For the first time in a long time, he's not waiting for me when I enter the room. Sending my guard a questioning look through my mask, he just gives me a slight nod and says, "He's running late."

Late ends up being an understatement.

I'm two glasses of champagne in, and my skin buzzes with anger when he walks through the door almost twenty minutes after our arranged meeting time.

"Nice of you to show up." My tone is bitter as I speak, the fizzing bubbles of my drink spurring on my fire-laced words.

He snorts and goes straight to the drink cart in the corner of the room, pouring a hefty amount of alcohol into his tumbler. "I don't think you're in the position to be upset, Little Ember. After all, it was *you* who did not show up last weekend."

"Last weekend, I took your advice and let my boyfriend plead his case."

It doesn't escape either of us that I say *my boyfriend* or that it's said in present tense as if Jackson is *still* mine.

My stranger freezes, but only briefly before he lifts his mask enough to drink the liquid in his glass like a shot. "And how did that go?"

"It fucking sucked. I asked him to treat me like all the other women he normally goes after, and I ended up leaving with multiple bruises and a bite mark the size of Texas. He was brutal and unkind, and we broke up."

He turns around as I tell him what happened, his body tight with something I can't read as his eyes sweep down the length of me. My robe is long tonight, though, and the only skin he can see is a triangle of cream where the sides of it overlap on my chest.

"Are you okay?" he asks softly.

"I'm *angry*. And I'm tired of being angry. I just want to forget it ever happened." Crossing my arms, I look down at the floor, gathering the courage to ask him to fuck me. Steeling myself for him to reject me *again*, like he always does when I ask him to sleep with me.

When my eyes find his again, he's looking at me expectantly. Almost as if he knows what I'm about to ask, and he's conveying his reply with his eyes.

Go ahead and ask, but you already know the answer.

"I want you to show me that there is something *more* than being treated like glass, but decidedly less than what happened last weekend. I know you weren't there, and you don't know just how…horrible…it was, but I can speak up if it becomes too much." My fingers twist in the robe's sash, and even from across the room, I can hear him let out a sigh.

Before he can answer, I snap, "If you don't, then there isn't really a reason for this to continue, is there? We do nothing but talk, and that's *if* we both show up. More often than not, we're arguing about something. So, if you don't want to, then I'll terminate our contract and find someone else to do it."

"You most certainly will *not* let another man touch you in

this club, Scarlett." His answer is harsh as he starts to walk toward me. His hands circle my wrists, pulling my hands away from where they are tangled up in the sash, and by doing so, my robe falls open to reveal my nearly naked flesh.

He sucks air through his teeth as his eyes travel down my body. My nipples harden as they are exposed to the air, and I can hear him groan softly as his fingers tighten around my wrists.

"Do not let your boyfriend turn you into someone you aren't. You are not the type of woman to let just any man touch her. To let just any man between her legs. That isn't *you*. And I will not be coerced to fuck you out of anger at the thought of another man's hands on you. That isn't *us*." His voice is low and restrained, and I glance down to see his erection straining against his pants.

Licking my lips, I lift my gaze to his again to find his eyes glued to my naked breasts. "He said the same thing. That what I asked for wasn't *us*. He told me I was different and that he was falling for me. But I don't know how he can say that after being in his car with another woman."

I don't even care that my words are in danger of revealing my identity. If my stranger reads the papers, then the coincidence of what I say aligning with Jackson's fuck up is too great to ignore.

"I think you're running from him, Little Ember, because you are scared. I think that he is showing you something very real, and you are frightened because you've never felt safe before. But you do with him, and he let you down. So now, you feel lost again. But this is what a relationship is, Scarlett. It is letting your walls down and knowing that you are giving the other person the power to hurt you." He pulls me into him, bringing my hands up to rest on his chest, before sliding his down to pull my robe back around me before retying the sash.

"I can't trust him," I whisper. My hips lean into his, trapping his hard cock between us. "Please, just give me what I want."

The way he sighs over my head tells me he isn't going to change his mind. But I'm not prepared when he spins me so that my back is to him, and his hand dives into the top of my robe to palm my breast. His thumb flicks my hardened nipple as his other hand holds my hip, anchoring my body to his.

"Do not move," he instructs before pulling his hands away.

I do as he says, my eyes widening in shock when I feel the touch of his lips against the nape of my neck. Air leaves my throat with a gasp, and I begin to tilt my head up to see his face, but his hand is suddenly cradling my jaw, holding it tightly enough so I can't move.

His other hand finds its way between the slit in my robe, and his fingers brush against my center as he murmurs in my ear, "It has been too long since I've touched you. But I will not fuck you. Not with my cock."

Arousal pools low in my belly, making his fingers slick as he continues to stroke me before pushing two inside my aching pussy. "If you want a cock to fill you, instead of my fingers, then I suggest you go back to your boyfriend and try again."

My hips rock into his fingers, his hand tightening on my jaw as I try to get free so that I can see his face. His teeth graze my earlobe before sucking the spot just beneath, causing a wave of wetness to rush from me.

"And what if I do just find some random man to give me what I want?" I tease. There's no truth behind my words because he and Jackson are both right. Now that I know what it's like to be touched by them, I don't think anyone else can even compare.

I'll break down my stranger's resolve if it's the last thing I do.

A third finger joins the other two inside me, pushing in as his thumb brushes my clit. "You won't," he whispers against my skin. "You can take all the time you want to think about it, but you know that there will only ever be he and I that get to touch you this way."

"Why are you so certain that I will go back to him? He told me he respected my decision to end things. He's probably already had multiple women in his bed since last week." The thought chases away my nearing climax like the light of the sun does the moon every morning.

My stranger picks up the pace, pumping his fingers quicker and deeper than before. "Because I know how to read you, Little Ember. You haven't given up on him. Deep down, you know he didn't betray you. You just need to admit it out loud."

His thumb presses against my clit, and I cry out as my release tears through me. My stranger's words of encouragement are whispers in my ear as I ride it out.

I never question why he's pushing so hard for me to go back to Jackson. Why he's pushing me into the arms of another man and continuing to refuse my requests to sleep with me.

All I know is when I'm with him, strangely, everything he says makes perfect sense.

Jackson

I'm not sure Ginny would have reached out had it not been for her stranger telling her to.

But now, as I stare at her message on my phone, I don't feel even the slightest bit bad about manipulating her to try again with me.

> I'll be looking for apartments this weekend.

At this point, she knows I don't own the apartment she's residing in. There's no reason to reach out and inform me of anything unless she truly wants to speak to me.

I leave the message on read—literally; I go into my settings and switch the read receipts on so that she knows I viewed it—choosing not to reply until after my morning workout two hours later. It's not meant to be a punishment or to make her wonder what exactly it is I'm doing this dreary Saturday morning. No, it's only because I'm not entirely sure how to respond, but I want her to know I saw it.

Ginny disregarded my text about respecting her decision. Though she mentioned it to her stranger, she never responded to me.

It makes me weary.

Should I push my luck and try and see if she'll talk to me? Is this a cry for me to take the reins and force myself into her space? Or am I reading too much into it, and she really just wants me to know she doesn't want to stay in the apartment anymore?

I've never been this tripped up over a woman before. I hate it—the second-guessing and the need to tiptoe around responses and decisions.

The fact that she lets her stranger get her off, but I get hung out to dry over a stupid mistake where literally nothing happened.

It's a double standard I find myself begrudgingly, but willingly, allowing.

But only because I *am* the stranger who gets to sink his fingers into her and feel her warm walls clench as I bring her to orgasm. The memory of last night charges to the forefront of my mind, and my cock swells as I remember all the little sounds she made as she came.

Palming it, I adjust myself before replying to her message. To hell with it. I'll take my chances that she wants to make up. I'd rather sink my cock into her than reacquaint it with my hand.

You don't have to move out.

Her reply is almost immediate.

Honestly, I don't want to. But it's weird…
being here…without you.

A smile finds its way to my lips. She misses me. And yes, she may not have said anything without prodding from her stranger. But none of that matters.

This is her telling me she wants to try.

Would you like me to come over?

The three little dots appear and vanish multiple times before she sends a simple *yes* as a response, and I'm out the door and on my way within the next three minutes.

I'm respectful of her personal space when she lets me into her apartment. My hands stay tucked in the pockets of my jacket, and I give her a wide berth as I make my way across the living room to take a seat at the end of the blue leather futon she and Lenni found at a flea market.

I begged her to let me buy whatever furniture she wanted, but she said she likes the charm and appeal of eclectic things, as the apartment now clearly shows. There's a cowhide rug beneath my feet and bright orange abstract paintings hanging on the wall on a set of three canvases.

It's very Ginny.

"How are you?" I ask as she leans against the kitchen island. She's wearing a pair of black leggings and an over-sized white shirt that's falling off one shoulder. Her hair is piled on top of her head, and she's fresh-faced, not a stitch of makeup anywhere.

Beautiful.

"I'm okay, I guess. Would you like anything to drink?"

Unless it's coming from between your thighs, I'm not interested.

"No, I'm alright. Thank you."

She nods slightly before pulling the corner of her bottom lip between her teeth. When she releases it, it's slightly wet and plump and pinker than normal, and I want to suck it into my mouth.

"You don't have to be uncomfortable around me, Ginny. I'm not going to hurt you." Leaning forward, I balance my elbows on my knees as I look at her.

She breaks our gaze to stare at the floor. "You did, though."

Her words feel like someone sucker punched me in the gut. But I'm proud of her for telling me. "I'm so sorry for last weekend. I should have never—"

"I asked for it. It wasn't entirely your fault," she cuts me off with a shrug.

Pushing up from the couch, I cross the room, deciding now is the time to invade her space. I reach out to grip her chin, gently lifting her head so that she's looking up at me. "It was *all* my fault. I should have never been that rough with you."

Tears line her eyes. "I really thought I wanted it. I should have told you to stop."

My heart feels like a block of ice is crushing it as the tears she's trying desperately to blink away fall down her cheeks. "And I should have never let it go that far. I'm sorry for hurting you. I went after you the second you left, but I couldn't get down the stairs in time."

Her cornflower blues widen, and her breath hitches. "You took the stairs to try and catch me? From your *penthouse*?"

"Trust me, Red. If I thought I'd have a chance at surviving it, I would have jumped from the balcony if it meant catching you before you could leave."

A short laugh leaves her lips before it turns into a sob as she wraps her arms around me, squeezing tight. "Why are we so fucked up?"

"It isn't you. I'm not...good with this. With intimacy. With *wanting* to put someone else before me. I'm not perfect, Ginny. You just need to decide if it's worth dealing with all my fuck ups as I try to figure it out." I wrap one arm around her waist and the other around her upper back to tangle my fingers in her hair as I hold her to me.

Her body fits against mine like a thousand-piece puzzle I've only ever found the edges to, and now, suddenly, the middle pieces are starting to connect.

We stand there for numerous seconds, just holding each other, before she finally pulls back and wipes at her face. "It's worth it. I'm sorry I didn't believe you about the woman in the car."

"*Do* you believe me?"

She nods as she looks up at me. "I do. We'd already slept together. If you wanted to go back to your old ways, you could have. You didn't need to come here and explain yourself. You didn't need to keep sending flowers or trying to see me. I'm sorry I overreacted."

Pressing up on her tiptoes, she reaches around my neck and pulls me down for a kiss. Her lips are soft against mine, surety in their motion as they open to allow my tongue entrance. Our kiss is unhurried, and when we part, she pulls me over to the futon.

"Can I ask you a question?" She settles against the arm, feet stretched out in front of her as she places them in my lap.

"You can ask me anything." Our position reminds me of the club, and I wonder if she's done it subconsciously or if it reminds her, too. Just like at Désirer, my hands find her calves as I watch her internally debate how to ask.

"Why do you like to be so aggressive?" Her tone is quiet, and she looks down at her hands in her lap as she asks.

No one has ever asked me that before, but the answer to that particular question is clear.

"It has a lot to do with my childhood, I think. I went to boarding school with a bunch of kids who were just as rich as me, so they weren't scared of my last name. Growing up, I was a runt. I didn't hit puberty until I was seventeen, so I got picked on a lot." I stare at one of the abstract paintings as I recall things I'd rather never remember.

My fingers start to trace absentminded patterns on her shins as I continue. "The other boys at school used to say that my father killed himself because I was too small and too weak to bear the Tailor name. They used to tie me to the flagpole and leave me there for hours, nearly naked in the cold. I'd pass the time by thinking of all the ways I'd get back at them. It harbored a lot of rage and pent-up frustration.

"When my balls finally dropped, I became popular with the girls. Years of jerking off to images I'm not proud of had ensured I wouldn't blow my load the second my dick was touched, and those girls were already experienced. All that pent-up anger just manifested itself sexually. The girls liked it. I wasn't *as* rough back then, but the older I got, the rougher I became. It was like I couldn't get off any other way."

"You came with me when we first slept together. You were gentle with me," Ginny muses.

"Because it's *you*, Red." Turning my head to look at her, I try to convey my feelings with my eyes. That everything about *her* has turned my world upside down, and everything I wanted before means nothing now.

"I'm really sorry that all happened to you, Jackson." A small smile plays on her lips before evolving into a bigger one. "What were the images you jerked off to?"

"Nope. Not admitting that." Shaking my head, I look away, knowing damn well that if she keeps asking, I'll tell her.

"Oh, come on! I wanna know. I won't tell anyone, I swear." She makes a zipping motion with her hand across her lips when I look back at her, and I can feel the blood rushing to my cheeks in preparation for utter embarrassment.

Sighing, I scrub at my face with both hands before looking away from her, choosing to stare out the window as I admit one of my most disturbing secrets. "My aunt's modeling photos."

Ginny snorts, and as I whip my head around to glare at her, her hands fly to cover her nose and mouth. "You jerked off to photos of your aunt?!"

"Hey, I was eleven when she married my uncle, okay? She's hot and was my first crush."

"I get it. She is hot. If she didn't terrify the absolute shit out of me, I'd probably have a crush on her, too."

"When have you met my aunt?" Curiosity spikes at her

comment as I recall my aunt's text message when she found out that I wanted the apartment for Ginny.

"Last year at Decadence. She was there to question Carmela about Scott. Just her mere presence was intimidating. She called me Scarlett since that's what my name tag reads, and then Carmela called me Ginny, and if looks could kill, I swear hers would have murdered me on the spot."

"Hmm." An errant thought skitters across my brain, linking Ginny and my uncle again.

I'm vaguely aware of her shifting, but I don't realize how close she is until she speaks softly into my ear. "Does looking at photos turn you on?"

She climbs into my lap, straddling me as her hands find my shoulders. "Should I book a photoshoot?"

My hands grip her hips as I push mine up into her, my dick already hard and straining to be in her. "Only if you want to be responsible for murder. I'll kill any man who tries to take naked photos of you."

Kissing her neck, I pull her hair from its tie, inhaling her sugary lemon scent as it falls around us. She rocks her hips and throws her head back, reaching down to lift her shirt over her head to reveal a black lace bralette underneath.

I pull the cups down, palming one breast while taking the other in my mouth and gently sucking as her hands tangle in my hair. "Who said they were gonna be naked photos?" she whispers.

"Anyone who tries to take photos of you of any kind better be female, or I'll rip their eyes from their head," I tell her before reaching up to cup her neck and pull her down for a kiss.

I stand, and she tightens her legs around me as I walk her to the bedroom, both of us clearly in the mood for much-needed make-up sex. After I lay her down on the bed, I peel off my jacket and rip my shirt over my head while she pushes my pants and boxer briefs down.

My cock springs up between us, and her eyes darken

while she licks her lips. Ginny reaches out and grips it, running her tongue along the underside of it before gently kissing the tip as she looks up at me through her lashes.

"Does that feel good?" she asks before taking me as far as she can down her throat. My hands itch to grip her hair and hold her down on me, but I fight the urge, instead, gently cupping her cheek as I pull out of her mouth slowly.

With my thumb, I trace her lower lip, glistening with her saliva. "Everything you do feels good."

Pulling her bralette off, I guide her to lie back, removing her leggings to find that she's bare underneath. She widens her legs as I skim my hands down her inner thighs and lower to my knees. One long lick up her center has her crying out, hands fisting in my hair as I shift her legs over my shoulders and suction my mouth around her clit.

I watch her face as I swipe the tip of my tongue up and down and side to side against her sensitive bundle of nerves, paying attention to her facial expressions and storing them away for later use.

She likes when I flick my tongue against her rapidly, but not when I fuck her with it. The left side of her clit is more sensitive than the right, and when I suck while fucking her with two fingers, she lets out these little sighs that are like music to my ears.

Her hands grip my neck and shoulders as she tries to pull me back up her body. "I want you inside me."

The second the words leave her lips, I realize I didn't bring any condoms. "We don't have protection."

Her cheeks glow pink as she wiggles beneath me, reaching over her head for the drawer on her nightstand. She opens it and pulls out a golden Trojan package. "I might have assumed we'd be doing this a lot here."

Smiling, I sit on my knees as she hands it over and waits for me to put it on. "I don't think I can handle how rough it was last time…do you think you can be a little more gentle? But maybe…not as much as the first time?"

Guiding myself to her entrance, I brace my weight on my forearm and brush her hair out of her eyes. "I'll be whatever you need me to be, baby. Just communicate with me, alright?"

I don't give her a chance to answer before I push in, groaning as she stretches around me, warm and tight and so fucking *mine*. Her head bends back toward the ceiling as her mouth opens in a silent cry. Angling my hips so that I'm hitting deep inside her as I thrust, I fist the sheets so I don't grip her skin too tightly.

"Fuck, Jackson! Right there! Oh my god, right there. Don't stop," she keens, legs wrapping around me to brace her feet on my glutes.

My teeth clench as she squeezes her walls around me purposefully. Her hands guide my face to hers, and she pulls my head down to capture my lips in a kiss.

"Is this okay?" I ask her when we part.

"You can go harder," she answers.

"Do you want to be on top? You can set the pace better." I slow my thrusts as she nods, the deep pink flush of her cheeks extending down her neck.

I roll us over, anchoring her to me so that I stay nestled deep inside her as we switch positions. She lets out a sharp, "Oh!" when she's seated on me and shamelessly starts to rock her hips back and forth.

Electric tingles spread from my lower spine down to my toes at the vision she makes. She grabs my hands, sliding them up her body to palm her breasts, holding them there as she lifts and grinds against me.

"I want you to watch."

My eyes immediately find the place where my cock keeps disappearing inside her wet pussy, and she slows her movements, dragging her hips in long strokes before lifting and engulfing my length again. There are white streaks of her arousal coating the thin condom, my cock bulging against it as if trying to break free.

"Do you like it when I watch you take your pleasure?" My

voice is low and husky as I ask, nearly ready to come as I continue watching her fuck me. She's bouncing on my cock, riding me faster and harder as she watches me watch the space between our legs.

"I love knowing it's *me* making you look like *that*," she says.

My eyes find hers. "Like what?"

"Like I'm the only thing in this world that you covet, and you'd burn it down for me." Her thrusts become erratic, and she bites her lip.

"I *would* burn the world for you, Ginny. Say the word, and I'll turn it all to ashes so you can recreate it into whatever you want." Our eyes connect—unshed tears springing to hers, utter devotion in mine.

"Are you close, baby? Do you want to come?" My hips rise to meet hers, holding her up as I reverse plank and drive so far into her that she cries out in pleasure.

Nodding furiously, her voice is hoarse as she replies, "Yes. I'm so close. I want you to come with me."

Her hands squeeze mine tighter into her as she grinds against me, head thrown back, making little whimpering noises with her eyes clenched shut. My balls tense, and I pinch her nipple lightly. "Watch me while you come, Ginny. I want to see your face when you coat my cock."

My words tip her over the edge, and she cries, "I'm coming! Fuck, Jackson, I'm coming!"

"That's right, baby. Come all over my cock." My dick twitches as I come with her, wishing that there wasn't a barrier between us. Wishing that I could fill her so full of my cum that it'll leak out of her for a week.

An image flashes through my mind of her on top of me with a swollen belly, and I swear it makes me come again, letting out a low moan through my clenched teeth as I empty into her.

When she starts to slow, I pull her down to my chest and

kiss her slowly. Our hips continue to move together, little waves of heat cresting one after the other.

"Eventually, I'll be able to fuck you exactly the way you want without you having to tell me. Until then, I'm going to have fun getting to know every moan, every flex of your fingers, every gasp that leaves your throat. I'll explore every inch of your body until I have my own personal atlas," I whisper when I release her lips from our kiss.

"Do you promise?"

"I promise."

$$Ginny$$

"Holy shit! I'm so glad you guys made up," Lenni exclaims as she sorts through gowns on a rack in the middle of my living room.

Looking through a different assortment, I raise my eyebrow and glance at her. "You said you would hate him until the day you die."

She shrugs. "If you forgive him, I forgive him. I can't believe he sent all of these over for you to choose from for tonight. Is this one of those situations where the dress will have a bodyguard, and it has to be home by midnight?"

A long satin number catches my eye, and I place it with the other dresses I want to try on. "No, that's the jewels."

At her incredulous look, I laugh and shake my head. "I'm kidding."

She pulls a long gold sequined gown from her rack and asks, "So, how *are* things with Jackson?"

A smile pulls at my lips, and I know that if I were to look in a mirror, I'd see a dopey, dreamy expression on my face. "Really good, actually. Really, *really* good."

The last week with Jackson has been a dream. Part of me feels slightly bad about canceling this weekend at the club, but my stranger *was* pushing me to make up with Jackson. Hopefully, he understands.

I think back to when Jackson asked me to go with him to this event. It was Wednesday night, and we were eating pizza and drinking wine in his game room with P-Kitty curled up between us.

"I know that we're working on getting back to a good place, but I'd really like it if you came to this party with me on Friday night."

I wonder if this is the party that Viktoriya was asking if he'd be at. As if he reads my thoughts, he explains, "It's Tripp's mother's birthday. He's my best friend, so I have to attend. We don't have to stay long if you don't want to."

"Of course, I'll go with you. Why would you think I wouldn't want to?"

"There's going to be a lot of paparazzi. There will probably be questions about the incident." He shrugs slightly as he speaks, stroking the patchy fur on P-Kitty's tail.

"I can handle it." Scooting across the couch, I nestle into his side and place a kiss on his cheek. "Thank you for inviting me."

"Well, good. I'm glad you're happy. Speaking of happy—this dress makes me unbelievably giddy," Lenni's voice pulls me from my thoughts. She's admiring a red mermaid-style gown with see-through tulle and glittery lace flower appliques.

"It's yours," Jackson's tenor drifts across the living room, and Lenni and I snap our heads in his direction.

Warmth fills my body like a warm picnic day as he crosses the space to place a chaste kiss on my lips. "Hi."

"Hi," is all I can manage as my insides turn to goo.

"What do you mean, it's *mine*? Are you serious?" she asks him, mouth gaping and eyes wide.

He chuckles and wraps an arm around me, thumbing through the dresses I've set aside to try. "Sure, why not? I'd invite you to come tonight, but the Kennedys are selective about who attends their parties, and I think it's too late to run a background check on you."

Lenni freezes momentarily, her eyes going blank as she goes somewhere else in her mind. I make a mental note to ask her what that's about later. After a few seconds, she blinks and shrugs.

"I'm fine with wearing this beauty around my house, watching *Pretty Woman*, and pretending that I, too, will one day find a billionaire boyfriend who will whisk me away from the dull life I lead." Her tone is whimsical as she whirls away in the direction of my bathroom with a hand held to her forehead like she's a damsel in distress.

When she disappears around the corner, Jackson whispers into my ear, "Is she always so theatrical?"

Laughing, I turn toward the dresses. "Always. Now, help me pick one of these out. I can't believe you had them all sent over. It's a little overkill, don't you think?"

He shakes his head, plucking a deep navy satin gown from the choices. It has off-the-shoulder sleeves and a form-fitting bodice. The material looks like it hugs the body until the knees, where it flares out, but not so tight that it will restrict my movement. "This one. I have a suit to match."

"Matching colors now, are we? Is there anything more official than that?" I tease and take the dress from him.

His eyes darken as he places a hand around my waist, drawing me into him. "I can think of something that ends with you wearing a glittering piece of jewelry on a very specific finger."

I'm sorry, what?

My breath hitches as he kisses me. That was…random. Did he just make a comment about putting a ring on my finger? Or did I imagine it?

I don't get the chance to say what's on my mind because Lenni waltzes back into the room with a flourish. "I've simply died and gone to heaven. I'm going to live in this dress now."

"I'll see you in a little bit. I'm going to get some work done at the office." Jackson pulls away and heads for the door, not even gracing Lenni with a look as he passes her.

"Thanks, bossman!" she yells at his back.

He raises his hand as he disappears through the open door that is propped open with another gown rack. Multiple others litter the hallway, and I pick up the phone to call the front desk to have them all sent back to wherever they came from.

"I think Jackson just made a comment about marrying me," I say in a daze once I've ended the call.

"Uh, that's a little fast. You guys just got back together." Lenni sits on the futon and dramatically drapes her legs over the side.

"I know..."

But, if I'm being honest with myself. I don't exactly *hate* the idea.

The party is at an event space close to Carnegie Hall. When Robert pulls up to the curb, anxiety races up my arms and down into my chest like a lightning strike. There are paparazzi everywhere, lights flashing from their cameras as guests enter the building. People are shouting and waving, trying to get the attention of whoever is ascending the stairs.

"What is this event for again?" I ask Jackson as I stare out the window, trying to ready myself for the inevitable frenzy that will happen as soon as the car door opens.

"Margo's birthday," Jackson says, voice dripping with amusement.

"Rich people are insane." My words are said under my breath, but Jackson chuckles anyway, reaching over to slide my hair over my shoulder so that he can lay a kiss on it.

"The Kennedys are good people. You'll like Margo."

"I didn't say rich people were *bad*, just insane."

He's quiet as I continue to watch the other guests walk in —women draped in lavish gowns and diamonds, the men in expensive-looking suits with feline grins that scream *up to no good.*

"If you'd like Robert to take you home, he can. I need to make an appearance, at least. But I can be in and out within an hour," Jackson offers softly.

My head swivels in his direction. He's watching me with a guarded expression, which makes my brow furrow. "Absolutely not. I told you I would come, so I'm going in. Just nervous, that's all. It's a lot to get used to."

"My uncle is already inside, so at least that's one other person you'll know." He presses the intercom button and says, "We're ready."

"Don't forget Viktoriya," I say, like I just took a bite of something nasty.

"You'd put her to shame if you were wearing a paper bag, Red. Don't worry about her."

"Don't lie to me," I say anxiously as Robert opens my door slightly, letting me decide when I'm ready to get out of the car.

"Here, let me out first." Jackson lifts me like I weigh nothing, pressing another kiss to my shoulder as he sits me on the other side of him. Before I can say a word, the door is open, and all the bright flashing lights point in our direction.

Jackson gives them his signature *I don't give a fuck* look as he buttons his jacket before turning to hold out a hand. Gracing me with a smile, he asks, "Ready?"

It's overwhelming, the way people shout questions and the blinding camera lights as we walk up the stairs. Jackson ignores them, so I try to as well, but it's hard when the questions are so invasive.

"Did you forgive him because he's rich, honey?"

"How does it feel to be the flavor of the week?"

"Jackson, Viktoriya Lukin is already inside. Any chance of reconciliation?"

"Ignore them," he whispers. His fingers stroke my side where his hand rests as we walk.

"It's a little hard," I grit out. Their questions are pissing me off, and instead of feeling anxious about going inside, I now feel like I have something to prove.

I'm worthy of being on Jackson's arm, even though I'm a nobody. Fuck anyone who thinks otherwise.

Turning my head, I smile at him and say, "Kiss me."

"You don't have to tell me twice," he responds before ducking to press his lips to mine. The paparazzi go crazy, and we smile at each other as we part.

Take that, assholes.

I'd never believe the party was a simple birthday if Jackson hadn't already told me. There has to be close to two hundred people scattered throughout the large room. Tables are placed randomly on the outskirts of the crowd, with champagne tablecloths and tall glass vases of large, plumed branches in the middle of them. Hundreds of black and champagne-colored balloons float along the ceiling, their streamers stopping just above people's heads.

There's a dance floor and a DJ booth, and doors open along one wall leading to an ivy-covered terrace. The lighting is low and intimate, setting off a romantic glow in the room. In the far corner, there's a giant backdrop of hanging lights behind a champagne glass tower.

"Wow," I murmur, taking it all in.

"Right? Like, okay, Mom, the people get it. No champagne problems for you at fifty-five." A voice comes from my right.

Jumping slightly, I look over to see a man smiling at me as he hands me a glass filled with bubbly pink liquid. He's about an inch shorter than Jackson, with deep-brown hair that looks freshly cut on the sides but wavy on top, and hazel eyes that make me think of moss-covered bark.

"I don't know, I think this is understated for Margo," Jackson responds as the man hands him a glass filled with scotch by the smell of it. "Tripp, this is Ginny. Ginny, Tripp Kennedy, my best friend."

Tripp sticks his hand out for a handshake. "I promise I'm a

lot nicer than Jackson. I'm not as rich, not as good-looking, and I absolutely hate being in the tabloids. But I make a mean cup of coffee in the morning, and I don't snore."

I like him immediately, giggling as he waggles his eyebrows at Jackson before letting go of my hand. "Seriously, though. It's nice to meet you. I've heard a lot about you."

"Nice to meet you too," I respond, stealing a glance at Jackson.

"I gotta warn you, my mother is going to ask you to lunch. Make an excuse not to go–it's an interrogation, and she can be terrifying, but that's her M.O. She wants to see if you crack under pressure. It's her thing," Tripp tells me.

"Stop trying to scare her. She's not going anywhere," Jackson says as he reaches for my hand and intertwines our fingers. "Come on. I'll introduce you."

"Don't feed her to the wolves!" Tripp calls out behind us, but his tone is light and playful, and I can hear the smile in his voice.

"He's fun. Lenni would like him," I muse as we make our way through the crowd.

"Dear god, if those two ever meet, they'll be annoying as shit together," he replies.

Jackson takes the time to stop and introduce me to random people who call out his name. He's polite, but not overly so, with the women. He makes it very clear that I'm his date, and he's not interested in the sultry looks they throw his way.

There's a blend of older people and ones our age, or his age anyway. All of which watch us together with thinly veiled intrigue. Finally, we make it to the other side of the room to see Scott talking with who I assume is Tripp's parents.

"Margo, looking beautiful as always. Happy birthday," Jackson says as he steps forward and places a chaste kiss on her cheek. She's thin, with her blonde hair pulled back in a fancy chignon and a black gown that looks like a cupcake.

"Thank you, Jackson. I was just telling Scott here that you

won yourself a beauty. You are stunning, dear." She comes at me like she's going to hug me but ends up leaning in to air kiss my cheek. "I'm Margo, and this is my husband, Weylan."

"Thank you. I'm Ginny. It's nice to meet you. Happy birthday." My eyes flit from her to her husband, who is talking to Scott. Scott's eyes are lit up with delight as he smiles at me, seemingly ignoring Weylan.

"Good to see you, Ginny," he says, raising his glass to me.

Weylan looks at me, his hand shooting out to shake mine. "Nice to meet you. So you're Jackson's new girl. Tell me, how on earth do you put up with this bastard?"

"Weylan! Language!" Margo scolds before her attention is caught by someone else, and she excuses herself.

Shrugging, I look up at Jackson. "Well, he's house-trained, and I like walks in the park, so really, he's well-behaved."

The guys all laugh, and Jackson's hazelnut orbs sparkle as he gazes down at me and murmurs, "You'll pay for that later, Red."

Weylan excuses himself as Margo calls for him from across the room, and Jackson's eyes snap over my shoulder, his warm smile turning ice cold in an instant.

I'm about to ask him what's wrong when I hear Viktoriya's voice ring out, "Jackson! I was beginning to think you weren't coming."

"Dear lord, not her again," Scott says into his glass.

Jackson straightens, and I turn to see her gliding toward us, eyes focused solely on him, just like that day at Citarella. Her hair is down in luxurious waves, and her strapless black dress looks like it was made just for her.

She reaches out to embrace Jackson, and without thinking, I step between them. Looking up at her, I paste my best *fuck off* grin on my face and say, "Hi. I'm Ginny, Jackson's *girlfriend.*"

Viktoriya doesn't even look phased as she stops to appraise me. "Viktoriya Lukin. Jackson and I go way back."

Her tone is smug, and when she looks over my head to

flash him her mouthful of pearly whites, I feel the stinging, cold shock of hatred deep down in my chest. "Save me a dance, love," she tells him before walking away.

Bristling, I turn, noticing that Scott has disappeared and Jackson is standing there just watching me with a pleased look. "I hate her."

"I think you handled yourself pretty well," he says as he steps into me, circling his arms around my waist. His body heat melts the chill away. "Does this mean *I* get to introduce you as my girlfriend?"

"Damn right, it does."

An hour passes by quickly. Jackson hasn't left my side all night, introducing me to more people before running into Tripp, where I get a few minutes of reprieve. Tripp is easygoing, and I don't feel like I have to prove anything to him.

Everyone else here is another story. Especially when Viktoriya keeps shooting Jackson longing glances from across the room. He doesn't seem to pick up on them.

Though, me and everyone else at the party do.

Jackson is immersed in a conversation with Tripp about what I'm fairly certain is a video game when I feel a tap on my shoulder.

Turning, I see Scott standing there, hand outstretched. "Come dance with me."

George Benson's "Nothing's Gonna Change My Love for You" starts to play as he smiles at me, and I return it as I put my hand in his. "I'll be back in a minute," I say over my shoulder to Jackson.

He doesn't know the extent of my friendship with his uncle, and I know it's something I'm going to have to tell him at some point. I'm surprised Scott is even asking me to dance, but this *is* his and Sadie's wedding song, and it's his favorite.

"How are you doing? How is everything going with you two?" Scott asks as he twirls me into his arms.

"Good. I feel like we're in a good place." Looking over his shoulder, I lock eyes with my man as he manages to hold his conversation while watching me.

"Have you told him? That you work at the club?" Scott's question isn't threatening but genuinely curious. However, it pulls my attention from Jackson to him.

Shaking my head, I stare at the buttons on his tuxedo jacket. "No, we haven't discussed *that* yet."

When he doesn't respond, I look up at him through my lashes. "Are you mad?"

"No, I'm not mad, Ginny. I just don't want to see either of you get hurt."

"I understand. That's fair."

Silence fills the space between us. I catch Jackson's eye again as he watches us from where he's moved to the edge of the dance floor, something warm and gentle in his gaze. "Have *you* told him?"

I already know the answer to my question before Scott sighs and says, "No."

I'm about to ask him not to tell Jackson I know anything, when I see Viktoriya approach my newly titled boyfriend. "Jesus Christ, does that woman ever give up?"

Scott turns his head to see what I'm looking at and grimaces. "She's a gold-digger, that one. She was only after the money. She didn't give a damn about Jackson."

"Why did he date her for so long?"

"I honestly think he tried to see beyond her bullshit. But who knows? He can't stand her–you have nothing to worry about. Come on, let's go save him." Scott ends our dance, placing his hand lightly on my back to guide me across the dance floor toward them.

Viktoriya's icy blue eyes are glued to the side of Jackson's face while she talks. But he only has eyes for me, and it fills me with delight when he reaches out a hand to pull me into his side.

"I'm gonna call it a night. Jackson, I'll see you in the office Monday. Ginny, thank you for the dance," Scott says, completely ignoring Viktoriya.

"So, what do you do, Ginny?" she asks me as he walks away.

"I work at a women's clinic. I'm a counselor," I answer, looking around for one of the waitstaff walking around with trays of champagne.

"Oh, what a dreadful job. So heavy. I could never. I'd be miserable all the time!" she exclaims.

"Imagine what the women who need my services feel like," I bite out.

Nasty bitch.

Jackson flags down a server and grabs a drink, passing it to me before kissing my temple. "Ginny's amazing at her job. One day, she'll own her own clinic."

It's an unspoken promise. A dream of mine that I told him during our pillow talk over the last week. A dream that he offered to fully fund if I wanted.

How do you say no to something like that?

Except, I don't want Jackson's money. And he needs to know that.

I just want him.

"Well, it sounds like you two just have your future all planned out, don't you?" Viktoriya asks flatly.

"Ginny!" a thick mid-western accent calls out.

Turning, I see a spindly brunette woman who works with Chris coming toward us through the crowd, causing my blood to freeze in my veins. "Barbara, hi. What are you doing here?"

"Oh, I'm old friends with Margo. Just popped in on my way to the airport. I'm heading out to join Christopher! I'll have to tell him I saw you. How do you know the

Kennedys?" She looks between me, Jackson, and Viktoriya—who is watching our interaction—curiously.

Jackson holds his hand out for a handshake. "I'm Jackson Tailor, Ginny's boyfriend. Tripp is an old friend of mine."

Barbara looks confused as she slowly shakes his hand. "Boyfriend? I thought you and Chris…"

"NO!" I shout so loudly she jumps. People around us turn to look, and I can feel Jackson at my back as tears threaten to prick my eyes.

"Chris is my *foster brother*," I stress.

"Okay," she says slowly. "Well, I'm sorry. I didn't know that. He always made it seem…you know what, never mind. It was good to see you. I really need to get going so I don't miss my flight. Nice to meet you, Jackson."

Barbara leaves, making her way through the crowd as I turn to see Viktoriya smirking at me with a raised eyebrow. My eyes are glassy, but I refuse to let the tears fall as I flee, heading for the terrace.

"Ginny!" I hear Jackson call out behind me, but I don't stop until I'm outside.

He follows me, closing the doors before pulling me to him. "Ginny, it's okay. You're okay."

"What if she tells him?"

When Jackson lets me go, I walk down the length of the building, where there's a slight corner that leads to a tight alcove. The ivy that wraps around the railing climbs up the wall and over the roof, and I let out a deep breath as I lean against the rail.

"It doesn't matter if she tells him. You don't ever have to worry about him again. Okay? I'll protect you, Red."

"It isn't just *him*. It's that stupid Viktoriya, too! She's been simpering after you all night, and everyone can see it. She's awful and doesn't deserve you, but I can't help but feel like everyone is looking at me thinking, why would he choose her when he could have the stunning blonde?" My head is spinning with all the looks I've received all night, angry tears threatening to fall as I attempt to control my breathing.

"Ginny, calm down. No one is thinking that. *No one.* And if they are? Fuck 'em. Trust me, you don't have anything to feel insecure about." He grabs me by the hips and lifts me to sit on the edge of the rail. "You're the only woman I've ever gotten on my knees for, Red. And I'll give them all a demonstration to prove it."

He gently pries my knees apart and starts to lift the skirt of my dress. My tears dry as I bat his hands away and look behind him. "Jackson! Someone could see!"

Suddenly, he cups under my knees and forces me back against the wall of the tiny corner. My hands grab his shoulders, anchoring myself so I don't fall into the small space between the rail and the wall. Jackson's grin is devilish as he continues to push my legs up before spreading them.

"That's the point, Red. This is the most perfect declaration of commitment." One hard slides my skirt up until it's pooling at my waist, and my flimsy thong is on display, soaked and probably see-through.

Jackson licks his lips as he stares down at the space between my legs. "I can just see the headlines now. *Jackson Tailor caught worshipping the fiery temptress that finally brought him to his knees.*"

The noise of the party fades into the background as he lightly runs his fingers over my center and asks, "Do you want me to stop?"

Feeling bold from how he's watching me with such apparent adherence, I stretch one leg out to hook over his shoulder and pull him down. "Don't you dare."

The look on his face is wicked as he bends to drag his tongue over my panties. He only does it once before nudging them to the side with his nose, his hands busy keeping me from falling off the rail.

My nails scratch down the length of the wall, hands fisting

in the ivy as he flicks his tongue against my clit before kissing it softly. "Jackson, stop playing."

Chuckling against me, he lays an open mouth kiss directly over my center before he starts to rapidly suck my clit, paying attention to my left side because he knows it drives me fucking wild. My hips chase his mouth when he pulls away for a moment, looking up at me between my legs.

"How is it that you taste so fucking good?"

Before I can reply, the sound of the doors opening draws my attention away from him and down the balcony. Peeking around the corner we're tucked away in, I see a few men lighting cigarettes while they laugh about something.

The sound of Jackson's mouth sucking at me pulls my gaze back to find him watching me. He stops to say, "It's thrilling, isn't it? The idea of being caught? Can you keep quiet while you come, or do you want them to find us?"

I slap a hand over my mouth as he resumes, picking up the pace, flicking his tongue against me quicker and harder as his hands squeeze my thighs. He moans against me, and the vibrations pull my orgasm from me instantly. A whine catches in my throat as I attempt not to alert the men of our presence, but Jackson keeps sucking at me as though he's *trying* to make me cry out.

My hips undulate against his mouth as I come again, and the sight of him swallowing me down is enough to pull a soft, "Fuck," from my lips.

When he lifts his head, his chin is glistening with my juices, and he wipes them away with his thumb before sticking it in his mouth to suck it clean. "I think it's time to go home now."

He helps me off the rail and makes sure my dress is back in place before I ask, "Don't you want me to return the favor?"

Grabbing my hand, he turns and pulls me out of our little nook. "Why do you think I want to go home, Red? There's no way in fucking hell I'd risk anyone seeing you on your knees."

My cheeks feel warm at his consideration, then burn as I look ahead to see the men staring at us. One of them nods to Jackson. "Tailor."

Jackson returns the nod but doesn't say anything to them as they openly stare at us while we walk back into the party. We say our goodbyes quickly, Tripp waggling his brows at me as Jackson pulls me away.

"Have fun, kids," he sings.

"Oh, we certainly plan on it," Jackson says under his breath as he smiles down at me.

Jackson

Ginny laughs softly as I push her against the wall of the elevator. "We could have had sex so many times by now. In the bathroom at the party, in the car on the way here, you could push that little red emergency button so we can do it *now*," she lilts as I pull the top of her dress down and graze my teeth across her nipple.

She rubs the length of my cock through my pants as I press my hips into her hand. Desperate to empty myself inside her. "Don't think the thought didn't cross my mind."

Kissing my way up her chest, I nip at her neck softly, just the way she likes it. Dragging her skirt up her thighs, I cup them and lift her until her legs are wrapped around my waist just as the elevator reaches my floor.

She sucks my lower lip into her mouth and bites down on it as I carry her through my penthouse and up the stairs. It pulls a moan from my throat when she adds more pressure, and the need to feel her skin against me is primal.

Over the last week, we've experimented with how to proceed with our sexual encounters. Anything Ginny does to me, I can do to her. It's an easy way of her letting me know just how rough I can be without me overstepping any boundaries and her having to tell me to stop something.

Though she knows if anything goes too far, she *has* to use her words to stop me.

Her hands move to the button of my pants as I set her down in my bedroom. While she's working on getting me out of them, I reach around and unzip her dress, letting it fall to the floor in a heap of satin, before I shrug out of my jacket and rip my dress shirt over my head.

Ginny's mouth is like fire against my skin. Moving down my chest and over my abs as she lowers herself to her knees, looking up at me before she takes my cock in her mouth. "Fuck, baby, just like that. I know I say it every time, but you're so fucking pretty on your knees."

She smiles around my length, bobbing her head and twisting what she can't fit in her mouth in her hand while the other massages my balls. With every drag of her mouth, her teeth lightly graze me while she sucks as hard as she can.

I'm convinced I've permanently bruised the roof of her mouth, and that's a fact I'm most proud of.

Searing heat soars through me as my balls tense, and I pull her up quickly. "I'll wreck that pretty mouth of yours later. Right now, I need to fuck you. Get on the bed and show me how wet your pussy is."

"I'm fucking drenched," she moans as she crawls on the bed backward and spreads her legs to show me that it's the truth. Her hand drifts down her naked body, where she begins to rub her clit, while she squeezes her breast with the other. "Hurry up, Jackson. I need you."

Shaking myself from my lust-induced stupor, I quickly grab a condom and put it on before crawling over her on the bed. She bends one knee as I position myself at her entrance and push in swiftly, her hands grabbing my shoulders as her head tilts back, and she lets out a hoarse cry.

"Fuck, yes!"

I groan and drop my head into the crook of her shoulder as my hips snap into hers. My thrusts are sharp and deep, her nails digging into my skin as she lets out a high-pitched squeal. Every part of my body feels like it's being bathed in a scorching blaze. Like she's lit a match to ignite the flame, and we're creating the firestorm I've imagined since the first time I saw her.

Sweat starts to glimmer on her skin, a light sheen that melts with my own as she wraps her arms around my neck and pulls me down for a deep kiss. The noises she makes against my mouth have my dick twitching, so I pull back abruptly, not ready for this to end.

"What are you doing?" she whines as I get off the bed and pull her by her legs to the edge.

"Trying something new," I tell her as I pull her legs straight in the air and over one shoulder.

She watches me curiously as I push into her again and look down, watching where I disappear into her. I've barely pumped into her three times before her body starts to shake, and I snap my eyes back up to see her trying not to laugh.

Freezing, I stare down at her incredulously. "Are you *giggling?*"

She slaps her hand over her mouth to stifle the sound before slowly stretching out her body. "I'm sorry." Her legs twitch over my shoulder. "It's just...do most women actually *like* this position?"

Unbelievable.

Grabbing her legs in my hands, I bring one on the other side of me and pull her closer, my cock bottoming out as her hips hitch over my thighs. She sucks in a sharp breath, teeth biting into her palm as her eyes roll back in her head. A moan escapes her puffy pink lips as I lean over her, grabbing her breasts as I start to thrust.

She makes an unintelligible sound accompanied by a hoarse, "Oh...*fuck.*"

"I'm not particularly fond of you laughing at me in bed, Ginny." My hips move sharply. Dragging slowly out from between her tight walls, only to slam back with such force, the bed groans beneath us.

I pause to haul her up to the pillows before resuming my pace. A smile curls her lips up as she wraps her arms around my neck to pull me closer.

"But *I'm* fond of the punishment you give me when I do," she says.

Little devil.

She kisses me, sucking my bottom lip harshly before pulling it between her teeth. Biting her back, I pick up the pace, eliciting another high-pitched squeal from her mouth. If she were any other woman, the noise would be a total turn-off.

From Ginny, it's like a fucking symphony. Knowing it's *me* who's making her sing so beautifully.

"Harder," she begs.

"Baby, if I fuck you any harder, I'm going to break the bed."

She chases her high, hips lifting to match mine thrust for thrust. Winding an arm under her waist, I pull her up so that she's straddling me. As I'm adjusting us, she throws her weight to the side, knocking us back to the bed so that she's on top. My cock meets resistance inside her, as though it literally can't go any further, but she just smiles as her hands twist up into her hair, and she starts to ride me.

"So let's break it. You're rich; you can buy a new bed." She grins at me before reaching up for the top of the headboard. Using it for leverage, she starts moving faster. Head thrown back, squeezing her walls around me with every press of her hips against mine.

"You're gonna be the death of me," I tell her, squeezing her ass so tight I know it'll be red later.

She's completely uninhibited. Hair wild, eyes glowing. It's the most beautiful sight I've ever seen.

My balls tense, cock twitching as it gets ready to release. But Ginny shows no signs of being near an orgasm. "Fuck, if you keep riding me like that, I'm going to come."

Immediately, her hips slow, and she tilts her head down

between her arms, still holding onto the headboard. Her hair falls around me, a bona fide siren as she singsongs, "Do you wanna come, Jackson?"

"Is that a rhetorical question?" I smirk up at her.

Her hips roll against me, slow and deep, and she drops her arms and kisses me. My tongue battles hers as I reach between her legs to pinch her clit, swallowing her gasp of surprise.

Moaning against my mouth, she begins to ride me again. Desperate and needy. When our lips break apart, she looks me dead in the eyes and says, "Then fuck me harder."

Raw, primal instinct rages through me as I flip us so that she's on her back again. My lips find hers again as I pound into her, sucking her bottom lip so hard she cries out but doesn't show any sign of wanting to stop. The sound of our bodies slapping together, flesh on flesh, pair with the beautiful words that pour from her mouth.

"Fuck, yes. Just like that. God, you're so fucking deep." She spurs me on, letting me know I'm not in danger of hurting her.

It's my turn to use the headboard for leverage as I fuck her so hard the headboard cracks as it detaches from the frame. My cock is so close to bursting it may very well break the condom from how hard I'm about to come.

My teeth clench as I squeeze my eyes, willing myself not to go before her. Her nails dig into my arms and over my back, leaving deep welts as she screams out my name. "Jackson, I'm coming!"

Digging her feet into my ass, she squeezes me closer as her pussy spasms around me. I hold out for two more thrusts before I'm spilling inside her, and I don't slow until my cock stops twitching. She rides out her release, coming once more before I finish. Our bodies continue to move against each other as I graze my lips up down her neck before pulling at her nipple with my teeth.

Her hands find the back of my head, holding me to her as

I suck on her breast before moving to the other to give it equal attention.

"Jackson?" she asks.

"Hmm?" Nuzzling my way up to the crook of her neck, I lay a gentle kiss there before pulling back to look at her.

She looks as though she wants to say something but is unsure. Hope springs through me that perhaps she'll come clean about the club. About her stranger. Opening the conversation and giving me an opportunity to tell her that it's been me all along.

Her fingers play with my hair, eyes bouncing back and forth between mine. Eventually, she pulls me in for a soft kiss. When we part, she looks as though she's about to cry.

"Hey. Ginny, what's wrong? What is it? Did I hurt you?" Concern bleeds into my tone as I wipe her sweaty hair off her forehead.

Shaking her head, she laughs as tears start to fall. "No, you didn't hurt me."

"Then why are you crying?" It's quickly becoming the thing I hate most—the sight of her sad.

"Because, you jerk." Her head falls to the side so she doesn't look at me as she says, "I think I've fallen in love with you."

If my heart could burst and I still be alive, this is what it would feel like—I'm sure of it.

"I *know* I've fallen in love with you, Ginny. I've fallen so fucking deep I'm drowning. And I will die a million deaths if it means I get to hear you tell me you love me every fucking day from now until eternity."

My confession doesn't dry the tears from her eyes, though. Instead, she starts to cry harder, pressing the heels of her hands into her eyes.

"You won't love me when you hear how awful I am. I'm afraid you won't want me anymore at all."

My brows clench together as I watch her come undone. Is

this when she's going to tell me about the club? Nothing would make me stop loving her—that or otherwise.

I open my mouth to tell her that exact thing when she blurts out, "Chris touches me!"

I'm glad her hands still cover her eyes because I know she's expecting me to be shocked, but since she's already confessed this to her stranger at the club, it takes me a moment to think about how to react.

Rage pours through me, just like the night I destroyed the room at Désirer. Now that Ginny is out of their apartment, that man has a whole lot of hurt coming to him when he gets back into town.

Ginny takes my silence as disgust.

She pushes me away, curling onto her side in the fetal position as she starts to cry harder. "I tried to ignore it. I tried for so long, but as we got older and I moved in with him out here…I *let* him do it."

I roll onto my back, removing the condom and tossing it down into the trash can beside my bed before moving back to wrap my arms around her and pull her into my chest. "Ginny, I'm so sorry that happened to you. Chris is a fucking weak excuse for a man, and trust me when I say he'll get what's coming to him."

"Didn't you hear me, Jackson? I said I let him do it. There were times when I *liked* it," she reiterates. Her crying is starting to cease, and she's taking long, gasping breaths between her stuttered words.

"Ginny, he abused you. He's older than you, and he knew what he was doing was wrong."

"But what does that say about me? That I liked it?"

"You mentioned that you tried to ignore it, and then you got older. I'm going to assume this started when you were a child?" I gently wipe her tear-stained cheek with my thumb as she nods in the affirmative.

"He fucking abused you, Ginny. It doesn't matter if you grew to like it. Our bodies find ways to cope with traumatic things. He's a fucking psychopath. He sure as hell shouldn't be allowed to be treating patients, let alone women and babies."

She tenses in my arms, and I gently nudge her to turn toward me. "I'm only going to tell you this once. If you want to speak to me about it, you can, but you don't have to. If you'd like, we can arrange for you to speak to a therapist, but only if you want to talk about it. I don't care about your past. I care about you. All I want is to chase away the darkness that haunts you. I see the fire inside you, and I want to light the world up with it. I love you for everything that you are and everything that you'll become. I'll be the pyre for your flames to reach the heavens. Whatever you want, it's yours to take."

She looks up at me through glassy eyes, her determination to heal shining brightly through as she says, "I don't want to take anything from you, Jackson. I just want to grow with you. I want to build a life with you. I've never been in love with anyone, but I love you so much it scares me."

"There's nothing to be scared of, baby. I've never been in love with anyone either, but loving you doesn't frighten me. It gives me hope."

Ginny reaches up to pull me down for a soft kiss that grows more heated as our tongues intertwine, and she rolls me onto my back.

She's the light that led me out of my darkness. I want to return the favor. The way I feel about her, as foreign as it is, makes my heart feel like it could burst at any given moment. When I look at her, I'm filled with love and the need to be good—everything I've always chased away until she came along.

Now that we've both admitted it, I have to end things with her at the club.

She can never know that it was me behind the mask all along.

It will be the only thing I ever keep from her from here on out.

<h1 style="text-align:center">Ginny</h1>

As I exit the elevator at Jackson's, my lips stretch into a smile to see him working at the kitchen island on his laptop. There's a large vase of long-stemmed white roses next to him, and a card leaning against it with my name scrawled across it.

"Be still, my heart! Are my many admirers sending flowers now instead of love letters?" I swoon, placing the back of my hand on my forehead and talking in the best Southern accent I can muster.

Jackson and I made a statement with the papers after the party last weekend. Jackson Tailor is officially a taken man—and I am the official owner of no less than five pounds of hate mail.

He smirks, eyes never leaving the screen as his fingers fly deftly over the keyboard. "Those are from me."

My cheeks warm as I pick up the card and slide the cardstock out of the envelope.

FOR A FRESH START AND A SYMBOL OF MY UNENDING LOYALTY.

"You're just a modern-day Shakespeare, you know that?" Slowly, I make my way over to him, waiting while he types the last of his document before he closes the computer and pulls me to him.

Jackson has many different ways he likes to kiss me. All of them are equally passionate, each having their appropriate time and place. But my favorite is when we're alone at home, and his eyes fill with pure lust, lips attacking mine like he's starved, tongue caressing like he's trying to memorize every dip and swell of my mouth while his fingers search for any patch of bare skin they can find.

When he grips the back of my bare thighs under my skirt and lifts me to sit on his lap, I feel his hard length against my clit and shamelessly rock against him once as my arms encircle his neck. Our kiss ends, and he hugs me to him, burying his face in my hair and inhaling my scent.

I don't know what it is about the way I smell, but it drives him wild, and there's something about the way he nuzzles my neck while he breathes me in that sends little tingles straight to my pussy.

"Do you like the flowers? Or are they too much?" he asks, lips moving softly against my skin.

"I love the flowers. And the card. And *you*."

"I love you too. How was your day?"

The next ten minutes are spent recounting our days, me perched on his lap like it's not giving both of us a core workout to stay balanced on the small stool not made for two people. Finally, I shift to move off him, walking around the island to the fridge to pull out some fresh fruit to snack on. "I'm going to go to Lenni's tonight. I'll probably be there late, so I'm just going to go to my place after."

It fills me with unease—the normalcy of how the lie falls from my lips.

Carmela called while I was at the clinic to tell me I was requested at Désirer tonight. Since my stranger is asking for me, I feel obligated to go. But I hate lying to Jackson about it.

Realistically, I know I can't have them both. It's not fair to anyone. But I also can't bring myself to end things with the man who has played such a huge part in the growth I've gone through these past two months.

"Lenni lives closer to me than you. Just come back here whenever. I'm going back to the office to get some work done anyway," Jackson says as he flips his computer back open and resumes whatever he was working on when I arrived.

"Are you sure? I don't want to wake you."

The smile he flashes me over the top of his screen is devious as he croons, "Red, you *better* wake me up when you get home. You can wake me up with your mouth on my cock."

If I could see them, I'd bet anything my cheeks are as red as the strawberry I'm about to put in my mouth. Instead, I throw it at him. "You are so dirty."

"You love it, don't lie."

Don't lie.

Fuck, I really need to figure my shit out.

"He what?" I'm confused by the request almost as much as I'm confused why Carmela called me to her office once I arrived at Désirer to tell me herself.

"He asked for you to wear a normal dress. No lingerie, no robe, no wings. And you're back in the Confessional wing tonight," she repeats while flipping through a bunch of papers attached to a clipboard.

"I think your man just wants to talk tonight. Is there anything wrong with that? Do you not want to go?"

"No, I'll go. It's fine." *Just random.*

Why are we going backward? There's no reason we couldn't have just talked in the Dreamers wing. But by requesting us to go back to the Confessional wing, he's made sure that we aren't able to touch.

Carmela pins me with a hard stare, her espresso eyes heavy with exhaustion. "Ginny, you don't have to if you don't want to."

"I know. I'm okay. I promise. Are *you* okay?" The lights are dimmed as low as they can go, and there's a rumpled gray faux rabbit throw on the black leather couch in the back corner. If I had to guess, I'd say she's burning the candle at both ends between the restaurant and the club. She looks like she needs a break.

She sets the clipboard on her desk and rubs at her eyes, careful not to smear her makeup. "I'm fine. Just tired. Nothing for you to be worried about. Go on and get ready."

It's her way of dismissing me. Carmela isn't an overly friendly boss. She's a no-nonsense, take no man's shit kind of woman. I've seen her put Scott and Mick in their place numerous times since I've worked for them. She's the kind of woman you fear if you get on her bad side. I'm thankful she's friendly with Lenni because I feel safe by association from her frigid temperament.

I change quickly, selecting a sleek black dress with a halter-style neckline from the wardrobe. The Grand Room is full tonight, clients and Angels mingling before they open the Desires wing for the monthly show. There's no one in the Confessional wing as I follow my guard to my old room, the sweet scent of the white roses that line the hall reminding me of the ones Jackson got me.

A symbol of my unending loyalty.

I'm such a terrible girlfriend.

Maybe my stranger and I returning to the Confessional wing is a good idea. Jackson and I *just* made things official. If I don't do anything physical anymore, would it still be that bad?

Something tells me the moment I step into the room that either way, tonight *isn't* going to go well.

The curtain is open, and my stranger is sitting on his side of the room—elbows on his knees and hands threaded together on the back of his head, staring at the floor.

"Is everything okay?"

He takes a deep breath, his chest rising and falling before slowly looking up. "Have a seat, Little Ember."

I begin to walk across the room to sit with him when he speaks again. "No. Have a seat on your side, love."

"What's going on?" My back is ramrod straight as I sit on the familiar clamshell loveseat. It's impossible to read him, with the mask covering every feature that may give something away.

"I think you know why we're here." He rubs the back of his neck as he blows out a breath.

Anxiety pours into my bloodstream like oil from a spilled barrel. Sludgy and toxic, making it feel like all of my internal organs have jumped into my throat to escape the poison. It takes me three tries before I finally manage, "No."

"Yes, Scarlett. It's time."

Slowly, I shake my head, moving it faster as I repeat, "No. No, it's not…I can't…"

"You're happy, are you not?"

Tears prick my eyes as I attempt to dislodge my heart from my throat. My tongue feels thick, making it hard to speak, everything taking a few attempts before I can form words. "I am but-"

"I will not fuck you, Little Ember. I've told you this. You've learned all you can from me. There is no reason for this—for *us*—to continue." His voice sounds pained, and I desperately want to race across the room and tear the mask from his face just to see if he truly looks as anguished as he sounds.

"Do you not want me anymore?" I sob, choking on the tears I can no longer hold back.

His head tilts to the side as his hands flex where they rest between his knees. "I don't think this arrangement is fair to your boyfriend."

"*YOU* PUSHED ME TO GO BACK TO HIM!" I yell, standing abruptly.

He sits back. "And would you have, still, if I had not said anything?"

"Yes." It feels like my heart is being crushed, pain exploding in my chest. "Yes, I would have gone back to him. I love him."

"Then why won't you let me go?"

There are no words that come to me. For seconds that stretch into minutes, I'm silent. Unable to answer. I've lived my life with him. He's been my way to cope for so long that I don't know *how* to live without him.

But the stranger I grew up with—that I made up—isn't really *him*.

"Scarlett. If you had to choose–"

"No!" My tone is rough and watery, and I'm starting to get a headache with all the pressure in my sinuses. "No, you will *not* ask me to choose."

It's his turn to fall silent. Minutes go by of audible attempts to control our breathing, my crying, and him cracking his knuckles. He finally speaks, his tone so thick with turmoil it shatters my heart. "Would you be so content to live for however long, only meeting me on the weekends? Still masked, never knowing our true identities? Never fucking. Because I will not do that in here. Not with you not knowing who I am. Would *that* be worth losing him? Because you cannot continue keeping it a secret. It will eat you alive."

Slowly, I sink to the floor, back against the couch, as I continue to sob. He's right. I know he's right. But I'm not ready to let him go.

"I'm not ready…" My words are a mix of inaudible and squeaky. Tears fall heavily from my eyes, washing away the liner and mascara. My fingers come away from my face with black smears as I wipe at my cheeks and cry harder.

The sound he makes behind his mask sounds like a harsh, ragged breath. His body shivers, as though he's trying not to cry. He pushes to his feet quickly, and for a moment, I think he will break the rules and pull me into his arms, but when I realize he's headed for the door, I cry out.

"No! Don't go!" Pathetically, I throw myself at his feet as he passes, clinging to his pants.

"I have to, Little Ember. This has to end. I was hoping it would have gone better than this."

He crouches, removing my hands from him and setting them in my lap. The sigh he lets out is heavy with emotion, but I'm crying so hard I can't see his eyes. "You'll be okay. I promise. Eventually, you'll realize this was for the best."

The cool metal of his mask touches my forehead, and then he rises. "I'm proud of you."

Blinking furiously to try and clear the tears from my eyes, I look up to see him with his hand on the doorknob. His head hangs like he's internally warring with himself over leaving. Eventually, he opens the door.

"Please, don't leave me," I whisper.

But he does.

And I feel like he takes a part of my soul with him.

Jackson

The last time I felt like this about a woman was *never*. My heart pounds in my chest like a judge with a gavel.

We find the defendant *guilty*.

His crime? Being a lovesick fool.

I was never going to be enough for her. It was stupid to think that she'd willingly give up the only thing that got her through her childhood trauma. I feel like I made a mistake walking out on her like I did.

Will she break again?

Will this set back her healing?

Did I ruin everything?

I have Robert drive me around the city, waiting another hour and a half before going back to my penthouse—spending the time trying to figure out how to move forward from here—giving her time to decide if she's staying at her place or mine. Because if she goes to mine, I don't know if I can look at her right now and not get angry.

By the time I get home, I've cooled down, and since I haven't heard from her, I expect she decided to go to her place.

But my heart jumps when I see the soft glow of the bedside lamp as soon as I step out of the elevator.

She came home.

Climbing the stairs slowly, I see her curled up on her side, P-Kitty snuggled into her like a little spoon. Her face is splotchy—eyes rimmed with red. It's obvious she's been crying, even though it looks like she's washed her face to try and hide the evidence.

"Hey," she says softly. "Where have you been? I thought you'd be here when I got back."

"Lost track of time." I'm emotionally exhausted and still smell like her stranger, so I head to the bathroom to rinse off. "Are you okay? You look like you've been crying."

"Lenni and I got into a stupid fight." The lie rolls off her tongue, bitter and flat. I wonder how long she took to come up with it.

"I'm sorry." My tone matches hers as I disappear into the shower and turn the water on. I discard my clothes quickly, stepping under the warm spray and reaching for my body wash. The quicker I get rid of the cologne I use at the club, the better.

Once I'm sure I've washed it away, I stand under the middle of the multiple shower heads, letting the steam engulf me because I don't know how to face Ginny.

I'm angry. My heart feels like it's been ripped from my chest. Yet, at the same time, how can I blame her?

All of this could have just been avoided if I'd just told her the truth when I started to catch fucking feelings.

"Hey, want some company?" Her voice echoes off the granite walls, and my hand shoots out to turn the water off.

Turning, I see her standing with the door open, naked. "No, I'm done. I'm too tired tonight, Gin. I'm gonna go to bed."

I open the door wider, grabbing a towel to wrap around my waist as she steps back.

"Are you mad at me?" she asks in a small voice, arms wrapping around herself insecurely.

Grabbing my robe from the back of the door, I wrap her in it before kissing her forehead. "No, I'm not mad at you. I'm just tired."

She doesn't say anything else as I move to the vanity to brush my teeth. By the time I walk back into the bedroom, she's put her nightdress back on and is lying on her side, away from me, with the lights off.

"Goodnight," I tell her as I get into the bed, mirroring her position.

"Night," she whispers.

All I want is to turn and pull her to me, but I'm afraid if I do, the emotions that have been building all night will spill over. It already feels like there's an ocean between us. The last thing I want to do is add more tears to its depths.

Besides, Tailor men don't cry.

UNCLE SCOTT

> I know it's the weekend, but I need you at Decadence for a meeting with Carmela and Mick tonight at six.

"What time are you working at the restaurant tonight?" I ask Ginny, setting my phone on the kitchen counter and grabbing a Gatorade from the fridge.

She's sitting at the island, right where she was when I left for my morning workout, with work files spread out in front of her. Using the towel around my neck, I wipe the sweat from my face before chugging half my drink.

"I'm supposed to go in at five. Why, what's up?" she answers without looking up from her notepad.

Things have been tense between us all morning. Both of us tiptoeing around the other, not sure how to act normal, how to act *in love* again. Not that we fell out of it, but I'm angry and guarded now, and she's depressed. It feels like we both lost last night.

She lost *him*, and now it feels like I've lost her.

"My uncle wants me there for a meeting. I'll drive you. There are some things I need to discuss with Carmela, anyway."

She freezes, unaware I'm watching her. Her pen has stilled over the notepad she's writing on, and her eyes are no longer moving over her notes. "What do you need to talk to Carmela about?"

"Business," I stress.

Sparks light in my chest, waiting to catch and combust into a raging fury, but I do my best to temper them as I stare at her. I want to ask her…want to know…

Why am I not enough for you?

Is she planning on continuing to work at the club? What would she do if I mentioned it to her now? Mentioned that my uncle is bringing me on board there and that she should go with me sometime.

How would she react?

"Jackson, are you okay?"

Snapping out of my thoughts, I shake my head to see her staring at me.

Her startling blue eyes are wide, brows knitted together in concern. "You spaced out there for a moment."

"I'm fine. I'm going to take a shower. Is there anything in particular you want to do today?" I throw over my shoulder as I walk away.

"No, I think I'm going to go home for a little bit, actually. I didn't sleep well last night. I want to get a nap in before work. I'll see you later."

She doesn't look at me when she speaks, and as I make my way upstairs, I mutter, "Yeah. See you later."

"Hi, Jackson. Carmela said to let you know you can go back to her office," the brunette who once tried to get a rise out of Ginny says as soon as I step through the door at Decadence.

Her eyes are heavy with desire, just like every other woman who thinks Ginny is just a passing fling. She ignores the fact that I'm dating her co-worker, stepping closer to me and whispering, "Ginny doesn't exactly seem very *adventurous*. When you get bored, let me know."

"Be careful. That's my future wife you're talking about." The words leave my mouth before I can think over my statement. Schooling my surprise, I turn away from her shocked face to look for my girlfriend so I can speak to her before I go into the meeting.

Ginny is leaning against the back wait station, watching my interaction with the hostess with interest. The restaurant isn't very busy as I make my way through the tables to where she is. "You know, you can quit working here if you want to. Focus on the clinic. Use your extra time looking for a space to remodel for your own."

She winds her arms around my neck and pushes up on her tiptoes for a kiss. "What did you say to Jacqueline? She looks like you just told her you killed her puppy."

"Just dashed her hopes and dreams of getting a piece of the Tailor fortune." I'm not about to tell her what I really said, and I doubt the overly confident woman will admit it to her.

"Why do you assume every woman wants your money? Maybe they just want to fuck you?" she jokes playfully.

"Should I buy into the sex toy industry? Get a mold of my cock done and dildos made so that the women of New York still have something to look forward to?" I quip.

She grips my tie and pulls me closer. "You can have a mold made for us. I've always wondered what it would be like to be fucked by two men at the same time."

Her comment takes me by surprise, and she nips at my lips before letting go and stepping back. "Now go, I have tables to take care of."

I've never been a fan of naps until now. It's like she's back to her usual self.

Letting out a chuckle, I shake my head and walk down the hall to Carmela's office. When I open the door, I see her working on her computer while my uncle has his set up on a smaller table that's been pulled over to her couch.

"Where's Mick?" I ask, shutting the door behind me and heading straight to the minibar to pour myself a drink.

"He'll be here in a bit. We have a crisis. I need your Englishman on a call," my uncle responds without looking away from his screen.

"Why couldn't we have met at the office if we're working?"

"Because we weren't supposed to be working. I need to talk to you three, but this just came up. Some asshole in Chicago is trying to withhold information about a company we're buying. I need you to call and pretend you're interested to see if you get different numbers."

Snapping into business mode, I speak with my smooth English accent. "Get them on the phone."

Carmela stops typing and looks over at me. "That's impressive. If I didn't know you were standing right there, I'd have never guessed that was you."

"That's the point," my uncle and I say simultaneously.

As the call is picked up by a secretary and patched through to the person in charge of the sale, I get settled on the couch, ready to bring my A-game and not let my uncle down again. "Here we go."

Ginny

"We're too slow to keep everyone. You can go home early if you want," Jacqueline's annoying valley girl lilt sounds behind me.

By the time I turn to answer her, she's already walking away, mumbling under her breath, "Not like you need the money, anyway."

Guess it was more of an order and not an option to leave.

Returning to dumping out the salt and pepper shakers that crowd the table in front of me, I look up to catch the attention of the kitchen manager, Jakob, who is talking to one of the cooks. "Do you guys need anything brought down to storage?"

"Nah, we got it. It's a slow night. We'll probably end up closing early," he replies.

"Sounds good." Placing the last of the empty shakers into the tray for the dishwasher, I bring it to the back before heading down the hall to the lockers where we keep our stuff.

"You're Jackson's new girlfriend, aren't you?" I hear behind me.

Turning, I see Senator Mick Charles walking the same way toward Carmela's office. I stop and reach my hand out to shake his. "Yeah, that's me. I'm Ginny. Nice to meet you."

In all the time I've worked at Decadence, and now at Désirer, I've never been introduced to Mick. Truthfully, he kind of grosses me out. I don't understand how he and Scott are friends. But if Jackson and I are going to stay together, I will have to learn how to deal with men like Mick.

"Nice to meet you, too. Scott is very fond of you. Nothing but nice things to say," he croons. I'm pretty sure he thinks he's being charming, but it comes off as creepy.

I don't respond, and we fall into step until we reach the office, where he opens the door, and I continue on my way.

Only, as soon as the door is open, I hear the unmistakable English accent of the man who left me crying on the floor of Désirer last night.

"... like a great deal to me. Are you sure there are no other companies interested? It was my understanding there was an offer on the..."

The air leaves my lungs as Mick shuts the door, cutting my stranger's voice off. All the sound is sucked from my head—replaced with the deafening thud of my heart against my ribcage.

My stranger is here?

Why?

I never saw anyone else enter the office, so he's had to have been here since before I got to work.

It sounds like there is some sort of business deal going on in Carmela's office, but all I can think about is the fact that my stranger and Jackson are in the same room. Do they work together?

Does he know who I am? Did he come here to tell Jackson about us? About me working at the club and everything we've been doing?

Or is he completely clueless?

My lungs begin to burn, reminding me to take a breath. As I suck in air, acid worms its way around my stomach, eating away at the lining and making me feel nauseous. Bile rises in my throat, and it's a struggle to keep it down.

After last night—when I finally decided to pick myself up off the floor—I'd decided to quit working at Désirer and take Jackson up on his offer to fund my clinic. There's no way I can work there and do anything like that with anyone other than whoever the man behind the mask was.

Also, I love Jackson.

I can't lose him. I don't think I'll survive losing them *both*.

Most of the night before was spent tossing and turning in Jackson's bed, wanting to reach across the giant space between us and just touch him. Feel him under my fingertips —real and *there*, right in front of me.

The stranger asked if I could live life not knowing who he was, if losing Jackson was worth that.

It isn't.

Jackson and I have grown so much together. All I want is for that to continue.

Am I devastated that my stranger ended things? Absolutely.

But I spent all night thinking about if I really *had* to choose, who would it be?

When the answer finally came, I accepted it without hesitation.

With the stranger being just on the other side of that door, though, I *have* to know who he is. I *need* to look him in the eye to be able to let him go.

All I want is just one glimpse, and then I'll move forward.

Jackson

"Do I even want to know if what you guys just did was legal?" Carmela asks as soon as the call ends.

"Perfectly legal. They lied. I had a hunch, and Jackson got the truth," my uncle replies, moving to the minibar to pour himself a drink.

"But you're pretending to be someone else–" she starts in again, but Mick cuts her off.

"First of all, I shouldn't be hearing any of this. Second, it's not like we're exactly running a legit operation at Désirer."

She throws her hands up. "Fair."

The way they interact with each other is informal. Too friendly to just be business partners and not tinged with the type of familiarity you have with people who are only friends.

I'll bet they've fucked.

"Okay, what are we all here for?" Mick asks, directing his attention away from Carmela to my uncle, who is still standing in the corner at the minibar.

He's holding his drink in his hand, the other stuffed in his pocket, as he leans against the bar with one ankle crossed in front of the other. He looks relaxed, but I know him better than that. Whatever he called us here for isn't good news.

"I'm pulling out of Désirer completely. I want Jackson to take over *now* instead of later." He looks into his bourbon as he speaks casually like it's not a big deal.

"No. He's not ready," Carmela exclaims flatly.

Gee, thanks.

"Why the sudden rush? This is the third business you've pulled out of this week, Scott. Something I need to know?" Mick asks, revealing information that's news to me.

What other businesses did he pull out of? And *why* is he doing this so suddenly?

An uneasy feeling starts to pool in my stomach, like butterflies with razor-sharp wings barely grazing the lining, testing my resolve. "What's going on, Scott?"

His eyes find mine at my use of his name. Rarely do I ever use it without the title Uncle in front of it, even at the office. "I've got cancer."

Carmela sucks in a sharp breath while Mick lets out his in a long exhale. Meanwhile, I feel like I've forgotten how to breathe.

The room is dead silent while we process what he's just told us. And the entire time, he just stands there like he's only told us he's about to retire early—a slight smile on his face while he waits for us to speak.

Finally, it's Mick who breaks the silence.

"What type?" he asks.

"Colon. Stage four."

"Fuck, Scott. When did you find out?" Carmela's voice is softer than I've ever heard, heavy with empathy.

I'm still sitting on the couch, shell-shocked at the news. I can't think properly, breaths coming in shallow waves as the conversation continues without me.

"I've known for a while. By the time they found it, it had already spread. It's in my lungs now, and they just found a spot in my brain."

"Okay, so what's the plan? What's the treatment? Who do we need to call? What strings need to be pulled? Clinical trials?" Mick sounds like any other rich man when faced with a problem.

Throw money at it, and it will go away.

"There is no plan. Even if I'd started treatment when I found out, it wouldn't have mattered. The best they could have done is give me more time, but that isn't how I want to live the rest of my life."

"Scott–" Carmela starts, but I cut her off this time as my voice finally returns to me.

"Why didn't you tell me?"

From my peripheral, I can see both Mick and Carmela startle and look my direction as if my speaking reminded them that I'm still here—his *family*.

"I didn't want to burden you, Jackson. It's why I've been pushing so hard for you to take over for me." His eyes are heavy with remorse, and suddenly, there's a fire in me that's raging.

"I don't give a shit about taking over for you! I give a shit about you staying alive! We could have been finding the best doctors with the best treatments for you. What have you been doing to treat it this whole time?" I stand from the couch because I can't sit anymore.

Mick walks over to Carmela, placing his hand on her back as he nods to the door. "We should give them a moment."

I begin to pace as they make their way to the exit, my uncle watching them go as if he's a kid about to be scolded by a parent, and he wants the other around to play the good guy.

When the door shuts behind them, he takes the lead, answering my earlier question. "Jackson, I'm sorry I didn't tell you. But I didn't say anything to you for the same reason I didn't tell your aunt. You both would have wanted me to do everything to beat it, but there is no beating it. By the time I knew, it was already too late. I've got a few years left in me. I don't want to spend them sick, chained to a hospice bed. That isn't how I want to go out."

My sinuses burn, and I breathe through my mouth harshly, bending over to put my hands on my knees as I hang my head. Tailor men don't cry, but tears are threatening to form, and my lunch wants to make a reappearance.

"How long have you known?"

"Jackson–"

"HOW LONG?"

Now he's looking at me with pity, and my hands ball into fists as I look around the office for something—anything—to take my rage out on.

"About a year and a half." He pushes off the minibar and walks closer to me, setting his drink down on Carmela's desk as he passes it. "This was exactly why I didn't want to tell you. I understand you're upset, but this isn't your decision."

"Oh, fuck you! It's never *my* decision, is it? You decide everything for me! Were you just never going to tell me? Never going to even *try* to fight it?" I throw my hand in the air and turn away from him, walking to stare out the window as I attempt to get my anger under control.

"I told you, fighting at this stage is pointless. You know a lot of people with cancer at this stage try to fight, and you know who it's for? Their family. It isn't for them. Do you think cancer patients *like* being sick? Do you think they *enjoy* feeling so weak they can't get out of bed? All the while, their families are out and about, talking about what they can do next to try and prolong their life. It's a selfish thing to ask, Jackson. And all for what? A few extra months? Maybe an extra year?"

Whirling back around, I glare at him. "So, you give up? Just like that?"

"In my eyes, it isn't giving up. It's living the life I have left the way *I* want to."

"That's a bullshit lie, and you know it." A realization

comes to me suddenly. "This is why you granted Aunt Sadie the divorce."

He doesn't say anything, affirming my assumption. "You know she'd never have left you if she knew."

"I know, which is exactly why I let her go. She was already miserable, but she would have stayed, and she would have asked me to fight. And I would have, shackling her to a sick man who would eventually get worse. She didn't deserve that." His eyes are glassy, his voice thick with despair.

We stand there, facing off, neither saying anything, both trying to fight back tears. I take a good look at him and see it written on his face. He's tired. I think back to all the times I noticed it in the last few months but dismissed it.

Guilt racks my body, but his next sentence pulls the anger right back to the forefront of my emotions.

"Ginny gave me a list of counselors that we could speak to together, if you want. Therapy is actually *therapeutic*, believe it or not," he tries to make a joke.

It's like everything is sucked from the room all at once— the air, the sounds—as my world goes deathly quiet.

Concern, followed by understanding, plays out in his eyes. He knows he just made a mistake but doesn't say anything as my blood begins to boil, and everything slowly bleeds back into existence.

"Ginny *knew*?" My words are low and asked through clenched teeth.

She knew, and she didn't tell me? *This* is the secret they've been keeping. Why they're so comfortable in each other's presence. The reason he was leaving Chillard that day I showed up.

"I asked her not to tell you, Jackson. Don't be mad at her–"

"I can't be here right now." Betrayal and rage pour through me as I push past him to leave.

"Jackson!" he calls out behind me.

Throwing open the door, I pause to see *her* leaning against the wall across from the door. She's smiling, but as her eyes take me in, then bounce behind me to my uncle, it falls from her face.

"Is everything okay?" she asks, pushing off the wall, concern bleeding into her beautiful blue eyes.

Eyes I can't even look at right now.

Ignoring her, I start down the hall to leave, but she grabs my arm to pull my attention back to her. "Jackson, what's wrong?"

"I can't speak to you right now, or I am going to say things I will regret later. Let me go, Ginny," I tell her without turning around.

She does as I ask, a quiet gasp leaving her lips as I walk away. Carmela and Mick sit nearby as I weave through the tables toward the exit. They watch me go with matching expressions of sorrow on their faces, which stokes the fire in my chest.

In a matter of minutes, my world has crumbled around me. The only person who ever gave a shit about me is choosing to leave me, just like my father did.

And the only person I've ever loved kept it from me.

As soon as I'm in the car, I tell Robert to take me home and raise the partition that separates us. Once I'm truly alone, I let grief win. There's no one here to see me cry, so I allow the little boy in me to resurface as I fall apart in the back seat.

Ginny

"What happened?" My voice is shaky as I ask Scott, watching Jackson disappear around the corner.

Scott comes to the doorway of Carmela's office, leaning against the frame as he rubs his eyes. "I told them. Jackson didn't take it well."

My heart breaks for my boyfriend. To know that he just learned of Scott's illness in a room with other people where he probably tried to keep it together when all he wanted to do was break down. Scott is the only family he has left since his aunt moved. He's probably devastated.

"I may have also accidentally let slip that you knew…I'm sorry, Ginny. I was trying to bring up going to therapy, and it just came out."

Fuck.

No wonder he said he couldn't talk to me.

Letting out a sigh, I shake my head. "It's okay. He would have found out at some point."

Every instinct I have is telling me to go after him. He shouldn't be alone right now. Even if he's upset with me, he needs someone to be with him. But before I go, I *have* to see my stranger.

Trying to act natural, I peer behind Scott, eyes sweeping the room to find an empty office. "What happened to the other man?"

"What other man?" Scott asks, turning to grab a tumbler from Carmela's desk. He tosses back what I assume is alcohol in one gulp as I take a step into the office.

Something crawls along my skin, anxious and aware. "The one with the English accent. I've been waiting outside the room since the senator went in. He and Carmela came back out, then Jackson and you. What happened to the other man?"

Things I subconsciously picked up on and paid no attention to flash through my mind.

"English accent?" Scott lets out a laugh. "That's Jackson. He does it when we think a company is withholding information to try and drive up a sale. Started when he was a kid fresh outta school. He used to joke around with the accent all the time. For whatever reason, we noticed people took him more seriously that way, and it just stuck."

My vision tunnels.

Shrapnel from the bomb Scott just set off travels throughout my body, causing my breath to catch in my throat as it carves up my insides.

I met Jackson and the stranger the same day.

He couldn't have me in the real world, not back then. But he had me at the club.

"Ginny?" Scott's voice sounds far away, like I'm underwater and he's above the surface.

The appearance of the full face mask after that first night. Jackson is smart. He didn't want me to see any of his facial features. The extra cologne bottle in his bathroom—my stranger had a different scent.

"My tastes are very…particular."

My stranger said it the first night we met. Jackon likes to be rough.

The way my stranger kept pushing me back toward

Jackson every time something happened…he urged me to find someone to protect me outside the club. He manipulated me from behind his mask before putting himself directly in my orbit in the real world.

"Ginny, are you okay?" Scott's voice sounds closer.

His hand on my arm pulls me back to the present, my vision clearing as I turn to find that I've walked down the hall and am almost halfway through the main room of the restaurant. Everyone is looking at me with odd looks on their faces.

"I'm fine," I whisper. "I need to go find Jackson."

Pulling away, I walk out the door and hail the first cab, not bothering to grab any of my belongings. After I give the driver Jackson's address, my thoughts start swirling again. One after the other, it's like a barrage of moments where Jackson took advantage of our situation.

Of course, he agreed to the thirty-day deal. He had me all along. Every touch, everything I said in our room at Désirer—he had his own personal Ginny handbook.

Yet…at the same time.

He got me away from Chris. Taught me how to be confident in myself and what I wanted with my body. He built me up—*continues* to build me up—and has genuinely attempted to start something real with me—something neither of us has ever had.

Jackson could have ended things after we slept together, only he didn't. And he may have only respected my space because he was still getting to see me at the club, but he fought for me.

He *fought* for me.

My stranger's words from the previous night replay with that realization.

"Scarlett. If you had to choose—"

I didn't fight for him. And he knows it.

The entire time we've been together, he's known that I work at the club and that I believed another man was the stranger. Our entire relationship, short as it may be, Jackson has known that I willingly let another man touch me and then went home to be with him.

Jackson has endured so much for me, and he had to sit there and listen while I told *the other man* I couldn't choose.

"We're here, Miss," the cab driver says.

Looking out my window, I see that we are in front of Jackson's building. Remembering I left my purse at the restaurant, I'm thankful my phone is in my back pocket and use the Curb app to pay quickly before heading inside.

My nerves are shot as the elevator pings slowly as it takes me up to the top level of Jackson's building. Turmoil surges inside me, guilt and anger warring between my stomach and chest.

A million big emotions play musical chairs inside me. Waiting for the music to stop as the doors open to Jackson's place. Waiting to see which one won't have a seat and will need an outlet.

Jackson is in the living room. One arm braced against the window as he looks out at the city below. P-Kitty is on the sill next to him, his patchy tail swishing back and forth as his head turns to me, and he lets out a soft meow in greeting.

"I told you I didn't want to talk to you right now," he says without turning around. He sounds like he's been crying, his voice tired and thick with despair.

For a moment, I'm puzzled how he knows it's me, but then I see my reflection in the window as I walk closer. He still doesn't turn, but I can see his lip curl in anger from where I stand.

"You're just a glutton for punishment, aren't you, Red?"

The music in my head stops. All the emotions I've been feeling for the past twenty minutes taking their seat, leaving only one standing.

"Don't you mean *Little Ember*?"

His head whips around, surprise sprawled across his handsome face. My anger may have won out, but I know in my heart that when it's all said and done, I still love him. However, here, in this moment, knowing that fuels my rage.

"How did you find out?" he asks quietly, pushing away from the window to face me.

"How did I find out?" I let out a laugh and cross my arms over my chest. "How about *I'm sorry I lied and manipulated you?*"

His jaw clenches as he swallows thickly. "I'm not sorry."

My eyes widen, my hostile expression morphing into one of disbelief. "Excuse me?"

Jackson takes a step closer. "You heard me, Ginny. I'm *not* sorry. Because everything that happened at Désirer led us here!"

"You *tricked* me, Jackson! How on earth do you think that's okay?" I understand what he's saying, but I need to hear him tell me he's sorry for lying. I need him to acknowledge that it's a giant betrayal of my trust, and we're already on a fine line with that as it is.

"I'm not saying it's okay, Ginny. I know it was wrong. But you wouldn't give me the time of day. And when I saw you there that night, I acted impulsively. Then you said everything you did, and I…I just had to have you. Simple as that. I wanted you. I was going to have you."

My cheeks grow warm, remembering how eager I was to divulge information about my lack of sexual experience that first night. "What was the plan, then? Fuck me and leave me, then move on to the next girl at the club? You told me it was your first night there, too. Was that another lie?"

Thoughts of him fucking the other Angels swim through my mind. What if he's slept with Carmela during one of her rare appearances? Or worse, what if he fucked Lenni?

Tears line my eyes, and I let them fall, not bothering to hide how upset I am.

"No, that wasn't a lie. It *was* my first night. The only woman I've been with in there is you." He's eerily calm, whereas I'm a wrathful storm inside.

318

"So, *what* was your plan?" I ask again.

"Honestly, Ginny? I did want to fuck you and leave you. You had such a smart little mouth on you, and I wanted to make you my next conquest. Dating was never on the table. It wasn't a thing that I did, you know that. When you made your proposal and said you'd go on a date with me if I could last thirty days without sex with another woman, I readily accepted because I thought of how fun it would be to have you both in the club and outside of it, and you'd never know. It *was* a game."

His words are like a red-hot spear to my heart. I'm under no delusions that it was love at first sight. I hated him when I first met him. But hearing him say it out loud hurts all the same.

"Until it wasn't," he continues. "And I'll admit right now that I started to fall for you pretty fucking quickly. Everything you did, I was in awe of. The more time we spent together, the more you began to occupy my thoughts, and then it was like I couldn't have a good day unless you were in it. My world was dark and bleak before you bled color into it. You branded yourself on my soul, Ginny. And I handed you the branding iron."

I'm so sick of crying, but I can't seem to stop. His words are a blend of pain and beautiful poetry, just like our story. "And where do we go from here, Jackson? *How* do we go from here?"

"Do you still love me?" He's speaking softly but guarded, bracing himself for the possibility of me telling him no.

"Of course, I still love you, but I can't *trust* you!" I sob.

"Yeah, well. The feeling is mutual." His tone turns flat, eyes cast to the floor.

I almost forgot that Scott told Jackson I knew about his uncle's illness. "It wasn't my place to tell you! And what you did doesn't even compare!"

"Doesn't it, though? He's going to die, Ginny! He's going to die, and we've spent more time fighting or talking about business this last year than we have acting like we're family! You could have warned me! Would I still be upset? Yes, but I would have had *time* with him!" Jackson shouts, voice cracking.

Tears spring to his eyes, the sight of them washing away some of my anger. "He just wanted to prepare you–"

"You don't get it, do you? He's all I have left!"

"You have me!" I shout back, closing the remaining distance between us to reach for his hand, but he pulls away and stares down at me coldly.

"Do I? Because last night you didn't want to make that choice."

His words cut deep. A reminder that he tried to end the lie he carried on for so long, and he had to hear me say I wasn't ready to let go of another man.

Shaking my head, I reach for him again. "Jackson, that isn't fair."

He turns away, hands going to the back of his head as he sits on the couch and stares out the window again. "I think we should take some time apart."

Panic races through my stomach and pushes my heart into my throat. "No…no, I don't want time apart."

"Just last night, you couldn't let go of another man. Do you really *love* me, Ginny? Or do you just not want to be alone?" His words are sharp as a blade, cutting through to what's left of my shredded heart.

Hysterically, I ask, "So now what? I lose you both?"

Jackson looks at me as I collapse next to him. "There is no plural, Ginny. It's just *me*. It's always just been me. I think you need to take some time to decide if that's enough for you…if *I'm* enough for you."

"You are!" I reach for him, but he catches my hands mid-air and holds them between us.

"Then why couldn't you let *him* go?" he asks softly.

"Jackson, that isn't fair. You manipulated me!" Pulling out of his grip, I launch back off the couch, turning to point at him as if somehow that will change what's happening. As if it will remind him that he hurt me, too.

"You're right, I did," he admits. "And I'm an asshole for that. It was fucked up, but I never thought it'd go this far. I never thought we would be here."

"But we *are*! How am I supposed to feel? What do you *want* from me?"

He stands and pulls me to him. His arms hold me tight, his lips against the top of my head as he explains, "I just want to know that I can be enough for you. That knowing it was me in that room won't have you run off to look for someone to replace your stranger. I'm all in, Ginny. I just need to know that you are, too."

"I am all in, Jackson." He starts to pull away, but I hold him tighter, not letting him go as he sighs.

"You say that now, Red. But when all the adrenaline dies down and you have a moment alone to think about what I did to you, you might not feel the same. So, go home. Let's take a few days to cool off. Okay?"

Pulling back, I wrap my arms around myself as he lets me go. My tears have turned to sniffles and deep huffs as I try to regain normal breathing. There are wet trails on his face but no longer tears in his eyes.

"I love you," he says, leaning down to lay a chaste kiss on my forehead.

"I love you too."

Wiping my face, I turn away from him. Every reluctant step closer to the elevator puts another crack in my heart. As much as I want to keep arguing with him, I know he's right. He's making a mature decision to ask for some space.

That doesn't mean I have to like it.

Jackson

Walking into my uncle's penthouse is like walking into a museum. It's quiet, not a speck of dust anywhere, thanks to Claudia, but it doesn't look like a home anymore. He never replaced anything my aunt took to Jacksonville, punishing himself with the reminder that he had lost the best thing that ever happened to him.

The sound of his coughing drifts from the kitchen, and I make my way there, calling out so that he knows I'm here. "Hey, you okay in there, old man?"

He laughs and turns as I walk in. He's wearing a pair of red flannel pajama pants and a plain black t-shirt. It's been years since I've seen him so dressed down.

"As good as every other morning. Are *you* okay? How did things go with Ginny?" He sets his coffee on the Calacatta marble countertop and moves to make me a cup.

"Here, you sit. I can do it myself."

"You ignored my question."

"I don't know how to answer your question," I say as I prepare myself a cup. He's still drinking my aunt's favorite brand and blend—Blue Mountain Panama Catuai.

"She heard me in Carmela's office using my accent," I tell him as I join him at the dining table.

He looks at me with a confused frown and a shrug of his shoulders.

"That's how I spoke to her at Désirer."

His eyes widen in understanding before he lets out a deep breath. "I told you, you should have told her sooner."

"Doesn't really matter. When I tried to end things at the club Friday night, she begged me not to. She needs *him* more than she needs me." I glance over to see him watching me with pity in his eyes.

I try to change the subject. "Why don't you want to tell Aunt Sadie? I get why you didn't then, but why not now?"

"What difference would it make? Knowing your aunt, she'd want to come up to knock some sense into me. I highly doubt her *husband* would appreciate that." He rolls his eyes as he speaks the title he once held.

I can't blame him because the man she married, Tyler, is younger than I am. I know they had some sort of incident that involved my uncle having the shit beat out of the guy. He admitted he put his hands on Aunt Sadie the same night, which helped fuel his decision to grant her the divorce she'd asked for.

As much as Aunt Sadie loves her new husband, I hate him. His overly positive attitude grates on my nerves, and I've only met the man once.

"I still think you should tell her. And I think you should at least *try* some sort of treatment."

"Jackson, don't start."

"Why are you being so difficult?"

"Why don't you understand that I don't want to live out my last years with someone having to help me wipe my ass?"

Clenching my jaw, I fall silent. I see where he's coming from, but it still doesn't stop me from wanting to do everything in my power to make sure he doesn't die.

"Look, I want you to know something, okay? This isn't...
I'm not your father, Jackson. I'm not dying by choice."

"Aren't you, though?"

"No, because treatment or no treatment, I *am* going to die.
So, I'm choosing how I want to go out."

He gets up to put his cup in the sink before pulling open
the freezer to take out one of the elderberry shots Claudia
makes for him.

"You know, you have your own place, so I'm leaving this
one to Sadie."

"Does Claudia know?" The woman has worked for them
for so long, but she's too young to retire. Regardless of my
uncle's answer, I make a mental note to have Stacey draw up
a new contract for the housekeeper to come to work for me,
whenever that may be.

"Yeah, she's the first one I told. She's been with us for so
long—I'm leaving her a sizable amount as well. If you want
to discuss her working for you, you can. But I'm leaving her
enough so that if she doesn't want to work anymore, she
won't have to."

No one could ever accuse Tailors of not being generous.
We take care of the people who are loyal to us. And Claudia is
one of the most loyal people I've ever met. Whatever my
uncle is leaving her, it's well deserved.

"Are you going to try to talk to Ginny?" he asks, dumping
the shot into a glass and breaking it up with a spoon.

His question reminds me that Ginny knew his secret
before I did. "Why did you tell her?"

A smile tugs at his lips as he glances over at me. "If I tell
you, you gotta promise not to get mad."

Well, I don't like the sound of that at all.

"I make no promises."

He laughs, chugging the smoothie-like shot before
returning to the table to sit. "Last year, when Mick brought
me in, I was in charge of *auditioning* the Confessional girls. It
was my job to see if they had conversational skills."

I vaguely recall interrupting a lunch he was having with Aunt Sadie, where they were discussing his communication skills. "So, you what? Just talked to them? Why would I be mad about you talking to Ginny?"

"Because she was one of the first girls I auditioned. At the club. In the rooms." He looks at me expectantly, waiting for me to read between the lines.

"You saw her in lingerie?" I should be irritated, but instead, I feel bad for her. She was nervous enough with me the first night in the room. I can't imagine how nervous she'd been with him.

"You better not have touched her."

"No! I didn't touch her! Jesus, Jackson. I told her to put her robe back on and never return wearing clothes like that again when I was in the room. I even started taking the women out for meals after that. I figured it was better than being in a dimly lit box with them half-clothed."

A series of coughs erupt from his throat, and he grabs a napkin. Even though I'm sitting across the table, I can see the bright red specks of blood on the ivory linen. It's a glaring piece of reality that he is indeed sick, and this isn't just a bad nightmare I haven't woken up from yet.

"That's why you were photographed with so many women last year." It's a statement, not a question. Even I had been surprised to see him publicly stepping out on Aunt Sadie so many times.

"Why did you let the press run with the cheating stories if that wasn't what was really happening?"

Wiping his mouth with the napkin, he shrugs and shakes his head. "Honestly? I was lonely. Your aunt was always away in Jacksonville. Looking back, I know it was fucked up, but I thought she might catch wind and return."

"You embarrassed the fuck out of her," I say gently but pointedly. There's no sense in making him feel bad about it again.

"I know I did. And to be honest, not *all* of my interactions with the women *were* by the book. But I will say that nothing happened with Ginny. She's just easy to talk to. I started seeing her at the clinic not long after that. I grew quite fond of her—actually told Sadie I thought she'd be good for *you*. Didn't expect you two to collide like you did, though."

"Neither did I. Didn't expect to fall in love with her, either." Reaching up, I rub my temples, the caffeine in the coffee not doing much for the headache between my eyes that's been there since last night after Ginny left.

"Love sucks, kid. We can try and harden ourselves to it all we want, but eventually, that one woman is gonna come along and break down the walls we built so high. Sometimes it works, and sometimes all it does is create utter fucking chaos."

Utter fucking chaos. What a great way to describe Ginny's and my relationship.

I don't want to keep thinking about the possibility of her telling me she's done with me, so I change the subject. "Will you be in the office tomorrow? I think we should probably tell the board."

"No, tomorrow I'm a guest speaker down at NYU. I'll get something set up for next week. Let's just take this one to let the information settle, okay?"

I nod in agreement as my phone vibrates in my pocket. My heart jumps, hands moving quickly to pull it out, hoping it's Ginny.

It isn't.

It's Stacey sending me a message to say she won't be in tomorrow because she and Kaia are both sick with the flu. I send one back, asking if they need anything, before shoving my phone back in my pocket.

"What do you think I should do? About Ginny. What if she decides she wants to go back to the club? What if I'm not enough for her?"

"Why don't you fight for her, Jackson? Fight like hell. Show her you *are* enough. Show her that you want her.

There's a time and place for giving a woman her space. This isn't it," he scolds lightly.

"I feel like she needs the time to think about what she wants," I tell him.

"Well, then give her the rest of the night. But tomorrow? Tomorrow, you show her what she means to you—got it? Don't let her get away. I'll be fucking pissed if you do. She's like the daughter I never had."

"Gee, thanks, old man."

"Shut up, you're not a woman. You know I've always treated you like you were my own son."

His words bring an unexpected sting to my sinuses—the familiar burn of tears starting to form, causing me to look away from him. Not once in my entire life has he ever referred to me as his son. Knowing he feels that way makes the news of his illness that much harder—like I'm losing my father all over again. Only this time, I'm aware enough to know what's going on.

"Come here, kid. There's no one here to see two grown men cry." He reaches across the table to lay a hand on my arm, pulling my attention back to him to see him getting up. "Don't make me pull you out of the chair, Jackson."

Standing, I let him pull me into his embrace. I don't remember the last time we hugged—it must have been when I graduated, and even then, it was only half-hearted, both of us too proud to do anything other than the awkward back pat.

With no one else around, however, we hug each other and release all the frustrated emotions that have been building up. When I was younger, he always told me, *'Tailors don't cry,'* but we spend the rest of the afternoon reminiscing about better times and letting our tears fall whenever they come.

Because apparently, Ginny told him that showing emotions is healthy.

"She isn't here, but I'll take the roses to her office if you'd like?" Michelle looks at the bouquet in my hands, her neon purple windbreaker suit making a crinkling noise as she gets up to enter the waiting room.

"No, that's fine. I'll just take them home. Isn't she supposed to be working here today? It's Monday." I knew Ginny's work schedule as well as I knew my own. On Monday afternoons, she's always at the clinic.

When I woke up this morning, it was with my uncle's words fresh in my mind. *Tomorrow, you show her what she means to you—got it? Don't let her get away.*

As soon as I could leave work, I picked up the roses and came straight here. I would have been here first thing this morning if it weren't for the fact that I plan to show my uncle he's leaving the company in good hands. It's time to grow up and stop acting like I can fuck off whenever I want to.

"She had no clients on the books, so she took a personal day. Said she wasn't feeling that well, but I know she has a shift at the restaurant today, too. Hopefully, she was able to get some rest, poor dear. That girl works way too hard if you ask me." Michelle sighs as she sits back down at her desk.

I'm already headed for the exit, pressing Ginny's name on my phone as Robert opens the door to the car. She doesn't answer, and I hang up without leaving a voicemail.

"Home, Mr. Tailor?" Robert asks.

"No. Decadence, please."

Laying the bouquet next to me, I send Ginny a message.

> I stopped by the clinic to see you. Michelle said you weren't feeling well. Can I bring you anything?

There's no reply by the time we pull up outside the restaurant. Leaving the roses in the car, I tell Robert to keep it running while I go inside to check if she's there.

It's steady, but not overly busy. Ginny's russet hair is nowhere to be found, but I see Lenni is at the hostess stand today.

"Hey, bossman. Looking for your girl?" she asks as soon as I step through the door.

If she's being this cheerful toward me, then Ginny must not have told her about what happened. "Yeah, is she here?"

"I'm surprised she hasn't called you. Her brother came in earlier to get her. He said there's some sort of family emergency, and she needed to leave with him immediately."

Ice shoots through my veins, gripping my heart to the point I have to let out a cough in an attempt to dislodge the uncomfortable feeling. "Her brother?"

"Yeah. Tall, dark hair, broody eyes. Cute. She looked pretty distraught when they left. I told her to call me later and let me know what's going on," she replies before helping a couple who just walked in.

Spinning, I run out of the restaurant and return to the car, telling Robert to take me to The Bryant. I try Ginny again, but she doesn't pick up. Panic laced with fear rushes through my bloodstream, and my hands start to shake as I find the number for the building.

When the man at the front desk picks up, I practically shout, "This is Jackson Tailor. I'm wondering if Ginny has left at all today."

"Good afternoon, Mr. Tailor. Miss Ginny left a few hours ago and hasn't returned yet. Did you need to leave a–"

Hanging up the phone, I tell Robert to go to Ginny's old apartment instead and dial my uncle.

"Hey, I was just abou–"

"Are you still at NYU?"

"Just finished up. What's wrong, Jackson? Why do you sound–"

"I need you to go to this address. It's Ginny's old apartment. I need you to get there as fast as you can."

I give him the address and hear him repeat it to his driver.

"Her foster brother picked her up from Decadence. He's a psycho. He's abused her since they were kids," I explain quickly.

"Shit," he swears softly. "Are you serious?"

"Yes. I'm going to fucking kill him. I'm on my way, but you're closer. Traffic is starting to get bad. Just get her out of there, please."

"Of course. I'll call you when we're leaving."

"Thank you."

It takes everything I have not to throw my phone across the seat. My knees start to bounce, and my heart jumps into my throat. I try Ginny repeatedly, getting her voicemail every time, feeling completely helpless as my mind starts to think about all the bad things that could be happening to her right now.

Hold on, Red. I'm coming.

Ginny

Chris' cold, clammy hand grips my arm, tugging me out of the cab and onto the familiar sidewalk that leads to the apartment I abandoned so many weeks ago. His silence during the ride after showing up at Decadence out of the blue is unsettling.

"Ginny, your brother is at the front for you. He's hot! I can't believe you never told me you had a hot brother," Lenni jokes as she pokes my side.

My heart seizes, head whipping to the front to see Chris standing there, eyes glued to me, a deadly serious look on his face.

What the fuck is he doing here? He isn't supposed to be back for months.

Did Barbara tell him about seeing me and Jackson? Is that why he's back?

Ignoring Lenni's disturbing comment, I make my way to the front slowly. When I reach him, his eyes roam over my body as if he's looking for any evidence of change. "What are you doing here? I thought you weren't coming back for a few more months?"

He steps closer and grabs me by the arm, pushing me a few steps from where Lenni has resumed her position at the hostess stand. "And I bet you would have been moved in with him by then, wouldn't you?"

Gulping, I shake my head. All the confidence I've found since working at Désirer bleeds out of me from the stab wound his reappearance has made. "What are you talking about?"

Lenni catches my eye, frowning when she sees the look on my face. Chris barks out a short laugh. "Oh, Guinevere. Barbara told me all about how you're dating Jackson. I told her she must be mistaken, but she assured me you were very much together. So, I decided to come all the way back here to prove her wrong. Imagine my surprise when I got home to find all of your stuff gone. Didn't wait long after I left, did you?"

"You need to leave." I don't answer his question, or ask how he found out I worked here at Decadence. I just want him gone as soon as possible.

"Oh, no. I don't think so, Gin. I think you're going to come home with me right now." His lowered tone rises as he says, "There's been an accident with Mom, so we need to get going."

He grabs my wrist and pulls me over to Lenni. "Will you be a doll and grab her stuff, please? My mother has had an accident, and we must leave immediately."

Lenni mistakes the shock on my face and runs to the back to grab my things without another word. When she returns, she shoves them into my hands. "Go. I'll tell Carmela what's going on. Call later and update me."

I could have told him no. I should have stayed there, where I was safe from whatever hell he's about to unleash on me. But the look in his eyes told me that if I were to deny him, he'd make a scene.

I'd discreetly tried to pull my phone out and call Jackson during the ride, but Chris had seen and snatched my phone away before I could.

As he drags me up the stairs, he finally grinds out, "Why is it that you can't just be a good girl, Ginny? Huh? Why do you *always* have to test me?"

Twisting my arm in an attempt to pull free, I spit back, "You're fucking delusional. You think I *wanted* all the shit you did to me? Newsflash, Chris, I didn't!"

He laughs, squeezing my arm tighter while he unlocks the door. "Oh, is that right? Is that why you always begged me to let you come? To fuck you so that you could finally know what it felt like to be filled up by a real man?"

"I never begged you to fuck me, you psycho!" I may have begged him to let me come because when you've been brought to the brink so many times, in the moment, you'll say whatever to get off, but I *never* begged him to fuck me.

Once we're inside the apartment and the door shuts, panic settles in. I start to struggle in his grip. Twisting and turning, I throw my weight to the floor to try and knock him off balance, but he just holds onto me tighter as he laughs at my feeble attempt to escape.

"Let go of me!"

Chris hauls me off the floor like I weigh nothing, pulling me through the kitchen on the way to his bedroom. "I told you when I got back, I would fuck you. Did you just want to get experience for me, Gin? You wanted to make me feel good when we finally fucked, didn't you?"

A memory pops up of the night he found out about me losing my virginity. He swore he'd never fuck me after that, and he was so upset that someone else had gotten to me first. So, I decide to rub it in his face that I've been with Jackson, seeing if it will buy me any sort of time to try and figure out how to get out of this situation.

"You'll never compare to him! You'll never be able to make me feel the way he does. *He's* got experience and knows his way around a woman's body. What do you have, Chris? Nothing but a small fucking dick!"

An angry slap reverberates against the cold, familiar wallpaper of the kitchen—skin on skin.

The cold metal of his grandfather's ring against my flesh as its diamond teeth bite my cheek.

The smell of copper. Warm, red, liquid life.

"I knew I should have never left! I *knew* that asshole was

lying to me! But *you?!* You fucking bitch! I should have put you in your place a long time ago!"

Unmistakable, the sound of his belt buckle pulling apart. I let out a cry as his rough hands spin me and shove my face down onto the island.

Crimson smears against the cream marble.

There have been times in our life where he's been normal. Asking about the book I'm reading. Helping me with homework.

Like a brother.

He works with babies, for Christ's sake. Helping mothers with high-risk pregnancies and successfully delivering complicated births.

Like a saint.

Lingering touches, loving caresses when the night has eaten the sun, and the dark chases reality from every corner of my bedroom.

Like a lover.

Now, he's my personal version of hell. A devil that is more corrupt than ever before.

Provoked. Tricked.

Fooled.

Fingers twist in my hair as he yanks my head back, holding me down with his hips. "You both had me so convinced. But you've always been such a great little actress, haven't you? Does he know that you like it when I'm knuckle-deep inside you? Does he know that you cry, and moan, and beg like the whore you are?"

Struggling against him, I twist and contort my body away from the other hand that is trying to undo my pants. Red-hot fury courses through my veins, pumping adrenaline and giving me a burst of strength and courage.

"He hears me beg and moan every time he fucks me!"

With a surprising bout of strength, I brace my arms against the counter and push back, sending him flying in his stunned state at my declaration.

Two steps.

That's all I take before he tackles me to the ground with a roar. Our bodies become a tangled pile of limbs as I struggle against him and try to get away. Eventually, he's able to overpower me, grabbing my wrists and slamming them against the floor as he pins my lower body down with his.

I can feel his erection, and it sickens me to know that he's getting any sort of perverse pleasure out of this. "Let me go, you fucking bastard!"

"Not before I take what's fucking *mine*!" he roars over me.

It's getting harder to breathe, my vision blackening at the edges as I try to buck him off me. But he's so much bigger than me. He barely budges as tears start to prick the corners of my eyes.

Lifting me by the wrists, he slams me back to the floor. My head smacks against the hardwood, and white spots dance behind my eyes, bursting one after the other, turning into a kaleidoscope of colors.

My head rolls to the side, and he must see the dazed look in my eyes because he lets go of my wrists, and suddenly I feel him unbuttoning my pants.

"No...Chris, don't." I'm barely able to voice the words. They come out soft and weak as my tears start to fall, dripping over the bridge of my nose and onto the floor.

"Shut the fuck up. I would much rather have had you enjoy this, but you're leaving me no choice, Ginny. I'm going to fuck you so hard. Jackson won't want your ruined pussy after I'm done with it. Then what will you do, huh?"

He starts to tug my pants down, pulling them enough to where he reaches in and cups between my thighs. I try to raise my head, searing pain shooting between my temples as I push at his hand while squeezing my legs together. "Don't touch me!"

Chris slaps my hand away, tightening his hold on me as he says, "Maybe if you're a good girl, I'll keep you afterward. If you beg me, I might just let you–"

A sharp knocking cuts him off, the sound of Scott's voice ringing out loudly, "Ginny? It's Scott, open up!"

Scott.

The only reason he'd be here is if Jackson sent him. Jackson knows. He's trying to save me.

Chris growls above me as his head snaps in the direction of the front door. "Scott, hmm? Fucking the whole family now?"

"The cops have been called and are on their way! I suggest someone come to the door now before I kick the damn thing down!" Scott sounds tough, but I know he's too weak to be able to take down our heavy door.

Praying that he really has called the cops, I push through the pain and start to struggle again. The weight of Chris' body leaves mine for a moment, and I open my eyes just before his fist connects with my cheek, sending my head banging back into the floor.

My vision blurs, the image of Chris' feet walking away from me as he heads to the entrance, going in and out. I fight to stay awake. The urge to go to sleep or roll over and throw up are both strong as I hear Chris open the door.

"Ginny isn't here. Now, I'd appreciate it if you stopped making a commotion, Mr. Tailor," Chris reprimands Scott.

"Ginny?" I hear Scott call out again, followed by the door banging against the wall.

"What the fuck? Get out of my house!" Chris yells. I hear footsteps, and then Scott's polished chestnut Oxfords come into blurry view.

"Fuck, Ginny! I got you. It's okay," he says soothingly. Warm arms wrap around me, pulling me up gently while supporting my head, and I close my eyes.

Only for a moment. Just to rest them for a little while.

"Jackson's on his way. So are the cops. You're safe now," he says quietly. Then, louder, he tells Chris, "You're a fucking dead man."

For a moment, I think I'm truly safe.

Then I hear Chris start to laugh.

It starts as a chuckle and grows into something that resembles an unhinged, maniacal lunatic. "She really has done a number on you guys, hasn't she? That's what she does, though, isn't it, Guinevere? See, Mr. Tailor, she's got a sickness inside her. I've had to deal with it almost all our lives. She pretends like she's such an innocent little girl, but then she looks at you with her big blue eyes, and you just know there's an evil little seductress in there waiting to be unleashed. Tell me, did she fuck you too?"

"You're fucking sick, you know that?" Scott's arms tighten around me, body tensing. "Shit," he swears.

Cracking open my eyes, I can tell my left one, where Chris hit me, is swollen nearly shut. Out of the other, I see Chris leaning against the wall where the kitchen leads into the entryway, holding a gun.

When and where *did he get a gun?*

"That's what she does, Scott. She gets in your head and rots your brain." He taps the gun against his head before pointing it at us.

"You don't want to do that, Christopher. Do you want to lose your license? You shoot either of us, and you'll never work in the medical field again." Scott tries to reason with him as he gently lays me back on the floor.

The few minutes of reprieve have chased my nausea away, and even though my head still hurts, I start trying to sit up. "Chris, this is crazy. Put the gun down."

Chris swings it in my direction, then immediately back to Scott when he starts to stand—hands raised in surrender. "Listen, let Ginny and I leave, and we can forget this all ever happened."

Chris' dark eyes are nearly black as they dart back and forth between us. His hair hangs down into his eyes, a sneer on his face making him look like some sort of crazed demon. "She's not going anywhere."

"Let him go then." Slowly, I rise to my feet, pulling my

pants back up over my hips with one hand as I use the other to brace my weight against the wall. The cut from Chris' ring earlier has split open further from the second time he hit me, rivulets of blood streaming down that side of my face, over my lips to drip onto the floor.

"Ginny—" Scott starts, but I cut him off.

"Let him go, and we can go home. Okay? We'll go home to Beverly Woods. I'm sure Calvin and Christine would like that. And then after we can go wherever you want. I'll do whatever you want, Chris. I promise. Just let Scott go." It takes me so long to speak, heaving breaths through my nose and out of my mouth between words.

Partially because all I want is to fall back to the floor and go to sleep, but mostly because I'm trying to buy us time. Jackson must be close, and Scott said the cops were too.

Chris stares at me for a while. There's a pregnant pause as his eyes bounce between me and Scott until he finally settles his gaze on me. "Will you be a good *fucking* girl for *once* in your goddamned life?" he finally spits at me.

I nod, the motion causing a fresh wave of pain to burst behind my eyes. When I open them again, Chris steps toward me before there's a loud bang, and his head snaps toward the door.

Scott rushes over to me, pulling me behind him as a dark blur slams into Chris. It takes me a few moments to realize it's Jackson, and my heart jumps, knowing he came for me.

"Where the fuck are the cops?" Scott says to himself as he helplessly watches Jackson struggle to get the gun out of Chris' hand.

"You fucking asshole! If you touched one fucking hair on her head, I'm going to tear you apart!" Jackson shouts as he shoulder-checks Chris into the wall before punching him in the face.

"Oh, I did more than that, didn't I, Gin? Wanna tell him *where* I touched you?" Chris laughs in Jackson's face, his hand never loosening on the gun that's pointed at the ceiling.

"Stop! Stop it!" I shout from behind Scott. At any moment, all it will take is for Chris to point it at Jackson and pull the trigger. He'd never survive it at that range.

"Ginny, come on," Scott urges. He turns and tries to push me back into the hall on the other side of the kitchen, but I struggle against him the best I can, not wanting to let Jackson out of my sight.

"No! Jackson!" The further Scott drags me away, the harder it is to hear what Jackson and Chris are saying to each other.

"He's got it, Ginny!" Scott tries to reason with me, but no sooner than the words are out of his mouth, my worst fear comes alive.

The gun goes off. Its thundering boom reverberates in the kitchen.

"Jackson!" I scream. Everything seems to move in slow motion as Scott blocks my view.

Multiple voices are shouting, "NYPD! Hands in the air!" seconds too late.

It feels like my heart has stopped. Adrenaline pumps through my veins, working overtime to keep my body from collapsing.

Scott's fingers tighten on my arms, and my gaze rises to his...just as he falls to his knees.

Blood blooms brightly through the breast of his white dress shirt, staining the tan suit jacket he's wearing as it pours from the bullet wound just below his heart. Slowly, I sink to the floor as he collapses. "Scott..."

"Scott!" Jackson yells. My eyes snap up to see Jackson, alive and unharmed, fighting against an officer.

"We need an ambulance!" someone shouts.

Everything that was moving in slow motion clicks into real-time. Jolting forward, I press my hands over Scott's bullet wound as Jackson kneels on the other side of his body.

"Hang on, help is coming," he tells his uncle.

"Jackson, I want you to know that I'm proud as hell of

you," Scott says weakly. He coughs, blood appearing at the corner of his mouth.

"Don't you dare fucking speak like that. You're going to be fine!" As Jackson speaks, his voice cracks, splintering my heart into a million pieces.

This is all my fault.

"Tell your aunt I love her. Tell her I never stopped. Even when I was at my lowest and I...I–"

"We'll tell her. Try to save your energy. The ambulance is almost here," I cut him off.

Where the fuck are they? Where did the cops go?

My hands are covered in his blood.

It should have been me.

"I think we all know I'm not going to make it, Ginny," he says softly.

"You better fucking hold on, old man. I can't lose you. It's not your time yet," Jackson cries.

"It's okay, son. You're gonna be okay. Ginny will keep you in line. Ain't that right?" Scott tries to joke. Calling Jackson his son makes the man I love cry harder. My tears fall faster as I look down at the man who has been more like a father to me in the past year than Calvin has most of my life.

"*You're* going to keep him in line, Scott. You're not going anywhere," I tell him as I put more pressure on his wound.

"Will you sing for me?" he asks. His eyes are glassy, and his attention moves from me to the ceiling. "You know the song."

"I'm a shit singer, and you know it," I attempt to joke. He tries to laugh but coughs instead, more blood bubbling from his mouth.

My voice hitches and keeps cracking as I poorly sing the first few bars of his and Sadie's wedding song. When I get to the chorus, Jackson surprises me by chiming in through his tears, and his voice is just as pitchy as mine as a smile spreads over Scott's face.

His body shudders, and our voices die out just as the commotion of the paramedics arriving fills the apartment.

Scott's chest stops moving as someone gently pushes me out of the way.

Jackson's cries grow louder, and he starts to fight against a man who is trying to pull him from his uncle's body.

"Is that her blood or his?" I hear someone ask. Their voice sounds far away, and the edges of my vision blur and darken.

"Ginny!" Jackson shouts.

Then everything goes dark.

Jackson

"I've told you multiple times, Mr. Tailor—"

"I'm the closest thing to family she has! Her foster brother was just arrested for trying to sexually assault her and for murdering my uncle!"

I fucking hate hospitals. I understand the protocol, but sometimes the rules are just fucking stupid.

Ginny's nurse fixes me with a stern gaze and raises an eyebrow. "Don't make me call security. The doctor is in with her now. When he's done, I will talk with her and determine if she wants you in there."

As she walks away, my phone goes off in my pocket, and I pull it out to see it's my uncle's lawyer, George Wilkins, returning the call I made on the ride to the hospital. "Hello?"

"My condolences, Jackson. I'm sorry to hear about your uncle. Per your request on the voicemail you left, I've contacted Sadie on your behalf. She'll be on the first flight out of Jacksonville. I'm currently out of the office, but I can arrange a time on Wednesday for us to go over the will if that works for you. I'll need time to sort out some things and contact the other beneficiary."

"Other beneficiary?" Who else would he have left something to?

"Uh, yes. A woman, I believe. The name escapes me right now, but it was a recent addition." The sound of papers being shuffled fills the speaker as he pauses.

"Ginny? Or Guinevere?" I ask softly.

"Yes. That's it. Said there was plenty to go around. She must be pretty special, eh? Never thought I'd see Scott go soft for a woman other than Sadie."

Rubbing my forehead, I sink into one of the uncomfortable blue chairs in the waiting room, not bothering to correct whatever idea he has about who Ginny is to my uncle. "As for the other thing I mentioned?"

"Jackson, I've been doing this a long time, and Scott was a dear friend. You don't have to worry about anything from this office being sold to the press. No details from your uncle's will are going to be leaked. I promise you that," George says sternly.

"Thank you, Mr. Wilkins."

The sound of my name being gently called by Ginny's nurse stirs me awake. I didn't even realize I'd fallen asleep. "Mr. Tailor, Ginny's asking for you."

Checking my watch, I see I've been asleep for over an hour. Standing, my neck sore from the awkward angle I slept in, I follow the nurse as she leads me to a room down the hall. The door is cracked, and the lights are off, but there's a faint glow from the machines Ginny's hooked up to.

"I'll come back by to check on her in a little while. She's got a concussion. She's doing okay, though." As the nurse leaves, I push the door open and enter the room, shutting it quietly behind me.

"Jackson?" Ginny's voice is soft and weak. When I round the curtain that's been pulled to give her privacy, my breath catches in my throat as my heart seizes in my chest.

Rage rolls through me at the sight of her.

Her left eye is swollen shut, and black and blue bruises lead down around the cut on her cheek that looks like it's been stitched up.

She looks too small, too weak, in the hospital bed. Chris will regret the day he decided to lay a hand on her.

"How are you feeling?"

"I'm okay. How are you?" she asks. She scoots over and pats the space next to her.

Instead of climbing into the bed, I take a seat next to it. If I get in with her, I know I will fall apart, and this isn't the time or the place for that.

Her lips turn down, and she sighs, settling in the middle of the bed again as I respond, "I'm okay. Were they able to reach your parents?"

She nods. "His parents? Yeah, they're going to catch the first flight they can."

"Would you like me to call Lenni?" Leaning forward, I rest my elbows on the edge of the bed and grab her hand.

"No, I'll call her when I get home. They said I'll need to stay overnight, but they'll discharge me tomorrow." She twists her hand, interlacing our fingers as she scoots closer.

"He left something for you in his will. We're going to go over it on Wednesday. As soon as I know a time, I'll let you know."

She looks surprised. "Why are you being so serious right now, Jackson? And why are you already worried about Scott's will?"

"As soon as word gets out that he's gone, the press will try and get their hands on it. There were too many witnesses in the halls of the apartment complex. Your neighbors are the ones who called the cops and reported a domestic distur-bance. I guess when Scott was yelling through your door, the neighbor told him the cops were on the way."

"Jackson, I'm so sorry. It's all my fault–"

"Don't," I cut her off. "Nothing is your fault, Ginny. You can't blame yourself. If anything, it's my fault. I should have been the one to call the ccps right away instead of sending him because he was close."

She bites her lip, looking like she wants to say more but is worried. It makes me physically ill, knowing that she's been through so much in the last few days and that I've been the cause of most of it.

"What is it?" I ask.

Shaking her head, she squeezes my hand tighter. "I don't want you to end up resenting me."

It's incredible how she's worried about my feelings when she's the one who's just been assaulted.

Tears start to flow down her face, and I reach up to wipe them away before kissing her gently. "I could never resent you."

Standing, I gently maneuver her back against her pillows. "Now get some rest. I have some things I need to take care of now that I know you're okay. I'll be back later, alright?"

She nods against the pillow, her good eye already closing as exhaustion overtakes her. I'd like nothing better than to crawl into the bed with her and hold her throughout the night, but I have calls to make.

The rest of Chris' life is in my hands now. And I'm going to make sure it's a living nightmare.

It doesn't occur to me that my uncle's blood is still staining the front of my shirt until I walk into my building and receive curious looks from the people in the lobby.

I don't think it's fully hit me yet that he's *gone*.

He's dead because of me.

If I had just gone to her instead of sending him…

But then, would Chris have raped her? Would the cops have made it sooner if *I* had called them instead of her neighbors? Would it be Ginny lying in a body bag in a morgue?

The questions swirl in my head, one after the other on a loop, but one fact sticks out above all the rest.

If I'd just told her about being the stranger sooner, none of this would have happened.

Even if Chris had found out and returned, even if she'd chosen to leave me, it would have given us time. Time to figure shit out and make it work. If she'd been in a better place…I wonder if she even would have left the restaurant with Chris.

My phone rings just as I step out of the elevator, P-Kitty greeting me with a soft meow like he always does. Seeing it's my aunt, I decide to answer, even though all I want is a shower and to make my own calls before going back to the hospital.

"Hey, how are you, kid?" she asks softly. Her voice is thick with grief, and I can tell she's been crying.

No one could ever accuse her of not loving my uncle. She loved that man so damn much. Sometimes, I wondered how anyone could love *that* hard. Whether they were divorced or not, I know she must be hurting as much as I am right now.

"Numb," I tell her truthfully. "It hasn't fully hit me yet. I called Wilkins to make sure nothing got leaked to the press. The reading should be Wednesday."

"Jackson, stop. I don't care about the will. I care about you. I tried to get the jet, but by the time they would have been able to get it ready, it just made more sense to take a flight from here. I'll be there soon, okay?" Her tone is soothing, and even though I'm nearly thirty-five, all I really want is to curl into a ball and have her stroke my hair like she did when I was a kid.

"Are you going to come to my place first?" I move to the kitchen as we talk, putting food in P-Kitty's bowl before shrugging out of my suit jacket and heading upstairs to start the shower.

"No, we're just going to head to the penthouse–" she starts, but her words make me freeze on the steps as another wave of rage courses through me.

"You're not staying there, are you?"

"Well, since Ginny is at The Bryant, yeah, I did plan on staying there."

"You said *we*. You better not be bringing *him*. Your little boy toy isn't stepping foot in his home!" I don't care that he's her husband. How dare she think she can bring Tyler into the place she shared with Scott for years.

"Jackson, I know you're upset but–"

"I'm not kidding, Aunt Sadie. I do not want that fucking kid in his house!"

She's silent for a few moments, and I can hear the low-mumbling of Tyler telling her that he can stay in a hotel.

"Yeah, sounds like a great plan," I mutter.

"Okay, Jackson. You win. We'll stay in a hotel," she says.

"*You* don't have to. It's *him* I don't want there. I can't even believe you were going to do that, how disrespectful–"

"I'm going to stop you right there," Tyler's voice comes over the line. "I understand you're hurting, Jackson. I really do. And I am sorry for your loss. I have no problem staying in a hotel because the last thing *I* want is to be disrespectful, but you will not speak to my wife that way. Is that clear?"

My fist flexes at my side. I raise my phone to my forehead while my jaw clenches, and I let the air in my lungs escape slowly through my nose, struggling not to shout at this man who thinks he can just waltz in and stomp all over my uncle's memory.

"Jackson?" My aunt's voice sounds from the speaker, and I slowly bring the phone back to my ear.

"Keep him away from me," I tell her, my voice low and as even as I can make it.

She doesn't get a chance to respond as I disconnect the call.

By the time I make it back to Ginny, her parents have arrived.

Christine is weeping at her bedside as Ginny does her best to console her, even though it should be the other way around. Calvin's gaze swings to me as I walk in, the shame apparent on his face.

"I'm sorry about your uncle, son," he murmurs, unable to look me in the eye as he says it.

"I'm not your son. Your son will live the rest of his life in a maximum security prison, at the mercy of men whom I've employed to ensure his time there serves as a reminder of what he took from Ginny and what he took from me."

Calvin swallows thickly, his bushy gray mustache twitching as he sniffs and nods. "If there's anything we can do–"

"You should have put him in line when they were younger," I snap.

Christine's cries have turned to soft whimpers as she watches the exchange between me and her husband, her hand lying limp in Ginny's, who has a tired expression plastered on her face as she lets me speak.

"You should have paid more attention to the way he treated her. It was your job to protect her. You're a fucking parent! It was your *job* to notice those kinds of things!" My voice rises as I continue.

Calvin nods and swallows a sob. "I know. I know we failed as parents–"

"You didn't just fail. You traumatized a little girl who will have to live with what was done to her for the rest of her life!"

"Jackson, I'm okay," Ginny says softly, pulling my attention to her.

Our eyes lock, and even though she only has one to see through, it's shining with strength as she nods slightly and repeats herself. "I'm okay. *We're* going to be okay."

Her will to make those words ring true chases away the anger that's building in my chest. It's believable now, the hope shining through her features. But it makes me wonder what will become of us once the adrenaline of our situation recedes and leaves us stripped raw.

We need time to process. Time to grieve. Will we be able to do those things together? Or will we constantly remind each other of everything terrible that's happened in the last few days?

Ginny spends the rest of the night and the next day resting before the hospital discharges her. As much as I don't want to leave her in the care of her parents, I'm kept busy by the never-ending phone calls ranging from dealing with business things to the press asking for my comments about my uncle's death.

So busy that I avoid my aunt until the reading of the will on Wednesday.

Ginny squeezes my hand as Robert parks outside the lawyer's office. "Are you sure I should be here?"

It's the first time we've spent more than an hour together in days—the first time Christine has left her side or let her out of her sight. As much as I want to do nothing more than dote on her as she heals, it's clear that Christine and Calvin finally taking responsibility for everything is what Ginny needs right now. And if that's what she needs to heal, then I'm not going to deprive her of that.

"He confirmed it's you that Scott added to the will. You

have a right to be here. There's nothing to be afraid of." I run my thumb over hers to try and soothe her nerves. I don't know why she's so afraid of seeing my aunt, but it's caused her nothing but anxiety since I picked her up earlier.

We're not in the waiting area of the office long before my aunt arrives. She waltzes through the doors like a cool breeze on a summer day. Stunning, as always, even with the heavy weight of grief present on her face.

The comfort I feel at her familiarity is quickly doused by the man who follows her inside.

"Why is *he* here?"

My aunt stops, taking in Ginny's appearance and landing on our joined hands. Her tone is soft and has no bite as she replies, "I could ask the same."

Ginny tenses beside me as Tyler draws up next to my aunt, his hand finding the small of her back. "I'm just here for moral support, Jackson. Calm down."

"Worst thing to say to someone who is the furthest thing from calm," Ginny says under her breath.

Tyler's eyes snap to her, a slight smirk pulling at his lips. "You're right, gingersnap. I'm sorry."

A door opens behind us, the weathered face and graying hair of George Wilkins coming into view as he steps out and takes a look between the four of us. "All ready?"

Ginny and I sit on one side of the long table in the room, with my aunt and Tyler on the other, his hand never leaving her back as he helps her into her chair. Even when he sits, I notice it still rests above her knee.

It makes me think of how I always feel the need to be touching Ginny.

Anchoring her.

"Right. Well, everything is pretty standard. Scott took care of all the funeral preparations already. As agreed in the divorce, Sadie, you'll get the penthouse and the beach house in Malibu. He left the Holland Park residence to Jackson since the business has offices in London, as well as the home in the

Hamptons. And the apartment at The Bryant was left to Guinevere Mills."

Ginny's breath catches, and she turns her wide eyes to me. "He left me the apartment?"

"Of course, he did," my aunt says under her breath.

George looks at them both over his readers before continuing. "There is also an account set up to maintain the bills for each residence. Jackson, he made you the executor to oversee the allocation of the funds. However, there is a stipulation."

My aunt lets out a soft laugh. "And, of course, he'd still be trying to control things."

The statement is said fondly with melancholy. We share a small smile before directing our attention back to George.

"At no time are you allowed to cut your aunt off from receiving any of the money set aside for the residences. Doing so will make your place as executor null, and it will immediately transfer to her...and she has no such stipulations." George chuckles.

"As if I'd ever do such a thing," I mutter, rubbing my eyes, vaguely offended that my uncle would think I'd do that to my aunt.

I'm tired, and everything is beginning to catch up with me. I feel like I could sleep for a week, and it still wouldn't be enough.

"Jackson, you will inherit all of Scott's shares in the company and forty percent of his assets, with Sadie receiving the remaining sixty percent. Sadie, I'm assuming Scott informed you that he changed the life insurance policy so that Jackson was his beneficiary?"

That's news to me. But the slight nod from my aunt says that she already knew.

"Well then, I think that settles the big stuff. Except for the family ring," George says, sending her a knowing look.

"I have it in safe keeping for Jackson when he's ready for it," Aunt Sadie says slyly, her eyes bouncing between me and Ginny like she's in on a secret we don't know.

Ginny's hand tightens in my own, and I look over to see that her cheeks look like a cherry has kissed them. When I return my gaze across the table, I see my aunt and Tyler sharing a knowing smile, and irritation prickles beneath my skin.

"I don't want it. The damn thing is obviously cursed." My words are out before I can stop them. Standing, I pull Ginny's chair out and offer her my hand. "If that's all, I'd like to get my girlfriend home so she can rest."

Walking down the hall, I text Robert to bring the car around. "I should stay and talk to Sadie. I'll have Robert take you home."

"I can wait for you at your place?" Ginny's tone is filled with a need I'm not sure I can meet right now.

"I think it's best if you go to yours. I'm not sure when I'll be home. And, honestly, I'm exhausted. I've barely slept. I haven't had any time to process...*anything*. Maybe it's best for us just to have a little space."

"I don't want space. I just want *you*," she pouts, wrapping her arms around herself.

I want to believe her. Every fiber in my being wants to reach out and pull her to me. To comfort her and be comforted by her. To start over and put everything behind us.

But we're still at this standstill. I still don't know if I can be enough for her, and she still doesn't know if she can trust me. Neither of us knows how to move on, and it's apparent on both our faces and in our body language.

"I think we both know that if we go home together, nothing will be solved. We're both exhausted, and I don't want to fall into a routine with you without having a proper conversation about everything. We can't just pretend like none of it happened. Let's just get through the rest of the week. Okay?"

Keep her close. Push her away. I'm sure I'm confusing her just as much as I'm confused. It isn't fair. All I want is to wipe our slate clean. But the blank canvas is filled with charcoal smudges from our past that keep making more of a mess the more I try to clear them away.

She nods in agreement. Her eyes turn glassy, and the sight makes my chest ache. I'm so tired of making her cry.

"I love you," I tell her, reaching out to wipe a tear away as it slowly trails down her cheek. The other is still stitched up, but looks like it's healing nicely—the skin around the cut is still bruised, but the swelling has gone down.

"I love you, too," she breathes out as she surges forward to wrap her arms around my waist. She lays her forehead against my chest as I return her embrace and kiss the top of her head.

"I'll see you in a few days," I tell her, opening the car door and making sure she's settled inside.

Grasping her chin between my index finger and thumb, I stroke her bottom lip with my thumbpad as she stares up at me with glassy eyes.

I want to say fuck it. I want to get in the car with her and take her home and never let her leave the bed. Wrap her in my arms and sleep the rest of the week away. Instead, I pull away and close the door, gently tapping the hood to let Robert know he's good to go.

Another black town car pulls up as he leaves, and I turn to see my aunt and Tyler walking toward me. Tyler and I lock eyes, both our gazes narrowing, before he rolls his and pulls Sadie to him to kiss her temple. "Call me later."

She nods as he walks away to fuck knows where. I don't care. She fixes me with a hard stare and nods to the car. "Come on. We're overdue for a talk."

"You know, I never meant to hurt you by leaving, Jackson," Aunt Sadie says as she shrugs out of her jacket and sets it with her purse on the table in the foyer.

It's weird to see her here again, especially when my uncle and I just sat together at the dining table a few days ago. Her absence has been felt here for so long, and now she's standing in the middle of her old home like she never left.

"I honestly didn't think you'd care this much. Why didn't you tell me you were upset?" she asks, moving to the bar cart to make herself a dirty martini.

"Would it have mattered? You both blindsided me with the divorce. Uncle Scott said I was an adult and needed to handle it like one. You sure as shit didn't seem to care how I felt." I loosen my tie and sink into my uncle's Eleanor Rigby Churchill recliner.

"Scott and I hid a lot from you. Things weren't great between us and hadn't been for a long time–"

"I know! Why do you think he kept it from you? The cancer? He wanted to set you free because he knew he fucked up! But if you just *stayed*–"

"Would you ever hit Ginny?" she asks, whirling around and taking a few steps toward me. Tears are in her eyes, and as my brows knit together at her question, the all-too-familiar sting hits my sinuses.

"No! What kind of question is that?"

"Once upon a time, Scott would have answered that question with the same conviction. And then he *did* put his hands on me. He threw a glass at the wall next to my head just steps from where we are now, and I will spare you the dirty details of what happened next, all while Tyler was getting the shit beat out of him in a random alleyway. Tyler could have *died*! And yet you think I should have stayed?

"And you know what the fucked up thing is, Jackson? It's that if he had told me he was sick, I *would* have because I *loved* him. But he didn't tell me because he loved me, too. And he knew he fucked up, so he let me go. Sometimes, you have to let things you love go because you know that if you try to keep them close to you, if you smother them, you will suffocate them."

Her words come out cracked through fresh tears and thick with warning tones. Is it a warning? What is she trying to tell me? That I'm no good for Ginny?

"I'm so sorry that I hurt you, Jackson. I never meant to. And looking back, I know it was wrong to cut communication. We're family. I should have been better. You're just always so hostile about Tyler–"

"I'm sorry," I cut her off. "I don't mean to be. He just irritates the ever-living fuck out of me. He's always so fucking happy, and his parents are the reason my father…"

I trail off, having never admitted it out loud. What my real issue with Tyler is.

Never admitted that my father was so greedy he tried to get his hands on Tyler's father's business, and when Thomas Michaelson wouldn't budge, he hired someone to scare the man, which resulted in a car crash that took three lives. Tyler's parents—and ultimately my father's, by his own hand. Because the guilt ate away at him until he couldn't take it anymore.

"Do not finish that sentence, Jackson. You know damn well Tyler's parents are not responsible for what happened to Simon. And Tyler sure as hell isn't. He lost his father, too. *And* his mother."

"Yeah, he took *that* away from me, too."

Her eyes grow wide, breath catching before she reaches down to swivel the recliner to face where she sits on the matching sofa. "Jackson…. You've never mentioned…that you thought of me that way."

Because by the time I realized I did, I was ashamed I'd jerked off to your photos. Talk about an Oedipus complex.

Shrugging, I look anywhere but at her, replying with, "You were the closest thing I had. Besides Grandma."

She blows out a breath, sitting back as she wipes her eyes. "Well, moving forward, do you think we can at least try to act like a family again?"

Nodding, I lean forward, motioning for her to do the

same. As we embrace, the tension bleeds from my body. Everything in my life feels like it's been shattered into a million little pieces, and I don't have any idea how I'm going to glue it all back together.

"Yeah, I'd like that."

But this seems like a good start.

Ginny

I t seems fitting that the day of Scott's funeral would be cold, gray, and gloomy.

Much like my entire personality right now.

Jackson has been…absent, for lack of a better word.

No. No, that's the exact word I would use to describe his actions. Part of me can't blame him. He's dealing with so much. Even though Scott made all of his own funeral preparations, there are still so many things Jackson has to deal with in terms of the business and all the legalities of transferring things over.

If my texts don't go unanswered completely, he replies with short sentences or just one or two words. It's hard.

It's hurtful.

All I want is him, and he keeps making every excuse to put distance between us. How am I supposed to feel about that? Scott is dead because of me. How could Jackson *not* feel a little resentful?

It's odd to think that just a few days ago, it was *me* who was the resentful one. Jackson turning out to be my stranger completely blindsided me, but now all of that anger feels so meaningless.

I want him. Pure and simple.

But he won't let me close enough to tell him that to his face.

The clouds in the sky are fat and heavy with the promise of rain, and the lawn of Green-Wood Cemetery is teeming with a sea of black as people gather for Scott's burial. As I get closer, I see the pure mahogany casket with the lid shut, covered in a spray of white roses and baby's breath.

Jackson stands near the front of the crowd, looking so tired I'm worried he may fall asleep where he stands. Dark circles ring his unfocused eyes, and his skin has a sickly pallor against the pure black suit he wears.

My heart breaks at the sight of him.

Stepping forward to claim my place by his side, I freeze as a familiar leggy blonde steps into view, throwing her arms around him as she cries into his neck.

Viktoriya.

A bomb goes off in my stomach, pushing my organs every which way as they twist and turn and threaten to combust at the sight of her wrapped around him.

He doesn't move back or pull her away. He continues to stand frozen, unblinking at the space where the casket will be lowered within the hour.

It's his aunt who pulls the boundary-crossing bitch off of him, physically making her find another place in the crowd.

"Hey, gingersnap," a smooth voice says over my shoulder. Tyler is there, reaching for my elbow and pulling me along with him as he directs us out of the section of the crowd we're in.

"My wifey wanted me to come get you. Says you're part of the family, so you should be standing next to them," he answers the question I don't voice.

It's the only thing he says as he leads me to them, where Sadie reaches for me and settles me next to Jackson, who doesn't acknowledge my presence. Up close, he looks even worse than he did from the other side of the crowd.

Leaning into him slightly, I reach for his hand, threading

our fingers together so that he knows I'm there to support him however I can.

His fingers tighten against mine as he takes a shuddered breath, eyes lining with tears that he blinks away furiously, refusing to let them fall in the public eye.

"I love you," I whisper. "I'm here."

Minutes tick by as more people show up. Sadie and Tyler quietly talk on the other side of us, pausing to acknowledge anyone who comes up to offer their condolences to her.

No one tries to approach Jackson.

Right before the officiant starts the service, Jackson turns and looks down at me. What I see on his face scares me. He doesn't look like a man about to be forced to say goodbye to his uncle.

He looks like the man I love, trying to figure out how to say goodbye to *me*.

Sadie pinches the arm of my peacoat as the service ends.

Jackson turns to leave, Tyler trailing behind him as she holds me in place. "Let him go."

Panic grips my rib cage and rattles the bones till I fear they might crack, but I let her keep me there, not bothering to move when she drops her hand away.

"Scott used to be the same way. When Simon, Jackson's father, died, Scott spent a week drunker than piss, and I could barely talk to him. He was nasty and cruel, and that week was the first time I ever caught myself hating him. But he was hurting, and I learned that it was just the way he dealt with things."

"Why are you telling me this?" The crowd thins until it's just the two of us standing there, watching them put Scott's casket in the ground as the rain starts to drizzle down slowly.

Sadie fishes an umbrella from her purse, opening it and

ushering me closer so we're both safe from the downpour as it starts to pick up. "Because losing people you love is hard. But you know that already, don't you? Jackson told me about your mother."

The weight of my head feels heavy as I nod. Out of my peripheral, I see her turn to look at me. "Don't give up on him. Today is the first day he's had a moment to breathe."

"I'm not giving up on him. I'm trying to be there for him, and he won't let me." Angry tears line my lashes, and I clench my teeth to keep them at bay.

"Jackson has grown tremendously since I last saw him. And I think you are the one responsible for that, Ginny. He's pushing you away because he's hurting, and he doesn't want to hurt you while he figures out how to deal with his feelings."

We stand in silence. The urge to return the way she's trying to bring me some peace violently crashes against the forefront of my mind. "Scott never wanted to hurt you. The day you came to Decadence, when Carmela told you he brought women to California? They were nurses disguised as escorts, so no one would figure out he was sick. He tried…in the beginning. He really did."

She didn't shed a tear the entire service, but my confession has her pulling her oversized sunglasses from her purse and putting them on, even though there's no sunshine in sight. "I know he loved me. And he knows I loved him. But sometimes that isn't enough."

Her body starts to shake as she looks away from me. Gently, I pry her hand from the umbrella and take over holding it above us. It's slightly difficult because she's almost as tall as Jackson, but I manage, stepping into her as I balance my weight on the balls of my feet.

She immediately notices and resumes hold of it, shaking her head as she says, "I can see why he liked you."

My ego inflates at her comment, but her next sentence makes my heart swell.

"Thank you, Ginny. For being there for him. For being there for both of them."

From the moment I first laid eyes on her, she's intimidated the hell out of me. But since I fully intend on sticking around and being a part of Jackson's life, I push my luck with the beautiful former model. "You know, I'd really like it if we could be friends."

"Friends?" she laughs. "I'm old enough to be your mom, gingersnap."

"Tyler is only a few years older than I am," I deadpan.

She shoots me a *very* unamused look. "Don't remind me."

$$Jackson$$

Everything hit me on the day of the funeral.

Every emotion I'd been keeping locked away. Every ounce of grief I tried to hide from the public eye. Every single part of me that wanted to keep it together…

It all fell apart as soon as I got back in the car after the service.

If Ginny hadn't been there, holding my hand through it, I'm sure I wouldn't have even made it through all the long talks about what a great man Scott was and the legacy he left behind.

The legacy he left to me.

The responsibility no one thinks I'm ready for.

But now, as I look around the boardroom the Monday after the funeral, there isn't one person willing to look me in the eye and challenge me as I step into my uncle's role.

"Well then. If no one has anything else to say, I think this meeting is over." There's no warmth in my tone, no inspiring speech about how I plan to make my uncle proud.

There's only the matter-of-fact statement that *I'm* in charge now.

Not one single member of the board believes in me—but

not a single one of them will stand up to me either, now that I'm the head of the Tailor empire.

They file out as Stacey moves from her seat behind me to take an empty chair at the table. It's not long before Tripp joins us, the three of us sitting silently until we're the only ones in the room.

"How are you?" Stacey asks, reaching over for my hand.

"I'm okay. Slept for two days straight. Claudia thought I was dead."

"Yeah, that was me who had her do a welfare check on you," Tripp says.

Stacey throws him an incredulous look. "You sent *Claudia* to see if he was dead? You put that responsibility on that poor woman instead of being a man and going to check yourself?"

"Hey, what if he was balls deep in Ginny, and I walked in on that shit? Better Claudia than me, okay?"

As they fall into their playful banter, my thoughts drift away at the mention of my girlfriend. The woman I've been avoiding because I don't know how to look her in the eye and ask her the same question as before.

Am I enough for you?

She's had days to heal, to sort out her feelings, without my presence clouding her judgment.

Not a day has passed when she hasn't sent me a text every morning and every night—fighting for me.

"Why don't you fight for her, Jackson? Fight like hell. Show her you are enough. Show her that you want her."

My uncle's words have come and gone all day.

The next few months will be busy, and I don't know if I want to subject Ginny to the whirlwind that will be my life while things transition over.

She deserves peace.

"She deserves to make that decision on her own." My uncle would have said.

"Earth to Jackson." Stacey snaps her fingers in front of my face, pulling me from my trance. "How *is* Ginny?"

"I don't know. I'm trying to give her space that she keeps saying she doesn't want, but so much has happened that I don't think she knows what she really wants."

"Jesus Christ, you idiot," Stacey mutters.

"Hey, don't be mean to him. Jackson doesn't understand how feelings work, Tace. You gotta explain it to him like he's five." Tripp reaches over and claps me on the back.

"It's okay, Jackson. I'll spell it out for you. If Ginny says she doesn't want space, don't give her space. She's going to think you don't want her. Listen to what she says she wants, and then give it to her. However, I can't promise that will always work because women are cold, cruel creatures who like to change their minds at the drop of a dime, and it very well could always turn out that what they say they want isn't *really* what they want and what they say they don't want is apparently somehow exactly what they want?" He takes a deep breath after finishing his run-on sentence as Stacey and I stare at him.

"You really need to get laid," Stacey says as she shakes her head.

"Yeah, that reminds me. Jackson, I demand an invite to this super exclusive sex club of yours," he says.

Of mine.

Désirer is now partly mine.

Or—at least I have a stake in it. I should talk to Carmela.

It hits me so suddenly, the answer to all the questions I've been asking Ginny. It's so simple I almost laugh at how stupid it is that I never thought of it before.

Reaching for my phone, I send off a message asking if Carmela is available to talk. Her reply is almost immediate.

"Where are you going?" Stacey asks as I get up. "It's the middle of the day, Jackson."

"He's the big boss now. He doesn't have to answer to anyone," I hear Tripp say behind me, explaining it to her like she isn't already aware of this fact.

She sighs. "Like he ever answered to anyone before?"

"I need you to secure a room for me tonight. And inform Ginny that she's been booked."

Carmela looks from her computer screen to me, raising an eyebrow as she replies, "It's not a Friday or a Saturday."

The way she says it is slightly accusatory—more than simply knowing those are the days Ginny worked at Désirer. The gleam in her eye is telling as her crimson-painted lips turn up in a smile.

"You knew?"

"I know everything that goes on in my club, Jackson. I knew the second you had two cards made the first night you were here. Morroni's men answer to me, not to Mick, and they certainly didn't answer to your uncle."

"Why didn't you tell him? My uncle?"

She sits back in her chair, fixing me with an introspective glare before she speaks again.

"I didn't like you at first, you know."

"Gee, really? I couldn't tell."

Carmela lets out a snort. "I always keep my cards close to my chest. Telling your uncle right away would have just caused more problems. I may not have liked you, but I wanted to give you a chance. And I watched the way you changed for her. She's made you a better person, Jackson. And while that's wonderful, have you made *her* better in return?"

"Yes." My reply is immediate. "She needed a place where she felt safe, but it could have been any man who walked into her room at Désirer. Any man who would have taken what they wanted from her without a second thought for her feelings. What I did with her, what I helped her realize about herself...even if she ends up walking away from me, she's confident enough now to know her boundaries and her limits. And even if she *does* decide I'm not what she wants, I'm proud as hell to be a part of her growth."

Carmela watches me for a long time without saying anything. So long that I begin to wonder if she will respond at all.

Finally, she says, "*I* know that. I just wanted to see if *you* did as well."

She pauses, pursing her lips as she steeples her fingers in front of them. "I can't promise that she'll agree to go. She quit, you know?"

For the first time in a long time, my signature cocky smirk finds its way to my face. "Tell her that her stranger will be waiting for her."

<h1 style="text-align:center">Ginny</h1>

S oft, giant, silvery wings are waiting for me outside my dressing area. These ones are bigger than the black and gold ones and have more meaning behind them.

Trust.

Experience.

"He requested you wear them. Along with the outfit he sent," Carmela says behind me.

My stranger.

Jackson.

When Carmela called and told me I'd been booked, I immediately said no. I'd already told her I was done working at the club.

But then she said *he'd* be waiting for me.

Hearing those words let all the stress and tension from the week prior melt from my body, leaving hope and anticipation in their wake.

And maybe just a little anxiety.

Why does he want to meet *here*?

Why didn't he tell Carmela to say *he* would be waiting, instead of specifically saying I'd be meeting *my stranger*?

Jackson has barely spoken to me in days—avoiding me so I can take our time apart to decide what I want.

I don't know how to get it through his thick skull that I just want *him*.

But now he's asking me to meet him here—the place where our storyline unfolded.

Before we both ripped the pages out and threw them into the flames.

Is this our elegy? Will this be a sad lament of a relationship that never truly got to flourish?

Does our story end tonight?

A female security guard enters the room, taking Carmela's attention away from her phone. "You have a visitor in your office, Ma'am."

"You gonna be okay?" Carmela asks me.

I'm not entirely sure why she's being so informal with me. I know she's close with Lenni, and technically, Jackson has a huge stake in Désirer now, but Carmela has never been so attentive before.

"I'll be fine. You don't need to worry about me," I tell her as I pull the outfit Jackson sent off the hanger. It's a simple slip dress—black satin with scalloped edges.

"I don't worry about you, Ginny. I've watched you blossom since you met him. You've become a strong woman —the perfect example of *why* I created Désirer. Everyone deserves a happy ending."

The way she says the last part has me asking, "Did you get your happy ending?"

Carmela smiles. It's the type of smile that is full of secrets she'll likely never tell me. Her eyes fall back to her phone. "You could say that. Now go get yours."

Every nerve ending in my body feels like it's been electrified as I walk down the Desires wing. The large, feathered wings on my back are heavy, but it's a comforting weight, grounding me in the moment.

This hall has vases of the reddest roses I've ever seen. Huge blooms, with a scent that is almost too strong to breathe in without their smell getting caught in the back of my throat —trying to overpower the heady musk of sex that permeates the air.

The smell doesn't seem to bother my guard as he opens my door and steps back to allow me in.

"You don't have to stay tonight," I tell him.

"It's my job, Miss Scarlett," he replies.

I think about telling him it's his boss in the room waiting for me but decide against it, stepping across the threshold and shutting the door behind me.

The Desires room is vastly different from the other two wings. There's a giant chandelier hanging in the center of the room. It's dimmed but illuminates the room with more light than the other two. There's something anchored to the ceiling around it—a sex swing maybe—and a giant four-poster bed against the far right wall.

Directly in front of me is an entire setup of sex toys. Nothing is hidden in drawers but set out on display. A massive black dresser with things I've never seen before sits in the corner, with a giant Saint Andrew's cross beside it.

Slowly, I run my fingers over the different items hanging on the left wall. Whips, chains, rope, and long satin ties are neatly lined up, just waiting to be used for whatever pleasure the people using the room desire.

With as rough as Jackson likes it, I wonder if he's ever used any of these things on a woman before.

The sound of ice clinking in a glass has me spinning to see him sitting on a velvet chaise along the wall behind the door. He's watching me, his face nearly visible behind the simple black mask he wore the first night we met.

He's dressed in black dress pants and a white dress shirt

like normal, only this time, the sleeves are rolled up to expose his forearms, and the top few buttons are undone, causing my stomach to start doing flips. Arousal swims low in my belly, and my mouth waters at the sight he makes.

"Hi," I offer lamely.

My greeting is met with silence, though I can see his eyes roving over my body as he calmly sips from his glass.

"I'm surprised you asked me to come here," I continue, the need to fill the silence spurring me on. "This is the place where everything fell apart."

He shifts, settling back as he uncrosses his legs and spreads them wide as if getting ready to watch a show.

And *I'm* the entertainment.

A flame ignites slowly, licking its way down my body to settle between my legs. The soft click of my heels on the hardwood is relaxed as I approach him, stopping when my bare knees brush the fabric of his pants.

"Would you be mad if I said I can see it now, and I don't know how I never noticed it before? I think...at a certain point...I might have subconsciously known. The way my body fit against yours, it was the same. The way your fingers felt inside me. But you were so careful to make sure I never noticed the little things like your voice and your scent. How you'd never look me in the eyes for long."

He still doesn't respond, just stares up at me as I speak, his glass nearly empty as he swirls what's left of the amber liquid around the giant ice ball.

"Jackson, will you please say something? *Anything*?" My voice is pleading. His unwillingness to talk is starting to make me nervous.

"The last time we were here, Little Ember, I told you that I'd never fuck you." He finally speaks—with his accent, which takes me by surprise.

"Jackson, you don't hav–"

"Thirty days," he interrupts, continuing his husky English intonation.

370

Slowly, he sits up, reaching for the hem of my slip to pull me closer. When I'm standing between his knees, he slides his hands beneath the fabric. His warm hands skate along the outside of my thighs and up to grip the swell of my ass.

"What?" I ask shakily, my hands finding the top of his shoulders as he skims his lips over my stomach. His hot breath dampens the silk, and my skin pebbles beneath it.

Jackson pulls me closer abruptly, lifting me by my thighs to settle me on his lap. I can feel the rock-hard ridge of his cock through his pants as he pulls me down onto him while his lips pepper kisses along my collarbone.

"Once, every thirty days, you can have *him*. This room. The masks. The personas. They all stay here." He pushes his hips up, the hand on the base of my spine pressing me into him as he rocks against my center. "At home, we're *us*. You and me. That *has* to be enough. *I* have to be enough for you. But until you're ready to let him go, I can offer you this."

There's no way to describe his tone other than vulnerable.

Sliding my hands into his hair, I gently pull his head away from my neck and press our foreheads together, our masks almost a perfect mirror. "I promise you, Jackson. I want *you*. Only *you*."

His hand slides between us, fingers brushing through my bare center and up to circle against my clit gently. My lips part, breath caught on a small gasp as he begins to stroke me. "Promise me again. Because if you decide you don't, and you end up needing someone to take the stranger's place, I don't think I'll survive it."

I stop trying to chase my pleasure, reaching down to still his hand against me. "Jackson, I love you. You're all I want. We don't have to do this."

"I want to give you everything you want, Ginny. I want to *be* everything you need. And if that means spending one night a month here at the club, fucking you however you wish, and speaking to you with this accent that seems to drive you wild. I'll do it. I'll do it happily if it's what you desire."

"My desire is *you*. I need *you*." Letting go of his shoulders, I drop my hands to the buttons of his shirt, undoing them to expose his naked chest.

"Tell me how you need me, baby. Tell me what you want your stranger to do to you," he says against my lips before kissing me deeply. He sits up further, shrugging out of his shirt before pulling the straps of my slip down until it pools at my waist.

Scooting off him, I stand, causing it to fall to the floor, leaving me completely naked except for my heels and wings. As soon as I try to remove the silvery feathers, he stands and pulls my hands away. "Leave them. I want to fuck my fire goddess tonight."

A moan leaves my mouth as I unfasten his pants and push them and his underwear down as he steps out of them. His cock springs up against my abdomen, long and thick with precum already glistening at the tip. My thighs are slick with want as I all but climb up his body. His hands wrap around my thighs to lift me, aligning us as I guide him to my entrance.

With one swift motion, he's inside me, and my head falls back in pleasure. "Fuck, Jackson."

He walks us to the bed, gently lowering me to the silky sheets as he thrusts into me. The heat from our bodies is stifling, sweat glistening in a thin sheen on our skin as we move together. With every press of his hips, I lift mine to meet him, and every single part of my body feels like it's on fire.

"You're so fucking beautiful, laid out with your wings spread behind you. My innocent little angel gripping Lucifer's cock with her greedy cunt." Jackson holds his weight on his forearms, picking up the pace as he snaps his hips, driving himself into me so deep that I feel him in my soul.

"You're not the devil, Jackson." Molding our lips together, I pull him to me before shifting my weight to throw him on his back as I climb on top of him.

"You're my savior." Sliding down onto his length, I ride him with a fevered passion, pulling a string of curses from his lips as his hands grip my thighs, helping me as I move.

His fingers flex against my skin, the telltale sign he's holding himself back.

"Do you want me to get on all fours? You're willing to be my stranger once a month. I can let you be as rough as you want. I trust you won't hurt me." I begin to move off him.

He shakes his head against the mattress and holds me in place, thrusting up into me as he growls, "No. I want to watch your face when you come all over my cock. I'm going to spend the rest of my life watching you take your pleasure from me, Little Ember."

"The rest of your life?" Our eyes lock as our bodies continue to move together, something more than lust or passion filling my veins and spreading outward as I sink onto him.

"Yes." He reaches up with one hand to thread our fingers together. "One day, this hand will have a ring on it."

The other slides down to rest against my stomach. "And one day, your belly will be full with our child. And every single day from now until the day we die, I'm going to bury my cock inside your sweet pussy and fill you so full, you'll never remember what it felt like to be empty."

His words pull my orgasm from me. "Fuck, Jackson, I'm coming! Come with me!"

He follows me over the edge, both of us gripping each other, our pleasure pouring from our bodies until we're a tangled mass of limbs in the middle of the giant bed.

"I love you," he whispers in his normal voice as he strokes my hair.

"I love you, too. Thank you." I slide the masks off both our faces before I kiss him.

"There's nothing to thank me for, Ginny. At the risk of sounding incredibly cheesy, you taught me how to love. I'll spend the rest of our lives thanking *you* for that gift." He chuckles and hugs me tighter as I bury my face against his sweaty chest, inhaling his regular spicy sandalwood and musky vanilla scent.

"You gave me a pretty great gift, too, you know."

"Oh yeah? What's that, Red?"

"You taught me how to heal."

Epilogue

SIX MONTHS LATER

JACKSON

"When I asked Ginny to marry me, I knew it took her by surprise when the first thing she said was, '*Are you insane? We've only been dating for a few months,*' but I think most of you understand that when it comes to this woman, I'm completely enraptured."

The crowd laughs. Glasses of champagne clink together, and lips turn up into smiles as camera flashes go off in our direction. Ginny stands beside me, breathtaking in a white lace dress, the glittering blue diamond of the Tailor family ring sparkling on her finger.

"Love is a labor, and I will work endlessly every day for the rest of our lives to prove my utter devotion to you, Ginny. Thank you for making me the happiest man alive, and for agreeing to become my prison warden until the end of our days."

"I love you," she says, tilting up to kiss me softly as everyone claps.

"I love you, too," I tell her before addressing the crowd once more. "Alright, now enjoy the party that my fiancée worked so hard to put together."

Everyone disperses from where they are gathered in front of us, breaking off into groups to mingle as others come to congratulate us. Through the crowd, I see Tripp making his way toward me. Looking over to see if Ginny needs a refill on her drink, I notice Lenni has also made her way to her friend's side.

Tripp and Lenni haven't met yet, and I've worked hard to keep it that way, but it looks like my luck is about to run out.

"Sorry, I'm late. Don't worry though, I didn't miss the big plate of cheese you served everyone," Tripp greets.

Ginny turns at the sound of his voice, leaning forward so they can air kiss in greeting. "Better late than never! I'm so excited to *finally* introduce you guys! Tripp, this is my best friend–"

"You!"

"It's you!"

They both exclaim at the same time. Ginny and I look at each other with matching looks of confusion at their outburst.

"You said your name was Bianca!"

"*You* said yours was Ken!"

"I've been looking for you for the last week! Do you know how much trouble I'm in because of you?" Tripp cries loudly.

"Me? What did I do besides give you the best night of your life?" Lenni asks smugly.

"Wait, *she's* the girl you hooked up with?" I ask my best friend incredulously. Over eight million people live in this city, and *Lenni* is the girl who's had Tripp *tripped* up for the last week?

Ginny begins to laugh. "Oh, this is too good."

Before he can shout at her again, I grab him by the arm and pull him away. "Stop making a scene at my engagement party, or I'll revoke your membership at Désirer."

"I haven't even gone yet, asshole. Wait…don't tell me she works there?" He pulls his arm out of my grip. "I'm so fucked."

"Why?"

His eyes drift back to Lenni and Ginny, who are still talking animatedly where we left them. Ginny's face is lit up with laughter while Lenni looks like she's finding this situation anything but funny.

"Okay, well, it started with her telling...."

<u>Ginny</u>

"Stop laughing!" My best friend groans, gulping down the rest of the pink bubbly rosé in her glass. "This is why I don't sleep with men outside the club."

"I love you, but this is hilarious. Do you know Jackson has *actively* tried to keep you two from meeting because he thinks that if you guys met, you'd be the most annoying pair in the world?"

"Gee, thanks, bossman," Lenni grumbles.

"You know he means it affectionately when he calls you annoying," I soothe. Jackson will never admit it, but he has a soft spot for my friend simply because she's my friend and makes me happy.

"Wonder what he's so worked up over?" she muses, grabbing another glass of champagne from a passing server.

"You told his ex that you two are engaged. I would assume that's probably it."

"How do *you* know that?"

"Because unlike you, who only told me you had a random hook-up outside the club, *he* has been recounting every detail of your encounter to Jackson daily. Except for your name, Jackson would have known it was you immediately. Good luck with that—you got yourself in a pickle."

My eyes drift to Jackson, who is watching me intently as Tripp rattles on next to him at the bar. We share a smile, and he discreetly nods his head toward the back of the room and walks away from Tripp without so much as a goodbye.

"What pickle? Why is there a pickle? Ginny, look at me and tell me about the pickle!" Lenni pokes my arm to get my attention.

"Go talk to Tripp. I'll find you in a little bit." I don't give her a chance to say anything else as I begin to make my way through the crowd to where Jackson is headed toward the giant windows that line the space, overlooking the bright lights of the city.

New York is dressed up in its usual Christmas decor, everything more colorful and sparkly during the holidays. And from the space Jackson rented for our engagement party, we can see it all from the panoramic view.

As soon as I reach him, he gathers me in his arms and kisses me deeply. "Do we have to stay? There are so many other things I'd rather be doing with you right now. I'm ready to go to the club *now*."

My pussy clenches at the promise of tonight.

True to his word, Jackson has taken me back to Désirer once a month, completely adopting the persona of my stranger and doing whatever I ask of him, staying in character until we've both come down from our highs and are ready to clean up and go back home.

It isn't even about *the stranger* anymore. It's about us and how we came together.

And like I told him half a year ago, I've trusted him enough to unleash himself on me when he needs to—both at the club and at home. It's much more enjoyable when he's making sure I'm getting pleasure from it, too.

It's been a healthy experience, learning what works and what doesn't. Even now, we're still continuing to explore our boundaries, finding new things we like *together*.

"Don't you think they'll notice if we leave early?" My voice is breathy as I speak, my need for him all-consuming as the rest of the room fades away.

The fire he ignites in me blazes all the time—a raging inferno of passion in everything he says and does. It's feral, the love I feel for this man. Savagely fierce and brutally obsessive at times, but it explains *us* perfectly.

"I don't give a fuck who notices. All I know is if I don't bury myself inside you soon, I might possibly die." He buries his face against my neck, nipping at my skin, burning my flesh with his touch.

I laugh at his theatrics, but it dies on a gasp when he sucks my skin into his mouth and bites down. "Jackson, people are watching."

He groans, pulling away and facing the window to adjust himself. "Give me a minute, but then we're saying our goodbyes and leaving."

This time, my laughter doesn't die as I lean against him, pressing up on my tiptoes to kiss his cheek. "Okay."

More than a minute passes. Someone I don't know comes up and attempts conversation, but leaves quickly when Jackson doesn't turn around. He chuckles and leans an arm against the window. "I think you need to go away because I just keep staring at your ass in that dress, and then I'm hard all over again."

Another five minutes pass before he finds me, and we say our goodbyes—no one questions why we're leaving so early. More than a few knowing glances are sent our way as Jackson leaves me to collect our jackets from the coat check.

Even as he walks away, I can still feel the heat from his body. It races through me when he simply looks at me, whether he's next to me or across the room.

Our love is like a blue flame, burning at the highest temperature all the time.

Jackson once said he'd burn the world for me.

I don't want to burn the world, though. I just want to bask in the glow of our flame forever.

Meanwhile in Prison

CHRIS

The sounds of angry men fill the cafeteria.

I keep my head down, poking at the inedible food, biding my time until they call me for a visit with my lawyer.

They won't keep me locked up long. I'm too good at what I do—a gifted surgeon.

The blood on my hands is tainted, anyway. Scott Tailor wasn't a good man, just like his nephew isn't one.

No, Jackson Tailor is a thief. He stole what's rightfully mine, and when I get out of here, I'm going to make sure he pays.

And then I'm going to claim my Guinevere.

I'm going to claim her until there's nothing left but a broken shell of her former self, and she relieves me from the rot she caused when we were kids.

It's going to be beautiful.

"Let's go." A guard approaches where I sit, nodding his head toward the exit that leads to the room where prisoners get visitors. Standing, I hold my hands out, ready for the handcuffs he places around my wrists.

It's about time.

My parents won't return my calls, so it took longer than I

thought it would to arrange for a good lawyer to get me out of this hellhole.

The room is dingy. Small, poorly lit, and devoid of the glass that looks like a mirror, but everyone knows is a way for the people on the outside to spy on what's happening inside the room.

The guard secures my shackles to the table, then pulls out another pair and twists them together, double locking me in.

"A little overkill, don't you think?" I sneer up at him.

He smirks. "You have no idea."

I don't waste time thinking about his remark. My feet tap impatiently, annoyed that the lawyer is keeping me waiting.

Finally, the door opens.

But it isn't my lawyer standing at the entrance to the room.

Two tall men covered in tattoos with arms the size of my head walk in, the guard behind them.

"Have fun," he says before he shuts the door.

The click of the lock echoes as the men smirk at each other before coming further into the small space.

"Who the fuck are you?" My pulse speeds up as I pull at my chains. They rattle and clang together but don't budge.

"Christopher Calloway?" one of them asks.

My heart beats erratically against my rib cage at their leering stares. One of them looks like he's ready to eat his last meal. "Yeah, that's me."

They grin at each other again.

"Jackson Tailor sent us to say hello."

They made up a lie, now they have to fake an engagement.

Read Tripp and Lenni's story, Lie With Me, now.

Afterword

As soon as Jackson made an appearance in Sweet as Sin, I knew he was going to get his own book. Cue Ginny a little later on, and I knew they were going to be a match made in Darbyverse heaven.

I had such a blast writing these two. Ginny was a little more vulnerable than I imagined, while Jackson literally did whatever he wanted to do, and I love them both so much for it. They wrote their own story and told me to sit back and relax.

Chris was hard for me to write because I put a little bit of my own trauma into his and Ginny's relationship. Writing their story was sort of cathartic in a way, though. My alphas wanted me to kill him off, but I knew he was going to need to suffer…and trust me, Jackson is going to make him suffer for a long, long time.

And then there's Scott.

When I wrote Sweet as Sin, I knew the entire time how Scott's story would end. It came about a little differently than I first planned, but I knew he would always have an end. Even while I was writing SaS, when everyone kept telling me how he was the absolute worst, in the back of my mind, I knew he really wasn't ALL that bad. He kept telling me during SaS that he loved Sadie, and he didn't really appreciate how he was being portrayed, but I just shrugged and said everyone needs a villain; just wait until you become the hero.

And in the end, I think Scott made a pretty damn good hero.

Now, who is ready for Tripp and Lenni?

Stay tuned.

Acknowledgments

First off, I always want to thank my alphas Alex, Jessica, and Cady. You ladies are amazing, and I am so appreciative of you being there for every little minute detail that I agonized over. For answering every text at all hours of the day and night when I had questions or got stuck. And for hopping on to read the moment I finished a chapter...even when I was busting them out at the end.

Thank you to my betas, Ashley and Cassee. I am forever grateful for your commentary and live for your notes.

To Virginia Carey, my editor, for always having nice things to say and for being so insanely quick with your turnaround. I appreciate you.

The Author Agency PR team for making the release of this book so easy and stress-free. I don't know how I did it without you ladies before, but I certainly know I don't want to do it without you again.

Thank you to all of the people on my promo team who help post and boost and share. Thank you for believing in me enough to want to help get my books out there.

Thank you to my husband for indulging my weird questions. I swear they continue getting weirder, but you never ask me what the reasoning is behind them, and I appreciate that.

Lastly, to the readers. Thank you for continuously taking a chance on us indie authors. All of this would be impossible without you.

About the Author

D.L. Darby lives in Anchorage, Alaska, with her husband and two fur babies.

By day, she's a hairstylist, and by night, she's continuously drafting new ideas on her "murder board" at home. While she writes across multiple romance sub-genres, you can always expect to find spicy alpha males and strong-willed women with a flair for dramatics in her stories.

www.ingramcontent.com/pod-product-compliance
Lightning Source LLC
Chambersburg PA
CBHW021406310726
48971CB00005B/1224